HER

BEAUTIFUL

MIND

JANET AKE

This book is dedicated to all the volunteers who work so tirelessly
to maintain America's system of long-distance hiking trails.
Thank you.

"And into the forest I go, to lose my mind and find my soul."
—John Muir

TABLE OF CONTENTS

CHAPTER 1

Springer Mountain

Ariella

Date: Tuesday, March 11

Starting Location: Springer Mountain, Georgia

Destination: Unknown

Total Trip Miles: 0

Spring comes slowly to the Appalachians. It creeps into the lower valleys, painting the trees in bright green and splashing the meadows with sunny yellow daffodils. White snowbells outline the ghosts of log cabin walls long since rotted and dissolved into the forest floor, forgotten in the graveyard of time—the delicate blooms a lonely testament to their passing.

Redbud trees, their leafless branches lined with purple blooms, and pink dogwoods edge the rutted backwoods' roads still rough and muddy from a winter's season of misuse. Hidden in the forest duff beneath them are tiny purple violets, each plant a nosegay of fragile blooms and foliage, seen only by those willing to pause in their wanderings and appreciate the woods around them.

Sometimes spring pauses there, delayed by a late snow or ice storm when winter fights to keep its frozen hold on the valleys and hollows of the ancient mountain range. Inevitably, it finally gives way, and spring slowly

1

resumes its relentless, slow march over the foothills, over the ridges, pushing ever upward until the very tops of the mountains are crowned with the green of new life.

It's spring in the valleys below Springer Mountain, but winter still rules on its summit. The trees are bare, and a cold, noisy wind scatters the dead leaves at my feet. A weak winter sun refuses to share its meager warmth. The view is breathtaking, however.

Range after range of hills and mountains march off into a misty blue distance, calling the adventurous to come explore them. Below the rocky summit, valleys are interspersed with shiny ribbons of creeks and rivers.

Only a dozen or so people are here on top of Springer. If this were a weekend in March or April, there would be two or three times that number. There would also have been more partying last night—both here, at the terminus of the trail, and at the nearby shelter—as hikers celebrated the beginning of a long-held dream of hiking the Appalachian Trail.

Today's group is a more serious bunch. Most of them are probably planning a thru-hike or at least a long section hike. Several parents are dropping off their sons and daughters. There are plenty of hugs and a few tears as moms and dads drive away, leaving their offspring to begin their journey. Most of them are around my age, twenty-somethings who have finished school and want an adventure before settling down to build a career, get married, or start a family.

A couple of guys, who appear to be in their early thirties, snap a salute to each other when they finish signing the trail register and shoulder their packs. They look fit and buff, their gear and clothing clearly suggesting ex-military. "Oorah!" they shout as they head north on the trail, confirming my suspicions that they are both Marines, perhaps newly released from their service. I wonder if this hike represents a chance for them to forget, or at least deal with, the horrors they probably saw in the Gulf War, in much the same way Earl Shaffer used his thru-hike in 1948 to manage the trauma of World War II.

I watch a middle-aged couple take pictures of each other posing beside the famous hiker plaque embedded in one of the large flat rocks—it marks the summit and the southern terminus of the Appalachian Trail. They gladly accept my offer to photograph them together. After snapping a few photos with the plaque, we move around the area so I can photograph them standing at the edge of the mountain, the distant hills in view behind them.

When I hand their camera back to them, the wife introduces herself as Janette and her husband as Jim.

"He's Allday, and I'm Dreamer." She laughs before asking me if I have a trail name yet.

"I'm Ariella!" I shout over the increasing roar of the wind. She looks confused for a moment, and I can tell she hasn't heard me clearly.

"Ella?" she asks, stepping closer. "As in Cinderella?"

I stop myself before I can correct her, realizing she has christened me with a trail name. One that suddenly seems very appropriate.

"Yes." I nod, stepping closer so she can hear me more clearly. "Because I'm living my very own fairytale. Maybe I'll find my Prince Charming out here and all my dreams will come true." My attempt at humor falls flat and even I can hear the sadness behind my words.

I haven't fooled Dreamer. She frowns for a moment as she studies me carefully before her face relaxes into a gentle smile. "You know, Prince Charmings are great and all," she answers with a wink before nodding toward her husband, who is busy with their packs, "but you don't really need them to be happy. Hiking by yourself means you're already a strong, confident woman, and you can make your own dreams come true." She pauses. "Hike your own hike," she adds, hinting at a deeper meaning to the often-used hiker phrase about not letting others' expectations control or affect how you conduct your hike.

"I will," I whisper back with a wan smile, letting her know I understand.

"Good for you. You'll be fine out here, but," she adds, her face more serious now, "if you ever feel uncomfortable or lonely, you're welcome to join Allday and me. We're old and slow; better safe than sorry, though, you know."

I nod, understanding what she's saying. Although my chances of being the victim of some type of crime were much higher in New York than here on the trail, there are places—especially at road-crossings and in towns—where being a single woman hiking alone can draw unwanted attention.

"Thank you," I reply.

I watch them shoulder their packs and start to leave the area. Before passing from view, they turn back to me with one last wave. Dreamer shouts something, pointing to the boulder beside me. "The register," she repeats louder. "Don't forget to sign the trail register." Then they're gone, following the trail as it twists its way northward.

The trail register is located in a compartment in a large rock beneath the painted, two-by-four-inch, white blaze marking the official route of the AT. For northbounders like me, it's the first of some 165,000 blazes guiding hikers to the northern end of the trail on top of Mt. Katahdin in Maine. For southbounders, who start their journey in Maine, it's the last blaze they'll see when they complete their hike here on Springer Mountain in Georgia. The significance of this spot as both a beginning and an ending is not lost on me.

~ * * * ~

Everyone has left and I'm alone on the summit. Nothing but gusty wind and creaky bare branches to mar the silence. Taking the register from its protective box, I thumb through the pages of the notebook, glancing at dates and thoughts left by the hikers who started before me. Some of the entries are short, just names and dates; others are longer … wishes, hopes, and dreams left by people I will probably never meet, yet who have left a personal part of themselves in this journal, on this mountain.

On one page is a carefully drawn Marine Corps emblem. The eagle, globe, and anchor are rendered in detail above two comical stick figures heavily laden with huge backpacks. Underneath them are two names, *Ghost* and *M&M*, with the date and *GAME*—the abbreviations for Georgia and Maine—carefully lettered below. As I suspected, they are ex-military planning to travel the entire distance from Springer Mountain to Mt. Katahdin. It will take them five to six months; I wish them well.

Farther down the page, I find a short poem left by Allday and Dreamer. I laugh when I read it.

Two mid-lifers who found themselves free,
Decided to hike the AT.
Their money all spent,
To Springer they went
And joined the class of two thousand and three.

They signed it with their names and good luck wishes to everyone who had gone before and to everyone who will come after. I'm still smiling as I read through the rest of the entries, looking for a blank page to share my thoughts.

Yet, when I pick up the pen to begin writing, my mind is suddenly blank. What do I want to say? I don't have any profound thoughts or clever sayings or funny limericks to leave behind. There's really only one person I should be talking to right now but can't because I've escaped to the woods rather than face the utter ruin of my life that his deceit has caused. I wish I could; if I were strong and fearless, I would look him in the eye and tell him. No, I would scream and yell and demand to know how, and what, and where, and finally … why?

If I were strong and fearless, I would never have left New York. When he, Gia, and all the executives from Banca Italia Internazionale left the stage on the last day of our business presentation after the stunning announcement that he'd accepted a position with them and was bringing our new security

5

software with him, I would have stormed into the meeting and demanded to know why.

I would have asked him how long he'd been planning his betrayal. Was our four-year-long friendship and working relationship an elaborate scheme to get control of my theories and ideas? Did he really just conveniently forget to have me sign the papers from our lawyer, which would have sealed any loopholes in our business arrangement, preventing either of us from selling our software without both of us agreeing—papers I only learned about after he joined Italia? And why, if he'd been living with Gia for two years, did he lead me on, finally spending the night with me, telling me he loved me even as I gave him my love, my body, and all the desire I tried to deny for so long?

I imagine standing before all of them in my righteous fury and getting answers to the questions that have plagued me since I fled the city a week ago. I imagine accusing them of deceit and betrayal and shaming them with their underhanded backstabbing, but I know I would never have been able to do it. My social anxiety would have made me stutter and stammer, and my backwoods Southern drawl—which I've worked so hard to lose—would have come creeping back, causing those executives to look away in discomfort and Gia to politely hide her amused smirk behind her perfectly manicured hand while he sat there tight-lipped and grim-faced, embarrassed at my fumbling, like he did during my presentation when I'd tried to explain the mathematical theories behind our new system.

For all my daydreaming and wishing, I know that's how it would have happened. Gia was right. Theirs is a world I don't understand. One in which I will never fit and never feel comfortable. So here I am back in the Georgia hills, back where I belong, back where I feel comfortable. I still need closure, however. I still need to ask how and what and why.

I look down at the notebook in my lap and the pen in my hand. Perhaps this is where I can ask my questions, vent my frustrations, and leave my thoughts. No one will know who I am; no one will know who he is. He will never read the words I leave here, but perhaps writing them down will ease the ache in my heart and the despair I carry within me. Perhaps this will be a way I can numb the sting of betrayal I feel. Adjusting my grip on the pen, I begin to write.

CHAPTER 2

Terminus

Date: Tuesday, March 11
Starting Location: Springer Mountain
Destination: Campsite near Springer Mountain Shelter
Total Trip Miles: 1

Dear Hudson,

As soon as I've written his name, I'm marking through it. Although I know he will never see this entry and I doubt anyone who reads it will have any idea who he is, he's still the son of a very prominent East Coast family. A family who happens to vacation with the Kennedys, has a summer home in the exclusive Hamptons, and attends all the important social events and philanthropic functions in New York City and Washington, DC. A family that has always been welcoming and gracious to me, although I have to wonder now how much they were involved in Hudson's duplicity.

No, I won't use his name, even if it is just his first. So, I begin to write again.

Dear Hud,

There, I think, chuckling to myself, I'll use the nickname he hates so much. It will be my passive-aggressive way of using some of my anger to spite him. With that decided, I find myself once again stumped for words. The energy of my previous furious thoughts has somehow drained away, and now all I feel is sadness and defeat.

It's getting later, too. Most of the afternoon has slipped away as I've sat here thinking about Hudson and the loss of four years' worth of work and dreams and possibilities. Colder temperatures and the melancholy of the day's end seep into me, almost paralyzing my ability to function, to make a decision … to do anything. The notebook sits in my lap waiting, the blank page another mocking reminder of my failure to express myself.

I take a deep breath, and I write.

Words have always been my nemesis. Perhaps not the words themselves but the necessity of having to speak them aloud to interact with people. I can write them; I just can't speak them. From the first time Dr. Albright introduced us at my eighteenth birthday party, to my disastrous performance during the sales presentation last week, you've always known and, at least in the past, have always been accepting and patient with my inability to communicate with words.

Words are not like numbers. Numbers don't lie. They don't break your heart. They don't accept the gift of your love only to throw it away the next day. They don't plot and scheme and take advantage of someone's naïveté and trust, only to cheat them of their future. Numbers can't have two meanings. They have only one truth, and that's why I have always loved numbers. It's why I've always put my trust in them. They, and the patterns and shapes they create, are my safe haven. They never lie.

I've thought about everything that happened last week, and I can't find the patterns or the numbers to help me understand. Nothing makes sense. My mind can't find a formula, an algorithm, or equation to explain your sudden change in character, and so I'm left floundering in this uncertainty of how, and what, and why.

Now, I find myself on this mountaintop in a place of one name with two meanings. Terminus: both an ending and a beginning. I should hate that word for its failure to be one or the other, but I find I don't mind that it has more than one meaning because I've also realized this word describes me and what is happening now. My old life in academia, in business, and with you is ending. I've come back to my roots, to the backwoods of Georgia, to start something new. I've come back for a new beginning in a place that was always my past.

And I'm okay with that.

So, here's to our terminus, our ending, and a different beginning for each of us.

Although I'm not feeling very charitable toward you right now, I will always cherish what I thought we once were.

Your A

The sun has almost set by the time I've finished writing. After placing the trail register back in its compartment, I shoulder my backpack, adjusting the straps to fit comfortably. My gear is old, well worn, and much loved, but I'm planning to replace some of it when I get to Neels Gap in three or four days.

Camping isn't allowed in this area. I'll need to leave soon to find a spot to put up my tent before it gets too dark to see. There are some campsites close to the nearest shelter, and water is available there, too. It's less than a mile or so up the trail and a fairly easy walk. I should be there in plenty of time. Taking one last look around the now deserted summit, I'm surprised to feel myself suddenly smiling. Writing my thoughts to Hudson has relieved some of the confusion and sadness I've been feeling for the last week. A sense of acceptance and purpose rises as I take my first steps northward on the Appalachian Trail.

Everything is going to be fine, I tell myself. I'm going to be fine. I'm going to be okay.

CHAPTER 3

Memories

Date: Wednesday, March 12

Starting Location: Springer Mountain Shelter

Destination: Hawk Mountain Shelter

Total Trip Miles: 7.6

After a restless night of howling winds determined to collapse my tent around me, I finally wake to a beautiful spring day. Cool, with a cloudless, clear blue sky and a gentle breeze to stir the tops of the still leafless trees, it's as if the forest is welcoming me back home with the perfect hiking day. The trail rewards me with an easy hike, a few ups and downs, and plenty of shade in the afternoon from towering old-growth evergreens.

A side trail leads me to Long Creek Falls where I take a much-needed break. Shoes and socks off, I let my tired feet soak in the icy water while rummaging in my pack for jerky, dried fruit, and some trail mix for dessert. The sound of the rushing water is soothing, and I lean back against the warm rocks, enjoying the sunshine on my face. The quiet is broken only by the sounds of nature: splashing water, singing birds, the rustle of leaves, and the sigh of the breeze. I've missed these sounds. New York City was loud—traffic and horns and sirens, people arguing on the sidewalks and in apartment hallways, TVs and music blaring—but here it is calm, peaceful. I feel the tranquility of this place seep into my bones.

~ * * * ~

I wake with a start, my movement surprising the tiny junco busy pecking the crumbs from my pant leg. He hops off my thigh but stays close, cocking his head to study me with his dark eyes. I have a few tiny pieces of dried fruit left, and I slowly, carefully, slide them onto the rock between us. After a moment, he cautiously approaches, watching me warily as he resumes eating. He moves on to the next piece, trusting but attentive to any movement on my part. I have to admire his bravery.

My Granny Cora loved dark-eyed juncos. They were regular visitors to our cabin during the winter when most of our songbirds left due to the cold mountain weather. Many afternoons, I would trudge home from school to find her waiting on the front porch steps surrounded by a flock of juncos eating the birdseed she would toss to them. Sometimes, the braver birds would even eat from her hand.

"Just look at them, Ariella," she would say. "So small, so plain, so easy to ignore beside all the fancier, more colorful birds. They aren't the best singers or the strongest flyers, yet they survive even in the worst weather and conditions because they don't know they are small, and plain, and vulnerable. They believe in themselves and their place in the world."

Then she would pat the step beside her, inviting me to sit and tell her all about my day.

She was easy to talk to, my Granny Cora. She never interrupted my rambling descriptions of what I learned or did in school, always patient with my stuttering and stammering. After my second-grade teacher discovered me working through the problems in an advanced high school algebra book, and after I'd been tested and then placed in a class for gifted math students, the vocabulary of my school-day descriptions became full of esoteric mathematical terms she had no way of understanding with her limited eighth-grade education. But even then, she always listened patiently, nodding at my accounts of asymptotes, or conic sections, or Fibonacci sequences.

I don't remember when I began living with her. She said I was a toddler when the police found me alone in an apartment after Charlotte, my mother and her daughter, was struck and killed by a car while crossing a street late one night. Gran hadn't seen Charlotte in years and didn't know of my existence. A search of the meager belongings in the run-down apartment turned up a birth certificate listing my biological father as Davis Johnson, but he was never found and I never had any contact with him. Granny knew nothing about him.

I was sixteen when she passed away. By then, I was already attending MIT and living with Dr. Albright, one of my professors, and his family. She had been ill for some time but managed to keep it a secret, not wanting to worry me or interrupt my education. Even now, eight years later, I still miss her.

The little junco has finished the crumbs I've given him, but he waits patiently beside me, as if asking for more. "Granny, is that you?" I whisper. He tilts his head again, his black eyes, so like hers, blinking at my question. Spreading his wings, he flits to the nearest tree before filling the air with his tinkling song as if to remind me the trail is waiting for me and it's time to move on.

Standing, I stretch before shouldering my backpack and heading along the side trail to the AT.

His song keeps me company as I hike north.

CHAPTER 4

Pain

Date: Thursday-Friday, March 13-14
Starting Location: Campsite five miles past Woody Gap Road
Destination: Neels Gap
Total Trip Miles: 30.7

On a hot afternoon two days later, I stumble down the steep, rocky descent from Blood Mountain to US Highway 19 at Neels Gap. The AT crosses the road at the Walasi-Yi Center, a stone and timber building constructed in the 1930s by the Civilian Conservation Corps. A visitor's center occupies one-half of the building while the other half houses an outdoor outfitter's store called Mountain Crossings. I plan to replace most of my old equipment and buy food and supplies here. There's also a basement hostel for hikers where I hope I can score a bunk and a much-needed hot shower.

I barely make it to the picnic table outside on the patio before I'm shrugging out of my backpack and pulling off my hiking shoes, groaning at the instant relief. I'm in pretty rough shape, a condition for which I have only myself to blame. Although I knew better, I made a common rookie hiker mistake—too many miles, too fast, too soon.

After an easy first day of approximately seven miles, I camped in the clearing surrounding Hawk Mountain Shelter. With only a handful of people staying in the shelter, there was plenty of room for me to join them, but I much preferred the privacy of my little one-person tent. Strangers, particularly men, always made me uneasy, and the thought of sleeping next to someone I barely knew was something I couldn't even consider.

With plenty of time and fuel, I took the opportunity to heat some water for a quick wash before cooking a freeze-dried meal of beef stroganoff. Afterward, I signed the shelter register, jotting down the date and a short mention of my nap at the waterfall before ending it with my new trail name, Ella. I noticed Allday and Dreamer had spent the previous night there, as well as the two Marines, Ghost and M&M.

An entry by two hikers, Yellow and Wonderland, dated several days previously, made me laugh at their description of being attacked by the shelter mice after they forgot to attach their food bags to the mouse-proof hangers suspended at the front of the shelter overhang. A mistake I was careful not to make. By dark, I was in my tent, snuggled into my warm down sleeping bag. Moments later, I was sound asleep.

Sunshine woke me early the next morning, and once again, I was blessed with the perfect hiking day. The trail was relatively easy, some ups and downs, followed by more ups and downs, with a few flat sections thrown in for teasers. The sun was warm and the breeze cool. I was rested and well fed. I kept my mind focused on the present, refusing to even think about anything other than the woods, the wildflowers, and the birdsong celebrating my passing.

The miles and hours sped by as I escaped into the physical demands of the hike. Cresting each hill and ridge meant a water and snack break. I munched on peanuts and sucked water, fresh and cold from a clear mountain stream, while the gentle wind dried the sweat from my body, and I marveled at the distant vistas opening before me. The rhythmic click, click, click of my hiking poles kept time with my footsteps and labored breathing as I powered along each level section.

The air was filled with the musty odor of decaying vegetation and sun-warmed earth. From time to time, the trail would cross over to a south-facing slope, and I would be greeted with a hillside covered in sweet-smelling wildflowers. Birds, and even a few butterflies, kept me company, and once, a small grass snake slithered quickly out of sight after I almost stepped on him. I wrapped myself in the peace and tranquility of the forest.

Gooch Mountain Shelter was a seven-mile hike from where I had spent the night. I ate a quick lunch there before hitting the trail again. By late afternoon, I cruised into Woody Gap, another six miles farther on the trail.

There was a roadside picnic area at the gap located just off the small parking lot where the trail crossed a two-lane country road before starting the climb up Big Cedar Mountain. An ice chest sitting on one of the tables caught my attention. I opened it to find cold sodas and a note from a previous hiker wishing us good luck on our hikes. Beside it was a sack full of small bags of chips. It was my first experience with trail magic—gifts of food or other supplies left on the trail for hikers. I crunched on salty chips and drank the caffeine and sugar-loaded cola, letting my sweat-soaked shirt dry in the afternoon breeze.

The thirty-minute break left me feeling refreshed and renewed, and I attacked the steep uphill climb after crossing the road, feeling powerful and unstoppable. Dusk came quickly, though, and I finally had to accept I needed to stop hiking and find someplace to camp.

When the AT crossed a small mountain creek, I followed it off-trail to a nice flat area where I quickly set up my camp, snacked on some trail mix, and after a speedy wash in the icy creek, changed into warm dry clothing, and slipped into my sleeping bag. I fell asleep, smug in the knowledge I managed to hike almost seventeen miles. I was genuinely proud of myself.

Two hours later, I was gasping in pain as I fought my way out of my sleeping bag and tent, lurching to my feet as I tried to stop the agonizing cramps in my calves and thighs. Everything hurt—my toes, my ankles, my hips, my shoulders, even the bottoms of my feet. I fumbled around in the dark, searching through my backpack for my first aid kit. After downing a couple ibuprofens and a long swig of water, I crawled back into my bag, tossing and turning to find a comfortable position on my sleeping pad. Exhausted, I fell asleep, only to repeat the whole thing again several hours later.

I checked my watch when the pain woke me a third time. It was four in the morning. This time, I donned shoes and a jacket and walked slowly around my campsite stretching and bending my protesting muscles, desperately trying anything to ease the pain. I laughed at myself as I hobbled around; I was only twenty-four but moved like I was ancient. This is what happens when you spend too much time sitting in a classroom, or at a computer, or in meetings all day, and then decide to go backpacking with no preparation.

Finally, I sat down on a nearby rock, closed my eyes, and listened to the night. It was quiet, almost eerily so. The silence had a weight to it. An almost intelligent presence seemed to hover just beyond my perception. I breathed in the cool night air, inviting the peace it seemed to offer into my mind and body.

Granny Dobbs believed in spirits, all kinds of spirits. Her favorites were the "Little People"—the traditional Cherokee name for spiritual beings who often lived in the woods and sometimes helped people who were lost. Not just physically lost, but those who were sad or confused and had lost their way in life. I laughed at her stories, the mathematician and scientist in me refusing to believe anything that couldn't be explained by logic or scientific reasoning.

One night, she took me by the arm, pulling me out into the meadow in front of our cabin and—pointing at the star-filled sky overhead—asked if my logic and reasoning could explain the beauty spread out above us. I started reciting explanations of stars and planetary orbits and theories of multiple universes, only to be interrupted by a blazing streak of light across the dark sky. It was followed by two more as Granny and I stared, speechless in wonder.

When I tried to explain them away as meteors burning in the Earth's atmosphere, she turned to me with a knowing smile. "Oh, child," she asked, "and how do you explain we were here, together, at this very moment, to see those meteors in the sky?"

I knew there were probably all sorts of statistics that could explain the probability of the two of us being in that exact spot, at that exact time, and seeing those exact meteors, but the numbers were too staggering to compute in my head.

The randomness of the events of that night stayed with me. I thought about Gran's question often. My need to merge the chaos of unpredictability with the ordered patterns of numbers led to the theories we used to develop our company's security software programs. The company and programs Hudson took with him when he accepted the position of Division President with Banca Italia Internazionale.

The sharp snap of a breaking stick halted my musing and I opened my eyes, turning quickly toward the sound. It was followed by the rustle of movement in the dried leaves on the forest floor. I couldn't see anything in the darkness. I told myself it was probably a small night creature checking out the large being who invaded its space.

The night chill settled into my bones, and I desperately needed more sleep before tackling the almost 4,500-foot elevation climb up Blood Mountain in the morning and the six miles it would take to reach Neels Gap later in the day. As I stood and stretched, a flash of light caught my eye and I watched in awe as a bright shooting star arced across the night sky above me. I followed its path, tracing the blazing streak as it headed north.

For a long time after it finally disappeared from view, I stood staring at the sky above me. With no moon and no city lights to dim their glory, the stars were polished diamonds glittering against thick, black velvet, a jeweled necklace looping across the ebony sky. I picked out a few of the constellations—recognizable designs interspersed among the haphazard stars surrounding them. Chaos and order, patterns and randomness, the dichotomy that rules my life and forces me to try to organize everything into neat, reasonable, logical occurrences. The quirk in my brain that strives to understand and control the events in my life.

With a tired shake of my head, I crawled into my tent. Settling into my warm sleeping bag, I sighed in relief, my tired muscles pain-free for the moment. I was almost asleep when I heard the sound of something scurrying in the underbrush close to my tent. To my exhausted brain it sounded like the pitter-patter of tiny little feet.

"Thank you," I whispered into the now quiet night.

CHAPTER 5

Pain & Memories

Date: Friday, March 14

Destination: Neels Gap

Starting Location: Campsite five miles past Woody Gap Road

Total Trip Miles: 30.7

Pack off, shoes off, my head resting wearily on the picnic table, I'm startled out of my near oblivion by the thump of something hard and the crinkle of plastic hitting the table near my face. When I crack one exhausted eye open, I can see an open bottle of lemonade and a bag of chips on the table in front of me. Condensation runs down the outside of the cold bottle, soaking my hand when I reach for it. A groan of pure pleasure escapes me after I swallow my first mouthful of the refreshingly sweet, lemony concoction, and a sigh of relief soon follows when I rub the chilled bottle over my face and neck.

A chuckle reminds me I'm not alone. When I glance up to see who has gifted me this most appreciated trail magic, I'm shocked to see someone I recognize.

"Liam. What are you … How did you …" The words are barely out of my mouth before he's pulling me to my feet in a crushing bear hug. For a moment, my emotions get the best of me and I lean into his welcome affection, unable to complete my question.

He draws away, laughing at my confusion. "It's good to see you too, little *gohusdi*."

His familiar use of the shortened Cherokee word for cousin instantly transports me back to long summer days and nights spent exploring the woods around Gran's cabin. Liam taught me how to catch fish with my bare hands, how to find morels in the woods, and more importantly, how to differentiate between safe-to-eat mushrooms and poisonous ones. We harvested wild ramps in early spring, picked blackberries in summer, and gathered muscadines and hickory nuts in the fall.

He was my first true friend, a constant companion, and a big brother in all but name. When bullying and teasing made school a daily torment, Liam had been my protector and champion. Five years older and at least a foot taller than me, he was a formidable opponent for anyone who thought a shy, socially awkward, part Cherokee math nerd would make an easy target. Growing up, I idolized him, even fantasized we might marry someday until I found out we *were* actually cousins. His grandfather Samuel was my granny Cora's brother.

Liam was already in college when I left to attend MIT. He combined a major in business with outdoor recreation leadership and environmental sustainability—a career path that seemed perfect for him with his interest in expanding Georgia's growing outdoor sports and recreation industry while preserving the environment that supported it. I'd only seen him a dozen times or so since I'd left. The last time was nearly two years ago at his wedding.

Now here he is, sitting across from me at a picnic table outside of the Walasi-Yi Center where the AT crosses a mountain road in the middle of nowhere Georgia. The mirth on his face and the laugh he's barely controlling tells me he's having way too much fun with my confusion. Before I can think of a clever retort, however, he glances over at my dilapidated backpack and discarded shoes.

"Whoa, Ari," he exclaims, reaching over to haul the remains of my gear onto the tabletop. "What happened here?"

He examines my makeshift repair on a broken shoulder strap. I've sewn it together with dental floss and wrapped it in duct tape to reinforce it, but I'll have to replace the complete strap soon. I'm hoping I can get one at the hiking store here, but the pack is old and I may have to special-order one—if they even make them anymore.

Before I can stop him, Liam has all my gear spread out on the table. I watch him examine each piece, shaking his head and muttering about the heavy, out-of-date, worn-out, get-yourself-killed-in-the-woods contents of my pack. His glare when he finally looks up lets me know he is not happy.

"How old is this stuff?" he demands.

I answer with a shrug. "This hike was a last-minute decision. I didn't have time to shop for anything new, so I picked up what was in the cabin before getting a ride to Springer."

His glare morphs into a stare of disbelief. "Are you telling me this is the same gear we used as kids? Good Lord, Ariella Coraline, what were you thinking?" he questions as he continues to examine everything on the table. The fact he has double-named me is not lost on me. He's seriously pissed.

He picks up my old down sleeping bag, shaking his head when he realizes the poor shape it's in—most of its loft and filling have disappeared over the last fourteen years. Although I've managed to stay warm for the last three nights, it won't be enough when I enter the taller, colder mountains of the Smokies. "You could get yourself seriously hurt, or even killed, by taking off into the woods unprepared like this."

"Liam, stop. It's only been three days, and you know damned well I can survive in the woods alone without any gear at all if I have to. You and Granny made sure I could. Besides, I was planning to replace most of it here. It's way too heavy to lug it all the way to Maine."

As soon as the last word is out of my mouth, I know I've made a mistake. My cousin's eyes narrow at me as he considers what I've just revealed.

"Maine? Isn't this about the time your company was supposed to be presenting the new security system to that big banking company? Why would you leave Hudson and New York for six months at such a crucial time?"

Liam knows Hudson. He met him when we visited for his and Emma's wedding. I was hesitant to bring him with me, but he wanted to see where I was from.

Gradually over the years, I shared some of my childhood memories with him: stories about Gran and my cousin, Liam; descriptions of our cabin and the woods surrounding it; legends from my Cherokee heritage; and anecdotes of life in the hills of Georgia. He surprised me by being interested in something so foreign to his upbringing. I was afraid he would find the people and the area boring and backward, but Hudson enjoyed himself very much. His innate good manners and friendliness charmed everyone, including my cousin and his very taciturn family.

During our visit, Liam and Hudson spent hours discussing business models, branding, marketing, human resources, stock options—all things foreign to me. The numbers I understood but not the human aspects of starting and maintaining a business.

Hudson was enrolled in Harvard's MBA program when I met him. Dr. Albright, my mentor and a long-time friend of his family, wanted us to meet and discuss the practical uses of my theories as a foundation for a new computer security program. He was looking for a project for his final thesis, and creating a start-up business plan for what would eventually become our company was exactly what he needed.

Liam and Hudson stayed in touch after our visit. I wasn't sure how much or how often. So, I'm not surprised he knows of our plans to offer it to Banca Italia Internazionale. I am surprised he knows it's happening now.

I'm not sure how to answer him.

My face must show my discomfort because Liam is staring at me intently. I stutter and stammer, my throat closing on the words I need to explain what happened. Liam quickly averts his gaze, understanding how difficult it is for me to speak when people are looking at me. Reaching across the table, he takes both my hands in his. He gently rubs the tops of them before urging me to take a deep breath and start over.

"Ariella, sweetheart, what's going on? Why are you here and not with Hudson? What happened to the meetings and the presentation to that banking company?"

"It's over, Liam. Everything's over. It's all fallen apart. He accepted a position with Banca Italia. I'm not part of it anymore. It's all … it's just all gone. He's gone."

The scarred tabletop in front of me is suddenly very interesting as I study the names carved over the years into its weathered surface, unwilling to look at my cousin when I think about what else happened between Hudson and me.

"I don't understand." Liam's voice is sharper, more insistent now. "I know you're business partners, but I also thought you two were a couple."

"We were … I mean, I thought so, too. He spent the night, and we … well, you know, we … umm." My cheeks are burning with embarrassment when I glance up at Liam, my natural reticence making me unable to confess Hudson and I had sex.

I'm met with an understanding smile. "It's okay. You're a big girl now. You're allowed to sleep with the man you love." His teasing tone turns into a chuckle when he confesses he's surprised we waited this long. "I could tell you loved the guy when you were here for the wedding, and I think he felt the same. So, no need to be embarrassed."

He gives my hands a reassuring squeeze before releasing them but hesitates when I've returned to examining the tabletop again.

"Ari? Ariella, did something happen? Oh, my God, did he hurt you?"

My head snaps up at Liam's angry shouting. "No, not physically. It's just—"

"What? What happened?" he interrupts.

24

Taking a deep breath, I face my oldest, dearest friend. "It's just … the next day, I found out he's engaged to Gia, Vincent Cattaneo's niece, and she's been living with him in his condo for the past two years."

Liam's suddenly slack face betrays the same shock I felt upon learning of Hudson's betrayal.

"Banca Italia is establishing a new international division that will be in charge of all their computer systems, worldwide. It'll be based at their headquarters in Italy, and Hudson is going to be the president of the division. Gia will be transferring to the headquarters with him as head of their Human Resources department. His employment offer was contingent upon him bringing our new security system with him."

Fresh out of words, I watch Liam's face morph from concern to bewilderment to anger. "But can't you stop him? Don't you own the company together? How can he possibly take it with him unless you agree?"

Shaking my head slowly, I confess Hudson's ultimate deceit and my ultimate naïveté. "Susan, our lawyer, found a loophole. She drew up the papers to prevent this from happening and gave them to him. He was supposed to bring them to me to sign. Instead, he came to my apartment with my favorite Chinese take-out and a bottle of champagne. We toasted what I thought would be a successful sale the next day, and then we ended up in my bedroom. He never mentioned the papers."

Liam's face mirrors Susan's when I said those same words to her.

Hudson had just finished his summation of the benefits of our system when Vincent stepped up to the microphone and made the announcement about his appointment. Applause filled the meeting room as we watched him escort Hudson, Gia, and the other Italia executives off the stage. Susan turned to me, frowning with confusion when she asked if I'd known and agreed to this. I shook my head, clearly as confused as she was. When she questioned me about the papers and I explained what happened the night before, she was just as bewildered and shocked as Liam is now.

I watch pure wrath overtake Liam's face.

His lips are clenched, and his nostrils flare. His eyes narrow in rage, and his hands ball into fists. For one brief moment, I'm reminded of the ancient warrior blood that still runs through his veins. Letting loose a stream of curse words that would make a sailor blush, he pounds his fist on the table between us.

"I'll kill him, Ari. So help me, I will. I'll hunt the damned motherfucker down and I'll drag his upper crust, lily-white *uka* all over these hills. I'll teach him what happens when he backstabs one of us. I'll teach him what real pain is."

No words leave my mouth as I stare at my infuriated cousin. I can only wonder how much angrier he would be if I confessed that Hudson had also told me he loved me.

CHAPTER 6
Wine & Candy

Date: Friday, March 14
Starting Location: Campsite five miles past Woody Gap Road
Destination: Neels Gap
Total Trip Miles: 30.7

By the time I've gathered my gear and hoisted my backpack, Liam has finally ended his rant against Hudson. I'm headed toward the entrance to the hiking store when I hear him call after me.

"Hey, where are you going?"

"I need to buy gear, I need a decent meal, and I really, really need a shower. There's a hostel in the basement, so I'm hoping I can score a bunk there and maybe take care of everything else while I'm here. Come on, maybe you can help me?"

"Ariella Coraline Dobbs. I'm not about to let you sleep in the basement. You can stay with Emma and me."

This time, I stop and turn to face him. "Liam Spencer Crow," I triple-name him in return. "You live on the other side of Gainesville, almost ninety minutes away. If I go home with you, you'll just have to bring me back up here tomorrow, and I'm sure you have work or something more important to do than haul my ass around."

By the time I finish, Liam is rolling his eyes and shaking his head. "Oh, cousin ... don't you ever read your emails?"

Now I'm confused and shaking my head. "I don't know ..."

Placing his hands on my shoulders, he turns me to face the building once more before pointing toward the large sign over the entrance. It's new; the words "Mountain Crossings" lettered in simple, bold script over a panoramic view of hazy hills in the background. But it's the smaller letters at the lower right edge of the sign that capture my attention. "Liam and Emma Crow, Owners" they proclaim to everyone who passes through the newly painted door.

"You ... you and Emma bought Mountain Crossings?" I can't contain my squeal of excitement. "When did this happen? Why didn't you tell me?"

"About six months ago, and I did in emails—you know those messages you get and are supposed to read, but never do? Come on," he urges, wrapping an arm around my shoulders and leading me through the door. "Emma and I live in the apartment in the back. There's a guest room with a shower *and* a tub where you can wash the hiker stink away. Emma has a hot meal waiting for you. After you've settled in, and maybe taken a short nap, we can work on some new gear for you."

I'm happy for my cousin and his wife. Owning one of the premier outdoor sporting goods stores in the South is the perfect opportunity for him to put his business degree to work while fulfilling his dreams of encouraging and promoting ecologically sound outdoor recreational opportunities for everyone.

Most hikers take three to five days to hike the thirty-two trail miles from Springer Mountain to the road crossing at Neels Gap—plenty of time for them to realize hiking the Appalachian Trail is not some "walk in the woods." Instead, it's hard work.

It's steep, lung-busting uphill and never-ending downhill switchbacks. It's too much heat or too much cold, gear-soaking rain, and skin-blistering sunshine. It's muscle cramps, and headaches, and gas from eating freeze-dried meals. It's snakes, bugs, and mice chewing holes in your pack at night. It's mile after mile of boring tree trunks and awe-inspiring views that surprise you at the top of the next ridge.

It's terrible and wonderful, torture and bliss.

Many of the hikers who stumble into Mountain Crossings are questioning their decision to spend time and money to pursue what their families and friends have already told them is a ridiculous daydream. They're suffering from sore hips, shoulder strain, and lower back pain from carrying packs that are too heavy with muscles that have had too little preparation. The staff at Mountain Crossings can help them lighten their packs, share advice on staying well fed and hydrated, and encourage those who are considering quitting by offering a bed and a shower—either in the basement hostel or in one of the nearby cabins. They can arrange a ride into town for a hot meal, laundry, or a few days recuperating in a motel. For those who have decided to quit, they will help arrange transportation to the nearest bus depot, train station, or airport. It's still a business and a service but performed with respect and care. It's the perfect fit for my cousin.

Several hours later, after a long soak in a hot tub, a two-hour nap, a steak dinner complete with baked potato, salad, and apple pie for dessert, Liam, Emma, and I sit on their back deck, watching the sunset, sipping a glass of wine, and catching up with all the local gossip and news. I learn the driver of the shuttle service I took to Amicalola Park, where Springer is located, is Emma's second cousin. Apparently, he recognized my name and called Emma to tell her I was on the trail. She and Liam had been expecting me, which was how he was able to surprise me earlier in the day.

I also find out Liam and some of his friends have been checking on Gran's cabin, doing minor repairs, and keeping the grass and weeds cut back. I was pleased to see it in such good shape when I stopped by to pick up my gear. Since her death, I've only been back a few times a year. Visiting is difficult; I miss her so much.

By some unspoken agreement, we don't mention Hudson or anything about New York and what happened there.

As the evening darkens and the temperature falls, Liam builds a fire in their outdoor fire pit. We drag our chairs closer to its warmth and wrap ourselves in worn, colorful old quilts, lapsing into companionable silence as we watch the stars appear in the dark Georgia sky above us.

There is something mesmerizing about the flickering flames. I can feel their calming influence settling into my mind, easing away my anxiety and fears about the future. I feel my kinship to the people sitting beside me, to the extended family living in these hills, to the ancestors who came before me. The patterns of our connection form and reform in my mind, numbers and formulas defining the relationships. They link me to the people, to the land, to the past, to the future … to the whole of nature.

Loud laughter from the basement hostel startles me from my musing, reminding me of where we are. Emma leans forward, refilling our empty wine glasses, and Liam begins to describe some of the interesting characters who have passed through since hiking season started in earnest.

The Appalachian Trail goes right through the middle of the Walasi-Yi building. In fact, there's a white blaze painted over the open-air breezeway that connects the visitor's center on one side to Mountain Crossings on the other. Every hiker who makes it to Neels Gap stops here, most to resupply or get something to eat or drink. The smart ones stop for a day to rest and take advantage of the opportunity to let Liam or his staff evaluate their gear and help them lighten their packs.

Hikers seem to fall into several broad categories.

There are the more experienced veterans of the trail, some younger, some older, who have winnowed their packs to the bare essentials, carrying only what they need to survive, knowing in most locations they are only a day's distance from a road or outside help should an emergency occur. They've arranged their lives so they can spend months in the woods, more at home here than in the confines of the cities they are trying to escape. Many of them have become legends of the trail, their names and exploits spoken of with awe and respect.

Section hikers often come to the trail every year, saving their vacations to spend a week or two hiking selected sections of the trail. Sometimes, they pick the most scenic or the more easily accessible segments. Or, they start at Springer or at Katahdin, working their way south or north as they systematically chip away at the more than 2,100-mile length, returning to start where they ended the previous trip. It takes determination and sheer stubborn grit to maintain the dedication to return year after year.

There are day hikers and weekend hikers. Adults and children who visit the trail to walk for a few hours or camp overnight in the woods, picking the perfect day and season to enjoy nature. Many times, this is their only opportunity to experience the forest in its ungroomed, natural state. I like to think many of them, especially the children, will one day come back to spend longer, more extended time in the woods.

Then there are the newbies. Young or old or in-between, who, for one reason or another, have decided they want to spend five or six months walking in the woods, sleeping on the ground, eating copious amounts of carbs and still losing weight, or maybe drift from one trail town to the next, from one party to the next. Maybe they've seen the movies, or read the books, or know someone who knew someone who hiked the whole thing and had the time of their lives. For some, it's a great adventure before settling down; for others it's an escape from the strangling confines of a mundane life that threatens to swallow their very soul.

The newbies are the ones who benefit most from Liam's expertise. They're the ones he persuades to send home the cast iron skillets and the three-pound first aid kits, the seven changes of clothing, and the three massive hardback books they've brought along to read. Without naming names, or getting too personal, Liam keeps us in stitches, laughing as he describes the strange things he's found in backpacks recently. When he mentions three pounds of M&M candy, my mind flashes back to the entry in the trail journal on Springer.

"The Marines?"

"You met them?" he asks.

"Not really. They were on Springer the day I started. They signed the register as Ghost and M&M."

"Well," he continues, "the big guy's name is Markham Mitchell Manning."

"Whew, that's a lot of M's," I interrupt.

"Apparently, a lot of his fellow soldiers thought so too." Liam laughs. "So they just started calling him 'M.' Guess what his favorite candy is."

"M&Ms," we both say at the same time, laughing.

"But three pounds of them?"

"Yeah." Liam chuckles. "Apparently, he started with something like five pounds, but he's been handing them out to everyone he meets."

"So where are they now?"

"Staying in one of the cabins down by the creek for a few days until the big guy heals up."

"Uh-oh, what happened?"

"Well, you know how steep the trail is coming down off Blood Mountain just before you hit the road?"

"Yes?"

"Seems he tripped and took a tumble ... bounced all the way down."

"Ouch." I can't help but flinch, remembering how I'd carefully picked my way down to the road. That part of the trail is rocks and roots, all the soil has been worn away from erosion and constant use over the years. "Couldn't he see how dangerous it was?"

"Yeah, but he wasn't paying attention because he was too busy stuffing his mouth with ..."

"M&Ms." We all shout together, finishing Liam's sentence. Maybe it's the late hour, maybe it's the camaraderie, or maybe it's the wine, but we double over in laughter imagining the big, tough Marine taking a tumble all because of a small, insignificant piece of candy.

Feeling guilty over laughing at a fellow hiker's misfortune, I ask Liam if M&M is going to be okay, and he assures me nothing was broken, just some bruises and a twisted ankle.

"I'm letting them stay in one of the cabins free of charge for the next four days. He should be fine by then. Besides, I got the impression he's had worse and seen worse while in service."

"Kuwait?"

"Yeah. Afghanistan, too."

We're silent then, each of us lost in our thoughts about the young men and women who are fighting in the never-ending, non-war our country is mired in. When I turn back to my cousin, I find him gazing at his wife. The love and appreciation I see reflected there has them wrapped in their own bubble of affection and admiration. For a fleeting moment, I'm both happy for them and envious of them. This is what I thought I would have with Hudson. Even though it didn't work out for me, I'm glad my cousin has found his life partner.

Leaving the two of them alone under the star-filled sky, I slip quietly away to the guest room. Sleep comes quickly and deeply, and for once, I don't dream of him.

I blame it on the wine.

CHAPTER 7

Rain

Date: Saturday, March 15
Starting Location: Neels Gap
Destination: Whitley Gap Shelter
Total Trip Miles: 38.4

Although Liam and Emma encourage me to stay with them, at least for another day, I hike out after lunch the following afternoon. I'm sporting a new internal frame backpack, having left my old external frame pack—which once belonged to Granny Dobbs and which Liam claims is an antique—hanging among the other dated and well-used gear on display along one wall of Mountain Crossings.

Allday and Dreamer arrive as I'm leaving. I must have managed to pass them somewhere on my seventeen-mile day. They look good, a little dirty and obviously in need of a shower, but otherwise happy and healthy as they enter Liam's store. She greets me with a cheerful smile, asking how I've been and if I'm doing all right. I can hear Allday inquiring about an overnight stay in a cabin and a shuttle to town for dinner. After a brief conversation and a goodbye hug, I leave them to their negotiations and start the steep climb out of the gap.

My new pack sits comfortably on the top of my hips—hips which, even in my skinny, awkward, and gawky adolescence, I hated for their unfashionable wide flair. Now that the rest of me has filled out and I don't look quite so bottom heavy, I've learned to accept their generous curve. Granny called them "child-bearin' hips" and told me I'd be grateful for their width when it came time to give birth. I'm not sure being a mother is something that will ever happen for me, but I'm currently grateful for the way they carry the weight of my pack. I've accepted that I'll never be like the tall, thin, elegant women who exist in Hudson's world. Out here in the woods, it doesn't seem as important as it once did.

Inside this pack is a new down sleeping bag with a water-resistant cover, a new blow-up air sleeping pad, and a small, very lightweight, one-person tent. Liam replaced my old canister stove with a fold-up stove the size of a deck of cards, which burns little squares of solid fuel. I have new rain gear, a new pair of synthetic shorts and T-shirt, a down-filled pullover sweater that weighs mere ounces, and an in-line water filter attached to the drinking tube of my water bladder. With four days' worth of meals and snacks and enough water to get me to the next shelter, my pack weighs around twenty-seven pounds. Almost ten pounds less than it did before Liam worked his magic.

I may have thrown a little hissy fit when he refused to charge me for the new gear. I know how expensive everything is. When I reminded him he was running a business and deserved to make a profit, he offered to let me work off the price of the equipment. He laughed when I rolled my eyes at his pathetic attempt to get me to stay, but then finally agreed to let me pay the wholesale cost of my new gear.

I'm not exactly destitute. Between life insurance policies and her savings, Granny left me a sizable inheritance. Hudson structured our business finances so we both, along with our two programmers, Oliver and David, were paid a decent wage. I own the intellectual property rights to the math theories our software is based on. Those alone have the potential to make me a wealthy woman … someday.

Selling our systems would have been a much more lucrative deal, but now, I'm not sure I'll ever see any income from what was once our business. The legal papers I never had a chance to sign also contained provisions to give Oliver and David shares in the company. Eventually, they, too, would have been financially secure.

There is a fundamental truth every hiker learns very soon after starting the trail: for every easy descent into a gap, road crossing, or shelter site, there is an equally brutal uphill climb out of that location. The climb out of Neels Gap is cruel, never-ending, and just plain hard. I huff and puff, sweat and swear, and lean heavily on my hiking poles as I trudge up the endless switchbacks. To make matters worse, it begins to rain.

Some hikers love walking in the rain; others hate it with a passion. I have mixed feelings. A light, misting rain can be a welcome relief on a hot, humid Southern afternoon; in those instances, the best thing to do is cover your pack and let Mother Nature give you and your clothing a nice refreshing shower. It's a completely different scenario if it's cold and wet.

The air temperature doesn't have to be below freezing for the symptoms of hypothermia to occur. All you need is cold air, a brisk breeze, and exposed wet skin to start the shivering and mental confusion characteristic of mild hypothermia. The physical exertion of hiking helps generate heat and protects the body's core, but dressing in the appropriate rain clothing is even more important.

As I continue to climb, the temperature drops and the light rain turns into a heavy deluge. This is obviously a major low front moving through, and there's no sign of the rain tapering off as I hike into the thickening fog. Before long, my teeth are chattering, and I know I should stop, refuel with some high-calorie food, and change into drier, warmer protective clothing.

Off to the right of the trail, I spot a cedar tree with low-lying limbs. Stepping under its sheltering branches gives me a break from the worst of the storm. Soon, I'm stripping off my wet clothes and pulling on the dry shorts and T-shirt, the down sweater, and the new rain pants and jacket Liam insisted I take.

I'm immediately glad I listened to him when I step back onto the trail. The rain still beats down on me, but I'm warm, dry, and my pack is protected as I shuffle along on the rain-slick pathway.

Time seems to drag as I continue doggedly forward in the rain and fog. My mind wanders, recalling scenes from my childhood—some clear, some muddled, some confusing glimpses of unknown faces I suspect might be my mother or perhaps my father. I have only a few distinct memories from my life before I began living with Gran.

I think about my college and post-graduate years, the fear and excitement of moving to Cambridge, and the acceptance I found there—from both the students and the faculty. Suddenly, it was okay to be different, to be smart, and to like math, science, and computers. Even though I was still a teenager, I felt like I belonged and relished the sense of being part of a bigger whole, of being with people who were like me. Living with Dr. Albright and his wife eased the transition from rural Georgia to urban Massachusetts, from the Deep South to New England. They welcomed me into their home, treating me like another daughter. I realize I haven't called them. They're sure to be worried about my sudden disappearance.

I should call Susan, too. Although she's our company lawyer, she's also my friend, and I haven't spoken to her since that last night in New York when I went to Hudson's condo to confront him about what happened during the day, only to find Gia living there. The things Gia had told me undermined all my false bravado, sending me back to my apartment in a frenzy to escape the city and my humiliation.

I called her then, explaining what I had learned from Gia and asking her not to fight Hudson's leaving. She begged me to stay, telling me I must have misunderstood when Gia informed me Hudson had stripped his trust fund to keep our business afloat and so, in effect, owned the company. We needed to speak to him directly, she argued, but I took the coward's way, leaving as soon as I could arrange a flight out of New York. I'm sure she must be worried, too.

I resolve to call Dr. Albright and Susan when I stop for supplies in a few days and have access to a phone.

So lost am I in my thoughts, I don't even realize I've crested the last ridge and I'm heading down into the valley where Whitley Gap Shelter is located. I've only taken a few steps downhill when I fall.

Everyone falls when they're hiking. It must be some unwritten, unspoken, universal rule—you are going to fall, especially when you aren't paying attention. Falling with a backpack on is a completely different experience than a normal trip and tumble. If you fall face first, the weight of your pack feels like a giant hand slamming you to the ground. It's almost impossible to stop yourself from getting a face full of dirt. If you fall on your back, you end up looking like an upended turtle, unable to right yourself until you can roll over and get your legs beneath you. Hiking poles can make things worse as you flail your arms trying to keep your balance and they end up whipping around through the air. If you're lucky, you just sit down … very, very hard, no broken bones, or sprained ankles.

This time I'm lucky.

Stepping over a pile of exposed rocks in the trail, I plant my foot, heel first, on a patch of soggy leaves covering the ground. The leaves have lost all adhesion to the wet clay under them, and before my conscious mind can register what is happening, I'm slipping and sliding, feet going in opposite directions as I struggle to find my balance on hiking poles trying their hardest to wrap themselves around my ankles. I sit with a thump, not hard enough to be seriously hurt but certainly enough to remind me to start paying better attention to my wet, slippery surroundings.

Getting up is tricky. My hiking poles, still attached to my wrists with their webbing loops, are somewhere behind me, and I wave them around, trying to position them in front of me before placing my feet on what I hope is firmer ground. With a grunt, I haul myself up, the pack on my back feeling like an anchor tethering me to the ground.

My once new, once clean, rain pants are streaked with mud, and my hand comes away covered in wet leaves when I brush off my seat. It could have been much worse, and I'm thankful it wasn't.

I'm very careful as I continue down the mountain.

It's evening before I reach the side trail leading to the shelter. The rain and the low-lying clouds have made it much darker than normal, and I almost miss the blue blaze that marks the turn-off. Under normal circumstances, I wouldn't consider staying at this shelter. The turn-off is less than a quarter mile from the nearest highway, although the shelter itself is over a mile from the trail. Apparently, it's not far enough to discourage the locals because, when I reach the shelter in the deepening chill, it's evident it's used as a secluded party destination.

Piles of trash litter the ground around the outside, and graffiti decorates the inside walls. The fire pit is full of burned beer cans. This isn't a safe place for a lone female hiker. Yet, I decide to stay. The cold temperatures and the heavy rain almost guarantee none of the locals will want to brave the walk to get here and only determined hikers would be trying to reach a shelter this late.

To give myself a little more privacy and a little more protection from the blowing rain, I erect my tent inside the three-sided building. It's not considered proper hiker etiquette to put a tent up inside a shelter, but with no one else here, I'm free to do what I think will help protect me. Anyone arriving after dark won't know there's a woman inside the tent.

While my dinner simmers in my new titanium pot, I peruse the shelter register, reading the entries left by previous hikers. I find Yellow and Wonderland's names and the date. Apparently, they ate lunch here two days before. I leave my trail name and the date, adding a note about the slippery trail conditions.

Finished with dinner, I sit on the edge of the raised sleeping platform listening to the rain beat a steady pattern on the tin roof, the plink-plink of drops on the beer cans in the fire pit a counterpoint to its constant rhythm.

Fog has settled into a solid blanket, wrapping the lean-to in a sound-muffling shroud of murky white. A fitful wind blows wisps of more opaque bits of cloud across the meadow in front of the shelter. Like ghosts, they twist and writhe, fighting to join me in my seclusion before a stronger gust sweeps them away. They're like the memories I've hiked with all afternoon, scattered fragments of people and places, painful events I've tried to bury in the deepest recesses of my mind. In this quiet, lonely setting, they demand to be set free … examined … acknowledged. Insisting I face the experiences that molded me.

The shelter register rests beside me on the wooden floor, a blank page calling to me. I situate it on my lap, pick up the attached pen, and begin to write.

CHAPTER 8

La Bella Mente

Date: Saturday, March 15

Starting Location: Neels Gap

Destination: Whitley Gap Shelter

Total Trip Miles: 38.4

Dear Hud,

You once told me I had a beautiful mind. Do you remember?

We were discussing the algorithms for the software, and I started explaining how patterns within patterns gave rise to more patterns, how chaos can interrupt and then change them into other patterns that can be predicted and manipulated. I remember being very excited to share the basis of my theories with someone other than my colleagues. I think I must have been quite animated and maybe a little loud—unusual behavior for me.

You, however, were very quiet. Realizing you hadn't said anything in some time, I looked up at you, only to find you staring at me in wonder. I remember blushing, mortified at my rambling, and then apologizing profusely for boring you. But you shook your head and smiled before telling me I had the most beautiful mind you'd ever known.

"La bella mente," you whispered.

Beautiful, Hud, you called my mind … beautiful. Not unusual, or weird, or messed-up. Not strange, bizarre, or different—all words I'd been labeled with at one time or another—but beautiful. You called me beautiful.

To my grandmother, I was Ariella, to my cousin and colleagues, I was Ari, but to you, I was la bella mente … a beautiful mind.

And in that moment, I did feel beautiful. Not just my mind … but every part of me. You gave me a new name and each time you said it, I felt special. I still do. Nothing about me was ever considered beautiful before.

I knew I was different. I knew my mind worked differently than other peoples' minds. No one seemed to see the patterns I saw. I'm not even sure when I first began to see the world around me as a series of patterns. I do know it was well before I had the verbal skills to articulate what I saw and felt.

My first clear memory is of a small room. One corner contained a soft pallet of blankets for napping. Beside the pallet are several bottles, topped with nipples and full of milk I drink when I'm thirsty or hungry. There's solid food, too. Soft, white bread, small squares of yellow cheese, and round slices of some type of meat. I don't know the words to describe their shapes or colors, but I recognize their differences.

When I'm not sleeping, I lie and watch the light coming in through the windows high on the walls above me. I watch it move across the tiles of the floor, brightening the colors I don't have words to name and bringing out the sparkles in the squares. I like the way they look in the sunshine.

The sunshine also creates patterns of dark and light as it creeps into the room, dividing the tiles into other shapes, which shift and change as it crosses the floor. I'm fascinated by the changes. I know it's important to watch the light because, when it reaches the far corner of the room, someone will come into the room.

That someone will remove my wet, uncomfortable clothes and let me play in warm water before dressing me in clean clothes and feeding me fresh food. If I'm happy smiles and don't cry, there will be talk and giggling, patty-cake, and cuddling in a soft bed when it gets dark. If I do cry, there will be loud words and angry faces. I learned early not to cry.

The next day, I'll be left in the quiet room again.

One day, as I'm watching the light move, I crawl over into it, becoming part of those patterns on the walls around me, on the ceiling above me, and on the floor beneath me. I've changed the patterns by being in them. I am the chaos that has interrupted their orderly progression.

I loved those patterns; I felt safe inside them.

I don't know how or when someone stopped coming, or how or when I left the room. Although I have other vague memories of that time, it's the only clear one of my life before I went to live with Gran. Over the years—when I've allowed myself to think about it—I've realized it must have been my mother who left me there each day when she went to work or to do whatever she did.

I'll never know why she didn't take me to a sitter or daycare. Her accidental death caused the police to find me and notify Granny of my existence.

I've always wondered if being a young child left alone in a room by herself all day affected my brain and the way I think and function. Perhaps it only exacerbated what was already there.

I do know being in the room made me quiet, withdrawn, and reluctant to cry. The pleasant expression I sometimes wear is a mask to hide the small, bewildered child who still needs "someone" to be nice to her.

Now that I've confessed my oldest, deepest, darkest secret to you, do you still find my mind beautiful? If you were here beside me, would you look away in disgust or stare at me in wonder again?

Perhaps it's a good thing we'll never know.

CHAPTER 9

Tears

Date: Sunday, March 16
Starting Location: Whitley Gap Shelter
Destination: Blue Mountain Shelter
Total Trip Miles: 48.5

I wake up sobbing.

Granny's funeral was the last time I cried so hard. Even when I'm upset, frustrated, nervous, or generally having a bad day, I always find some other way to handle my emotions. I don't cry. But I woke this morning … crying in my sleep. Weird dreams haunted me all night. I was either running toward something or away from it, being chased or chasing someone. An overwhelming sadness and loneliness gripped me until I awoke, sitting upright in my tent and sobbing for something just out of my reach.

It's early. Fog still wraps the surrounding woods in whiteness. It's barely light enough to see, but I'm ready to move on. I quickly pack my gear, and then glance around to make sure I have all my things. My gaze falls on the shelter register I'd written in the night before. For a moment, I consider tearing out the page I filled with my memories but decide to let it be. I haven't signed or dated it, and no one will ever know who Hud is. Perhaps it's best to just leave this misused shelter, the wet, sodden forest, and those memories from so long ago.

I hike out. The road crossing comes quickly. I scurry across, senses alert for any sound of traffic in the blinding fog. Then I disappear into the mist-shrouded forest on the other side.

The hours pass. I hike through fog and mist, light rain, and then a sudden, drenching downpour, which is over almost as soon as it begins. The sun finally makes its appearance mid-morning before hiding behind more clouds. It plays peek-a-boo all afternoon with the wind-swept clouds passing overhead.

There are more road crossings, some paved, some gravel, each one a link to the outside world I'm hiding from. I struggle up steep, slippery slopes, traverse rocky ridgelines, and descend into shady gaps. Almost every mile contains a clear, cold mountain stream to be forded, some by hopping from stone to stone, some on worn, wooden bridges built by volunteer maintenance crews designed to protect both the stream and the hiker crossing it. I skirt cliff faces, pick my way gingerly across rock falls, and cross open meadows. False summit after false summit teases me until I finally emerge onto a sunny bald with views stretching on forever.

Sometimes, the trail circles back on itself, heading south for a while before turning east or west as it circumvents a dangerous or unclimbable obstacle in its path, but eventually it turns north again. I let it lead me north, always north, following the memory of the junco's song, the falling star, and those tiny footsteps.

The day is long, unhurried, and slow. Every hour, I find someplace—a log, a rock, a tree stump or grassy area—where I can sit, rest, eat, and drink. I try not to think about Hudson or New York, but my thoughts, like a hamster in its cage, spin round and around and around, working furiously but never getting anywhere. I find them impossible to stop. When I top a small rise and find a bench cut from a downed tree overlooking a green valley below, I sit and let the memories wash over me.

Finding Gia and then confronting her as she stood in the doorway of Hudson's condo was one of the hardest things I'd ever done. Like me, she'd changed from the business clothes she'd worn to the meeting. But while I wore jeans, a tee shirt, and a hoodie, she was dressed in tailored wool slacks and a cashmere sweater. My ratty high-tops were a stark contrast to her red-soled heels. I'd stuck my shaking hands in my pockets and swallowed the bile that rose in my throat as I faced her disapproving glare.

Somehow, I'd found the courage to argue with her when she claimed Hudson had only been using me, but my bravado had quickly wilted in the face of her pitying, condescending look. "Oh, Ariella; sweet, innocent, naïve Ariella." I can still hear her voice in my head. "Did you really think Hudson and his family would just welcome you with loving arms? Did you think you could fit into their elite society? Hudson needs a woman who is his equal, a woman who knows how to act and talk properly, and knows which fork to use. A woman who is an asset, who understands how to further his career. Did you seriously think it was you?"

Courage gone, I'd turned from her in defeat, but her cloyingly sweet voice had followed me down the hallway. "I'm sorry you had to hear this from me," she continued. "Hudson has a wonderful future ahead of him, and I'm the kind of woman who will help him reach his full potential. A woman like you, who can barely speak in front of people, who looks like a frightened mouse most of the time, is not the woman Hudson needs or deserves."

Her words were hard to hear then and they're hard to remember now. I'd often wondered the same thing. How could someone like him be interested in someone like me? It was easy to accept the truth of them. Hudson does deserve someone better than me, and I care enough about him to accept that I'm not that person. The sting is still there, the harsh words still hurt. But strangely, the pain is dulled, and I don't feel as miserable as I did when I first left New York.

With a sigh and a shake of my head, I stand, adjust the straps on my back, pick up my hiking poles, and begin walking. With all my focus on the trail beneath my feet, it's much easier to ignore the stray thoughts clamoring for my attention.

By late afternoon, I've finished twelve miles and find myself at Blue Mountain Shelter. A group of five hikers, all male, are sitting at the picnic table in front of the lean-to, each one cooking a hot dinner on their various camping stoves. The aroma hits me, and my stomach growls in displeasure at my failure to feed it anything but snacks and junk food all day. I find a place at the end of the table and pull out my dinner supplies and stove, quickly boiling enough water for the evening's packaged noodle meal before adding a packet of tuna for extra protein, calories, and fat.

The hikers are friendly, greeting me with smiles and introducing themselves. They all use trail names, hiding their real identities behind an assumed persona, just as I do when I introduce myself as Ella. I listen to their conversation, only taking part when asked a direct question, and gradually, I'm mostly ignored as I eat my meal. I'm surprised, however, when they all repack their backpacks and begin to leave. The nice evening has persuaded them to try to reach another shelter a few more miles up the trail. Although I'm invited to hike along, I decline.

Once again, I have a shelter all to myself. I consider sleeping in it, but I'm still a little nervous from spending time with five strangers, so I opt instead to set up camp in a small clearing some distance from the shelter. There are enough trees and undergrowth to hide me from any hikers who might wander in later. It's also in the opposite direction from the privy, another definite advantage.

I find the scarf, rolled up and sealed in a plastic baggie, at the bottom of my clothes bag. I'd forgotten I'd tucked it into the bag, piling shorts, shirts, woolen sleeping tights, and extra socks on top of it. Frustrated because I couldn't find the wool pullover I normally slept in, I dumped the whole bag, and it fell out on top of the pile. Besides the clothes I'd been wearing when I left New York, it was the only thing I brought with me.

Cautiously, I open the storage bag, making sure my hands are clean before I pull it out. It's exquisite, one of the most beautiful things I've ever owned. A long, rectangular, handwoven and hand-embroidered scarf crafted from wool and silk threads so fine, so sheer, it almost floats in the air as I gently shake it to release the folds. The blues, peaches, and corals in the abstract floral pattern glow in the light from the setting sun streaming through my tent door. Intricately knotted fringe on each end tickles my fingers as I pull the length slowly across my hands.

I fold it carefully, looping its length around my neck, remembering the way Hudson's hands felt when he placed it there. He'd reached behind my head, freeing my heavy braid, which was caught under it. His hand lingered there as we stared at each other, our faces close, our lips almost touching. My eyes fluttered closed as I leaned in toward him, longing for my first kiss, wanting it from him. But he stepped back, putting distance between us, and I opened my eyes, mortified at what I'd done.

Emotions flickered across his face as mine flamed with embarrassment. "Ariella," he whispered, "I'm sorry ... I shouldn't have." Then he took another step away before turning to the artist whose handiwork I was wearing around my neck and handing her his credit card. She smiled as she rang up the purchase, telling me how lovely it looked on me and complimenting him on his excellent taste in clothing and girlfriends. Laughing, he agreed with her before taking my hand and leading me off to explore the rest of the street fair.

I wore the scarf all afternoon as we wandered through the artists' booths, admiring the stunning variety of artwork and handmade crafts while stuffing ourselves with fresh pastries and ethnic goodies. It was a glorious autumn afternoon in New York City, sunny but cool, a gentle breeze ruffling the Technicolor leaves of Central Park. We finished the day dancing to a street band, watching the moon rise over the city before he took me home.

There was another moment as we stood in front of my apartment door when I thought he might kiss me, but he lightly bussed my forehead instead before thanking me for a wonderful day and saying he would see me at work on Monday. Disappointment bloomed within me as I watched him walk down the hallway and enter the elevator, turning with a slight goodbye wave before the doors closed on him.

Later, when I was placing the scarf in a drawer, I found the very discreet price tag for $500. Hudson hadn't even asked how much it was, just purchasing it because it was lovely and looked beautiful on me. I shook my head, marveling again at the differences in our backgrounds and upbringing.

I wore the scarf many times over the next year, sometimes casually with jeans, sometimes with work dresses or skirts. The size was perfect for looping around my neck or wrapping around my shoulders. Once, I even knotted it around my hips. I always received compliments when I wore it, and Hudson always smiled when he saw it on me. There were wonderful memories attached to his special gift.

I wore it that last day in New York.

It was the morning after he spent the night with me. We showered together, and I finally found out why so many of the romance books I sometimes secretly indulged in included a sex-in-the-shower scene. Unlike our first time the night before when he had taken his time with slow, soothing touches, massaging my back and shoulders, kissing his way from my neck to my toes, caressing and fondling my body with his fingers. Unlike the gentle way he finally entered me, waiting for me to relax and adjust to him, staring into my eyes the entire time as he whispered words of love and adoration. Unlike our perfect first time, this time was … different. His hands were a little rougher, more demanding, needier.

He touched me everywhere—fingers, mouth, and teeth—bringing me to the point where I was almost incoherent with want. One hand wrapped itself in my hair, tilting my head to the side as his mouth latched onto mine, his tongue invading me even as I felt his other hand slide across my wet belly and slip between my legs. Garbled moans and cries filled my ears, and I realized with a start that I was the one making those pleading noises.

His mouth pulled away from mine, and I opened my eyes to find him staring at me. "Tell me this is okay. Please ... Please, tell me I can have you again." His pleading words only increased my desire, my mumbled response changing to a desperate, "Yes," when his lips found my hardened nipple.

Hudson's strong body pushed mine against the shower wall. I wrapped my arms around his shoulders and he raised my foot to rest on the shower bench. His gruff, desperate voice told me to hold on, and then he was inside me.

I forgot my worries about the important, final meeting waiting for us later in the day, forgot all thoughts about what I should wear, what I should say, how I should act. There was only the here and now as my world shrank to the glass walls around us. I was barely aware of the warm water hitting my shoulders, the slick tiles against my feet, and the clean, herbal scent of my soap. My existence, my entire focus, was on the feel of him inside me and the tension growing in the pit of my stomach.

Lips and hands roamed. Squeezing, rubbing, nipping, almost demanding in their insistence that something happen. I was vaguely aware of the gasping sounds coming from my lips as I felt pressure build and build.

For a moment, it was as if all time stopped, as if my brain no longer thought, my lungs no longer breathed, my heart no longer pumped; instead, my whole being was frozen, focused on Hudson and the place we were joined. His mouth moved across the side of my neck, hot breath blowing on my wet skin before I felt a sharp sting and his teeth sink into the straining muscle at the top of my shoulder. That was all it took for the growing pressure to release, exploding through my body in rhythmic contractions and a long wail of overwhelming pleasure even as a rushing heat swept over my chest and neck. I felt him swell within me, and then his pulsing orgasm as I continued to clench around him.

We were both breathing heavily when we finally eased apart. Hudson wrapped his arms around me and pulled me to his chest where I rested my head over his rapidly beating heart. We stood for a few long moments, letting the warm water cascade over our heads. Finally, he reached for my shampoo bottle, squeezing a generous amount onto his hands before he began to rub them soothingly through my hair and down across my shoulders and back. His touch was gentle, almost hesitant, and I shivered against him, moving closer before wrapping my arms around his waist.

"Are you okay?" he whispered softly. "Did I hurt you?"

"No," I whispered back before tilting my head up to look at him. "It was good. I mean, I liked it, and I … Well, you know, I guess I orgasmed," I mumbled in embarrassment.

"Yeah, I know." He chuckled, a proud, self-satisfied, pleased-with-myself smirk on his face. "I could feel it, and, well, so did I."

"I know." I laughed back at him. "I could feel it, too."

Hudson's eyes widened and a horrified expression wiped the pleased smile from his face. "Oh, shit, Ariella. I didn't use a condom. Oh, God, I'm sorry. I got carried away, and I didn't stop to think and—"

"It's okay." I tried to reassure him. "I'm on the pill, and you know there wasn't anyone else before you."

"Yes, but still …" Placing his hands on each side of my face, he stared at me intently. "I promise you I'm clean. I've always been very, very careful, and there hasn't been anyone else, not in a long, long time."

Not knowing what to say, I nodded silently before moving into his embrace once more. A tiny, possessive part of me was very happy to hear there has been no one else for some time.

We finally parted, finishing our showers and our preparations for the day. Later, when I was in my closet slipping into the new, dark teal dress and jacket I planned to wear, Hudson sought me out, smiling at the color he loved so much on me. When I reached for a necklace, he stilled my hands, asking me to please wear my scarf instead.

I did as he wished, wrapping and arranging it around my neck, savoring the loving look on his face as I did so. It was only later, after I fled the

51

meeting room and office building where everything had gone so terribly wrong, that I realized why he asked me to wear the scarf. As I stood facing my bathroom mirror, shock and anger making me tremble in disbelief, I reached up and tore the scarf from my throat to be confronted with more evidence of his manipulation. There, just above the neckline of the dress but hidden all day by the folds of silk and wool, was a bruise—a love bite, the shape of his mouth plainly visible on my skin.

Involuntarily, my hand rises to cover the area where the bruise has finally faded. Gia had seen it that night in the hallway as I turned to leave. The fury on her face had been a frightening thing.

"Hudson always did like to mark his conquests," she spat at me. "I bet he left another one right over your heart while he whispered how much he loved you and how wonderful you were."

My face flamed with embarrassment because that's exactly what had happened. But how could she have known?

"Oh, please," she sneered. "Did you think I didn't know where he went last night? He's been lusting after you since he first met your sweet, little virgin ass. I finally told him to go enjoy himself to get you out of his system. Hudson's always been quite good in bed. I'm sure he left you with some moments to remember him by when he finally leaves with me."

Her words left me reeling. I didn't want to believe them. Didn't want to believe the depth of his deceit. Yet, I couldn't deny them.

Now, sitting in my tent, staring at this lovely piece of cloth in my hands, I remember why I brought it with me. To remind me that every beautiful thing can have its ugly side, that nothing is permanent and everything can change. I may not be able to control the chaos that surrounds me, but I can control how I let it affect me.

A drop of moisture lands on the back of my hand, and I peek outside my tent door to see if it's raining but find only a clear twilight sky awash with the blazing colors of a fiery sunset. Reaching up to touch my face, I realize I'm crying again, tears trickling down my cheeks to drip onto my hands.

Anger—fierce, hot, and overwhelming—rushes through me. Anger with myself, with Hudson, with Gia, at my circumstances, at my weakness … at my tears. Scrambling out of my tent, I stomp my way to the shelter, pick up the register, and fill page after page with my fury. The pent-up rage makes its way from my brain to my hand, to the pencil, to the paper. Word after word, line after line, I release my frustrations until I'm left drained and exhausted.

Only when it's too dark to see do I finally stop. As I make my way back to my hidden campsite, one thought is utmost in my mind: there will be no more tears.

CHAPTER 10

New Friends

Date: Monday, March 17
Starting Location: Blue Mountain Shelter
Destination: Deep Gap Shelter
Total Trip Miles: 63.3

There are infinite ways to wake up each morning on the trail. The soft warmth of the early morning sun working its way through your tent door, the cheerful chirping of songbirds welcoming the new day, the restful sighing of a mountain breeze rustling its way through the dried grass, and even the low-pitched, whispering voices of your fellow hikers preparing to start their day. All of these are welcoming, friendly, agreeable ways to begin each day.

Then there are the not so pleasant: the flash of lightning followed immediately by the deafening crack of thunder, leaving you momentarily blind and deaf; gale-force winds threatening to shred your tent into tiny fragments while you cower helplessly inside; copious amounts of ice, hail, or snow, collapsing your tent around you even as you struggle to escape its synthetic-fabric clutches.

Trail shelters are notorious for being loud: from the snores of exhausted fellow hikers, to the scratching of mice claws as they scramble over wooden floors and walls; from the nighttime screeches of owls hunting those same mice and the snakes slithering after them, to the whining hum of mosquitoes buzzing your exposed head and ears; all of these and so many more can and do conspire to rob you of sleep at night and force you to start your day before it's barely light enough to see.

But perhaps the worst way to end your restful, or maybe not-so-restful slumber, is with the sudden onset of stomach cramps. I start my morning with a desperate dash to the privy. Still half-asleep, untied shoes flapping about my feet, toilet supplies clutched in my right hand, I barely make it to the half-walled, wooden outhouse in time to drop my sleeping tights and avoid a rather embarrassing and messy situation.

Later, after I've cleaned up a bit and feel more in control of myself, I'm tiptoeing quietly past the still dark shelter when I hear a voice inside.

"Glad to see you made it. Taking a dump inside your pants is a real mess. I had to strip off and take a bath in a stream a couple of days ago after I shat myself right there in the middle of the trail."

The shock of hearing an unexpected voice, and then those very candid, very personal words, freezes me in my tracks. I'm left standing in front of the shelter, peering into its still-shadowed depths. I can barely make out two human-sized lumps cocooned in swaths of fabric like large caterpillars. Gear, clothing, and food bags dangle from chains attached to the front overhang, each one with its mouse-proof, inverted empty tuna can. The lump on the left wiggles, and a human sits up, emerging halfway from his synthetic casing.

Reaching up, he pulls off a knitted sleeping cap, scratching his head vigorously, revealing a shiny, bald head. "Ah," he says grinning sheepishly. "I've rendered you speechless, haven't I? Sorry." He chuckles. "I'm afraid I have that effect on people."

Before I can answer, his shelter-mate rolls over with a groan, muttering something about "too early" and "more sleep" and "shut the fuck up." This causes another bout of laughter, but he keeps it subdued.

"Seriously, though, are you okay?"

This time, I manage to find my voice. "Yes, just a little hiker digestive issue. Thanks for asking, though."

The sun has topped the horizon while we've been talking, sunlight beginning to peek into the clearing surrounding the shelter. I can see my conversation companion more clearly now. He looks tall, with wide shoulders, brown eyes, and that smooth head, but what catches my eye is his thick handlebar mustache. His upper lip is covered in a wide band of hair, which lengthens and twists into an upward curl at each end. I can't remember the last time I've seen a man with this type of facial hair. My stare is interrupted when he introduces himself as "No Filter."

"No Filter?" I question, wondering if I've heard him correctly.

A wide grin splits his face, making the curled ends of his mustache twitch as he chuckles again. "Yeah, I didn't have a water filter when I started hiking, so I was always borrowing someone else's. And then there's my bad habit of saying whatever pops into my head. Kind of like I did just now." He shrugs his shoulders, rolling his eyes and waggling his eyebrows dramatically. "Mouth got no filter, you know."

Although I try, I can't control the giggle escaping me. The horrible start to this day, the absurdity of this whole conversation, the genius of his trail name, strike me as hilarious. Soon, I'm laughing so hard I have to sit down on one of the benches attached to the picnic table. "That's … that has to be the best, most appropriate trail name I've ever heard," I manage to gasp in between my bouts of laughter.

No Filter is still grinning at me when I finally calm down enough to catch my breath and wipe the tears from my eyes. "Well, now I've told you mine, you have to tell me yours. You got a name, girl?"

"Ella."

"Ella, huh? As in Cinderella, umbrella, portabella, citronella, or maybe mozzarella? You like the cheese, girl? Or … wait, I know … salmonella." His eyebrows are doing their crazy dance again, and the mustache jitterbugs across his face as we both laugh at his silliness.

"Goodness, I hope not," I finally manage to answer once we've both calmed down a bit. Shaking my head and shuddering at the thought of dealing with food poisoning while in the woods, I add, "I think it was the big meal I ate last night."

"Let me guess. You skipped breakfast, snacked on junk all day, and then, because you were starving, stuffed yourself with the biggest, richest dinner in your food bag, and you paid the price this morning."

"How did you … yeah, I guess you're right. Not very smart, was I?"

"No, you need to spread those calories out during the day. With the physical demands you're putting on your body, your metabolism is starting to really kick in, and you need to feed it regularly, not overload it in one big meal. Of course, as soon as the hiker-hunger hits, you'll be eating all the time."

Another open, friendly smile lights up his face. "Tell you what … why don't you go back to your sweet, little campsite and pack up. Come back in about thirty minutes, and I'll treat you to one of my fabulous, rib-sticking, fill-your-belly, No Filter special breakfasts."

"You knew I was down there?" I ask, nodding toward my secluded spot.

"I always check out my surroundings. An aware camper is a safe camper."

His words hint at some deeper meaning, but No Filter's expression doesn't change as I study him intently.

"Okay." I finally agree, heading back to my tent. "See you in a little while."

As I walk off, I can hear him yelling at his companion. "Get up, lazy slug, you're wasting daylight, and we have a lady guest joining us for breakfast."

~ * * ~

Thirty minutes later, I'm staring at an unappetizing glob of gray goop No Filter has dumped into my pot. "This is your special breakfast?" I ask incredulously.

"Oh, ye of little faith," he chastises with an eye roll. Opening his food bag, he removes a bundle of filled baggies and a small scoop. "Peaches or cherries?" he asks. When I reply peaches, he fills the scoop with pale, dime-sized flakes from one of the bags and dumps them onto the blob in my pot. Next, he adds two scoops of brown sugar, a heaping scoop of chopped pecans, and then two scoops of white powder.

"Powdered milk?" I ask.

"No, no, no, my dear, nothing so mundane. Dried, full fat, sweet cream powder. Now stir," he commands while pointing to my spoon.

As I stir, No Filter slowly pours hot water into the concoction in my pot. It gradually changes from a lumpy glob into a bowl of smooth, creamy, hot oatmeal, chock full of plump bits of rehydrated peaches and crunchy pecans.

"Now for the finishing touch," he announces, sprinkling a light dusting of cinnamon over the top. "Voila!" he exclaims, throwing his hands up before bowing over his creation. "And there you have it—a *No Filter Breakfast Special Extraordinaire.* Eat up, girl."

The first taste is pure heaven, and I groan in appreciation of the sweet, rich, creamy delight.

"Like eating peach cobbler topped with nuts and melted ice cream for breakfast," says the man who sits down across the table from me. "Good morning," he continues. "I'm Curly Dan, or at least that's what No Filter calls me."

"I ... what?" I manage to ask in surprise, staring at his smoothly shaved head. My tablemate is a young man of medium height and weight. His large, expressive, dark brown eyes are framed by the longest lashes I've ever seen on a man, but it's his warm cinnamon-colored skin that draws my attention.

The word beautiful pops into my mind as I study him closely. Normally not a term I would use to describe a man, but he is truly beautiful with his full lips, symmetrical features, those amazing eyes, and richly colored skin. He's also one of the few people I've met on the trail whose skin is darker than mine. For some unknown reason, minorities rarely participate in long-distance backpacking. A situation Liam hopes to change.

My thoughts are interrupted when he explains his trail name.

"Well, I started this hike with a full head of curly hair, and my name is Daniel, so when we shaved our heads at Springer, No Filter christened me as Curly because I'm now bald, and Dan because I despise that nickname."

"But—"

He shakes his head, chuckling at my confusion. "I've learned to live with his craziness. Life's easier and a lot more fun that way. Besides," he continues, "he has a real knack for trail names. I wouldn't be surprised if he hasn't already thought of a new one for you."

"Well, I might consider a new one as long as it's not Salmonella," I reply.

We're still grinning at each other when No Filter joins us, setting a full bowl of his amazing breakfast in front of Curly Dan and taking one for himself. "I've decided against the Salmonella name," he informs us as he sits down. "I thought about Cinderella, but Disney princesses are *sooo* boring." Rolling his eyes dramatically, he grins mischievously at me before adding he's reserving the right to christen me with the perfect trail name at a later time. Turning to Curly Dan, he adds, "You win again; she did pick peaches."

"Told you." Curly Dan responds with a triumphant grin. "I believe the score is now fifteen for Curly Dan and zero for No Filter. Someday, you'll learn not to bet against me."

Their conversation makes no sense to me as I watch their good-natured teasing. Finally, Dan takes pity on my confusion, and turning away from No Filter, he explains they have a theory about which fruit people will choose based on the part of the country they're from. People from the northern and western states will pick cherries while people from the South pick peaches.

"How do you decide where people are from?" I ask.

"Ah, that's where I have the advantage over Mr. Mustache here. I'm actually a linguist. Language and the way humans use it, change it, and speak it is my specialty. I have a very good ear for accents. They can tell us so much about a person, where they were raised, and where they have lived. Sometimes, even their ethnic background."

"And you decided I was from the South by the way I talk?"

"Yes," he slowly replies, carefully watching my reaction as he speaks. "There's a slight drawl to some of your words. Not very many though. You're covering it up most of the time. It's hard to hear unless you know what to listen for. I'd say you are probably from somewhere in the Appalachians, perhaps Georgia or West Virginia, but you've been living in the Northeast. And I think you may have taken some diction lessons at one time. Also …" He stops, frowning a bit as he continues. "Did you spend some time in Massachusetts? Not Boston specifically, but somewhere nearby?"

"Yes, I … Wow, that's amazing. I had no idea you could hear so much in my speech."

"I love accents, all kinds, but I have a special appreciation for the soft, slow drawl of America's Deep South. That one pours over you like thick honey, sweetening the conversation and wrapping around you like a warm blanket. Yours is beautiful, too, if you'll let it out a little bit more."

I've spent years trying to control and cover up what I thought was an embarrassing, backwoods, hillbilly accent, yet here is a man I've just met encouraging me to embrace my speech patterns and my heritage. Ducking my head, I take a few more bites of my breakfast, not knowing how to respond.

"Ella? I'm sorry," he continues when I glance up at him. "It was very presumptuous of me to tell you how to speak or offer advice to someone I've just met. Please forgive me. I find accents fascinating. For me, they're the spice that adds interest and flavor to our speech. If we all spoke the same, our conversations would sound very boring indeed. However, sometimes, I let my enthusiasm overwhelm my good manners, and I overstep the boundaries of common courtesy."

"I will on one condition," I answer. "You have a very interesting accent yourself. Will you tell me where you're from?"

"I'm from northern England," he replies. "A wonderful place for someone who loves accents because we have such a melting pot of regional dialects. From the Scottish brogue to the Liverpool Scouse, the very proper Queen's English or Posh, and the working-class Cockney. Throw in some Geordie, some Ulster, and some Glaswegian and you have a veritable feast of wonderful language. My mother was English, and my father was from India, so I grew up speaking multiple languages."

Listening to Curly Dan is mesmerizing. He switches accents easily as he lists the different dialects and explains where he's from. By the time he's finished, I'm openly gawking and No Filter is laughing.

We've almost completed our breakfasts when No Filter startles us by slamming his hands on the table before turning to Curly Dan. "I found another entry," he announces loudly. "And boy, this one is a doozy," he continues. "She really let him have it this time."

"Oh. Can't wait to hear." exclaims Curly Dan. "What are you waiting for? Go get the register and read it to us."

While No Filter returns to the shelter, Curly Dan turns to me, explaining they've been following a woman who is writing anonymous entries in the registers to an unknown man. "We found the first one on Springer, and then another one at Whitley Gap. This poor girl," he adds, shaking his head sadly. "Apparently, he cheated her out of a business deal and broke her heart along with it. He must be a real asshole."

No Filter slips back onto the bench and starts flipping through the notebook in his hands. Clearing his throat, he begins to read. *"Dear Hud."*

My mind whirls, and I can barely suppress my startled reaction as he speaks the words I wrote last night.

CHAPTER 11

Nice Ass

Date: Monday, March 17
Starting Location: Blue Mountain Shelter
Destination: Deep Gap Shelter
Total Trip Miles: 63.3

I struggle not to react, keeping my eyes on the table in front of me and glancing up only briefly to gauge Curly Dan's reactions. He doesn't seem to notice me, however. All his attention is focused on No Filter as he reads the words on the page. I'm shocked to hear them. They're intense. Angry, hurtful, slashing words explode in the air as he speaks them aloud. Accusations and insults and blame wrapped in enough profanity to surprise even Liam. I can barely believe I wrote those words.

The hushed silence when he finishes reading is finally broken by No Filter's loud, whooshing, "Whoa. That guy is one lousy motherfucker, and she is one badass, really angry woman."

We laugh, our chuckles breaking the tension. Before anyone else can comment, Curly Dan jumps up from the table, announcing we're wasting daylight, and it's time to hike. Soon we're cleaning our surroundings, shouldering our backpacks, and heading up the trail.

I find myself sandwiched between the two men. When I step to one side to let No Filter pass me—proper etiquette for slower hikers—he waves me on, telling me he always brings up the rear.

"I've been following Curly's ass for more miles than I care to think about. It'll be a nice change to have a different one to stare at; although, I have to say Daniel does have a very fine butt."

He laughs when I involuntarily glance toward Curly, who is quickly disappearing down the trail ahead of us. "Told you so."

Shaking my head at his nonsense, I turn and begin heading up the trail. We hike in silence for some time, but something he said keeps mulling over in my head. Finally, I stop and turn back to him.

"We're less than fifty miles from Springer. How could you have been following Curly Dan for more miles than you care to think about, if that's where you started?"

"Ah, who says we started hiking at Springer?" he questions me teasingly. "Sorry," he adds at my answering frown. "Actually, you could probably say this journey started about five years ago at Campo."

"Campo, on the PCT?" I ask, referring to the small border town where the Pacific Crest Trail begins its trek from Mexico to Canada. "You and Curly hiked the PCT?"

"Yes." No Filter chuckles at my astonished question. "And then we went to Montana and hiked south to Crazy Cook Monument in New Mexico on the Continental Divide Trail."

"Oh … my … God," I whisper, staring at him in absolute awe. "The PCT, the CDT, and now the AT—you and Curly are triple crowners."

"Well, we have to get to Katahdin first," he agrees with a chuckle. "But, yes, eventually, we'll be triple crowners."

"Wow," I murmur, shaking my head in disbelief. "You *have* been following that ass for a lot of miles. Almost 8,000 by the time you're finished,"

I add, calculating the distance they will have to walk. "You two are like hiking royalty."

No Filter grins broadly at me. "It's no big deal, girl. Just one step at a time; one step at a time."

"But it is kind of a big deal," I argue. "Just the two of you hiking so far, having to get along, the resupplies, the logistics, it's ... well, it's an amazing feat."

No Filter glances away from me, his normally pleasant expression morphing into one of sadness. Shifting his feet nervously, he looks back at me, studying my face intently.

"Did I say something wrong?" I ask. "I'm sorry if—"

"No, no," he interrupts. "We, uh ... there used to be three of us." Sighing, he reaches up to run his fingers through his nonexistent hair, chuckling when he remembers he's bald. "Sorry, can't seem to kick the nervous habit. Anyway," he begins again, "I met Daniel and Jeffrey during the PCT kickoff party at Lake Morena. We were all so different, but we clicked, you know. We became friends, hiking buddies, and then ... ah ... partners."

He hesitates, watching me for some type of reaction, but I smile, nodding at him to continue. Motioning toward a couple of trailside boulders, No Filter invites me to sit beside him, saying it's time for a snack break. We rummage through our food bags, grinning at each other when we both pull out a Snickers bar. While we eat and drink, No Filter continues his story.

"We were the Three Amigos, the Three Musketeers, the Three Stooges. We were brothers-in-backpacks, lovers, family. I've never been ashamed of my sexuality, never tried to hide it or pretend to be something I'm not, but for all my bluntness and lack of filter, I keep some things to myself. Jeffrey was openly gay, sometimes almost flamboyantly so. He was out and proud." A big grin splits No Filter's face as he reminisces. "Dear Lord, but he was one crazy dude.

"He'd strut down the trail like he was on a catwalk, greeting people we met with this high, falsetto voice calling everyone 'darling' and 'sugar' just to see their reaction. He loved ridges and rock falls. He used to skip and hop across them, sometimes doing pirouettes on the tallest rocks, laughing when Daniel and I would yell at him to be careful. Sometimes, he would sing. He'd belt out show tunes at the top of his voice as he hiked. He was so full of life and joy … you know. I called him Rock Dancer, and he loved it."

No Filter stares off into the forest around us for a long moment before shifting his focus back to me. "Sorry," he says. "My mouth is running again. I shouldn't burden you with this story."

"No, it's okay. What … May I ask what happened?"

With another sigh, he begins the rest of his story.

"Well, we finished the PCT together, and it was such an amazing adventure we decided to do the CDT. So, we moved to Portland, worked and saved our money for a year, and then went to Canada and started hiking south through Montana. One weekend, we left the trail to resupply in this little mountain town in New Mexico. We checked into a hotel, cleaned up, and went for hamburgers and beer at a local hangout. Rock Dancer was his usual crazy self, maybe even more so because of the negative reactions he got from some of the locals.

"Anyway, the next day, the sheriff gave us a ride back to the trail, which was basically a dirt road at that point, and told us to keep going south. We'd been hiking for several miles when we heard a vehicle behind us. Curly and I were ahead and off to one side talking about something or other and not paying a lot of attention. Rock Dancer was behind us. I remember he was belting out Smash Mouth's *All Star*, dancing down the middle of the road and singing about being a shooting star when the sound got louder. We turned in time to see an old, dirt-covered truck speed up and head straight toward Jeffrey."

No Filter's eyes flick back to me when I gasp. "Oh, no."

He nods, sorrow filling his eyes. "He tried to get out of the way, but it was too late. They never swerved or tried to miss him. They didn't stop, either, but barreled on by us yelling 'fucking faggots' and disappeared down the dirt road in a cloud of dust. It took hours to get help, and by then, it was too late. It was a senseless, stupid murder, all because he was gay."

He leans forward, elbows on knees, resting his head in his hands. His voice breaks with anger and pain, and he takes several shuddering breaths before he speaks again. "Curly says I blame myself for not paying enough attention to our surroundings. But I have to think if we'd all been a bit more aware of what was going on, Rock Dancer would be doing this hike with us."

For a few long moments, we sit silently, each of us lost in our thoughts. I struggle to think of something to say to ease the pain of those memories. I've only known No Filter for a few hours, but he's already a friend. Before I can speak, however, he straightens, swallows roughly, and then turns to me with a sad smile.

"It took a few months, but we went back to the same spot, erected a small monument to Jeffrey, and then Daniel and I finished the CDT. Doing the AT and becoming triple crowners was always Rock Dancer's dream, so we're doing this in his honor. We're carrying a small rock with his name engraved on it. When we reach the sign on top of Katahdin, we'll leave it there."

"Oh, I like that, and I hope I can be there when you leave it." I smile back at him. "Do you mind if I ask you one more question though?"

"Sure, go ahead."

"The bald head. Curly said you guys shaved your heads on top of Springer. Was that for Rock Dancer, too?"

This time No Filter's laughter fills the woods around us. "No," he finally manages to answer. "No, it was payment for a dare Curly lost. It's a pretty good tale. Come on," he says, getting up. "I'll tell you as we hike."

Grabbing his arm, I stop him before he goes any farther. "Thank you for sharing your story. I want you to know your secrets are safe with me. I'm not a big talker, and I would never break your trust."

He nods back at me, smiling in agreement. "I know. And I want you to know your secrets are safe with me, too, RAW."

"RAW? What do you mean?"

The mischief is back in his eyes as No Filter smirks at me. "RAW," he answers. "*Really Angry Woman.* Go on." He waves at me, shooing me up the trail and laughing at my dumbfounded look as I realize he is referring to my anonymous entry in the shelter register. "Move it, hikergurrrl," he growls, deliberately drawing out the "ur" sound. "Curly Dan is so far ahead of us, he'll think we've fallen off the trail or something."

Shaking my head at his silliness and still trying to figure out how he knew I was the one writing the entries, I turn and begin climbing the winding trail in front of me. I can hear No Filter chuckling behind me. When I peek over my shoulder to see what is going on, he just smiles at me. "Nice ass," he says.

His chuckles turn into a full belly laugh when I raise my middle finger and flip him off.

CHAPTER 12

And into the Forest I Go

Date: Monday, March 17
Starting Location: Blue Mountain Shelter
Destination: Deep Gap Shelter
Total Trip Miles: 63.3

I've never really backpacked with a companion before; actually, I've never done any long-distance, multi-day hiking before this last minute, spur-of-the-moment trip. Liam and I spent hours roaming and exploring the woods around Gran's cabin, camping out overnight when the mood struck us, and swimming in the creek when we needed to cool off. Occasionally, Hudson and I would day hike at nearby state parks. One summer, he took Susan, Oliver, David, and me on a working vacation at his family's cabin in Maine. We planned and brainstormed in the morning, swam, fished, and hiked in the afternoons.

When we visited Georgia for Liam and Emma's wedding, we hiked part of the AT approach trail at Amicalola Falls State Park to view the famous waterfalls. At one point, we sat on a viewing bench, and I pointed out where the Appalachian Trail started at the top of the mountain towering above us. But this is the first time I've backpacked with anyone, and I'm surprised to find I like it a lot. Or maybe it's the person I'm hiking with.

No Filter keeps me entertained with stories about the PCT. I listen to him describe encountering Mojave green rattlesnakes while crossing the desert sections, post holing in the deep Sierra snow fields, and scrambling over the rocky crags of Washington. The three of them became well known on the trail for their practical jokes, their ridiculous dares, and their crazy pranks. I understand why they earned their Three Stooges nickname.

The trail also helps the morning pass quickly. Since leaving the shelter, we've been steadily dropping in elevation as we hike toward Unicoi Gap. At one point, we pass over a narrow ridgeline and descend into a small, sheltered hollow. No Filter almost runs into me when I suddenly stop in the middle of the trail, staring at the scene before me. We've left winter and entered spring.

The dirt path in front of me and the tree trunks lining it are the only shades of brown I can see … everything else is green. *Emerald, chartreuse, jade, citron, lime,* the words tumble around in my head as I gaze at this beautiful place. Ahead, the trail weaves a serpentine path through tall oaks and small shrubs before disappearing from view in the thick woods at the other end of the narrow vale. Thick grass edges the dirt walkway, and the verdant green of new leaves covers every twig, branch, and treetop. Directly in front of us, a majestic, ancient oak tree spreads its gnarled limbs into a woven roof overhead. Halfway up its wide trunk is a white blaze, a two-by-four inch painted stripe proudly proclaiming to everyone who is privileged to pass by that this is the Appalachian Trail, the famous granddaddy of all the long-distance hiking trails.

Early morning fog still lingers in this secluded hollow. The mist captures the sun's rays, transforming them into an otherworldly luminescence that spreads its glow over every leaf, twig, branch, and blade until the very air seems to pulse with the promise of new life. It's quiet. A hushed silence, broken only by an occasional rustle of leaves or chirp of a hidden bird, steals the breath from my lungs as I stare at this gift before me. I can feel No Filter behind me, but he makes no sound as we stand frozen in awe.

A slight movement behind the old oak catches my eye, and I wonder what could be hiding there. For a moment, I consider fairies, wood nymphs, or unicorns—anything seems possible in this magical place. My inner scientist rolls its eyes at this ridiculous thought, but for the briefest second, something in me yearns for the mystical to appear.

It's a doe that emerges from behind the trunk. Stepping timidly on her graceful legs, she watches us warily with her curious eyes. She pauses in the middle of the trail and flicks her ears before looking over her shoulder toward the oak behind her where a soft rustling of dry leaves indicates something else is hidden there.

I'm holding my breath, anxiously waiting to see what could be following her. It's six to eight weeks too early for does to start dropping their young, but nature never operates on a strict timetable, and it's indeed a small, spotted fawn that toddles on shaking legs toward its mother. It can't be more than a few hours old. Its legs still tremble, and it can barely keep its balance as it slowly stumbles to its mother's side. It nudges at her belly, looking for a meal, but she steps away before giving its face a careful grooming with her tongue. Then, pushing it with her head, they amble off into the underbrush. Before disappearing from view, the two turn to gaze at us one more time.

For a brief moment, we're four living things accepting each other without fear or threat, all part of the beauty of nature and the cycle of life. Two more steps and they're gone, quietly blending into the foliage as though they were never there.

Only after they've completely disappeared do I turn to look at No Filter. His face radiates pure joy as he grins down at me before mumbling something. "What?" I ask.

"My favorite John Muir quote," he explains, nodding toward the wonderland in front of us. "And into the forest I go, to lose my mind and find my soul."

His words repeat on a loop in my head as we resume our walk toward Unicoi Gap.

CHAPTER 13

To Lose My Mind

Date: Monday, March 17
Starting Location: Blue Mountain Shelter
Destination: Deep Gap Shelter
Total Trip Miles: 63.3

We catch up to Curly Dan at the parking area where the AT crosses state highway 75. Once again, trail magic in the form of bottled apple juice and individual bags of mixed nuts is waiting for us on one of the nearby picnic tables. Before we can drop our packs and join him, he's already talking about the hidden hollow.

"Did you see?" he questions. "And the light and the fog making everything glow," he exclaims. Excited, he can barely get one thought out before he's moving on to another.

No Filter eases onto the bench across from him, laughing at his friend's enthusiasm. They both begin to discuss what they saw and how they felt, so in tune with each other they finish the other's sentences. At one point, Dan reaches across and grabs No Filter's hand and apologizes for not waiting on him because they could have seen it together. There's so much love and affection in the gesture and in the look they give each other that I have to glance away, suddenly overcome with the longing to share this hike with someone I love.

My thoughts are interrupted by Curly Dan when he asks if I need to go into town to resupply. He has *The Hiker's Handbook* open in front of him, and he and No Filter are discussing the trail ahead of us and their food situation. From this road crossing, it's possible to catch a ride into Helen or Hiawassee, Georgia. A town resupply usually involves a night in a motel room, a chance to do laundry, and the opportunity to buy food for the next section of your hike. But I still have enough food for at least another day. When I tell him this, we all agree to wait until we reach the next road crossing at Dicks Creek Gap. It's another sixteen miles farther on the trail. If we spend tonight at Deep Gap Shelter, we'll have an easy three-mile hike to the gap where US Highway 76 crosses the AT.

Decision made, No Filter digs into the trail magic, passing bottles of juice and bags of nuts to each of us as Curly Dan reads descriptions of the trail ahead from the handbook. Twenty minutes later, we dump our trash, shoulder our backpacks, and prepare to leave. Dan takes the lead, I fall in behind him, and No Filter brings up the rear. And as simple as that, I become part of their group. Strangers only hours ago, they've become trail friends and hiking buddies. It feels right. It feels comfortable. I cross the road with a smile on my face.

As usual after a road crossing, the trail climbs, and climbs, and climbs. We take it easy, ambling along at a comfortable pace. If I'm slowing them down, they don't mention it. Conversation flows, each of us sharing stories about ourselves. I say very little about my adult life, only mentioning I'm taking a break from post-graduate work at MIT.

Although No Filter has somehow figured out I'm the one writing the anonymous journal entries—or at least he thinks he has—I'm not ready to share how long I've been at MIT or that my published papers on Chaos Theory have already earned me a PhD. Instead, I share my knowledge of the flora surrounding us. I point out the differences between scarlet oaks and blackjack oaks, shortleaf pines and Virginia pines.

We spy a few dogwoods that have burst into flower on the sunnier south-facing slopes, and we walk through a rhododendron tunnel so thick with the shiny, leathery evergreen leaves they block out the sunlight above us. In two or three months, they'll be covered in showy clusters of pink and purple flowers.

As the temperature rises, we're treated to the buzzing of bees, a swarm of bright butterflies erupting from a bush as we pass, and even a few pesky gnats we have to brush away from our noses and mouths. But perhaps the best of all is the red eft No Filter almost steps on. His surprised yelp has us turning back toward him only to see him bent over examining the immature newt. Against the dark browns and grays of the forest floor, its bright orange-red body seems to glow. We watch until it wiggles away, searching for its dinner of insects and worms.

We're serenaded by red-eyed vireos, yellow-bellied sapsuckers, and black-capped chickadees, their whistled "fee-bee, fee-bee" following us down the trail. The deep thump, thump, thump of the male ruffed grouse beating its wings against its body to attract a mate causes Curly Dan to turn to me in surprise. It sounds very much like the turning blades of a helicopter. There are more wildflowers to be appreciated: tiny yellow dogtooth violets, deep purple dwarf irises, and the pink bloodroot. Rounding a bend in the trail, we're greeted with an open meadow of my favorite wildflower.

"Trilliums. Trillium grandiflorum." My excited shout brings Curly Dan and No Filter to my side as I make my way off trail to enjoy their beauty. "Look," I command, squatting down to examine the flower in front of me. "These are the most amazing plants. The stem isn't really a stem but a peduncle because the rhizome, which is the part in the ground, is considered the stem. Then it has a set of three large leaves, which aren't really leaves at all but green bracts. Above them," I continue, tracing the pseudo-stem with my finger, "is a set of three sepals, which look like little green baby leaves but are actually part of the flower. Finally, you get to this beautiful white flower with three petals and six stamens divided into two whorls. Nothing is what it appears to be; it's all chaos yet organized in patterns and sets of threes. Each one growing offset on the stem to let the sunlight hit all the parts of the plant."

My explanation finished, I stand, letting my eyes roam over the beauty before me. "There are other colors of trilliums, but the white ones were my granny's favorites. I think I was probably around seven when she took me into the woods and explained to me what I've just shown you. I remember she also said they were spring ephemerals." Something niggles at the back of my mind, and I turn slowly, frowning as I survey the woods and the meadow where we stand.

"What is a spring ephemeral?" asks No Filter.

"It's a plant whose life-cycle is synchronized with the forest where it grows. Something—" I glance around again, still frowning, still trying to identify what is bothering me.

"Ella?" Curly Dan interrupts my thoughts. "Is something wrong?"

"It's six weeks too early for these flowers to bloom, just like it's still too early for the doe to fawn. The timing is all off, and the patterns are disrupted."

"Maybe we're getting an early spring this year."

"No," I answer, slowly shaking my head. "Winter doesn't give up so easily. We need to be extra careful about the weather for the next few weeks." Turning to them both, I smile, shrugging my shoulders. "Nothing we can do now but hike."

So, we do.

Three hours, six miles, and almost two thousand feet in elevation gain, we emerge from the forest onto the rocky summit of Tray Mountain. The sky is a clear, bright blue, the sun almost hot, and the view is an amazing, 360-degree panoramic display. Looking south, we can see Blood Mountain, and to the north is Standing Indian Mountain almost thirty trail miles away. Farther north, we can make out the dark blur of the Smoky Mountains on the distant horizon. We stare and stare until our growling stomachs remind us it's lunchtime.

Lunch is a shared affair, the contents of our almost empty food bags dumped out and sifted through to find enough food for our empty bellies. I'm in the middle of my piece of jerky when No Filter hands me a baggie full of colorful bits. "Eat your veggies," he tells me. "They're good for you."

I turn the bag over in my hand, examining it closely. "What are they?"

"Freeze-dried veggies," he replies. "Corn, carrots, peas, and green beans. They're good—sweet and crunchy; just be sure to drink a lot of water."

He's right, they are delicious, especially the corn. It tastes like sweet popped corn. While I munch down on them, I watch him open a vacuum-sealed pouch and crumble the contents into a plastic jar. He fills it with water, and then gives it a good shake. My curiosity gets the best of me, and I have to ask what he is doing. "Making dinner" is his reply.

He laughs when I roll my eyes at his cryptic remark. "It's meat sauce. Ground beef cooked, drained, and rinsed, then mixed with a good flavorful sauce and dehydrated on drying sheets, either in an oven or a dehydrator. It will rehydrate all afternoon as we're hiking. Tonight, when we get to the shelter, we'll dump it into a pan of boiling water along with some quick-cooking angel hair pasta, sprinkle it with parmesan, and have a delicious, rib-sticking, belly-busting dinner to finish our day. And," he adds, ginning at me, "Curly Dan and I would be honored to have your company for dinner."

"Well, I would be honored to accept your invitation." I grin back. "But I have to ask. How did you learn to make all this food?"

"By necessity, mostly. When you've hiked as many miles as we have, the prepackaged meals, the noodle and mashed potato mixes, the jerky and chips and trail mixes get really old and boring. So, I started making our meals, drying and vacuum sealing them, and then sending them in our mail drops. Besides, I'm a pretty good cook."

Curly Dan's loud guffaw and No Filter's smirking grin are good indicators I'm missing something here. "What's up with you two?"

"Sorry," Curly apologizes. "No Filter's being a little brat. He's more than just a 'good cook.' He's actually a graduate of the Institute of Culinary Education."

"The one in New York?" I ask incredulously. "That's like the number one culinary school in the US. Good cook, my ass. You're a chef." No Filter has the grace to look embarrassed as I yell at him, but he joins in when we all laugh at his discomfort.

"Come on, Little Brat," I say to the chef, "it's time to hike." Stuffing my food bag back in my pack, I stand, shouldering my pack and adjusting the straps.

"Little Brat, huh." No Filter huffs under his breath. "And to think I said you had a nice ass."

The climb down Tray Mountain is just as steep as the climb up. Sometimes, the trail is a series of switchbacks giving our knees some reprieve from the constant descent, and sometimes, it's a scramble over bare rocks. We pick our way carefully over the rockfalls, balancing the need for safety and the desire to get off the mountain. Down, down, down the trail leads, passing through Sassafras Gap and then Addis Gap. Finally, after six miles and the loss of all our elevation gain, we arrive at the base of Kelly Knob.

The climb up Kelly Knob is brutal. It's 1,000 feet straight up in less than a mile. We're also very tired from a long day of hiking. By the time we get to the shelter located just past the summit, we'll have hiked almost fifteen miles today. Although I'm carrying very little food or water, my pack feels like a boulder on my back.

Years ago, Gran taught me to *rest step* up steep, difficult hills. Basically, it's a technique to give your muscles a two or three second rest in the leg you're stepping forward on. The rear leg is locked, all your weight transferred to your leg bones as you swing the front leg forward and relax your leg, back, and hip muscles. Then, when you place your foot down, all the weight is transferred to it. The pause in between steps can last as long as needed depending on the terrain and your energy. I rest step *all* the way up Kelly Knob.

When we finally arrive at Deep Gap Shelter, we're exhausted. No Filter pulls out his cooking supplies and begins working on dinner. Curly Dan sets up their pads and sleeping bags, unpacking their backpacks, and hanging their gear from the mouse-proof chains. He makes a trip to the spring, filtering enough water for the night and the next morning. They work seamlessly together, their routine perfected by months of practice. Without even stopping to think about it, I join them in the shelter, arranging my bedding beside No Filter's.

Dinner is as delicious as he said it would be. After a huge helping of pasta topped with the tomato-based meat sauce and sprinkled liberally with parmesan cheese, No Filter serves us instant chocolate pudding made with his powdered cream and topped with dried cherries and slivered almonds. I'm in a food coma even before I crawl into my sleeping bag.

Night comes quickly, and a cold breeze rustles the leaves and works its way into the shelter. Warm and snug in my sleeping bag, knitted hat keeping my head and ears protected, I watch the last rays of the setting sun paint a golden glow across the horizon. Last night, I was alone in my tent crying as the sun set. Tonight, I'm sleeping in a shelter with two men. Complete strangers only this morning, now dear friends with whom I feel safe and comfortable.

There's an old hiker saying that whatever you need, the trail will provide. Did it know I was lonely? Did it know I needed new friends—accepting, welcoming friends who liked me for who I am? Did it know I needed a day to just forget everyone and everything that happened in New York, a chance to turn off the worries and anxieties, to lose myself and my mind in the natural world around me?

My sleepy brain wanders over all the surprises of the day. The secret hollow, the doe with her new fawn, the meadow of trilliums. The trail had gifted me with the most amazing day, one I will cherish forever.

The shelter is quiet. A night bird calls somewhere nearby, and I hear Dan's sleeping bag rustle as he rolls over, shifting around to find a more comfortable position. Just as I'm about to surrender to the pull of slumber, No Filter lets loose with a loud, rip-roaring fart. He must have been asleep because he sits up quickly with a "huh?" I clap my hand over my mouth, desperately trying to control my laughter, but it's a lost cause when Curly Dan begins to howl hilariously. Soon, the two of us are rolling around on the floor, laughing so hard we have to wipe the tears from our eyes.

"Oh, shut up." No Filter grouses before rolling over and scrunching down into his bag, muttering about wise asses and nice asses.

Oblivion takes me, and I sleep soundly until the next morning.

CHAPTER 14

And Find My Soul

Date: Tuesday, March 18
Starting Location: Deep Gap Shelter
Destination: Plumorchard Shelter
Total Trip Miles: 71.1

With only three and a half miles to Dicks Creek Gap where we plan to leave the trail and hitchhike into Hiawassee, we take our time the next morning, sleeping late, recovering from yesterday's 15 miles, and lingering over the last of No Filter's breakfasts. I donate my two remaining packets of hot chocolate mix to our meal. It's a leisurely start to what I hope will be another interesting day.

The guys have a mail drop waiting for them at The Blueberry Patch, an organic farm that houses hikers during the peak hiking season. For a small, reasonable fee, you can stay in their bunkhouse or set your tent up in a nearby field. Showers, laundry service, breakfast, and shuttle rides are included. I've never stayed in a hostel before, but I'm surprised to find I'm not nervous about the experience. A hot shower and clean clothes sound wonderful, and I need to go into town to resupply.

The next two hours pass in companionable conversation. No Filter shares some of his trail cooking secrets and recipes. Even though I'm pleasantly full from our breakfast, I find myself looking forward to another meal. We discuss my buying options for supplies in Hiawassee.

Curly Dan tells me about research he's been studying that indicates the backwoods, Appalachian dialect I grew up speaking can be traced almost directly to Elizabethan English. "Did your granny ever use the word 'afeared'?" At my nod, he continues. "And did you grow up saying, 'warsh rag' for wash cloths, 'tarred' for tired, 'far' for fire?"

He chuckles at the astonished look I give him. "How did you know?"

"Appalachian-English is one of the oldest dialects in the US. Most experts think the ruggedness of the mountains served as an isolating factor, keeping the people who settled here cut off from most of the outside world. Not only did it preserve their customs and beliefs, but their manner of speaking, too. Sadly, it's all but disappeared. Earlier researchers were able to document most of it, though.

"Just think," he continues, after stopping for a moment to catch his breath. "You and Shakespeare have something in common. A truly wonderful thing, if you ask me."

The idea that words, phrases, and speech patterns I've tried to distance myself from were those Shakespeare may have used is almost more than I can grasp. My mind instantly forms patterns, relationships, and abstractions. But for once, I turn it off, concentrating on listening to Dan, letting my emotions react to the astonishing things he's telling me.

When it's my turn, I share more about the local forest and the legends of the area.

"Have you heard the story of how Blood Mountain got its name?" I ask. When he shakes his head, I continue. "Well, about 400 years ago, there was a great battle between the Creek and Cherokee warriors. So fierce was the fighting and so brave were the warriors the hills ran red with their blood. Slaughter Mountain is nearby, and I guess adds to the legend. Of course, the elders also claim all the Cherokee gold was hidden on the mountain when we were forced from our land in the early 1800s."

"Has anyone tried to find the gold?" Dan asks with a knowing grin.

"Of course." I laugh. "More fools than you can count over the last two hundred years."

It's becoming more obvious from my stories and from my conversation about the trilliums and the doe yesterday that I'm the one who's been writing to *Hud* in the registers, but neither one of them says anything about the subject. I appreciate their silence and their willingness to accept me for who I am.

~ * * * ~

We can hear the traffic from the highway before we reach it. Curly Dan has lengthened his lead in front of us when I see him stop and survey what must be ahead. He turns and begins to backtrack to where No Filter and I are still walking. The two of them share a silent look before he speaks. "There's a guy sitting at one of the tables. He seems to be by himself, but I thought it might be best if we approached the crossing together." Curly Dan smiles at me and shrugs. "Just a precaution," he adds. No Filter agrees, so the three of us stay close as we continue along the trail, rounding a bend before entering the roadside picnic area near the parking area.

Dicks Creek Gap is a busy place. It's a convenient trailhead for day or section hikers who want to hike south to the top of Kelly Knob or north toward Bly Gap where an iconic, much photographed, gnarled oak marks the border between Georgia and North Carolina. Both are popular hikes, and the parking lot is already filled with cars and hikers. The fact that it's Spring Break for many of the nearby schools and a cool, sunny day means a lot of teenagers and college students begin to pass us on their way to the knob.

The man Curly Dan mentioned is at one of the picnic tables off to the side. He does look a little out of place, sitting there by himself, and he's staring intently at the trail rather than watching the activity in the parking lot. There's something vaguely familiar about him when I lean around Dan to get a better view. No Filter must think the same because I hear him say, "Is that—"

"Liam," I continue, interrupting him.

"You know Liam Crow from Mountain Crossings?" he asks, glancing toward me.

"He's my cousin."

"Did you know he was going to be here?" Curly Dan asks.

"No." As we start walking again, I can't help but wonder if something has happened. "I hope everything's okay," I murmur to myself. Both guys give me a worried glance but don't say anything.

As soon as Liam recognizes me, he's standing, rounding the table, and walking toward us. I can see his worried expression relax as he realizes who I'm with. One more tiny proof I've not misjudged my hiking companions.

He greets them with a handshake, calling them by their trail names before giving me a hard hug. "Been worried about you," he whispers before letting me go. There's an awkward pause as the four of us stand there, no one quite sure what to do or say. Finally, I bluntly ask him what he is doing here.

Liam shifts nervously, his eyes darting over Curly Dan and No Filter before settling on me. "Something's come up, and I really need to talk to you, Ari. In private," he adds, turning to the guys standing next to me.

"Oh, of course, sorry." No Filter nods to Liam. "Tell you what. Dan and I are going to see if we can hitch a ride to the Blueberry Patch with someone out there in the parking lot. You're more than welcome to join us later, if you want, Ella. Or is it Ari?" He grins at me, twitching his mustache before becoming more serious. "If we see you there, great, but if not, we'll catch you somewhere up ahead on the trail. Okay?" When I nod, he turns back to Liam. "Nice to see you again, Crow." Then, with a nod and a wave, they make their way to the roadside where they strike up a conversation with a van driver who is apparently giving rides into town.

Two minutes later, they're both gone, and I turn back to Liam. "What's going on? Has anything happened to Uncle Billy or Emma?"

"No, they're fine," he answers, shaking his head. "I just really need you to come home with me."

"What? You drove all the way here to tell me you really need me to come home with you? What exactly does that mean, Liam?"

My cousin has the decency to look apologetic at my demand, but he doesn't back down.

"Look," he says, starting again. "You left things in a mess in New York. You need to come back to Neels Gap with me. We'll get on the phone, talk to Susan and Hudson, and get this all straightened out. You need to be taking care of business instead of out here hiking."

"I need to be taking care of business, huh? Well, let me tell you something, Liam Crow." There's fury in my voice as I step toward my cousin. "All I've done for the last nine years is *take care of business*. First, it was classes at MIT and research and papers and presentations and dissertations." I continue to shout as I advance closer to him, and he slowly backs away. My voice has gotten loud enough for several people to glance our way, but I pay them no mind as I continue to unload on my startled cousin.

"And, yes, I enjoyed it, and it was good, but it was *business*. And then there was Hudson and *real business*—programming and writing code and figuring out how to make something real and useful from my theories. It was business, business, business, always business.

"But you know what happened while I was taking care of business, Liam?" My fury has suddenly run its course, and I plop myself down on the table's bench, staring at the ground below me. "Do you know what happened? I forgot to take care of me, Liam … I forgot to take care of me."

He takes a seat beside me, reaching over to take one of my shaking hands in his. "I'm sorry. I didn't mean—"

But I shake him off, ignoring his apology. I'm still too angry, my emotions too raw. I can feel tears pricking my eyes, and they only make me more upset. No more tears, I promised myself. With a shuddering sigh, I lean back against the tabletop, then turn and face my worried cousin.

"I tried so hard to fit in. Changed the way I spoke, the way I dressed, the way I ate, and what I thought. But by doing so, I lost who I was—who I am. I lost me, Liam."

My cousin's dear face reflects the sorrow and regret in my own. "I'm sorry. I'm so sorry. I didn't know, didn't understand. But—"

Once again, I interrupt what I know is going to be another plea for me to return home with him. "Something happened yesterday. Something wonderful and magical, and I want you to listen to me until I'm finished, okay?"

Liam cocks his head, studying me closely. "Wonderful and magical?" he teases. "I thought you didn't believe in magic?"

Rolling my eyes at his pathetic attempt at humor, I once more ask him to listen to my story. "No interruptions."

When he nods in agreement, I begin telling him about meeting No Filter and Curly Dan and the instant friendship we developed. I describe the hidden hollow we hiked through. The luminescent fog, the brilliant, glowing green of each leaf, the magnificent old oak with its white blaze, the doe with her too-early fawn, and the brief moment when I wished for a unicorn, or wood nymph, or fairy to appear.

I express my delight at finding the meadow abloom with trilliums and the memories of Granny they invoked. And then I repeat No Filter's favorite John Muir quote. "'And into the forest I go, to lose my mind and find my soul.'

"That's what happened to me yesterday, Liam. I let go of my mind. For once, I just existed and was happy. I didn't think about algorithms or computer codes. I didn't see the world around me as patterns and formulas. I didn't worry about chaos and interruptions. I lost my mind, and with it, I lost all worry about the business I should be in New York taking care of. I lost my mind, and I started finding my soul."

The tears I've been trying to hold back are trickling down my cheeks. Liam reaches out with his thumb and gently wipes them away. "I'm sorry, cousin. I'm so sorry," he whispers before hugging me to him. "What can I do to make this better?"

Drawing away, I look up at him. "Don't ask me to go back. I love Hudson, I always will, but I'll never go back to New York. I *need* this hike. I *need* to find myself. And I *have* been thinking about the business, Liam. I truly have. I own the intellectual property rights to the math theories the whole system is based on. He can go to Italy with Gia, if it makes him happy. He can *try* to use our program if he wants to. It might take some legal work, but I can make it *very* difficult and *very* expensive for them to use any part of the program without my consent. And I have every intention of doing just that!"

The biggest smile spreads across my cousin's face, and then he begins to laugh, a deep, gut-busting, joyful laugh that fills the space around us. It's impossible to ignore, and soon, we're both wiping tears from our eyes as we grin at each other.

"Oh, there's the girl I remember," Liam manages to choke out. "And that's the badass, competent, woods-wise woman she grew up to be."

CHAPTER 15

Cinderella at the Ball

Date: Tuesday, March 18
Starting Location: Deep Gap Shelter
Destination: Plumorchard Shelter
Total Trip Miles: 71.1

If I thought getting away from Liam was going to be easy, I was sorely mistaken.

After we both calm down a bit from my emotional outburst, after he agrees not to ask me to return to New York, and after he finally accepts I'm going to continue my hike, we begin discussing my options for resupplying. Liam volunteers to take me into town, either to the Blueberry Patch where Dan and No Filter are going, or to a hotel where I could get a room for myself. He even offers to get a room, too, so we can spend some time together, and he can give me a ride back to the trail tomorrow.

For some reason, I have a hard time deciding what I want to do. Suddenly, I don't want to leave the trail; I want to keep hiking. I need to be back in the woods. When I finally confess that's what I really want to do, Liam tells me he probably has enough supplies in his truck to get me to Franklin, North Carolina, another forty miles on the trail. Apparently, he always carries a week's worth of food and supplies in his truck in case he and Emma decide to go camping or if he finds a hiker who needs some help. I suspect some of the homeless in the area towns probably benefit from Liam's generosity, too.

Having decided I'll make use of his emergency supplies, I stand and start toward the parking lot, but Liam doesn't follow me. Instead, he continues to sit at the table. I watch him fidget, shifting his body, glancing from side-to-side, and then back to me, running his hands through his hair. It is so unlike him. I know something is still bothering him and our discussion isn't over yet. Finally, I sit down across from him, and demand he tells me what's going on.

He continues to shift around uneasily before finally confessing he still needs to talk to me about something.

"What is it, Liam? Just spit it out, okay?"

Nodding, he takes a deep breath before focusing on me. "Tell me about Gia and what happened your last night in New York. Tell me why you think Hudson is engaged to her and they've been living together for two years."

Anger sparks at his request. "Why?" I demand.

My cousin raises his hands in supplication. "Just trust me, please. I just need to talk this through with you."

Scowling at him, I finally nod, resigned to finishing what he came here to talk about.

"You've known him for what, almost six years now, and he's been my friend for over two. Does any of this—the engagement, living together, stealing the business—sound like the Hudson we know? He's always been an upstanding guy. I like him. You just said you love him. Does this sound like something he would do? Does it?"

Liam has a point. I've looked for patterns in Hudson's behavior, tried to understand how and why, but I've only become more confused than ever. Conceding he may have a point, I nod for him to continue.

"So, let's focus on Gia. Do you remember when you first met her?"

Frowning, I concentrate, trying to remember when I was introduced to her. "I think … I think it was at the fancy charity ball his parents sponsor every year. Yes, yes, it was. Remember three years ago? I sent you a picture.

"Hudson invited me the previous year, but I was too nervous to go. That year, he persuaded me to go with him. He promised to stay by my side and said it would be a chance for me to meet some of the people who were investing in our company. He told me I needed to get used to hobnobbing with the 'rich and famous' because we were going to be very rich and very famous someday." I chuckle softly at the memory.

"I went to his parents' penthouse to get ready for the party. His sister, Kathryn, was there as well as a makeup artist, a hairdresser, a manicurist, and a personal shopper with a rack of evening dresses and accessories to choose from. You know, Liam"—I turn to my cousin with a wry smile—"it's true. The rich really are different from the rest of us."

He answers me with a chuckle of his own.

"Although I was dreading the afternoon, it turned out to be a lot of fun. There was champagne, fancy hors d'oeuvres, and a lot of pampering. It was the girls-only, getting-ready-for-the prom, mother and daughter bonding that I never experienced. I remember wishing Granny could have been there."

"You looked so beautiful and so happy in the photo."

"I was. I felt like Cinderella with her Prince Charming all evening." My mind wanders to the lovely peach silk dress the stylist picked for me, the soft, loose waves of my hairdo, and the sight of Hudson in his tailored tuxedo.

"And you met Gia that night?" Liam interrupts my musing.

"Yes, she and her parents were seated at the Calders' table. Kathryn introduced her as a family friend she grew up with."

"Did you get the impression Hudson was interested in her or had some type of history with her?"

"No, thinking about it now, he didn't have much to say to her. In fact, I remember he was a bit rude when she spoke to him. I thought it was because she was a few years older than him and was actually Kathryn's friend."

"How did she act toward you?"

"Polite but cool. I think she dismissed me fairly quickly as someone who wasn't worth her time."

"When did you see her again?"

"Liam. Is this really necessary? What good is it going to do talking about all this now? They're engaged. She's living in his condo." Frustrated with his interrogation, I start to stand, but he grabs my hand.

"Please, a few more questions. Okay?"

"All right." I huff, plopping back down on the bench. "Make it quick."

"When did you see Gia again?"

"It wasn't until we started serious negotiations with Italia. I knew she worked there. Vincent Cattaneo is her uncle, and the whole family is involved in the business, but I hadn't seen her before then. I … Oh …"

Something I'd forgotten, a memory I'd tucked away and conveniently refused to think about rears its ugly head, nagging at me to remember.

"What is it?" Liam stares at me intently. "Where did you just go?"

"It was a year later, time for the charity ball, and I thought maybe we would go again. Despite my nervousness, we actually had fun the year before. By the time the evening was over, he'd somehow persuaded me to dance with him. Me dancing. Can you believe it?" Shaking my head, I smile sadly at my cousin.

"But he didn't mention it, and I finally asked if we were going. He stuttered a bit, and then mumbled something about having to go out of town for the weekend. I didn't question him. The financials for the business were a little shaky, and I knew he'd been busy with investor meetings and was stressed. I didn't want to push."

When I stop, staring at the weathered tabletop between us, Liam takes one of my hands in his, prompting me to finish my story. "What happened? What are you not telling me?"

With a resigned sigh, I continue. "*The Times* ran a huge article about the fundraiser in their Sunday section. There were lots of photos. Hudson was in one of them. He was talking to Vincent Cattaneo, and Gia was standing next to him. She was smiling at him, and they were holding hands."

The tears I thought were gone are back, filling up my eyes and threatening to spill over. Taking a deep breath, I swallow them down before I finish. "I never told him I saw the picture. I pretended nothing happened, and he never mentioned it. It was two years ago, probably about the time they would have gotten engaged and she moved in with him.

"I was such a coward, Liam. If I'd said something, anything. If I'd only called him on his lie, none of this would have happened. Poor ... pathetic ... stupid ... hillbilly Ariella. I wonder if they laughed about it."

"That damned, lying, motherfucking, son-of-a-bitch."

While I stare at the woods around us, lost in my memories, my cousin sits across the table from me and curses Hudson to all kinds of living hell.

CHAPTER 16

No Fairy Tale Princess

Date: Tuesday, March 18
Starting Location: Deep Gap Shelter
Destination: Plumorchard Shelter
Total Trip Miles: 71.1

My conversation with Liam lasted most of the afternoon. He wanted to know everything that happened on my last day in New York. What did Vincent Cattaneo actually say when he announced Hudson was accepting a position with them? Where was Gia, and what was she doing during the announcement? Why didn't Susan and I follow the executives to the reception? He wanted every detail.

I closed my eyes, trying to picture the scene in my mind, describing what I'd seen, heard, felt.

Applause filled the room as Hudson finished the last of his comments and began taking questions from the audience. Susan and I were sitting at the rear of the room, watching everything, when she leaned over, whispering in my ear. "He did an amazing job, Ariella."

"Yes, he did," I concurred, smiling back at her. "He's always amazing." Memories from the night before and the shower that morning widened my grin

as I heard her chuckle softly. It's impossible not to admire how comfortable and at ease he is in front of an audience.

Years of elite boarding schools, skiing trips to the Alps, summers in the Hamptons, and extensive world travel had prepared him for the role he's now filling. It doesn't hurt that he's astonishingly handsome. Blessed by good genes, good health, and good tailoring, Hudson is the epitome of what most people think a Harvard-educated, MBA-trained, business leader should look and act. It's not hard to understand why his parents have political aspirations for him. "And," I thought smugly to myself in that moment, "he's all mine."

The questions over, Vincent Cattaneo joined Hudson at the podium. Several other executives stood around them, including Gia, who wrapped her arm around Hudson's. An uneasy feeling twisted my stomach, but my attention was focused on Vincent, who began by thanking Hudson and his staff for the informative presentations. I listened in astonishment as he announced that Hudson had accepted the newly created position of President of International Security and, after his move to Italy, would begin the immediate installation of the new software program. He ended his remarks by inviting everyone to a celebratory reception to honor Hudson and welcome him to the company. Then, he turned and ushered everyone off the stage where they were joined by more executives before exiting through a side door.

I stood on tiptoe, craning my head and moving from side to side, desperately trying to see what was happening. For a moment, the crowd shifted, and I could see Hudson. He pulled his arm away from Gia before placing his hand at the small of her back and guiding her through the open doorway in front of them. The movement was all Hudson, all gentleman. I've had his hand on my lower back so many times; I can almost feel it now. His hand there always made me feel protected and cherished.

Seeing him touch Gia in that way made me lightheaded, and I sat down quickly, grabbing the edge of the seat to keep my balance. I lost sight of them as the rest of the attendees began to exit the room.

Susan and I were left sitting there, both of us staring in bewilderment at the empty room. The uneasy feeling had exploded into an overwhelming nausea, *making me gasp in pain as I turned to her for an explanation. "What did Vincent mean? Did he say Hudson was leaving?"*

She took my hands, trying to calm me. "It's okay," she reassured me. "The papers he brought over and you signed yesterday evening closed all the loopholes we found in your partnership contract with Hudson and the investors. Even if he wanted to, he can't steal your part of the business. You're protected. Please, I'm sure it's just a misunderstanding."

And then I told her Hudson did come to my apartment. I told her about everything we did, but none of it involved signing any papers.

"Oh, dear," she mumbled to herself when I finished. "Okay, this is what we're going to do," she said after a couple of long, silent minutes. "We're going to march into the reception and demand to speak to him. We're going to get this all straightened out, and I promise you, Ariella, everything is going to be all right. I'm not going to let him or Italia get away with cheating you out of your share of the business."

She was facing me then, all righteous anger and determination, but I couldn't go with her into that room. The thought of seeing all those strangers caused the bile to rise in my throat. Clamping a hand over my mouth, I rushed from the room, desperately seeking an escape from the panic threatening to overwhelm me.

I could hear Susan calling to me as I ran out the front doors of the building, tripping and falling my way to the street to hail a cab. I slid into the backseat of the closest one and gasped out my address. When I heard her voice again, I turned and looked out the back window. She was standing in the middle of the front steps, holding one of my shoes, watching my taxi pull away. It was then I realized I was wearing only one shoe and must have left the other behind me when I fell down the steps. The whole thing struck me as ironic, and I laughed hysterically even as tears filled my eyes. Like Cinderella, I was running from my Prince Charming. And just like Cinderella, I'd been to a ball where I didn't belong. Unlike a fairy-tale princess, however, I didn't see a happy ending in my future.

Liam is quiet when I finish my story. He's been slowly assembling a lunch for us as I talked about the meeting, and we eat in companionable silence before he asks if that was the reason I chose Ella as a trail name. I laugh before confessing Dreamer gave me the name on top of Springer when she misunderstood Ariella. "It seemed like an appropriate choice," I tell him.

He nods, smiling, and we spend a few minutes talking about Dreamer and Allday. They're still in Neels Gap sharing a cabin with Ghost and M&M. Allday is recovering from a bad sinus infection, and M&M is still resting his ankle.

"You should see Dreamer." He grins. "She's mothering all of them, and they're happily enjoying it. She taught Emma how to make her secret recipe for chocolate chip cookies, and they've been handing them out to all the hikers. I managed to save you some for dessert," he adds before handing me a full baggie. "I'm thinking about offering her a job as a greeter," he adds laughing.

I know Liam wants more answers, but I manage to put him off until we finish eating, and I feel brave enough to share what happened at Hudson's condo. Finally, after devouring a handful of Dreamer's cookies, I turn to him and begin.

"So, when I got back to my apartment, I changed clothes, made a cup of tea, and managed to calm down. I was pacing, thinking of everything that was said, everything that happened, and I realized Susan was right. There must have been some kind of misunderstanding. Maybe Vincent meant Hudson and our company would be working *with* them rather than *for* them as they installed our new programs. Maybe we would *all* be going to Italy to help set up and arrange their new security division.

"As I walked through the apartment, I saw his belongings everywhere. His shaving kit in the bathroom where we prepared for the day, his coffee cup and half-eaten piece of toast in the kitchen. He brought an overnight bag with him, and his clothes and shoes from the day before were neatly folded inside it. Hanging in the closet was the garment bag, which contained the suit, tie, and dress shirt he wore to the meeting. There was a clear pattern here, I realized. Hudson knew he was going to spend the night. He knew when he came with Chinese take-out and champagne he wasn't leaving.

"What I couldn't figure out, Liam, was if this was the pattern of a man in love who wanted to celebrate with the woman who loved him in return, or the pattern of a man who needed to distract a naïve, clueless woman in order to steal her business. I couldn't solve the equation. There were too many variables missing."

My cousin and I sit facing each other as we both think about what I've told him. He frowns slightly, and I know he must feel as confused as I felt that night. I reach for my water bottle, downing half of it while he watches me.

"So, you decided to go to his condo and confront him?"

"Yes."

"And you found Gia living there?"

"Yes."

"Okay, so this is what I don't understand." Liam shifts slightly, leaning across the table to get closer to me. "How could you not know she was living there for two whole years? Did she hide or something when you were there?"

"I didn't go to Hudson's condo very often, and it was always with the rest of our staff. It's been at least three years or more since I was there."

"What? Didn't you find that odd?" Liam questions, frowning.

"Not really, I mean … Crap, Liam. I didn't know how rich people lived. I thought maybe he was trying to keep his personal life separate from his business life, or maybe he didn't want to flaunt his wealth. I never thought about it or questioned it."

"But you knew where he lived?"

"Yes. His condo is in one of those beautiful old buildings overlooking Central Park and has an amazing view from the terrace. The inside looks like something from a magazine—designer furniture, real art, beautiful fabrics and colors. The four of us—Susan, Oliver, David, and I—were there for a couple of short meetings a few times when something unexpected came up and it was too late to go back to the office. I was never there by myself."

My cousin shakes his head, muttering to himself as he tries to rub the frown lines from his forehead. With a huge sigh, he leans back, staring at me from across the table. "None of this makes any sense," he finally says.

"It gets worse," I admit, thinking about what happened after I arrived at Hudson's home.

"Maybe you should just tell me what she said," Liam states. "Everything, please."

With a resigned sigh and a nod, I begin. "I took a cab to his place. I was mad, angry, and ready to demand some answers from him. Calvin, the same doorman, was still working there, and he recognized me. He helped me from the cab and asked if there was something he could do for me. I told him I needed to speak to Hudson about something business-related, and I was wondering if he was here.

"He frowned and said, 'Mr. Calder isn't here. However, I believe Miss Cattaneo is home. Perhaps you'd like to speak to her?' His answer confused me, and I wondered which Cattaneo he was referring to. So, I asked him if he meant Gia Cattaneo, and he told me, yes.

"I followed him into the lobby and he used his pass key to bring the elevator down. There are only two condos on each floor of Hudson's building. When I exited the elevator, I turned toward his door, only to find Gia standing in his open entryway. She asked me what I was doing here, and I told her I wanted to speak to Hudson about what had happened at the meeting earlier in the afternoon. She told me he wasn't home yet, and perhaps I should speak to him tomorrow."

"She didn't invite you in?" Liam asks.

"No. She just stood there with the door open."

"Could you see inside? Did it look any different from when you had been there before?"

Glancing at my cousin, I wonder why he would ask but shrug and continue. "She took a step backward, pushing slightly on the door behind her, and I could see more of the interior. It was just as I remembered. Tastefully decorated with beautiful furniture and warm, inviting colors. There were some new additions—a different painting over the fireplace, different throw pillows on the sofas. Multiple photos in silver frames were arranged on top of the piano. Some were famous landmarks from Italy. I recognized Gia's family in a couple of them, but most were of her and Hudson. There were pictures from skiing trips, beach vacations, and charity functions. But the one that captured my attention, the one I couldn't tear my eyes from, was a close-up of two overlapping hands, a male hand and a female hand with a large diamond engagement ring prominently displayed on the woman's finger.

"I was staring at the photo when she said something about Hudson being late because he was working out the remaining details of their move to Italy. 'Are you moving, too?' I asked her.

"She laughed at me and said of course she was moving with her fiancé. Then she added that while Hudson was establishing the new security division, she was being promoted to head of their Human Resources Division. I was so shocked I just stood there staring at her. That's when she lifted her left hand and flashed the diamond ring at me."

My voice is dry and scratchy, my emotions making it hard to continue. Picking up my water bottle, I sip it slowly, trying to quell the bile rising in my throat as I remember the other things she said that night. Things I'm not going to share with my cousin.

"Then what happened? Did she say anything else?"

I turn to him and shrug. "Some personal stuff and a warning about ruining Hudson financially if I tried to stop him leaving."

"So, you never saw or spoke to him that night?"

"I did see him, but I didn't speak to him. When I got off the elevator, Calvin offered to call a cab, but I told him no, I wanted to walk a bit because something was bothering me. Before I left, I asked him how long Gia had been living there. He told me she moved in a little over two years before.

"I went to the corner and crossed the street. I'd just stepped beneath a large tree when I heard brakes squeal and a door slam. When I looked back at the building, I saw him getting out of a cab. He and Calvin were talking, and Hudson was looking around frantically. It was pretty dark by then, and I edged over into the shadows where he couldn't see me. Then I watched him run into the building and enter the elevator. I stayed long enough to see his and Gia's shadows as they moved around the condo. Then I went home and called Susan."

"Had she been able to talk to Hudson?" Liam asks.

"No. She said he was in Vincent's office, and the receptionist wouldn't let her in to see him. I told her what I found out from Gia and asked her not to fight Hudson over his leaving. He owned the company, and he deserved to be happy."

"Did she—" Liam begins, but I interrupt him.

"Please, no more. I can't take any more, Liam. Just let it go. I feel like I've been through a police interrogation."

My cousin takes pity on me and stops asking questions. Throwing his arm around my shoulders, he leads me to his truck where I fill my food bag with enough meals and snacks to get me through the next four days.

"Call me when you get to Franklin?" he asks when I shoulder my pack and start to leave. "Please."

With a thumbs up, I turn my back on him and start across the highway.

CHAPTER 17

Find a Penny and Pick It Up

Date: Tuesday, March 18
Starting Location: Deep Gap Shelter
Destination: Plumorchard Shelter
Total Trip Miles: 71.1

Granny Cora always picked up money she found lying on the ground. Most often, they were pennies, but sometimes, she would find other coins, and occasionally, a one- or maybe a five-dollar bill. Paper money, she called them. Once, she even found a folded one-hundred-dollar bill. "Find a penny and pick it up, and all the day, you'll have good luck," she would say before slipping the money into her pocket.

We kept a jar at home where we collected this "found money." When it was full, Granny would dump the jar onto the kitchen table, letting me play with the coins, sorting them by size and color before counting them, and deciding what we would buy. Since it was "found money," it had to be used for treats. Usually, it was an ice cream cone on a hot summer day, maybe a trip to the donut shop early on a Saturday morning for a fresh, chocolate-frosted, cream-filled long john. We used the hundred-dollar bill for hamburgers and a frosted mug at the old A&W root beer drive-in before we went to the local theater to watch a movie, and then played putt-putt golf.

It was her one rule about the money—it had to be used for something special, something fun. It couldn't be used for essentials or things we needed to survive.

I never considered we might be poor. We were never hungry. There were vegetables from the garden, fruit from the old orchard, and fresh venison in the fall after Uncle Billy went to deer camp. The woods supplied us with mushrooms, berries, and nuts. We gathered poke sallet, watercress, and dandelion greens in the early spring along with wild ramps to season them. It never felt like work either. Granny told me stories and made up I Spy games while we tramped through the woods or worked in the garden.

I don't remember being cold or uncomfortable. Liam and his father kept us supplied with split wood for the central wood-burning stove, which heated the cabin in the wintertime. I had new shoes when I wore out my old ones and new clothes or a new coat when I went through a "growing spurt."

Granny was "careful" with her money, and we had everything we needed, but she still picked up every penny she ever found. Over the years, it became a habit, a game we played, and a fond memory of the only mother figure in my life.

I'm halfway across the road when I hear Liam calling my name. Desperate to escape his questions and the painful memories they invoke, I ignore him, speeding up in an attempt to reach the other side. When I hear his pounding footsteps behind me, I stop and turn, glaring at him in hopes he will let me leave.

Holding up his hands in defense, he grins at me. "One more question. I promise, just one more."

Sighing in defeat, I wave my hand, giving him permission to ask.

He hesitates, shifting from foot to foot, and it occurs to me something is definitely going on with my cousin, something he hasn't told me yet. The thought is immediately forgotten when he blurts out his question.

"What do you want me to tell Hudson when he comes looking for you?"

"Are you crazy? Did you not listen to anything I told you? He's engaged to Gia, he owns the company, and he's taking it with him when they move to Italy. He won't be coming here looking for me."

"But what if everything Gia said was a lie? What if she was trying to set you up to leave?"

"Did Calvin lie when he said she'd been living there for two years? Did Vincent Cattaneo, the respected CEO of one of the largest banking corporations in the world, lie when he announced Hudson was joining them? I'm sorry, Liam. I know you want to think the best of him, but he's gone. He won't be coming here to look for me."

Seeing the unhappiness on Liam's face, I move closer to him and put my hand on his shoulder to reassure him. "I'm going to be fine. This hike? It's good for me, and when I decide to leave the trail, there's a position on the faculty at MIT waiting for me. Or I might find someplace down here, closer to you and Emma. Stop worrying."

Liam nods, then gives me a crooked grin. "But if ..."

Rolling my eyes so hard they almost hurt, I laugh at my persistent cousin. "Okay, fine. If Hudson shows up looking for me, you know what I'm doing and where I am. If I'm *that* important to him, he can come find me."

Then, because my cousin still wears a worried expression, I step closer, wrapping my arms around his waist. "I love you, big *gohusdi*. Thank you for caring about me."

Liam hugs me back. "I love you, too, my little cousin," he whispers into my hair. "Please be careful and call me when you reach Franklin."

Nodding, I turn, and then with a final wave, set off down the dirt pathway in front of me.

For once, the AT doesn't immediately start climbing the steep mountain on the other side of the road. Instead, it stays on the side of the hill following Dicks Creek, the stream that cuts its way through the mountains into the gap bearing its name. The trail is on the left and above it, giving the hiker a great view of the rocks and rushing water below. A narrow dirt road borders the creek on the opposite side. Several access points have been built along the creek bank to allow fishermen or swimmers to reach the water.

As I walk, I let my eyes wander along the road until it ends in a small turnaround just before an elevated footbridge crosses the creek and connects to the trail on the left side. It looks like the AT takes a sharp left turn away from the creek at the bridge and begins a steep climb up the mountain. I can barely make out an old pickup parked on one side of the turnaround.

A large boulder juts out into the trail obstructing my forward view. As I start to take a step around it, I notice the bright, shiny penny in the dirt. When I see the copper penny laying in the dirt in the middle of the trail, I stop to pick it up, and because I stopped, and because I bent over and picked it up, and because I held it in my hand wondering how and why it had been dropped here in the middle of the trail, because I did all that … it might have saved my life.

I'm smiling to myself, thinking of Gran and her theory of "found money," when I hear their voices.

"Is she coming?"

"Yeah, she's on the other side of the bend where the boulder is."

"You sure she's alone?"

"I told you she was. Wearin' a brand-new pack and clothes. I bet there's some money in there, too."

The voices are male. The first one sounds older, gravelly, like it's been soaked in nicotine and whiskey too long. The other voice is younger, impatient, and more menacing.

Staying bent over and out of sight, I crawl closer to the boulder, wedging myself between the rock and the mountainside. It's obvious they're talking about me and are somewhere on the trail ahead. I'm surprised I can hear them though. The narrow valley must be funneling or magnifying their voices somehow, or perhaps the large boulder is cutting off the sounds of the creek, making them easier to hear.

"Remember, you promised not to hurt this one. Not like you did the last time." It's the gravelly voice again.

I can feel my heart rate speed up.

"Oh, shut your yap, you old coot. I ain't gonna hurt her. Might have a little fun first before sendin' her on her way though. Besides, I don't remember you complaining about getting your dick wet the last time."

Now I'm gasping for breath, my heart pounding in my chest, the sick bile of fear rising in my throat. I'm scared, petrified. A sudden sting makes me look down at my hand. I've been rubbing the penny so hard and furiously between my fingers I've broken the skin. "Granny, oh, Granny," I whisper to myself. "What am I going to do?"

Tell me, child, what's the first rule about being a'scared in the woods? Suddenly, I'm back in the forest with Gran. We're picking spring mushrooms, and I've wandered off and lost sight of her. I panic, my screams bringing her quickly to my side.

Ariella, what is the first rule? I can hear her voice so clearly, demanding I answer her.

"Don't panic," I whisper to myself and to her. "Panic kills. Relax, look around, and think logically." So, I do.

Taking a long, deep breath, I will my heart to slow, my brain to think. I can see back to the road crossing and the parking area. It's completely deserted. I could take a chance by going back, but I can't count on anyone being there to help me.

I could try to run down the road toward town, but the pickup I saw probably belongs to the men waiting for me. A vehicle makes it easy for them to catch me if I try to escape that way. Memories of No Filter's story about Rock Dancer make me shudder at the thought of trying to evade a speeding vehicle. Going forward is completely out of the question, so it leaves only one direction—up.

The mountain face beside me is almost straight up. It's a challenging tumble of rocks and boulders, trees, vines, and bushes. It's easy to understand why the trail builders followed the streambed instead of trying to carve a trail out of the cliff-like jumble above me. As I study it intently, I can hear Granny's voice urging me to start moving. *You don't have long, child. They're gonna figure out something has happened real soon. Get up, Ariella. Go up. No one ever looks up. They stare at the ground or look off into the distance, but they never look up. Move!*

I'm on my feet, climbing and moving upward even as her voice urges me on. The route seems to open in front of me—a toehold here, hands there, grab that tree limb and swing yourself over to the ledge. Granny's voice is in my head, directing my movements as I scramble up the cliff face. *Now go around to the other side of the boulder. Yes. See the rhododendron grove? If you can get behind it, they'll never see you. Good, child, good. What's that sound? Stop. Get down.*

Crouching behind a rock, I peer down at the trail below me. I knew it wouldn't take long before the two men came looking for me. Just like Granny always said—they don't look above them. Instead, they search the creek below and watch the road crossing and parking area. I study them while they stand there arguing about where I could have disappeared to.

The gravel-voiced man is older, pot-bellied, with lank gray hair and short, bristled stubble on his face and neck. He's wearing a too short, too tight T-shirt, which leaves a large swath of hairy stomach exposed. As I watch, he spits a large chaw of tobacco on the ground. My stomach turns at the sight of him. He's like all the other old men who sat on the dead pecker bench in front of the local barbershop, chewing and spitting and ogling my 14-year-old body. The ones who sneered and whispered "squaw" as Granny and I walked by. He's no threat to me now. I'm nearly 100 feet above him, and he couldn't climb this mountainside if he wanted to.

The other one—the younger man—is the dangerous one. Taller, fitter, with a full beard and long hair, he paces the ground angrily, trying to figure out how I got away. Briefly, he studies the cliff face, letting his eyes follow it upward, but he shakes his head as if to dismiss the possibility that a single woman could have climbed it. He's the ringleader from elementary school, the one who led the chants of "half-breed" and thought the tomahawk hand chop and the Indian war whoop were *sooo* funny. The one who tripped me on the school bus, the one who pulled my braid so hard my eyes watered. He's the one who could climb this rocky cliffside if he wanted to.

They represent everything I thought I was escaping when I left Appalachia and went to MIT. The narrow-minded, self-righteous bullies who couldn't see beyond their gender, race, or religion. Bullies aren't confined to the backwoods small towns of my childhood, however. I found them in the educated East Coast elite, too. They may wear tailored wool slacks, cashmere sweaters, and red-soled stilettos, but for all their meticulously groomed perfection, they're still bullies. Gia was a bully, and I let her degrade and manipulate me. I ran from everything I created and loved. And I'm sick of bullies.

I can hear Granny's voice as I contemplate what I'm about to do. *No, child. Don't look at them. Don't let them know you heard them. Hold your head high and walk past them. No, Ariella, stay down; stay hidden.* Her warning voice screams in my head. *Stay safe.*

But I'm tired of turning away, of being safe. I'm tired of running.

My movement causes dirt and a few pebbles to bounce down the cliff face, alerting the two men below me. When they look up, I kick a few larger rocks and laugh when they have to scurry out of the way.

The old man stares at me, opened-mouthed in disbelief. The younger one scowls and flashes me a look of pure hatred when I stand upright and glare down at them.

Raising both arms above my head, I extend my middle fingers in the universal salute of contempt. "Hey, assholes. You tryin' to prove how big and strong you are by picking on someone smaller and weaker than you? Huh?

Well, here I am, you inbred, limp-dicked, dumber than a sack of rocks, egg-suckin', mealy-mouthed motherfuckers. Come and get me!"

With one last kick, I send a large rock hurtling down the cliff face toward them. Then I turn and start climbing.

CHAPTER 18

And All the Day You'll Have Good Luck

Date: Tuesday, March 18
Starting Location: Deep Gap Shelter
Destination: Plumorchard Shelter
Total Trip Miles: 71.1

I climb as if my life depends on it, and I guess it actually does. My taunting has probably made the two men, particularly the younger one, very angry. I can't risk him catching me. Another thirty feet and I've reached the top of the mountain where it begins to level off. Ducking behind a tree, I check the rocky cliff below.

The older man has given up. I can see him walking along the trail toward the bridge and the truck parked there, but the younger one has decided to come after me. Thirty feet or so up the climb, he's already chosen the wrong route. Stranded on a ledge, his only way off is to use a small sapling growing between some rocks and try to move sideways to a different group of boulders. The tree isn't nearly big enough to support his weight, and it pulls loose when he grabs it.

He tumbles down the mountainside, barely managing to right himself before sliding on his butt to a halt at the bottom. When he tries to stand, his leg gives way. I can hear his yelp of pain and cursing fit even from where

I'm hiding. I watch a few more minutes as he tries to hobble toward the road crossing. Satisfied he's no longer a threat, I begin making my way through the woods toward the Appalachian Trail.

I know the trail is somewhere to my right. To keep myself from straying too far off course, I pick several points of reference in the direction I want to go. An unusually tall evergreen, a large rock formation, a glimpse of color from blooming wildflowers, anything unique I can use to orient myself. As I reach each one, I look for the next and continue.

There's very little undergrowth this time of year, so I'm able to hike without too much effort. I'm still very aware of where I step and continually search the area in front of me for any hidden hazards. Before long, I find a narrow animal trail heading in the direction I want to go, and I'm able to increase my pace. When I reach a large rock formation near the summit of the mountain, I scramble to the top and see the AT below me on the side of the hill. Fifteen minutes later, I'm headed north toward Plumorchard Gap Shelter.

~ * * * ~

With three different levels of sleeping platforms, Plumorchard is one of the bigger, nicer shelters on the AT. The highest is tucked away under the overhang at the front of the shelter and is reached by a ladder attached to one of the side walls. The other two platforms face the open front. Concrete covers the ground at the entryway and helps prevent mud and dirt from being tracked in. A wooden picnic table offers hikers a place to cook and sit. The shelter is packed when I get there.

A Boy Scout troop has taken over the highest platform under the overhang, and a high school hiking club with their chaperones is on the lowest level. The leaders are currently making all the boys move to one side of the platform and the girls to the other side while they lay out their sleeping bags between the two groups. I chuckle to myself, wondering how much sneaking around will go on after the adults go to sleep.

Just when I'm about to decide to pitch my tent outside, a voice above my head invites me to join them on the middle level. When I look up, I see a woman's face smiling down at me. "There's still some room up here," she says. "And you're more than welcome to join us. You'll have to use the ladder to get up here though."

The sleeping platform is deep enough to allow plenty of room to navigate around the hikers who are busy unpacking and settling in for the night. They all look like seasoned backpackers as they arrange their space and store their gear efficiently, hanging their food bags from chains attached to the ceiling. Most of them greet me with a nod or hello as I make my way across the wooden deck toward the two women smiling and waving me over.

"There should be enough room for you here," the first one says as she moves gear around to open a space beside her.

"Thanks," I reply, shrugging out of my backpack and pulling out my sleeping pad and bag.

"Oh, no problem," she answers with a grin. "I'm Wonderland, by the way, and this is—"

"Yellow," I interrupt, finishing her sentence. "Sorry, I've seen your entries in the registers, and your trail names caught my attention. I've been trying to think of some meaning behind 'Yellow,' but I never thought about yellow hair."

Yellow grins at me, laughing as she tells me I'm not the first person who's told her that. "I've had people ask me if my name meant I only wore yellow clothes, or if my favorite color is yellow. But I tell them all, 'Sorry, hun, it's just my yeller hair.'"

When she speaks, it's obvious where Yellow is from. Her Texas accent is quite pronounced.

"Curly Dan would love you," I can't help saying out loud. At her questioning look, I hurry to explain. "I met Curly Dan and No Filter a couple days ago. Curly is a linguist from England, and we've had some interesting discussions about accents and dialects. He would love your accent."

"You mean my 'Texas twang.'" She laughs again.

"Exactly," I agree, smiling back at her. "So, Yellow from Texas, and you're Wonderland from … Wait, your real name wouldn't happen to be Rose, would it?"

My question sends both women into gales of laughter. "Oh, I like this one," says Yellow, nudging Wonderland. "Can we keep her?" She gives me a sheepish look when they finally calm down. "Sorry, we're bein' a bit rude here. It's just you're the first person who's asked that question. We've been wonderin' when someone would. I was losin' faith in the IQs of my fellow hikers until you came along. I guess you're smarter than the average hiker. My name is actually Rosemary. Nice ta meet ya …"

"Ella," I reply to her unspoken question.

The smile she gives me is as warm and friendly as a Texas summer day. She makes me feel welcomed, much the way I felt with No Filter and Curly Dan. I hope I'll be able to spend more time with her.

"Can you guess Wonderland's real name?" Rosemary interrupts my thoughts when she turns to her friend.

"Well, my first thought was Dorothy because we're all walking through a nature wonderland. Like, you know, the 'Land of Awes' or something. But now I'm wondering if she fell down the rabbit hole to get here instead of flying in on a tornado." Rosemary's grin tells me I'm on the right track. "So, I'm thinking you must be Alice."

Wonderland's grin tells me I'm getting close. "It's actually Allison." She laughs. "As in Allison Wonderland."

Then it's my turn to laugh. "Clever, very clever."

She turns to Yellow with a grin. "Yeah, I agree; this one's smart. We should keep her, sis."

I frown briefly, wondering if they could be sisters. They don't look alike or sound alike. Before I can ask, Wonderland turns to me and asks if my trail name is for Cinderella.

"Could be," I admit. "Although No Filter wanted to call me Salmonella because of a hiker upset stomach." Realizing they've both shared their real names with me I add, "My real name is Ariella."

"Oh, that's better," she replies. "We could call you Ari, or better yet Bella as in Beauty and the Beast."

"That was Belle, not Bella," Yellow scolds her hiking partner. "Get your stories straight, Disney girl. She could be Beauty from Sleeping Beauty."

"I thought that was Aurora," Wonderland argues, turning to face Yellow.

"No, Briar Rose," Yellow answers.

"Maybe that's what we should have named you." Wonderland scowls. "You're getting as prickly as a thorn bush. You probably need to get—"

"Now listen here ..."

Gathering my food bag, stove, and cooking pot, I start making my way toward the ladder and the picnic table below. When I glance back, the two are still arguing about Disney princesses. Maybe they really are sisters. I smile to myself.

It's only later, sitting at the table waiting for my dinner to cook, when the full implications of what I did this afternoon begins to hit me. Although it felt really good to stand up to the bullies, taunting the two men wasn't the smartest or the safest thing to do. I could have stayed hidden and they would never have known where I was, what I looked like, or what direction I was heading.

My mind starts imagining all sorts of scenarios. Could they be at the next road crossing, waiting for me? Did I make them angry enough to hurt the next hiker who came along? I know some of the people in this shelter are probably headed south toward Dicks Creek Gap. What if one of them gets hurt because of me? My heart races and my hands shake as I frantically think about what I should do.

I'm startled out of my panic when two warm hands reach out to hold mine.

"Ella? What's going on, sweetie?"

I look up to find Yellow's worried face across the table from me. "Oh, Rosemary, I think I've done something really stupid, and I don't know what to do about it," I manage to whisper.

"Well, my nana always told me two heads were better'n one. So maybe you should tell me what happened, and we can figure it out together."

At her urging, I tell the whole story. Everything that happened, everything that was said, and my fear I may have made the situation worse; I let the words spill out, holding nothing back. Yellow listens until I'm finished before saying anything. She asks for more details about the location, what the men looked like, what they were wearing, what I heard, what I said, would I recognize them if I saw them again? Her questions are pointed, direct, and designed to help me recall every detail. Her manner changes completely as we talk. Gone is the laid-back, friendly hiker. Instead, she's efficient, skillful, and professional. Even her accent has disappeared.

By the time we finish talking, my dinner is ready. While I eat, Yellow sits quietly, frowning slightly as she considers everything I've told her. Abruptly, she gets up, walks over to the side of the shelter, and returns with the register.

"Okay, first thing, I want you to write everything you've told me in the register. Sign your trail name and date it. If those two come looking for you, which I doubt, they won't be able to learn your real name. Every southbounder who stops here will see the entry and be warned about what could be waiting for them at Dicks Creek.

"Second, I'm going to get everyone's attention, and I want you to tell your story again. You don't have to give all the details this time, just enough so everyone understands what happened and how serious the situation is.

113

"Then, I'm going to get the leaders, chaperones, and the hikers down here and come up with a plan for getting this reported to the proper authorities."

I must look slightly aghast at her suggestions because she stares at me pointedly. "This is serious shit we're talking about here. These guys didn't just threaten you; they've already hurt someone. We need to stop them before it escalates into something worse. Next time this happens, someone could die."

She puts two fingers in her mouth and whistles so loudly it hurts my ears. The shelter immediately goes quiet. "Hey, listen up," she yells. "Ella here had a dangerous encounter at Dicks Creek Gap this evening. She's going to tell y'all what happened, and you need to listen up, 'specially you south-bounders. When she gets finished, I want all the leaders, chaperones, and hikers down here for a quick meeting so we can decide how to alert the police and sheriffs' departments."

Everywhere I look, faces are watching me, waiting for me to speak. Fifteen teenage Boy Scouts and their three leaders stare down at me from the top sleeping deck. The high school students and their teachers are sitting on the lower level, ready for my words. Hikers gather on the edge of the middle platform. I can feel their eyes on me and their expectations. For a moment, I'm back in New York, reliving my disastrous presentation. But as I look around, I don't see judgement or disdain or pity; instead, there is only interest and a willingness to listen to what I have to say. Swallowing my nervousness, I tell my story.

Afterward, Yellow meets with the adults, and I start writing everything in the register. I'm not quite finished writing when the meeting is over, and everyone returns to their spots and starts settling in for the night. Most of them take a moment to thank me for sharing my story and wish me a safe hike. Yellow stops and discusses what was decided.

The Scouts are headed south. One of the leaders will get in touch with the local sheriff when they get to Dicks Creek. The high school students are from the area but are headed north. My description of the two men sounds like a few people they might know. When their hike is finished and they return home, they'll also talk to the police. Southbound and northbound hikers will help spread the word by telling everyone they meet and by writing a warning in the shelter registers. Wishing me goodnight, she leaves me to my writing.

By the time I finally finish, it's dark and the shelter is quiet. A few soft snores, a cough or two, and the grunt of someone shifting around on their sleeping pad are the only sounds. It's cooling off quickly, but I take a few moments to enjoy the stillness and reflect on this long, eventful day.

I spent the morning with two new friends, and the afternoon with my cousin rehashing and reliving events from my past. I found a penny and picked it up, then faced down two bullies. I ended the day by speaking to a shelter full of people, and I didn't panic. When I go to sleep tonight, it will be beside two new friends. Perhaps I really did have good luck "all the day."

A warm sleeping bag is waiting for me when the cold temperature finally forces me to end my musing. Wonderland opens her eyes when she hears me settling in beside her.

"That was a scary story," she whispers. "I'm glad you escaped unharmed, but I don't know if I could have been so brave."

"I think I may have had a little help from my granny today," I whisper back. "It felt like she was right there with me, climbing the mountain."

"Ah," she yawns sleepily. Her eyes close, and she pulls the hood of her sleeping bag up over her head, snuggling down into its warmth.

"Wonderland?" I ask quietly, a few minutes later. "What does Yellow do for a living?"

She chuckles softly before answering. "Rosemary Buckman is an assistant district attorney for Tarrant County, Texas."

"And you? What do you do for a living?" I ask into the darkness but get no answer.

My shelter mate has entered a wonderland of dreams and is sound asleep.

CHAPTER 19

Goodbye, Hud

Date: Wednesday, March 19
Starting Location: Plumorchard Gap Shelter
Destination: Standing Indian Mountain
Total Trip Miles: 84.8

The temperature plummets during the night and I wake cold and shivering in the early predawn darkness. Rummaging through my clothes bag, I pull on my down sweater, wool socks, and wool cap. I also shift my sleeping pad and bag around so I'm closer to the back wall and away from the open edge of the platform.

The next time I wake, sunshine is warming the shelter, and I'm too hot. I'm also alone. I can hear the hiking group below me as the teachers give last-minute instructions, and they prepare to leave. They remind their students to always hike with a buddy and make sure they're wearing their safety whistles. When they leave, I'm surrounded by silence.

I sit up and stretch, groaning at the stiffness in my shoulders and arms. Pulling myself up the mountainside yesterday used long-ignored muscles, not only in my upper body but in my butt and thighs, too. It takes me a few minutes of hobbling around before I can stand and move comfortably.

There's a piece of folded paper on the floor near me. It's a note from Yellow, telling me they decided to let me sleep since I seemed to need the extra rest, and they hope to see me at Bly Gap where they plan to eat an early lunch. Wonderland has added "and take a nap" with a smiley face at the bottom of the page.

When I begin to pack up, I realize how tired I am—physically, emotionally, and mentally. Yesterday was more draining than I realized at the time. Yet the extra sleep has helped. By the time I climb down to the bottom level and begin organizing my food, I'm ready and eager to start the day.

While I eat my breakfast bar and dried fruit, I thumb through the shelter register. I find entries by most of the hikers and both groups here last night. A few have been added this morning. Most of them mention my narrow escape from the bullies. Some call me brave or lucky. Someone points out how important it is to always be aware of your surroundings. The entry that makes me laugh, however, is from Wonderland, who calls me a badass, take-no-shit hiking girl.

I reread my story from last night, checking to make sure I've described everything accurately, and then I find myself flipping to a page near the back, pen in hand, and writing to Hudson.

Dear Hud,

Yesterday was one of those days. You know the ones you look back on and realize how so many events in your life have been leading to that day. How all the "cause" in your life came together to form one beautiful "effect," and how a different pattern for your life was revealed, ready to be explored and enjoyed. That's what yesterday was.

Three things happened.

The first was I stopped being a victim. No one can bully me if I don't let them. I stopped ignoring them, stopped pretending I didn't hear them or that their words and actions didn't hurt. I talked back. I told them to put up or shut up, and I fought back. It felt so freeing to be rid of the weight, to shift it to their shoulders where it's always belonged. No one—not the tormentors of my youth or the Gias of New York—will ever make me feel inadequate again.

I hope you would have been proud of me for the second. I stood in front of a group of strangers, and I told a story. I spoke clearly and calmly, without stuttering or stammering, shaking or sweating. If my accent was more pronounced, I didn't care. It didn't matter what I looked like, how I was dressed, or in this case, how bad I smelled. Ha! I had something important to say, and I said it. They listened to me and thanked me for sharing.

The third thing happened during a long talk with LC. He wanted to know all the details about New York. During our long discussion, I told him I loved you. How sad is it I told him but not you? It's not as if I didn't have the opportunity. I could have said those words when you told me how you felt. I could have told you the next morning when you showed me how you felt. But I didn't. Granny loved me, of that I have no doubt, but she was never one to talk about feelings. None of her family did. So, when you said you loved me, I didn't say anything, just kept my words to myself. I'm sorry. People should know how you feel about them; children need to know they are loved. Not just shown but told.

So, here goes … I love you. I love you enough to forgive you for everything that happened in New York. I love you enough to want you to be happy. If it means marrying G and having a career with BII, then that's what I want for you. I love you enough to let you go, and I love me enough to move on without you.

There is one more thing. (I know I said three things, and this is four. Sorry.) Before he left yesterday, LC asked what he should say if you came looking for me. I laughed at him, sure it was the last thing you would do. Yet I have to confess some small part of me, some last, small hope left inside, wants to think you will come looking for me. A little part hopes I was, and still am, important enough for you to follow me.

There's a journey waiting for me. If I had a choice, I would make the journey with you by my side. With or without you, I'm going forward, and I'm going to savor every moment of it.

Goodbye, Hud.

CHAPTER 20

Girlfriends

Date: Wednesday, March 19
Starting Location: Plumorchard Gap Shelter
Destination: Standing Indian Mountain
Total Trip Miles: 84.4

Bly Gap is famous for three things.

The first is a much-photographed, gnarled oak tree that grows in the open meadow. Sometime in its past, the tree was bent, causing the trunk to grow horizontally along the ground. The limbs grow perpendicular at one end of the trunk. From some angles, it looks like a large reclining deer or elk with a huge set of antlers, one of which sports a white blaze.

There's no road access to the gap. Instead, you have to actually climb up to the flat area, which has a spring and nearby tent sites. The flat, grassy field has amazing vistas to the north and is, for all practical purposes, the border between Georgia and North Carolina. Northbounders can celebrate one completed state with only thirteen more to go before they reach Katahdin. Southbounders celebrate because they have only one state left to hike, and their goal is almost within sight. One more reason for its popularity. I catch up to Yellow and Wonderland at Bly Gap.

Despite the cold night, the day has warmed quickly. The sky is a perfect, clear blue. With very little humidity, the slight breeze quickly dries the sweat generated by the heat and the physical activity. The girls are taking advantage of the beautiful weather by sunbathing. They've found a rocky outcropping on one side of the meadow and they lie stretched out in the sun, using their sleeping pads for a little cushioning.

Wonderland appears to be asleep. Lying on her stomach, head resting on her arms, she's stripped down to her sports bra and underwear. Her skin is very pale, and I'm instantly worried about sunburn.

Yellow must feel the same way because I hear her scolding and telling her to cover up when I approach them. Yellow is wearing a long-sleeved T-shirt and hiking pants, which she's rolled up to mid-thigh. She quickly rolls them down when she spots me but not before I notice what looks like a raised, jagged scar running from one knee to ankle.

Both of them seem pleased to see me, and soon the three of us are happily sharing a picnic lunch. We talk, we laugh, and we enjoy the sunshine and each other's company. I can feel something bubbling up inside me, and I realize it's pure joy. Joy at being here, at this place, at this time, with these new friends. After the drama of yesterday—the long, difficult conversation with Liam, the frightening confrontation with the two men, and the public speech in front of so many people—I welcome this new feeling. It makes me want to laugh, to giggle. The trail has given me another wonderful gift.

All too soon, we've finished lunch, and it's time to face the third thing that Bly Gap is famous for—the beginning of a nine-mile hike to the top of Standing Indian Mountain. At 5,498 feet in elevation, Standing Indian will be the tallest mountain we've climbed so far. There are steeper and longer ascents in the Smoky Mountains and in New England, but this is the first time the trail goes over five thousand feet. There are no carefully engineered switchbacks on this section; instead, the trail goes straight up the ridge. It climbs over several smaller peaks located on the flanks of the massive mountain before beginning the final assault of the summit. The first of these is Sharp Top. As the name implies, it's steep.

Without the benefit of leaves, the trees give little shade. The trail is fairly open, and the views are amazing. But no leaves mean no shade, and it's not long before we're sweltering in the early afternoon sun. It takes over two hours of endless plodding for us to cover the three miles from Bly Gap to Muskrat Creek Shelter. When we get there, the small shelter and the meadow around it are full of hot, tired hikers.

A swiftly flowing creek runs nearby. Without even stopping, Wonderland turns and follows it downstream until she finds a small, secluded pool. Pack comes off first, then socks and shoes, shirt and shorts. Seconds later she's in the icy water up to her neck. With a squeal, she ducks her head under, soaking her hair in the process before lunging to her feet and grinning with glee.

"It's cold but wonderful," she exclaims. "Come on, get in."

I'm shucking off my outer clothing and heading into the water when I look back at Yellow. In her long pants and sweat-soaked, long-sleeved shirt, she looks hot and uncomfortable. Yet she's still standing on the bank, hesitating.

"Rosemary, honey, there's no one else here. It's just Ella and me. Join us ... please," Wonderland pleads with her friend. "It'll make you feel a lot better, and you don't even have to take off your clothes—leave them on and come cool off."

Finally, Yellow nods and, after taking off her shoes and socks, steps gingerly into the cold water. She walks to the far side of the pool and, with a sigh, sinks down into the cold water. Her hair is in two braids today, and she loosens them both before leaning back into the water and scrubbing the sweat and dirt from her head and hair. With closed eyes and a small, pleased smile, she lets the cold water run over her neck and shoulders.

Wonderland has decided our clothes need a rinsing, too. She tosses my shirt and shorts to me, and we spend the next few minutes trying to wash some of the hiker funk away. By the time we finish, we're chilled and beginning to shiver. It's time to get out and resume hiking. We still have almost six miles to the next shelter.

I get a good look at her back as we dress and start packing up. It's obviously sunburned. She must have been miserable wearing her backpack and hiking in the heat, but she never complained.

Yellow seems to need some time alone, so Wonderland and I hike together while Rosemary gradually pulls ahead of us. We get glimpses of her from time to time as the trail twists and turns. She stumbles more than once, and I notice a pronounced limp. I want to say something, to ask if Yellow's okay, but I'm not sure how or what to say. I've never had "girlfriends" before. I've never hung out, or gone to sleepovers, or done any of the normal things female friends do. My social skills are sorely lacking.

Worry twists my stomach, and finally, I stop and turn to Wonderland before blurting out, "Is Yellow okay? I know it isn't any of my business, but she's limping, and I noticed the scar, and then in the water she wouldn't ..." Shrugging my shoulders, I try to find the appropriate words. "I'm sorry," I start again. "I'm just really worried."

She studies me intently for a few moments while she gathers her thoughts. "Yellow hasn't had an easy life," she begins. "I'm sure if we stay together she'll eventually share more of her story when she feels comfortable around you. I know she already likes you a lot. There are all kinds of scars. Some are on the outside, and some are on the inside. Some of them eventually heal, and others never do. She has all of those scars and more, but she's dealing with them the best she can. This hike is already helping her both physically and mentally. Thank you for caring about her. It's okay to ask." With a nod and a smile, she starts walking again, and I join her.

Nothing else is said for the next thirty minutes or so as it takes all our breath just to scramble up the steep incline. Finally, the trail levels off and begins a slight downward slope. When I can talk again, I ask Wonderland about last night.

"You said Yellow is an assistant district attorney? She seemed different last night—really professional, very organized, and direct."

"Oh, yes." Wonderland chuckles. "You saw the formidable Rosemary Buckman in action last night. Known far and wide throughout North Texas for inspiring fear in even the toughest opponents." She grins. "Her expertise is domestic violence, and she can go all mother bear to protect people she thinks have been threatened or abused, particularly children."

"And what do you do?"

"I work in the emergency room at Harris Methodist Hospital in Fort Worth. I'm a trauma nurse."

"Oh, did you treat Yellow there?" Realizing I've asked something that isn't any of my business, I stop and start to apologize again. "I'm sorry. I shouldn't have asked."

"It's okay, really. Rosemary can share the details when she's ready, but I can tell you I did meet her and her family when she was in my care."

"So, she's not your sister?"

"What?" Wonderland stops abruptly and turns to face me. "Sisters?"

"Yes. I thought I heard you call her 'sis' last night."

Wonderland's giggling lights up her whole face. "Oh, you are a smart one. You must notice everything around you. Is there anything you miss?"

"Well." I stutter in embarrassment. "I've always been pretty observant."

"A good thing," she grins, nodding. "When I met Rosemary, I also met her brother. We're engaged," she confesses with an even bigger grin. "Technically, we'll be sisters-in-law, but she's as close and as dear to me as a sister can be."

"Congratulations. Is he going to be joining you for part of the hike?"

Her happy face falls at my question. "No, it doesn't look like it. We planned to do this together. A kind of '*spend lots of time in the great outdoors, get reacquainted, vacation/reunion,*' but Travis is a Marine, and his discharge papers were delayed for some reason, so he couldn't join me. My leave of absence was already arranged and approved, and I really wanted to do this hike. Rosemary volunteered to come with me, and here we are."

"I'm sorry," I offer, not knowing what else to say. "Maybe another year, after he gets home?"

"Maybe," she answers with a shrug before we turn our attention back to the trail and continue hiking.

The trail offers us a reprieve when it dips down into a slight break in the ridgeline. We can see Yellow ahead of us. She's stopped in the middle of the trail, hunched over what appears to be a wooden trail sign. Her shoulders are shaking, but it's impossible to tell if she's been hurt or injured.

"Rosemary?" Wonderland questions before rushing toward her friend. We run down the trail, packs bouncing on our backs. When we get closer, we can hear her sobs. Just before we reach her, she clutches her stomach, bends over, and dry-heaves onto the ground.

"Rosemary?" Allison reaches out to her friend, laying a comforting hand on her shoulder. "Sweetie, what happened? Are you all right?"

If I live forever, I will never forget the look on Yellow's face when she turns to look at us—such pain, such sorrow, such utter defeat. Her face is pale, sweaty, hair plastered to her forehead. She steps away from the sign, pointing to it, and begins to laugh hysterically, tears running down her face as she gasps for breath.

"Look at it, Allison; look at *that* motherfucking sign!" she shouts. "A thousand miles from Texas in the middle of the woods of North Carolina, and I still can't get away from *that* goddamned nickname."

Wonderland and I look at the wooden sign. It marks the spot where the Chunky Gal Trail crosses the AT before heading off in an easterly direction. I have no idea what could have upset her so much, but apparently, Allison does. "No, no, no," she whispers before leading Yellow away from the sign and farther down the trail. She pulls her into a hug, rubbing her back soothingly while she murmurs to her. "You're okay, hun. He can't hurt you anymore. Shh, Rosemary, it's all right. You're beautiful and wonderful, intelligent and smart, and stronger than any childhood nickname. Shh, shh."

Once again, I curse my lack of social skills as I watch the two friends. I want to offer comfort, but I'm uncertain about what is appropriate.

Yellow gradually calms. She lifts her head from Wonderland's shoulder and gives me a tentative smile. Then she straightens, opens one arm to me, and I step into their three-way embrace.

Girlfriends, another gift from the trail.

~ * * * ~

It takes the rest of the afternoon and early evening to reach the top of Standing Indian Mountain. Neither Wonderland nor Yellow seem inclined to talk, so we mostly hike in silence. From time to time, I point out a new wildflower or identify a bird, but little else is said. I'm left to my thoughts and worries.

My mind won't let go of the conundrum that is Rosemary Buckman. On one hand, I see a tall, very attractive, well-educated, fiercely intelligent attorney, but on the other is the vulnerable woman who is afraid to show her scars and falls apart at a seemingly innocent trail sign. Something about the Chunky Gal name reminded her of some hurt in her past, but looking at her now, it's hard to imagine how or why. Yellow is what Granny would have called "statuesque." Tall, curvy, with long blonde hair and startling, corn-flower blue eyes, she's the perfect reincarnation of a 1950s pin-up girl. She's the beauty standard I longed for as a young teenager.

Wonderland is pretty, too. Shorter and thinner than Yellow, her brown hair is just long enough to pull into a short ponytail that's perfect for long-distance hiking. Her eyes are brown, too, and her skin is already tan from days in the sun.

As I study them, I can already see the effects of two weeks of hiking on their bodies. Men and women react differently to daily long-distance hiking.

Men usually lose weight, particularly upper-body muscle and fat, much more quickly than women. They develop huge calves and strong legs, but all the rest seems to shrink, as if their body doesn't want to carry big biceps, shoulders, or six-packs up and down mountains for six months. Staying clean-shaven is usually too much trouble, so beards and long hair become normal.

Sometimes, women don't lose any weight at all, at least according to the scales. But their bodies do change. Fat layers thin, waists become more defined. Testosterone levels rise, and muscles are more pronounced. Thighs, calves, butts—all the muscle groups involved in walking, hiking, and climbing—become harder, stronger, and bigger. I can already see some of those changes in Wonderland and Yellow. By the time they finish their hike on Katahdin, they'll look like Amazonian warriors, superheroes, or Wonder Woman. Still curvy but with a strong aura of power about them.

When we finally reach the shelter on top of Standing Indian, it's full to overflowing. Tents fill the meager meadow around the building. Wonderland points to a nearby sign marking a side path to the actual summit. "Let's camp up there," she suggests.

We find a flat, grassy area on the top, perfect for gazing at the stars, which are beginning to become visible. The night is clear and cooling rapidly, but we decide to sleep under the stars instead of erecting our tents. I laugh when Yellow calls it "cowboy camping." Using our flat tents as ground cover, we lay out our pads and sleeping bags, then quickly change into woolen sleeping tights and pullovers, socks, and knitted hats.

Dinner is a hurried affair of shared snacks and plenty of water; we promise ourselves to cook at least one good meal tomorrow. By the time we've repacked our food supplies, cleaned ourselves, and brushed our teeth, then taken a quick trip to the bushes, it's fully dark and getting much colder.

Lying on our backs, we watch the stars appear, oohing and ahhing at the occasional falling star. Neither Yellow nor Wonderland know much about the constellations, so I point them out. When they ask if I know any star stories, I share the Cherokee legend of how a spirit dog made the Milky Way by spilling cornmeal he tried to steal from an old couple.

"The old man and woman worked hard to dry the corn and grind it into meal to support themselves, so they were dismayed to find some of their cornmeal missing one morning. Knowing Cherokees do not steal from each other, they decided to lay a trap for the thief. They put on their turtle shell rattles, got their drums, and hid by the full baskets. Late that night, they heard a great whooshing noise and looked up to see a giant spirit dog gulping down mouthfuls of their cornmeal. They jumped up, shaking their rattles, pounding on their drums, and screaming. The loud noise scared the spirit dog, and he ran across the night sky. The cornmeal that spilled from his mouth turned into the stars of the Milky Way."

"I like that story," Wonderland says when I finish. "Thank you for sharing it." After a moment, she adds, laughing, "You know it does kinda look like someone spilled shiny cornmeal across the sky."

Something about the way she says it strikes me as funny, and I start to giggle. Maybe it's the aftermath of the physical, emotional, or mental stress of the day, maybe we just need some relief from the tension, but before long, all three of us are laughing and giggling.

Yellow makes it worse when she says she always thought it was Tinker Bell's fairy dust. Wonderland responds with another crazy theory, and soon we're trying to one-up each other with the silliest ideas for what the Milky Way is made of. It's Wonderland, however, who finally wins the contest when she announces the Milky Way is most definitely made from unicorn piss. The mental image of a unicorn flying across the sky leaving behind a sparkling, golden shower sends us all into another fit of laughter. There's no topping her theory.

The long, hard day finally takes its toll, and sooner than we'd like, we're yawning and telling each other goodnight. I hear Wonderland mumble something, and then giggle softly. "She talks in her sleep," whispers Yellow, who is lying next to me.

"Does she ever say anything incriminating?"

Yellow chuckles. "Sometimes, she'll say Travis's name, but most of the time nothing makes any sense. He's my brother, by the way."

"She told me they were engaged, and he was supposed to be here to hike with her, but his discharge papers were delayed. She said you volunteered to come with her. That's a pretty nice thing to do."

"Well, I owe her big time, and, to be honest, I had some other reasons to get away from Texas."

An owl hoots nearby, and we're both quiet for a while. Just when I think she might have drifted off to sleep, Yellow whispers to me again. "Are you close to your family, Ella?"

"I don't really have a lot of family left. Some cousins and an uncle or two. I never knew my father, and my mother died when I was very young. My grandmother raised me, but she passed away eight years ago."

"I'm sorry. You must be a strong, determined young woman to be living on your own for so long."

Not sure how to respond to her compliment, I change the subject. "My granny was an amazing woman. She taught me a lot about hard work and surviving."

"I have a wonderful nana. Sometimes, I'm not sure I would be here now without her love and support."

For a while, neither of us says anything. I consider her words, wondering if they really mean what I think they do. Perhaps it's my turn to offer support. Before I can speak, she continues.

"I hate my father."

Her simple statement startles me, and I turn to look at her in the darkness. There's enough starlight to see the shimmer of liquid in her eyes as she stares at the sky.

"He's an asshole, a bully, an emotional, physical, and sexual abuser." She turns her head to look at me now, and there's no mistaking the meaning of her words. "I was thirteen, scared to death, afraid to tell anyone. Food became my solace, that and cutting. He used to call me his chunky gal. 'How's my little chunky gal?' he'd say when he climbed into my bed at night. My God, how I hated him!"

"Yellow?"

"It's okay. Most of the time, I don't think about him. I refuse to let him affect my life anymore, but today, when I saw the sign … Well, it just brought it all back." She wipes away the tear trickling down her cheek, then looks up at the stars again.

"Travis was the one who figured out something was going on. He caught me binge eating in my closet one day after I cut myself several times. There was blood all over my arm and chocolate cake all over my face. Then he saw our father coming out of my room late one night. Mother was an alcoholic who was too drunk to be of any help, so he went to our nana. She got the authorities involved, but I was too afraid to testify against him. They worked out a deal for me to live with her. I have no doubt she saved my life."

"Do you mind if I ask what happened then?"

"No," she answers, rolling over to face me once more. She shifts onto her side, sliding her hands under her head. "I grew up, but it wasn't easy. Nana made sure I got professional help, and she loved me, unconditionally, even when I couldn't love myself. There were some drugs, lots of alcohol, and more than a few random men, but she never gave up on me. And then I became a lawyer."

Rosemary chuckles, a smirking grin on her face. "I became a lawyer, and I took the bastard to court and put him away for a long time. And, you know, Texas prisons aren't the nicest places to be when you're guilty of incest and rape."

This time she laughs out loud, and I can't help but join her. We both stood up to the bullies of our past, and it feels good—freeing and wonderful.

"Yellow?"

"Uhm?"

"I think you're a strong and determined young woman, too."

"Thank you," she whispers back.

Above us the stars continue their dance across the sky, and the spirit dog continues to form the Milky Way from his stolen cornmeal, just as they have for eons upon eons. Asleep in our warm layers of wool and down, neither of us notices.

CHAPTER 21
Happy Days

Date: Thursday-Friday, March 20 & 21

Starting Location: Campsite on Standing Indian Mountain

Destination: Franklin, North Carolina

Total Trip Miles: 106.8

The next two days are some of the happiest of my life. Everything—from the weather, to the trail, to the company, to the food—everything is wonderful. It's as if all the variables in the universe came together at one time to form the perfect equation for happiness.

The weather stays unseasonably warm. Sunny days, cool nights, and low humidity make the best hiking conditions. We take advantage of them by deciding to cover the twenty-two miles from Standing Indian Mountain to Winding Stair Gap in the next two days. From the gap, we can hitchhike into Franklin, North Carolina, for a town break.

The abundant sunshine brings new life back to the forest. Bright green leaves seem to burst from each stem and branch. The gentle breeze is redolent with the perfume of wildflowers. More than once, Wonderland surprises us by stopping in the middle of the trail to breathe in great gulps of air. The delighted glee on her face almost makes us think she's getting high from the scent.

We see more animals, too. The meadows, full of wildflowers, are also covered in bees, butterflies, and other flying insects. Squirrels chitter at us as we pass, birds serenade us, and once, we round a bend to see a red fox standing in the middle of the trail. Three humans and one fox freeze in place as we carefully study each other. It's beautiful. The flaming ginger of its coat seems to glow in the sunlight, and the snowy white of its chest is matched by the tip of its tail. Satisfied we mean it no harm, it finally trots off into the woods, leaving the three humans to grin happily at each other.

Snakes make their appearance, too. Grass snakes, gopher snakes, and once, a baby rattlesnake, all slither away at our approach. The sighting of each one elicits a scream and a curse or two from Yellow. She *hates* snakes.

Winter is gone, and we walk north with spring.

From our campsite on top of Standing Indian Mountain, we watch the sun come up. The summit gifts us with magnificent views in all directions. I sit, along with Yellow and Wonderland, as the new day begins in a glow of apricot and peach, scarlet and vermilion. When the sun tips the horizon, the sky blazes canary, amber, and gold.

It's a new day, a new beginning, a new chance to rewrite the equations of my life. At Plumorchard, I said goodbye to Hudson. At Standing Indian, I say hello to a new me. I chuckle to myself at the implications of the mountain's name.

Six miles later, we stop for lunch at Carter Gap Shelter. After eating snacks and cold food yesterday, we had promised ourselves a leisurely, hot lunch today. When I dump out the contents of my food bag, I realize how well my cousin has taken care of me.

Liam told me he received samples from companies making packaged lightweight trail food for climbers, hikers, and outdoor enthusiasts. As owner of Mountain Crossings, his opinion mattered. A recommendation, a favorable review, and a spot on his shelves could mean success, especially for a small company trying to get started in the business.

He's included several dinners from companies I've never heard of. None of them require actual cooking. All I have to do is pour boiling water into their heatproof bags, wait a few minutes, and enjoy. The only cleanup is washing my spoon and disposing of the trash at the next road crossing.

When I offer Yellow and Wonderland a choice, they jump at the chance to try something new. We're famished, so we quickly pick out three selections. Fifteen minutes later, we're sharing the meals, tasting each one, and comparing the flavors. The unanimous decision is they are all delicious. Dessert is gourmet chocolate from Yellow's stash and a thirty-minute nap.

Four more miles and we cross Betty Creek. Yellow already warned me to expect to stop at every stream big enough to swim in, so I'm not surprised when Wonderland starts stripping off again. Into the water she goes, submerging herself completely in the icy water before emerging with a gasping grin.

My entrance is a bit slower and much more hesitant. I turn at a noise behind me, to find Yellow shrugging out of her clothes, too. Perhaps it was the emotional release of sharing her story with me last night, or the physical release of hours of constant hiking, but she's calmer, happier today.

Although I try not to look, it's impossible not to notice her scars. Tiny, almost invisible white lines crisscross the inside of both arms and thighs. When she moves through a patch of sunlight, they become even more noticeable. She has other scars, too. Besides the jagged one along her outer left calf, there's another along her left ribcage and left shoulder. Two smaller round scars mar the skin on her chest above her sports bra. I try to quickly look away, but she knows I've seen them.

"Ella?"

"Sorry, Yellow. I didn't mean … You just caught me by surprise," I manage to say.

"It's okay. I know they can be pretty shocking when you're not expecting them. I told you about the little ones, the ones from cutting myself, but I didn't tell you about the others."

"You don't have—"

"Hey," she interrupts. "It's all right. Really, I don't mind. These are from a car wreck," she explains, pointing to the bigger scars on her left side. "I took some kids away from their asshole, meth-dealing parents who decided to try to get them back by T-boning my car. As if *that* would help their case— stupid dipshits. The police were there before they could even *try* to drive away. The judge took one look at the traffic camera footage and gave custody to a grandmother who desperately wanted them. Last time I checked, the idiots were still in prison."

"And you went back to your job, even after they tried to kill you?"

"Well, it took me awhile to get out of the hospital, but yeah, I finally did." Walking past me, she gives me a wink before entering the water. "Haven't you ever heard of 'don't mess with Texas'?" Laughing, she jumps into the stream, splashing Wonderland, who retaliates by trying to dunk her.

Big Spring Shelter is our destination for the night, but first we have to climb Albert Mountain. Two hours after leaving the creek, we're standing at the base of the mountain, looking at the short but extremely steep, extremely rocky, climb in front of us. Less than a quarter of a mile separates us from the summit, which is topped by a fire tower, typical of many that once dotted the Southern forests but now manned only during very dry years.

Some stairs are built into the almost straight up path, but most of the way is just a scramble from one rock to the next. Coming at the end of a long day, it seems to take forever to finally reach the flat summit. When we do, we're rewarded with amazing views in every direction.

We decide to climb the stairs leading to the building at the top of the tower. The small residence is locked, but we walk around the surrounding viewing platform, marveling at the seemingly unending forest stretching out across the hills and valleys in every direction. Sitting on the edge, we dangle our feet over the long drop to the ground while we eat a snack.

I tell them the Cherokee legend of the Thunder Boys who made so much noise the people made them live in the high mountains away from the villages in the valleys. Then, I embellish it a bit by claiming the forestry service can no longer get people to stay in the tower because the Thunder Boys won't let them sleep at night. We share a laugh before we climb down.

Half a mile later, we arrive at the shelter. It's full with spring breakers, gear and bags hanging everywhere. While Wonderland and I discuss our camping options, Yellow takes out her water filter and begins walking to the spring. A startled shriek has us running around the corner of the building to check on her.

A large black snake, easily four or five feet in length, is crawling up the side of the shelter. The warm weather has brought it from its winter den, and now it's hunting the mice swarming the shelter.

"I'm not staying in *that* shelter or anywhere close to it," she declares when she sees us. "So you need to find somewhere else to camp." Turning, she stomps off toward the water source, muttering about damned snakes. "I *hate* snakes!" she shouts one last time.

I find a secluded clearing some distance from the shelter where Wonderland and I set up camp. We take some time to clean up trash left behind by previous campers and clear the area of large stones and sticks we'll put back in place before we leave in the morning.

Yellow and Wonderland share a tent. It's bigger than mine and has two side doors, which allow them to enter and exit without crawling over each other to do so. The door overhangs also provide a protected space for their gear.

My tent is tubular shaped with the door at one end. It's barely tall enough for me to sit up, and there is space, both at the narrow foot and in the doorway, for me to stash my gear. It's a little harder to enter and exit.

We eat, we clean up, we hang our food bags at the shelter, and we sleep. A deep, restful, dreamless sleep that restores the body and mind and prepares us for another day on the trail.

~ * * * ~

Songbirds have become my alarm clock. Long before the sun makes its appearance, even before the slightest gray colors the eastern sky, the birds are awake and singing. With the warmer temperatures, there are a lot of birds here, and they're really, really loud.

Comfortable in my little tent, I listen to the birdsongs, picking out the familiar notes from my childhood. A mockingbird cycles through his repertoire, and I follow his tweets, trills, and warbles. The pattern of his note progressions takes form in my mind, and I contemplate the possibilities of incorporating music into random sequence codes. The sound of a zipper opening on Yellow and Wonderland's tent lets me know they're awake, so I file the music theory away and begin to prepare for the day.

We have nine miles to travel today. Not an insignificant number but still easy to manage, particularly in this amazing weather and with the trail slowly dropping in elevation. The plan is to reach the highway by mid-afternoon. It gives us enough time to find a ride, get to a motel, and clean up before going out for dinner. The girls have a mail drop to pick up at the post office, which they'll be able to do tomorrow morning only since it's closed on Saturday afternoon.

It's another beautiful day on the trail, perfect weather, perfect pathway, and perfect companions. In no time, we've covered six miles and pull into a shelter for a food break. Yesterday's hot lunch made us feel so good, we decide to splurge again and cook something to eat. Pulling out our food bags, we rummage through them, picking out favorites and pulling together a shared picnic lunch. A nap soon follows.

The road crossing at Winding Stair Gap comes quickly. A man sits in an open van door, watching a young child play on the ground near his feet. When he sees us, he stands and approaches us with a friendly smile.

"Ariella Dobbs?" he asks, glancing down at a card in his hand, and then back up at me.

"Yes?"

"I'm Tator. I do a little trail angelin' around here. Rides to town and stuff. Liam Crow down at Neels Gap called and asked me to meet you this afternoon and make sure you get into Franklin safely."

He hands me a small business card with his name and phone number printed on the front. "He told me to tell you to call him at the number on the back, and he still thinks you should come home."

Chuckling, I flip the card over, finding Liam's private cell phone number and email address.

"Do you have room for all of us?" I ask Tator, who nods and leads us to his van.

Tator picks up the little girl, who watches us load our packs into the rear of the van. "This is my granddaughter," he explains, smiling proudly at the little girl who appears to be about four years old. "You want to tell the ladies your trail name?"

His granddaughter ducks her head shyly, hiding her face against his neck.

"Would you like to know my trail name?" Yellow steps closer to the little girl and holds up one of her braids. "It's Yellow, like the color of my hair. Please tell me your name."

The little girl smiles at Yellow, then leans forward conspiratorially and whispers, "It's Tator Tot."

We're all laughing as we arrange ourselves in the van and start down the road to Franklin. We've only gone a short distance before Tator is discreetly lowering his window to let in some fresh air. In the warm, confined space of the van, it doesn't take long before we're also reaching for the window controls.

Tator Tot's face is scrunched in a disgusted scowl as she surveys us. From her car seat in the back, she leans forward toward her grandfather. "Stinky hikers, Papa," she complains.

She keeps us entertained all the way to Franklin.

CHAPTER 22

Town Days

Date: Friday-Saturday, March 21 & 22
Starting Location: Franklin, North Carolina
Destination: Franklin, North Carolina
Total Trip Miles: 106.8

Tator drives us directly to the Franklin Motel where Liam has reserved a room for me. It's a good thing, too, because hotel rooms are in short supply this weekend. Hikers, outdoor enthusiasts, and tourists have invaded the little town due, in part, to the great weather and the town's proximity to the Nantahala Outdoor Center.

When we find out the room has two queen beds, Yellow and Wonderland agree to share with me. Tator refuses any payment or tip, claiming it's all been taken care of. Before he leaves, he makes sure I have his phone number and reminds me to call for a ride back to the trail.

Liam also left a box for me. We open it to find more packaged, freeze-dried dinners, an assortment of snacks and trail bars, and a huge bag of Dreamer's homemade chocolate chip cookies. Best of all is a sack of fresh fruit. Grapes, apples, an orange or two, and a carton of fresh blackberries. We moan in pleasure while we gorge ourselves on the juicy grapes. Fresh fruit is too heavy to carry on a multi-day hike.

Yellow wins our coin toss and gets the first shower. While she washes away the hiker funk, Wonderland and I tackle the backpacks. Dirty clothes go in one pile, trash in another, and leftover food makes up the third pile. Sleeping bags are pulled from their stuff bags and unzipped. The bags are then draped over the beds for a good airing. We take the tents outside and shake as much dirt as possible from them. They, too, are left out of their stuff sacks and folded neatly in one corner of the room.

Their gear is similar to mine: newer, lighter weight, innovative fabrics, and unique construction details. Each piece of clothing or gear in their packs has been carefully chosen with an eye toward usefulness and overall weight. So I'm more than surprised when Wonderland pulls out the biggest first-aid kit I've ever seen. It looks like she's brought an entire emergency room with her. She laughs at my gawking. "Same reaction I get from everyone, but I can't help it. I'm a trauma nurse, and if someone were to get hurt, I'd be the first one to help. I could never forgive myself if I didn't have something that could save someone's life. I just hope I never have to use it."

Yellow emerges in a cloud of steam, groaning in pleasure from the hot water. "I swear, sometimes I think hot water and ice cubes are mankind's greatest inventions," she says as she plops down on one of the beds. "I need a Coke on ice." Then, with a muttered curse, she quickly opens a window. "Damn, this place stinks." She laughs.

Before Wonderland can get in the shower, I hand her all our dirty socks. "Put these in the tub while you shower so they can start soaking."

She gives me a questioning look but takes them with her anyway. Two minutes later, I'm laughing at her surprised yelp, and Yellow is running into the bathroom to see what is happening.

"Holy shit!" I hear Yellow exclaim.

Socks take the brunt of day-to-day hiking. Dust from the trail filters into the yarns, building up from daily use. I've seen socks so stiff from dirt and sweat they almost stand up by themselves. Most hikers bring at least three pairs with them—two to hike in, and one clean pair to sleep in and wear in town while the other two are in the laundry. Getting them clean is the problem. If you dump them in with the rest of your clothes, they'll turn the wash water into a muddy mess unless you pre-wash some of the dirt out of them. Which is what Wonderland is doing right now by letting them soak in the tub while she showers. Of course, it also means she's standing in a big puddle of muddy water.

Then, it's my turn. I luxuriate in the hot water, letting the pressure soothe my sore shoulders and stiff neck. I have to shampoo my hair twice before it feels clean. Finally, feeling relaxed and refreshed, I turn my attention to those nasty socks. Each one is rinsed under the faucet and squeezed, then added to the pile of clothes waiting to be washed.

Like me, Yellow and Wonderland have saved one set of clean underwear and one clean shirt to wear in town. We'll wear our rain pants while everything else goes into the laundry.

The motel has one coin-operated washer and dryer, as well as a dated computer with dial-up internet access available for their guests. Both are located off the main lobby. While I get the laundry started, Wonderland uses the computer to email her fiancé. She's been unable to get in touch with him since they began hiking and is clearly worried. Yellow adds a note to her brother before they finish.

When the hotel attendant offers to watch our laundry, we decide to get something to eat. An hour later, we're stuffed with chicken fried steak, mashed potatoes with gravy, green beans, and cornbread. We each get a piece of homemade berry pie to take to the room.

After we pick up our freshly washed, dried, and folded laundry, it's back to the room and into bed. For a while, we flip through the channels on the TV, but the busy day soon takes its toll, and we're asleep by the time the sun sets outside.

~ * * * ~

Yellow and Wonderland head to the post office early the next morning, taking along an empty backpack to carry their mail drop. We've decided to save any supply shopping until after we see what they have. Between what Liam left me and what's in their package, we probably have plenty of food to get us through the next 28 miles to the Outdoor Center where we plan to spend the night and resupply. We could be there in two long days, but just in case, we'll take enough food for three.

While they're gone, I use the computer in the lobby and email Dr. Albright, telling him I've taken a vacation in Georgia to visit family and will get in touch when I return. Then, I send Susan a message, letting her know I'm fine. I also tell her that although I won't fight Hudson's leaving, I will definitely be defending my intellectual property rights and expect a very generous compensation for their use. A quick note to Liam, telling him I'm here and safe, thanking him for the ride and food, and promising to call later when I can find a payphone, and I'm finished.

Later, while getting our money's worth at an all-you-can eat lunch buffet, Wonderland tells us she wants to get her hair trimmed at a salon they passed on the way to the post office. They're giving free haircuts to anyone who donates to Locks of Love. Even though she doesn't have enough hair to donate, she wants to support them.

Everything is within walking distance, and we soon find ourselves in front of the beauty salon. Sure enough, a large sign in the window announces free haircuts for anyone donating their hair. We follow Wonderland inside while she arranges for a cut. Yellow declines, saying she's fine with her length.

The receptionist's eyes widen when she sees my braid. "Oh, honey, are you thinking of cutting off your braid?"

Up until her question, I hadn't thought of getting a haircut. I was just following Wonderland. But now, I wonder what it would be like to have shorter hair. It would certainly be easier to deal with on the trail. "I think maybe I am," I reply.

She gets me settled into a chair, and soon, a stylist is behind me releasing my braid. "You have beautiful hair," she tells me, running her fingers through its length. "Has it ever been cut?" When I shake my head, she studies me carefully in the mirror. "This is a big step, and you need to be sure. I won't cut it unless you're absolutely positive."

My reflection looks back at me from the mirror while I watch her run a comb through my hair. "Such beautiful hair," I hear her mutter to herself. Suddenly, I'm back in my apartment, sitting in front of my bathroom vanity getting ready for the meeting.

"May I?" Hudson asks, taking the comb from my hand. He runs it carefully through my hair from the top of my head to the very tip where it falls against my waist. "So beautiful, so beautiful," he whispers to himself. Brow furrowed in concentration, he repeats each stroke, bringing the comb deliberately from crown to tip and letting the strands fall through his fingers. He glances toward the mirror where I watch him.

"I've always loved your hair," he tells me. "And I've wanted to do this for a long time."

"Why did you wait?"

His eyes search mine before he speaks. "You were so young when I met you. I was afraid you might think I was too old. Then, when we started working together, I didn't want you or anyone else to think I was trying to take advantage of you. But I wanted to, Ariella. I wanted to hold your hand, wanted to kiss you, wanted to run my fingers through your hair."

"Hudson, you're only four years older than I am. Twenty-eight to my twenty-four. That's not a big age difference."

"It isn't now," he agrees, smiling at my reflection. "But it was when you were eighteen and I was twenty-two. You were so——" He breaks off, frowning.

"Naïve?" I answer for him. "Backward, countrified, gullible, inexperienced?"

142

"Absolutely not." He glares at me. *"Don't ever call yourself that. I thought you were wonderful … so real, so innocent and unspoiled. I was in awe of you and your beautiful mind."* He chuckles before starting to comb my hair again. *"And this beautiful hair, too."*

Once more our eyes lock in the mirror before he leans over and kisses me lightly on the top of my head. "Promise me you'll never change from the wonderful girl I fell in love with, and promise me you'll never cut your hair."

"You decided yet, hun?"

The stylist's words cut short my memories. She's still standing behind me, studying my reflection in the mirror and waiting for my decision. "Cut it off," I answer.

Forty-five minutes later, I'm still staring at my reflection but for a completely different reason. I barely recognize the person in the mirror. After she had cut off the heavy length, the hairdresser began arranging my hair, trying to get an idea of how it would lay on its own before she started shaping it. She studied the shorter hair in the back, frowning a bit before asking me if I had curly hair. When I replied no, she sprayed some water on it, crunched it a bit, and then turned me around so I could see the back in the mirror. Freed from the weight of the braid, the shorter hair curled around on itself and lay in soft waves against my head.

Grabbing a magazine lying beside her station, she quickly thumbed through it before showing me a photo. "This is how I'd like to cut your hair." Yellow and Wonderland glanced at the photo, and then at me before smiling and nodding.

And now I have a new hairdo. Shorter in the back and over my ears, the layers gradually lengthen on top. It's curly and spiky, messy and casual. Best of all, I can wash it, finger comb it, let it dry, and be done. The hairdresser rubs a little product through it, spiking it up a bit and feathering the ends.

When she's almost finished, the bell over the door dings and a loud voice startles us.

"I told you it was Ella. Oh, dear Lord above, girl. What have you done to your hair?" No Filter and Curly Dan rush over to stand behind my chair. They join Yellow, Wonderland, and the stylist, who are all grouped around me staring at my reflection.

"Would you look at those cheekbones," No Filter continues. "And those eyes. I swear they take up half her face. A little liner, a little mascara, and some lip gloss, and you'd be ready to go." He grins at me, then sobers a bit. "You really do look amazing. And who knew there were curls hiding in that braid. Great haircut," he adds, turning to the hairdresser. "Would you like to fix mine?" He winks, running his hand over his bald head.

She rolls her eyes at him, then slaps his arm playfully before glancing at Curly Dan. "Does he belong to you?" She nods toward No Filter.

"Yes, madam, I am happy to acknowledge he does indeed belong to me," Dan answers her in his best upper-crust British accent.

"Hikers," she laughs, shaking her head before shooing us out the door.

As soon as I've introduced everyone, No Filter turns to me with a glare. "I want you to know I just about had a heart attack when I read your entry in the register at Plumorchard. You've got a lot of explaining to do." Glancing around, he spies a nearby coffee shop. "Come on, girl, let's talk." Grabbing my hand, he leads us across the street and into the shop.

Over the next two hours, we laugh, talk, and get reacquainted. When I didn't join them at the Blueberry Patch, they assumed I'd left with my cousin. They weren't worried until they saw the entry in the shelter register and began hearing stories from hikers they were meeting. "Everyone is talking about it, trying to spread the word. The authorities are tracking down leads, and local trail angels are watching the road crossings for anyone acting suspicious. What you did was a good thing. Hopefully, they can catch these two scumbags before they hurt anyone else. However"—he cocks his head at me, twitching his mustache—"I think you probably left out a few deets, and I want them all."

I repeat my story about the bullies, filling in all the details I left out of the register, including pushing the rocks down the cliff and the insults I hurled at them. No Filter laughs so hard he has to wipe the tears from his eyes.

"Mealy-mouthed?" Curly Dan asks. "You called them mealy-mouthed?"

"Yes."

"Oh, good one. Do you know what it means?'"

"Not really. Granny used to say it all the time. I always assumed it was some kind of insult. 'Mealy-mouthed motherfucker' just sounded really good together," I add, sending No Filter into another fit of laughter.

Dan grins at his friend, then turns back to me. "It's an old, old saying," he explains. "Dating back well into the 1600s. It means someone who is afraid to speak plainly or directly. I don't think anyone could ever accuse you of being mealy-mouthed, Miss Ella."

After numerous cups of coffee, a large assortment of homemade muffins and pastries, and more laughter and more talking, it's time to head back to our hotel for an afternoon nap. The guys are staying in a local B & B where their host is taking care of their laundry. They still need to pick up supplies before the stores close, but they agree to meet us for a late dinner. Curly Dan has fallen in love with authentic Southern chicken fried steak and wants to find a restaurant that serves the dish. A request that makes No Filter roll his eyes and shudder dramatically.

When we reach the hotel, Wonderland checks her email one more time, but there's no word from her fiancé. She's clearly upset and worried, but there really isn't anything she can do.

Saturday night means the restaurants are full and very busy. We meet No Filter and Curly Dan at the same little diner where we ate the night before. An almost hour wait means we have plenty of time to visit and compare hiking experiences. The night is pleasant, and we sit outside while we wait for our table. Yellow and Wonderland grill the guys about the PCT.

Finally, No Filter asks if they're thinking about hiking the trail. "Maybe." Wonderland grins. "It might make a good honeymoon journey."

"Oh, spill the beans, girl. You thinking about tying the knot? I can see it now," he continues before she can even nod an answer. "You could have the ceremony at the monument at Campo, and then hike off into the sunset in your wedding gown and backpack. We'd get a custom-made backpack, white with sequins and lace."

Thankfully, the hostess interrupts him by calling our names. Curly Dan grabs No Filter's hand. "Come on," he urges. "We need to feed you before you get too far into crazy land."

Later, stomachs full and the merits of deep-fried versus griddle-fried versus pan-fried steak endlessly debated, we wander down the main street. It's easy to pick out our fellow hikers—we all seem to wear the same uniform. Hiking boots or trail shoes, moisture wicking T-shirts, pants that can be converted to shorts by zipping off the legs at mid-thigh. We're greeted with smiles and nods by both hikers and townies.

Loud music pours from an open doorway. "Brooks and Dunn," shouts Yellow. "Come on, they're playin' my kind of music. Let's do some boot scootin'." She grabs my hand, pulling me and Wonderland into the crowded dance hall. Deftly skirting around the edge of the dancers, she finds us a table for five in a quieter area toward the back.

When a waitress shows up, they quickly order their favorite drinks, but when she turns to me, I don't know what to say. "Ella, what do you want to order?" Yellow asks.

"I don't … I mean, I've never."

Sensing my distress, Curly Dan leans in closer to me. "Have you ever had an alcoholic drink?"

"Some wine a few times and a beer once or twice."

Four sets of eyes regard me, five if you count the waitress. "Tell you what, hun," she says. "Let me turn in this order and you think about what you'd like to try. I'll bring you some water when I come back, and you can tell me what you want then." With a nod, she hurries off.

My face feels hot, and I'm completely mortified as I look around at my companions.

Wonderland is the first to speak. "Have you ever been to a bar before?"

"No."

"Dance hall, honky-tonk, nightclub?"

"No."

"I have a plan," No Filter announces, slamming his hands on the table and breaking the uncomfortable silence. "Each one of us will order another of our favorite drinks. Then we'll have one to drink and one for Ella to try. She can taste them, and if she doesn't like it, then we'll already have a second drink. If she likes it, she can have it, and we can order more later. Then," he adds, "when she's relaxed a little, I'm going to teach her how to two-step. And you two lovely ladies can see if you can teach Curly Dan his right foot from his left."

The night turns into more fun than I thought possible. I manage part of the margarita Wonderland hands me. Dan's top-shelf Scotch makes me gag and choke. No Filter's highball is okay, but I really like the drink Yellow gives me. Coca-Cola with a little kick—it's cold, sweet, and goes down easily. She declares me a true Southern belle when I order another.

"What is it?" I ask while she laughs.

"Coke and Southern Comfort with a little twist of lime." She grins. "The ultimate Southern party girl drink. So, drink up and let's party," she shouts.

And we do.

Although I wouldn't have believed it possible, No Filter actually manages to teach me how to two-step. I find it quite easy. The rhythm is three quick steps and then a slow one. Three quick and one slow, three quick and one slow. He pushes me around the floor, smoothly guiding me in and around couples as we make a giant circle around the dance floor. Soon, he's twirling me, swinging me around and under his arm, and I'm laughing at how much fun it is.

A young man taps No Filter on the shoulder, asking him if he can cut in. When I smile and nod, he hands me off to him, and we dance two more songs before another man asks for the next dance. I spend the next hour dancing with one young man after another. All of them are polite, no one gets handsy or grabby, and all of them call me ma'am and thank me for each dance.

When the music finally changes to a slow waltz, No Filter finds me again. "Are you having fun?" he asks.

"Yes," I manage to answer, finally catching my breath. "More fun than I think I've ever had before."

"Good. I'm glad." He sways me gently back and forth before speaking again. "I read your other entry in the register at Plumorchard; the one you wrote in the back."

When I only nod, he continues speaking. "You told Hud you loved him."

"Yes."

"And then you told him goodbye."

"Yes." Perhaps it's the alcohol, perhaps the excitement of the night, or perhaps the fatigue I'm suddenly feeling, but tears well up in my eyes as I look up at my friend. "I had to. I need to move on."

He nods in agreement before pulling me in closer to him. Resting my head on his chest, I listen to his deep and steady heartbeat. "It's not easy though," he tells me. "And it takes a while, but eventually, the pain goes away. We never forget our first love, though."

We sway together for a few more minutes before he laughs. "Hey, at least, you're not angry. Looks like I'll have to think of a new trail name. RAW doesn't work anymore."

The music ends, and we begin to make our way back to the table where our friends wait for us. Before we get there, he stops and turns me toward him. "There's something you need to know, Ella. You look stunning tonight. The haircut is a killer, girl; a true killer. But more than that, you're laughing and happy, and your face is flushed with joy. Those men, the ones who asked you to dance? They watched you all night. Any of them—hell, all of them—would have been proud to call you 'girlfriend.' You deserve someone who thinks you're the most precious thing in the world. Don't settle for anything less."

I grab his hand to keep him beside me. "No Filter, if Curly Dan ever gets tired of you, can I have you?"

He grins back at me. "Sorry, girl, you know your plumbing doesn't work for me, but I'll always be your friend."

CHAPTER 23
Becoming Beautiful

Date: Sunday, March 23
Starting Location: Franklin, North Carolina
Destination: Siler Bald Shelter
Total Trip Miles: 110.5 miles

Our plans were to get an early start on Sunday morning. After getting a ride back to the trail, we intended to hike at least to Wayah Bald and, hopefully, several miles past it. That didn't happen.

It's mid-morning before I open my eyes, groaning at the harsh light and the pounding in my head. "Good morning, boot scootin' party girl," Yellow greets me when I turn my back to the open window. "Wonderland is in the shower, and it's your turn next. There's a bottle of water and a couple Tylenol on the nightstand next to you. You're supposed to drink it all. I'm on my way to the lobby for coffee, and I'll bring you back a cup. Sugar and cream?"

I manage a frowning nod, which she laughs at before leaving the room. The slamming door elicits another groan. When she returns with the coffee, I've managed to sit up and down most of the water. The pills, the shower, and the hot, sweet coffee make me feel almost normal again, but my stomach is still unsettled. Both of them assure me I just need something hot and greasy to soak up the rest of the alcohol in my system. So, while they giggle and crack jokes about "Ella's first time," we make our way down the street to a nearby café for breakfast. Dry toast, coffee, and bacon—a lot of bacon—are all I can manage. I have to turn my head away from Yellow's runny, sunny-side-up eggs.

There's a TV playing above the cash register, and I catch a glimpse of a weather map. The forecaster is pointing at and saying something about a strong winter storm spreading across the northern plains. Getting out of my chair, I walk closer to the screen so I can hear above the noise of the diners. The screen advances through the next twenty-four hours, showing the storm getting closer to our location. Just as he's about to give the forecast for our area, he's interrupted with a breaking news bulletin.

A serious-looking news anchor faces the camera, behind him footage of tanks rolling through desert towns and soldiers in combat gear plays. "The Pentagon has announced the first casualties in the latest fighting in the Gulf region. Eighteen US Marines and eleven US soldiers have died in what has been described as the fiercest fighting since Operation Iraqi Freedom began three days ago. The names of the deceased are being withheld until notification of next of kin."

Silence has filled the café during his announcement. I turn, as if in slow motion, to Wonderland and Yellow, who have risen from our table. I watch their eyes widen, then fill with shock and horror. And then Wonderland begins wailing.

Yellow manages to hold it together longer than Wonderland, but she's crying and sobbing as they hold on to each other. The owner of the café reaches them at the same time I do, and together, we lead them through the kitchen and into a small office. There is a small couch we get them settled onto. She leaves and returns with glasses of cold water, which she urges the girls to drink.

"Is there someone they can call?" she asks me.

"A grandmother, I think."

151

"I'll leave you alone then. Y'all use the phone on the desk and make whatever calls you need to make. Don't worry about anything and stay as long as you need." When I nod, she leaves the room.

"Rosemary? Rosemary. Listen to me." Nodding, she gives me her attention. "You don't know your brother is there. Just because you haven't heard from him doesn't mean he's over there. Use the phone and call your grandmother. Find out if she's heard anything."

"You're right; you're right," she mutters before crossing over to the desk and picking up the receiver.

While she's punching in the numbers, I sit beside Wonderland, pulling her into a hug. She leans against me, hiccupping as her sobs slowly subside. "Allison, Travis could be anywhere. He could be stateside; he could be in transit; we don't know anything at this point. There must be hundreds, if not thousands, of Marines over there. Please, it's going to be okay."

"I know," she finally says. "It's just I've been so worried. I guess the stress of not knowing anything is finally getting to me. Dear God, why do we have to go to war again?"

Rosemary must have reached someone on the phone, and the news must be good because she turns toward us, nodding and smiling as she listens. "Okay," she finally says. "I'll tell her. We'll call you in three days when we get to Nantahala. Love you, too, Nana."

She joins us on the couch hugging her soon-to-be sister-in-law.

"He's safe, Allison. He called her a week ago, but she couldn't remember where he said he was, except it was in Georgia somewhere. His papers were sitting on some officer's desk and overlooked because of the preparations for the invasion. She thinks he may be trying to find us."

After a much calmer Yellow and Wonderland leave to return to the motel, I find the owner and thank her for her help. When I try to pay for our meals and the phone call, she waves me away, telling me the bill has been covered by one of the other diners. "You girls take care of yourselves and stay safe now, you hear," she says. "And if you ever meet that young man they're so worried about, you tell him he's one lucky fella to have two sweet girls like that afeared for him. Thank him for his service, too, would ya?"

We're a very subdued trio that Tator picks up to take back to the trail crossing. We discussed staying another night in town, but we seem to need the physical release hiking offers, so we decided to hike the four miles to Siler Bald Shelter and spend the night there. It's only after we've been hiking awhile that I realize we didn't see No Filter or Curly Dan again, I didn't call Liam or Susan, and I forgot to find out more about the bad weather headed this way. We should be at our next stop in a couple days, so I'll call them then.

The guidebook doesn't have very much information about the four miles to the shelter. The trail goes up, of course—it always does. We cross several streams, one with a small log bridge and the others by hopping from stone to stone. At one point, we cross a beautiful mountain meadow, but we don't linger to admire the flowers or the open views. Lost in our thoughts, no one says much. I'm sure Wonderland is thinking about her fiancé and Yellow about her brother, or maybe she has someone special in her life, although she's never spoken of anyone.

As for me, I can't stop thinking about Hudson. Seeing how upset Yellow and Wonderland were about the possibility of losing Travis makes me realize how much he still means to me. I would be devastated if something were to happen to him. Have I deluded myself into thinking I needed this hike, that I would be stronger because of it? Or maybe it *is* time to go home like Liam wanted me to. Maybe it *is* time to take care of the mess I left in New York. Could the stronger, wiser, more confident me be ready to deal with Hudson and the fallout from his betrayal? Or was everything a sham and lies orchestrated by Gia, as Liam seemed to think?

Thoughts of Hudson and New York are soon forgotten when the trail transitions from a moderate uphill hike to a very steep, very rocky, ridgeline scramble. There's no trail here, just white blazes painted on jumbled boulders. We gingerly make our way over, and around, and under them. Sometimes, we have to hop across a gap from one rock to the next. When I look down into one, I can see patches of ground far below me. I shudder to think what a fall or slip would mean. Back and forth we scramble, like ants making their way along the bony spine of a skeleton. We can see down into the valleys below us as the hillsides fall sharply away on both sides. On a warm sunny day, this might be fun, but the sky has clouded over and a brisk wind smacks us in the face. Thankfully, the rocky section is a short one, and soon, we're lowering ourselves over the last boulder and back to a more normal rocky trail.

The shelter is located on a side trail before reaching the actual summit of the mountain. It's tucked into a protected little hollow, which shields it from the worst of the north wind. There's a nice grassy meadow in front and a piped spring located on the opposite side from the privy.

We have the shelter to ourselves. With spring break over and the weather cooling off, there are fewer hikers on the trail. In fact, we haven't seen anyone else all day. We eat the rest of Liam's fresh fruit, share a couple of hot dinners, and finish the chocolate chip cookies for dessert.

Although it's dark, although we're in our sleeping bags, although we've had a hard day, I can't go to sleep. Lying on the wooden floor, I stare up at the ceiling, trying to still my mind and will myself to sleep. By their occasional sighs and constant shifting, I can tell Yellow and Wonderland are having as much trouble as I am. Sometimes when my anxieties or nightmares kept me awake, Granny would slip into my bed, hold me close, and tell me stories and legends of our people. Listening to her soothing voice always relaxed me, and eventually, I would fall asleep. I miss her.

Sighing, I roll to my side, only to find Wonderland looking at me in the darkness. "Can't sleep?" I ask.

"No," she replies. "My mind is going ninety miles an hour. I can't stop thinking about Travis, and the war, and … well, everything."

"My gran used to tell me stories when I couldn't sleep. Would you like to hear one?"

"Please." She smiles back.

"Okay. So, this is the legend of the Cherokee Rose," I begin.

"Louder," Yellow interrupts. "I can't sleep either."

Wonderland and I both laugh. I begin again, this time a little louder.

"In 1838, the People were driven from their homes and forced to begin the long walk to the west. The way was hard, and many fell sick and died. Their hearts were heavy with sadness, and their tears mingled with the dust of the trail.

"The Elders knew the survival of the children depended upon the strength of the women. One evening, they called upon Heaven Dweller, *galvladiehi*, and told Him of the People's suffering and tears. They were afraid the children would not survive to rebuild the Cherokee Nation and its seven clans.

"The next morning when the People woke, they looked at the trail behind them, longing to return to their homes. What they saw instead was a fast-growing, vining plant covering the ground where their tears had fallen. As they watched, flowers formed and opened, releasing their sweet perfume into the air.

"Each blossom was white for the tears they shed. The golden center represented the gold taken by the white man's greed. The seven leaves on the plant represented the seven clans of the Cherokee Nation, and the sturdy vine was covered in sharp thorns, which defied anything that tried to destroy it.

"The People forgot their sadness, and the women began to feel strong and beautiful again. Just as the plant protected its blossoms, they knew they could protect the children who would form a new nation in the west. The wild Cherokee rose still grows along the route of the Trail of Tears into eastern Oklahoma. To honor our heritage, the state of Georgia chose the rose as its state flower."

It's quiet when I finish. Finally, Wonderland whispers, "Thank you. It was beautiful."

"Yes, it was. Thank you," Yellow agrees. "You know," she adds after a long pause, "I think you need a new trail name. Something that honors the beautiful stories you tell us. Maybe Bella instead of Ella. It suits you, and I don't think Cinderella does anymore."

Wonderland and Yellow fall asleep quickly, but I lie awake in the dark for a long time, listening to the wind moaning in the pines and thinking about their words.

CHAPTER 24

The Calm Before

Date: Monday, March 24
Starting Location: Siler Bald Shelter
Destination: Siler Bald Shelter
Total Trip Miles: 110.6

It was late when I finally went to sleep and early when I woke. I tossed and turned in the still dark shelter, trying to find a comfortable position on my sleeping pad, which did little to soften the hard, wooden floor beneath me. Maybe I was spoiled from two nights' sleep on a real bed, or maybe I missed the luxury of cool, clean sheets against my body. Whatever it was, my sleep was fitful at best.

When the sky lightens enough I can barely make out my surroundings, I crawl from my sleeping bag, visit the privy, and begin packing my gear. I'm quiet, for the most part, until I take my food bag off the mouse-proof hanger. The chain rattles enough to wake Yellow, who peeks at me with one eye, then rolls over, and immediately goes back to sleep. Wonderland never moves. Hitching up my backpack, I adjust the straps, grab my poles, and start hiking.

The eastern horizon is a soft predawn gray when I reach the summit of Siler Bald Mountain. At almost 5,000 feet, the grassy bald has beautiful views in all directions. With the stars above me and the lights of Franklin in the dark valley below, I feel like I'm suspended between heaven and earth, an outside observer floating between the two, separated by space and time. As the sun rises and the sky turns pink then gold, I watch the stars dim and finally disappear, conceding their dominance of the sky to the bigger star we call the sun. Granny was always a dawn watcher. I think of her as I eat my breakfast and watch the new day begin.

I don't know why I'm so unsettled, so uneasy, why my thoughts keep returning to her. Finally, with a sigh, I begin hiking again.

Time goes by.

The trail drops down off the top of the mountain and skirts the side of the ridges, staying on their protected east side and under tree cover. I snack, drink, and focus on the trail, enjoying the solitude of hiking by myself after being with friends for so many days. At heart, I'm an introvert. I had fun hiking with my new companions, but it's nice to be alone for a while.

The sound of running water grabs my attention, and I turn onto a short side trail leading to a fresh spring bubbling out of the ground. The source itself has been enclosed to protect it from contamination, but a pipe funnels the water from the spring to a small pool. Pulling out my water bottle, I fill it from the pipe, adding a purification tablet and some powdered drink to flavor it.

It's while I'm sitting on a nearby rock, sipping my drink, that I realize something is wrong, seriously wrong. The air is too still, too quiet. It has a heaviness about it that makes me feel like I'm being watched. Standing up, I whirl around, scanning my surroundings for a glimpse of someone or something. There's nothing there. No breeze sways the branches above me. No birdsong fills the air. No small animals scurry through the dead leaves at my feet. A chill settles around me. Quickly donning my backpack, I begin to run up the trail.

I've almost reached the top of Wayah Mountain when I round a bend in the trail and I'm hit with a gust of cold wind. It's not just cold—it's freezing.

158

Even as I stand there catching my breath, I can feel the temperature dropping, and the first drops of sleet hit my face.

There's a stone observation tower on top of Wayah Bald. The vistas are amazing, and it's a great place to spend some time on a warm, sunny day. When I emerge from the forest into the open area around the tower, the strength of the wind catches me off guard, and I'm almost knocked over. The sleet is unlike anything I've ever experienced. It falls in a solid sheet of ice, accumulating quickly. Even as I struggle to reach the shelter of the tower, each blade of grass, each twig, each rock is encased in its frozen grip.

Inside the protected base of the tower, I quickly scramble into my warmest clothes and cap, then cover them with my rain pants, rain jacket, and hood. I don't have any gloves, so I use a pair of wool socks to protect my hands.

And then I think.

Panic kills, and so does this weather. In these conditions, it wouldn't take much time for either one to do the job. I can go north, or I can go south, or I can try to get off the mountain.

There's a dirt forest road that leads to the top of Wayah Bald and this observation tower. It's closed from November through March. The chances of meeting any vehicle or person who could be of help are practically zero. No one in their right mind would be out driving in this. Following it would mean miles and miles of walking in the storm.

Going north means walking *into* the storm, which is intensifying even as I sit here. According to the guidebook, the trail stays close to this elevation for most of the next seventeen miles until it drops down to the Nantahala River and the Outdoor Center. The only smart thing is to head south, either back to the shelter or back to Franklin. The idea of trying to cross the rocky ridgeline in this storm makes me shudder with the thought of how dangerous it would be in these conditions. So, it's back to the shelter. At least, it's somewhat protected from the brunt of the wind, and I know what to do to make it more comfortable and safer until conditions improve.

The final deciding factor, however, is Yellow and Wonderland. If I head south, I'll meet them. If I head in another direction before they get here, I can't be sure they'll make the right choice, and I can't leave them alone to survive in this storm.

Trying to navigate across the open clearing to reach the trail is almost impossible. Several times, a gust of wind pushes me to my knees, and the icy ground is so slick I can barely stand. The wind shrieks and moans, the ice a constant din as it hits the ground. At times, it seems more like hail than sleet.

Finally, I resort to crawling back to the path. As soon as the trail descends below the summit and I'm out of the worst of the wind, conditions improve. It's still bitterly cold, but the sleet gradually changes to snow, and it's easier to keep my balance as I hurry back down the trail.

Forty-five minutes later, I meet Yellow and Wonderland. They're huddled under a rhododendron tunnel, the thick mesh of leaves and branches giving them some protection from the worst of the storm. I'm relieved to see they've layered up in their warmest clothes. They're obviously arguing. Wonderland is waving her arms around, but I can't hear them over the howling of the wind.

"Thank God, you're here," she says as soon as she sees me. "I told Yellow you were smart enough to turn back, but she wouldn't leave without trying to find you. Now, can we please get back to Franklin?"

"We'll never reach Franklin. Remember those boulders we climbed over yesterday? They'll be lethal in this weather. One slip and—" I shrug, throwing up my arms. "No, the best thing, the safest thing, is to go back to the shelter."

I can tell it's not the answer they're hoping for.

"Ella, it's going to get really cold tonight, and who knows how much snow is going to fall. It could be several feet before it's over. I don't see how we can survive in the open shelter." Yellow's concerned face matches her words.

"I know it's not ideal, but trust me, please. I know what to do." With a worried nod, they follow me back down the trail toward the shelter.

Rather than hike over the top of Siler Bald, we take a shorter side trail that bypasses the summit and leads directly to the shelter. During our rushed hike south, I make sure we take a couple breaks to drink and eat and to regulate our body temperature. We're practically running, and it is important not to overheat and sweat too much in our layers.

We've almost reached the shelter when a loud, male voice stops us in our tracks. "Oh, hell. We just missed her. She was here last night. Hurry up, Ghost. Maybe if we leave right now, we can catch her."

His voice fills the clearing in front of the shelter, and we instinctively slow our progress, stopping right at the edge of the forest where he can't see us.

"Did you hear me, Ghost?" he shouts again. "Wonderland signed the shelter register last night. She was here with her friends. Get a move on, man. We need to hustle if we're going to catch them."

At the mention of her name, Wonderland glances at Yellow and me, a worried look on her face. Most of the time, signing the register is a good thing—it can help the authorities track a missing hiker. But it can also make it easier for a stalker to find you, and the man with the loud voice in the shelter sounds a little obsessive about finding Wonderland right now. The path to the privy is off to our right, and with a tilt of her head, Yellow begins to lead us quietly toward it. The privy door opens, and then slams shut as a tall man exits, yelling an answer to the guy in the shelter.

"I heard you, M. Calm the fuck down. I'll be there in a minute." He's busy zipping up his pants and almost runs into us before looking up. He comes to an abrupt halt when he sees the three of us silently watching him. I hear Wonderland gasp beside me. "Well, well, ladies," he drawls, a smirk on his face as he blatantly eyes us up and down before settling his gaze on Wonderland. "This is an unexpected but very welcome surprise."

He's tall and lean, with startling blue eyes. Short blond hair peeks out from under a weather-stained cowboy hat. His smirk has morphed into a predatory gleam as he swaggers toward Wonderland, who has remained frozen beside me. There's something familiar about him, and then it clicks. Ghost and M&M are the Marines who were at Springer the day I started, and they were staying in one of the cabins at Neels Gap. But why is he acting like this? His aggressive actions don't seem to match the little I know about him. My instincts are screaming at me to run, and I find myself lifting my hiking poles in front of me defensively.

Before I can say anything to Wonderland, however, she's running toward him screaming, "Travis!" She throws herself at him, wrapping her arms around his neck and her legs around his waist. He catches her, holding her with one arm while he tries to fend off Yellow, who is now slapping at his head and shoulder and calling him an asshole.

"Quit, Rosemary. That shit hurts," he yells in between laughing and kissing Allison. "I'm sorry, okay. Is that anyway to greet your dear brother?" And then they're all laughing, and crying, and hugging each other, and it makes me smile to see them so happy.

Finally, after they've calmed down a bit, Yellow turns to me. "Ariella, I'd like you to meet my infuriatingly obnoxious but very charming *older* brother, Travis."

Travis, who now has both arms wrapped around Wonderland's ass, holding her close to him, gives me a sweet, genuine smile before apologizing for his rude behavior. "I'm really a good ole Texas boy," he claims. "Just ask my girl here. She'll tell you." He gives her one last kiss before setting her back down on the ground. "Now, ladies," he asks in a suddenly serious voice. "Can you tell me why you're hiking in the wrong direction?"

A blast of frigid air roars overhead, and the snow, which has been falling steadily, increases dramatically. Pings of ice begin to bounce on the ground around us. Before I can say anything, Travis answers his own question. "Ah, the storm, right. I bet it's much worse farther up the mountain."

"It is. I made it to the top of Wayah and could barely stand. We need to start making plans and taking precautions right now before it gets any worse."

"So back to Franklin?" he asks.

"No, too dangerous. Remember the ridgeline between here and Franklin? As soon as this ice starts coating those rocks, they'll be impassable. Our best bet is to ride it out in the shelter. Its location protects it a bit from the wind, and I know some things we can do to make it more comfortable."

I watch Travis closely while I speak, looking for any indication he doesn't want to take advice from a woman he's just met. Although he's apologized for his behavior, he still makes me a bit nervous. He seems to accept what I have to say, nodding while I explain things we need to be doing.

As we walk toward the shelter, I tell him I was on Springer the day he started with M&M. "Is that who's in the shelter and was yelling at you a few minutes ago?"

Suddenly, Rosemary stops walking. When we turn around to see why, she's glaring at Travis. "Tell me Markham isn't with you," she demands of her brother.

"Now, Rosemary—"

"No, Travis, no. I'm not ready for this."

"Dammit, you've been writing to the guy for two years. You know him, probably better than he knows himself, and he knows you. Hell, the guy's half in love with you already, even though you refused to send him a photo. You can't put off meeting him any longer."

Travis steps closer to his sister, reaching out to take her hands in his. "He saved my life, sis; you know this. He's my best friend, and he'll be my best man at the wedding. He's going to be around a long time. I want my best buddy and my best sister to be best friends, too."

Rosemary gives her brother a wry smile. "I haven't had a bath in two days."

"It's been longer for him." Travis laughs.

"It's been hours since I brushed my teeth or combed my hair."

"Then don't kiss him."

"Bubba." Rosemary's voice drops to the barest of whispers. "I have scars."

"Oh, sis," he says, hugging her to him and kissing the top of her head. "We all have scars, inside and out, and Markham has his fair share, too. He won't care."

Another gust of wind rocks the branches above us, sending snow cascading down. Rosemary and I begin heading toward the shelter while Travis and Allison follow behind.

"You know, Al," we hear Travis drawl. "My old war wounds have been bothering me somethin' fierce. I think I might need me some lovin' nursing care."

"I'm an emergency room nurse," she answers. "I only treat emergencies."

"Oh, darlin', you can be sure this *is* an emergency."

I bite my lip to keep from laughing, and when I glance at Rosemary, she has the same smirk on her face. Both of us begin giggling. "We may have to put them outside in their own tent tonight," she says.

"Too cold," I reply.

"Not sure they'll notice," she whispers, glancing at the two behind us.

Wonderland and Ghost are locked in a tight embrace, kissing each other as if their very lives depend on it. We watch them for a moment before smiling at each other.

"I love my brother," Yellow says as we make our way toward the shelter.

CHAPTER 25
The Storm

Date: Monday, March 24
Starting Location: Siler Bald Shelter
Destination: Siler Bald Shelter
Total Trip Miles: 110.6

As soon as we leave the cover of the woods, we're exposed to the full force of the wind. It's not quite as bad as the top of Wayah, but it's getting there. Snow and ice pelt us, and the wind shoves us as we run across the open meadow toward the shelter. Yellow and I are hanging on to each other, slipping and sliding, shrieking and laughing, as we struggle across the icy ground. I can hear Travis and Allison doing the same behind us.

The big Marine I remember from Springer is busy stuffing his food bag back into his pack when we burst into the shelter. "Damn, Ghost, took you long enough," he complains without looking up. "Thought maybe you fell in. Come on, we need to hurry. This storm sounds like it's getting worse." He turns toward us, swinging his pack on, and freezes so suddenly, and with such a confused look on his face, we all start laughing again.

"Three?" His gaze darts questioningly between the four of us. "You go to the privy and come back with three—" Before he can finish his question he leans closer, peering at Allison, who is taking off her hood and cap. "Al, is that you?"

With a nod and a laugh, Allison steps forward to hug M&M, laughing at the pleased surprise on his face. "Yes, you finally found me."

"Thank God," he replies. "Travis has been driving us all crazy, trying to catch up with you and your friends." He grins at Ghost, who's still standing off to one side next to his sister.

Yellow slowly reaches up to take off her hood and cap, carefully watching M&M, who's staring at her, a puzzled frown on his face. It's easy to see the resemblance between brother and sister as they stand next to each other. There's a hushed silence in the shelter as they gaze at each other. Emotions flash across M&M's face: confusion, surprise, hope, and finally, excitement and anticipation.

Travis is the first to break the quiet. "M, I'd like you to meet my—"

"Rosemary?" he interrupts. "Oh, Rosie, is it really you?"

She nods slowly, a small, almost timid smile lifting the corners of her mouth. "M," she whispers.

Two long steps and he's in front of her. He reaches out with both hands, almost trembling with his need to touch her, but he stops himself, content for the moment to study her face. "You know," he finally says, "I knew you'd probably look a lot like Travis, but I had no idea you'd be so beautiful. Oh, God, Rosie, can I please hug you?"

It's Yellow who's trembling now, her eyes glossy with unshed tears as she opens her arms to the big Marine. "Yes, Markham. Oh, yes."

He sweeps her up in his arms, lifting her clear off the ground, crushing her to him as he buries his face in her neck. "Finally, finally." I hear him mutter as he slowly rocks them back and forth.

Allison grabs Travis's hand, leading him to the far side of the shelter where I'm standing. "Let's give them a little privacy," she suggests, smiling as she looks over her shoulder at the two who are still locked in a fierce hug.

They break apart, M&M leading Yellow over to the edge of the sleeping platform, pulling her down to sit beside him. He's holding her hand, smiling when she moves closer to him and leans against his shoulder. We can hear soft words, a giggle or two, and then a quiet sob.

Travis's smile matches Allison's as he watches his sister and his best friend, but when he turns to face me, he sobers quickly. "We need to get started, don't we?" he asks. When I nod, he continues. "Okay, tell us what to do."

While Rosemary and Markham continue to talk, we gather all the backpacks and dump their contents onto the picnic table.

"We need to close off this opening," I explain. "So, we're going to take our tents and hang them like a flat curtain from the ceiling to the platform. There should be some nails up there, and we can use tent stakes to secure them, too. If we have enough tents, we can overlap them and cover any holes or openings that the wind might get through. Use rope or string or even dental floss to tie them together."

Travis examines the ceiling as I talk, nodding while I describe where to hang the tents. "We'll use any leftover tents, tarps, ground covers, or those reflective safety blankets to cover the floor and give us another layer of protection from the cold. We need to check under the platform, too. Sometimes there are large pieces of plastic stored under there."

M&M and Yellow have joined us as we talk. While he and Travis start on the curtain, I gather all the water bottles, bladders, and water filters.

"What should we be doing?" Allison says.

"It's going to be important to have enough water to get through the night and possibly the next day. As the storm worsens and visibility drops, no one will be leaving the shelter. Drinking something hot will warm our body core and prevent dehydration. And these hydration bladders," I add, picking up one of the soft, flexible plastic bags, "can be used as hot water bottles if we take off the drinking tubes, fill them with boiling water, and use the screw-on lids to close them. Tuck one of these in the foot of your sleeping bag, and you can stay warm all night."

"We'll take them," Wonderland offers, grabbing two empty backpacks to carry everything. "I imagine you have other things to do, and Yellow and I can handle the water."

"Be careful," I warn as they pack up. "Stay together, and whatever you do, don't get off the path. It only takes a few minutes to become disoriented and lost in this kind of weather."

Nodding, they put their caps back on, tightening their hoods, and pulling socks over their hands. "Hey," I add, as they're about to leave. "Do you have your whistles?"

Rosemary pulls hers out of her shirt where it hangs on a cord around her neck. "Yep," she answers. "Three short blasts for an emergency, right?"

"Right." They step out of the shelter into the blowing snow, bending over to protect their faces. I watch for a few moments until they disappear into the swirling whiteness.

There's a large piece of heavy plastic, rolled, tied, and stored under the sleeping platform. I get busy, layering it with a couple of tarps the guys aren't using to cover the floor. Hopefully, this will prevent errant gusts of wind blowing through any cracks in the wooden slats. It's while I'm laying out all our sleeping pads, trying to arrange them as close to each other as possible, that Markham tells me they have another person hiking with them.

"What?"

"We've been hiking with this other guy named Easy. He's always a little slower, but he should be along anytime now, so you need to leave room for his pad."

Shaking my head, I slowly stand, glaring at him as I listen to his words. "Are you telling me you have a third hiker with you, and you left him alone out there in *that*?" I shout.

Before he can answer, the girls burst into the shelter, covered in snow and gasping for breath.

"Man, is it nasty out there," Rosemary exclaims before shrugging out of her backpack.

Allison is watching us, her eyes darting between Travis, Markham, and me. "What's going on?" she asks, sensing the tension in the air.

"They left a hiker out there," I blurt out.

A surprised Allison turns to her fiancé. "Travis?"

"It's not as bad as it sounds," he begins to explain. "He was waiting for supplies. Easy's slower and takes more time, but he eventually makes it. The trail wasn't too bad coming up out of the gap, and the storm didn't really hit until we got here. He should be fine."

"Ariella?"

"I don't like it, Allison. That ridge is tough under the best circumstances, but hiking into this north wind with the freezing precipitation. I just … I don't feel good about this. Do you think he's smart enough and aware enough to turn back and try to get to Franklin if the trail gets too dangerous?" I ask.

"Probably not," Markham answers me. "The guy's a real city boy, not a lot of common sense when it comes to the woods. He's been pushing pretty hard, trying to catch up with a friend who's hiking ahead of us."

"What do you think, Travis? Would he turn around?"

Travis shakes his head. "I don't know." He frowns, worry creeping across his face as he stares at the open meadow in front of the shelter. Several inches of snow have accumulated since we arrived and more is falling, along with the temperature. "M," he finally says. "We gotta go back. We can't leave him out there by himself."

I expect M&M to argue, but he doesn't. Instead, he nods, pulls on his cap and jacket, and picks up his hiking poles. Travis bundles up, too. Before they leave, I grab a length of small rope and tie the ends to each of their left hands.

"This will keep you together," I explain before making sure they both have emergency whistles. "Three short blasts every five minutes. If anyone is in the vicinity, they should answer with the same. It's the best way to locate someone when the conditions are bad or the wind is too loud. Calling and yelling won't work; your voice isn't strong enough. Check your watch, hike for thirty minutes. If the conditions aren't too bad, hike another thirty, but don't go past those boulders. At the end of an hour, you start back. It'll be dark in three hours. You *have* to be back by then."

Allison grabs Travis, kissing him fiercely before telling him to be careful. Markham hesitates for a moment before bending forward to buss Rosemary's cheek, but she turns her head, meeting his lips with her own. Her hand grips the back of his neck holding him to her. "What Allison said," she tells him when they finally break apart. His grin is pure happiness before he turns to follow Travis into the blowing snow. We watch them cross the meadow and disappear into the woods.

As soon as they're gone, I turn back to Allison and Rosemary and begin explaining what else we need to do. Keeping them busy will take their minds off what the guys are doing and make the time go by faster.

Before long, we have two stoves going and water boiling in the cooking pots. Hot food for the evening has been decided upon, and a big pot of cocoa mixed. Sleeping pads and bags are arranged on top of the layers of plastic and fabric. The two couples are next to each other, and I'm at one end. Each person's clothes bag is tucked into the hood of their sleeping bag for use as a pillow and to have extra clothing close by if needed during the night.

We've stored unused gear and backpacks along the north wall at the back of the platform. They'll help, in a small way, to block any wind coming through the cracks. Both Rosemary and Travis are carrying collapsible candle lanterns, and we've hung those from the ceiling, ready to be lit when it gets dark.

I'm pleased as I survey our preparations. Travis and Markham did a great job connecting the mismatched tents into a tight, wind-blocking curtain. Our little sleeping area is cozy and neat. Everything we need to survive the night in relative comfort has been done. I've even dug a privy hole outside one corner of the shelter. We're as ready as I can make us. I think Granny and Liam would be happy with our efforts.

The girls and I are sitting at the shelter table, busy with boiling water and making dinner when I first hear it. Allison starts to say something, but I raise my hand to stop her. We sit in absolute silence, holding our breaths in an effort not to make a sound. At first, all we hear is the wind moaning, the trees creaking, and an occasional flap of the tent curtain. Then ... there it is again, three short blasts from a whistle, muffled by the storm but still distinctive enough to recognize.

Allison jumps up, screaming, "Travis," as she begins to run toward the meadow, but I grab her arm, pulling her back.

"No, Allison, don't go out there. They can't hear you, and you won't be able to find them. Rosemary, do you have—"

Rosemary is already putting her whistle to her lips as I ask. She steps to the edge of the overhang, and I barely have time to cover my ears as she blows out three of the loudest notes I've ever heard. We wait in silence. A minute passes ... and another. And then, we hear it again. Three more blasts, closer this time, and off to the right a bit.

"Okay, now we go," I shout, handing them their hiking poles. "Again, Rosemary."

As soon as we step out from under the overhang, she blows her whistle again. This time, the answer comes almost immediately, louder and still to our right.

"They're using the side trail that bypasses the summit. Come on," I urge, turning toward the back of the shelter and breaking into a run. "Keep blowing."

As soon as we enter the woods behind the shelter, the visibility improves and the wind drops. We pass the privy, then veer to the left when we reach the junction with the bypass trail. The signaling continues until it sounds as if they are right in front of us. We round a bend … and there they are.

Four figures, bundled in layers of clothing with only their eyes showing, stumble toward us. They're carrying something large and cylinder-shaped between them, one at each end and one on each side. The narrow trail makes it difficult to walk easily as they support their burden. The person in front lifts the whistle to his lips again, but stops when he sees us in front of them.

"Are we almost there?" he shouts, and I realize it's Travis.

"Travis?" Allison calls to her fiancé. "What is it? Can we help?"

"It's Easy," he yells back. "We found him, but he's hurt." He glances behind to the package they're carrying, and I realize it's a person, wrapped in sleeping bags and being carried on a stretcher made from another bag. "Go back to the shelter and get your first-aid supplies ready. He's pretty bad."

Allison takes charge as soon as we reach the shelter. "Give me some pads to put him on," she shouts. "I'll need lots of light. Gather up all the flashlights and bring those lanterns over here." One by one, she lists all the things she's going to need as Rosemary and I scramble to help her prepare. "Hot water," she adds. "Lots of it, and see if you can find all the other first-aid kits. I'm not sure what I'm going to need."

Her makeshift emergency room is all set up by the time the guys stumble in with Easy. They lift him, still shrouded in the sleeping bag, onto the pads Allison has readied for him. Rosemary and I step to one end of the platform, out of the way, along with Travis and the two other people who were helping him. When they pull their hoods and caps off, I realize it's No Filter and Curly Dan.

With a happy shriek, I'm hugging both of them, demanding to know why they would leave Franklin in this storm. "Trying to keep up with that nice ass of yours," No Filter replies with a grin.

"Don't let him fool you," Curly Dan whispers to me. "He's been worried sick since we found out you left Franklin yesterday. We've had some experience with this kind of weather, though, and we came prepared." He points to his feet where I can see straps crisscrossing the tops of his boots.

"Crampons?"

"Yes. We couldn't have made it across those boulders without them. Too bad that bloke wasn't wearing some."

Allison's voice pulls our attention back to the patient on the floor. "What have we got here, Markham?" she says to the man kneeling beside her as they start to remove the sleeping bag from the injured hiker.

"Head wound, probable concussion," he starts. "That's where most of the bleeding is coming from. Looks like he fell on his left side, scrapes and bruising to that side of his face. Possible broken ribs, maybe a dislocated shoulder, but the worst is his leg, Allison. It's broken—you can see the bone."

Allison grimaces. "Any evidence of arterial bleeding?"

"No."

"Has he been conscious at all?"

"Some. He tried to talk a little when we first moved him and some groans from time to time, but nothing for the last thirty minutes."

By now, they have the sleeping bag open. His pants have been cut away, and we can see the broken leg Markham was describing. I have to turn my head away from the sight of the bone protruding from the torn and bleeding skin.

"I tried to stabilize it with hiking poles and straps but didn't want to do more than that until we got him to you," he explains.

"Good job," Allison nods. "I'm going to need more light. Get those lanterns over here. Travis and Dan grab flashlights and shine them on his face so I can start cleaning it. Here," she adds, handing M&M her stethoscope. "Monitor his breathing and heart rate. Let me know if there are any significant changes. Okay, let's get to work on the head wound."

Using a pot of boiled water and soft cloths, Allison begins to clean the blood covering Easy's face. It's only when she asks for a clean pot that I step forward and get a good look at him. There's a large gash on his forehead still bleeding slowly. The left side of his face is scraped raw, the eye swollen shut, and the lips broken and bleeding. But it doesn't matter because I'd recognize him in whatever condition he's in.

"No, no, no, oh please, no," I beg, my voice beginning to rise as I stare at his face. "No, please, God, no, not him."

No Filter grabs my arms, turning me toward him, shaking me a bit to get my attention. "Do you know him? Who is it?"

"It's Hudson," I cry. "Hudson."

"Who?"

"Hud. It's Hud."

"Oh, shit," he mutters.

"You know him?" Allison asks. "Then get down here," she commands when I nod. "Hold his hand, talk to him, see if you can get him to respond."

I drop to my knees, picking up his right hand. It's cold, and I cradle it in both my hands as I lean over and begin speaking. "Hudson? Hudson, it's Ariella. Can you hear me, sweetheart? Open your eyes. Please, Hudson, please."

He doesn't respond at first, but when I continue talking, he groans, moaning as he tries to answer. Finally, he opens one eye, the other too swollen to move, and he blinks frantically before focusing on me. "Ah ..." he manages to whisper before swallowing roughly. "Ariella ... found you."

"Shh, shh, don't talk. Save your strength. You're going to be okay, Hudson. We're going to take care of you."

"Need ... need to tell you," he gasps again. "Lies, all lies." He coughs, moaning in pain, and a trickle of blood seeps from the corner of his mouth.

"Hudson?"

His eye flutters, then rolls back in his head as he passes out again.

"Hudson!"

And then I'm crying.

Begging, screaming, pleading for Allison to help him, for someone to do something, for him to come back to me. I'm vaguely aware of No Filter's arms around me, lifting me up and pulling me away as Allison and Markham work frantically.

"Hudson, Hudson." My sobbing screams fill the small shelter and the meadow beyond where the wind grabs them, flinging them away into the cold, uncaring winter storm.

CHAPTER 26

Time Traveler

Hudson

Date: Sunday, March 16

Starting Location: Springer Mountain, Georgia

Destination: Hawk Mountain Shelter

Total Trip Miles: 7.6

Ariella once told me mountaintops were magical places. She claimed you could see both the future and the past from their summits, just like a time traveler. All you had to do was decide which direction you wanted to go.

We were in Georgia for her cousin Liam's wedding and stayed to visit some of the places she remembered from her childhood. One day, we drove to Amicalola Falls State Park, and after eating lunch in the lodge, we climbed the path that led to several viewing spots of the impressive waterfalls. While sitting on one of the benches along the path, she'd pointed toward the top of the mountain and explained if we continued on we would eventually reach the summit and the terminus of the famous Appalachian Trail. Then, she called it a magical place.

She grinned at my questioning frown and explained that even though it was a beautiful spring day where we sat, it was still winter at the summit. A few months from now, in late summer, we would be able to come to this same place and see autumn and then winter at the top, even though it would still be months before cold weather finally invaded the valleys around us. "See." She laughed. "The past and the future … just like magical time travel."

I teased her, the hard-nosed, science-loving, math genius believing in something as fantastical as magic. She laughed right back at me before finally confessing it was Granny Cora who explained the magic of mountaintops. She said she always wanted to see Springer's summit, to stand in winter but look down at spring. We debated driving to the top, taking the backwoods' forest road, which would get us within a mile of the famous long-distance hiking trail, but finally decided it was getting too late, and we would save it for another day.

Instead, we drove back to the cabin where I spent another restless night in her grandmother's bedroom, tossing, turning, and thinking about the woman who was sleeping down the hallway in her childhood bed. The woman I was desperately trying to keep my distance from even as I fell more deeply in love with her every day.

I never thought I would fall for someone like Ariella. When Dr. Albright persuaded me to attend her eighteenth birthday party, I went for one selfish reason only: I needed an idea for a startup business. To complete my MBA at Harvard, I had to submit a business plan for starting and managing an actual company. The requirements were very specific. Everything required—from product to investors, from manufacturing to distributions, from legal to practical—had to be written, described, and included. I knew I could do all of it, I just needed an idea, a real idea, not some bullshit made-up scenario like some of my classmates had chosen.

So, I went to the party, and I met not the geeky, socially awkward, badly dressed, math genius I expected, but a shy, very lovely young woman who had no idea how special she truly was. She seemed so real, so innocent and open, so trusting and unspoiled. There was no hardness about her, no veneer of false sophistication or manipulation so many of the young women in my social and educational circles seemed to have acquired over the years.

I was interested and intrigued, and then I fell in love. She became my bella mente—beautiful mind, beautiful heart, beautiful person, and a beautiful name that only I called her. But she was also my business partner, and that was a line I could not, and would not, cross.

When we became partners, Albright sought me out, warning me about taking advantage of her. He told me a little of her difficult past and upbringing, hinted vaguely at her medical diagnosis, and reminded me how my wealth and social connections made me more powerful than her. He needn't have worried. I'd never consider hurting her in any way, but I also understood how it could appear to the outside world.

I was a wealthy man from a wealthy family, and that meant power in our country and society, but I also knew all that wealth had been handed to me—I'd done nothing to earn it. I grew up with trust funds, real estate investments, and stock portfolios. With my connections, it would have been simple to gain control of her theories and discoveries. Starting a romantic relationship would have made it even easier. So, I stayed away, trying to be a good friend even when I wanted so much more.

We never made it back to Springer. Other activities filled our time until we returned to New York. Instead of making the trip with her, I traveled the forest road with Liam, who dropped me off at the dirt parking lot with a gruff "good luck" before handing me a loaded backpack and pointing to the path I needed to follow to reach the summit. At least, he used words this time and not his fist.

Thinking about his violent greeting when I entered the store at Neels Gap has me rubbing my sore jaw and shaking my head at the memories. It took me nearly a week to finally get away from New York and follow her to Georgia. Every time I tried to go, something would demand my attention and prevent me from leaving. Meetings with Vincent, with Susan, with the police, with the FBI, and finally, with the US Military had me so anxious and on edge I could barely remain civil.

Keyed up and agitated, I stormed into Mountain Crossings, demanding to know where she was, only to be met by a furious Liam Crow and a mean right hook I managed to avoid only at the last minute. He still caught me with a glancing blow, which sat me on my ass. I'm sure the next punch would probably have broken my jaw if Emma hadn't stopped him. The disgusted look she gave me hurt almost as much as Liam's fist.

"Take it to the back," she demanded, pushing the two of us ahead of her and out onto the patio. Pointing to two chairs, she told us to sit. "And you," she said, glaring at me, "you better start explaining yourself, and it better be good, or so help me, I'll beat your ass myself."

"Have you seen her? Has she been here? Is she okay?"

Liam couldn't hold back. "What do you care, you lying, cheating, backstabbing, son of a—"

"Liam," Emma warned. "That's not helping matters. Let him talk."

He sat back, arms crossed on his chest, staring at me with a scowl, daring me to say something wrong.

"I do care. Look," I said, leaning toward him, "I'm not sure what she told you, or what she believes, but I can explain everything."

"Then explain it to me," he spat out through gritted teeth. "Explain how you forgot to have her sign those papers protecting her interests in the company. Explain how you accepted a position with Banca Italia and basically stole the company from her. And then"—he stood, taking a threatening step toward me—"you can explain to me why you slept with my little cousin while you've been living with your bitch of a fiancée in your condo for the last two years. Explain *that*, Hudson."

Liam glowered down at me, hands fisted, jaw clenched. For a moment, I think I knew what true fear was. Then, he sat back down, still scowling, still waiting for me to say something to make him angrier.

His accusations made me realize how terrible this whole situation must appear to Ariella. I wasn't exactly sure what Gia had said to her. I knew it was bad, but I hadn't known the extent of her deceit.

"Oh, God," I groaned, rubbing the worry lines I was sure were permanently etched into my forehead. "They're lies, Liam. Everything is a lie. I didn't take a job with Italia, Gia is not my fiancée, I don't own the condo and haven't for over two years. And I swear to you, I swear, I would never cheat or steal the company from her."

My words didn't appear to satisfy Liam or Emma. Both were still glaring at me, waiting for me to say something else to convince them.

"I love her. I wouldn't be here if I didn't. She's more important to me than any condo, any business deal, or any other person in my life. Please," I begged, glancing between them, "please tell me you've seen her. Tell me she's okay, that I still have time to make this right."

"She's been here," Emma finally answered me. "She left earlier this afternoon."

"Do you know where she's going? Can you tell me how to find her?" I said, jumping out of my chair, ready to go wherever she was.

"Sit down, Hudson," Liam commanded. "You're not going anywhere yet."

"Dammit, Liam. What do I have to do to make you believe me? Tell me," I begged. "I'll do anything."

For a long time, Liam stared at me. His stone face gave away nothing, no hint of what he was thinking. "Anything?" he finally said.

"Anything," I replied. "Just tell me how to find her. I have to fix this."

"Okay," he said and stood up. "Have you had anything to eat this evening?"

"What?"

"I said ... have you had anything to eat this evening?"

"No, but—"

"Emma made venison stew today. I'm sure there's some left you can have. You're welcome to sleep in the guest room, and we'll continue this tomorrow. I have to go back to work."

He turned his back on me and walked toward the back entrance to his store. I started to follow him, but Emma stopped me.

"Don't," she warned. "He's been torn up about all this. You're his friend, and he wants to believe you, but Ari is family, and family is important to us."

"Emma, tell me, please. How is she? Where is she?"

"To tell you the truth, Hudson, she looked horrible. She's sad, confused, depressed. She stayed with us a couple days, and I think it helped, but I've never seen her so quiet, so withdrawn."

Her words hurt. I frowned, wondering how I could have let this happen. I'd been such a clueless fool. Despite my money, education, and family connections, despite all the privileges I'd grown up with, all the business acumen I thought I had, I'd been played, royally played, by a conniving bitch I thought was out of my life for good.

"She's hiking the Appalachian Trail," Emma continued. "Being in the woods is good for her. I'm sure Liam will figure out the road crossing closest to her location and take you there tomorrow. But for now, let's get you fed and into bed. Knowing Liam, he'll have you up at the crack of dawn." I followed her into the kitchen, and then spent another restless night worrying about Ariella.

Liam did wake me at sunrise, but he didn't take me to a road crossing to find her. Instead, he brought me to Springer. He stopped in the parking lot before telling me to get out. I wasn't stupid. I knew what he was doing. When I told him I would do anything to find her, he'd taken me at my word. This was a test—a test of my determination, of my willingness to do whatever I needed to do to find her. A trial of sorts to win Liam's trust and friendship again.

He pulled an old, beat-up, heavily laden pack out of the truck. I swung it up onto my back, staggering a little from its unexpected weight. I caught a glimpse of his pleased smirk before he handed me a small paperback book.

"This is a trail guide. It should tell you everything you need to know about the trail, where to camp, where to find water, where the shelters are. Today's Sunday. You have three days to make it to Neels Gap. I'll pick up Ari on Tuesday morning and have her there when you arrive. If you get there," he added with another infuriating smirk. "Good luck."

Then he climbed into his truck and drove off, leaving me standing in the middle of the parking area covered in his dust. I followed the sign to the summit, thinking of Ariella, and wondering how to get through the next three days until I could see her again.

~ * * * ~

This place is busy. Groups of people wander around the area, posing for photos, admiring the scenery. Some are backpackers laden with gear, excited to be starting their hikes. Others are family members saying goodbye to those hikers, and others are sightseers, enjoying a beautiful day on top of the famous mountain. I notice more than a few passing around a battered notebook, thumbing through it before sitting down to write something with the attached pen.

There's a lookout point at the edge of the mountain, and I walk over to stand on the flat rock and gaze at the scenery below. It's just like Ariella said—"winter here, but spring below." I'm standing alone without her on this magical mountaintop, looking out over the rivers, the valleys, and the forest. I'm looking at the future when all I want to do is change the past.

If I were a real time traveler, I'd go back. I'd tell her everything, share everything, and make her a true partner, both in our personal and professional lives. I'd acknowledge what a strong, fully capable person she is, a woman who doesn't need my misplaced, misguided protection. When I find her again, there will only ever be trust and truth, the whole truth, between us.

Shaking my head at my melancholic thoughts, I find a rock to sit on and drink from the water bottle stored in one of the pack's side pockets. Lost in my reflections, I don't notice the person standing in front of me until he speaks.

"Hey, you okay?" he asks.

I look up to find a young man staring at me. He's lean, fit, dressed in standard hiking garb of convertible pants and moisture-wicking shirt. There's a small, well-worn pack on his back and trail runners on his feet. Something about him reminds me of Liam, perhaps his skin tone, high cheekbones, or his long dark hair. I wonder if he shares the same Cherokee heritage with Liam and Ariella.

"Oh, uh, yes, thanks," I manage to mumble.

Instead of walking away, he continues to examine me, his gaze wandering over my pack and clothing. Suddenly, he sticks out his hand. "Randall Green. I'm the ridgerunner for this section of the AT."

"Ridgerunner?"

"Yeah. During hiking season, I work this section of the trail, mostly to keep it clean and do some maintenance. I pick up the trash people leave behind and shovel shit out of the privies when they get too full." He laughs at my grimace. "But my main job is to help hikers who run into problems or look like they could use some, uh, guidance. And, to tell the truth, you don't look like a very experienced hiker. So, tell me—"

"Hudson. Hudson Calder," I answer, standing and extending my hand.

Randall's grip is firm when he shakes my hand. "Tell me, Hudson, have you done any long-distance or overnight hiking before?"

"No, not really. What gave me away?"

He shakes his head, grinning as he chuckles at my question. "Well, just about everything, especially those clothes you're wearing. Your jeans look nice, expensive, too, but denim is a bad choice for the outdoors. It takes forever to dry if it gets wet, and those shoes aren't exactly made for hiking over rough ground.

"And then there's this pack. It's a beautiful, old classic backpack, but nobody ... What the hell?" he exclaims when he bends over to pick it up, grunting at the weight of it. "What have you got in here? Rocks?"

"I don't really know," I confess sheepishly. "I didn't know we were coming here. I was dropped off, handed the pack, and told to be in Neels Gap by Tuesday. I have no idea what's in it."

"This some kind of prank or something?" He glares at me, his voice loud enough for people around us to hear. "Because let me tell you, Hudson, people die out here, and I'm not about to be responsible for your dead ass because some stupid, city boy decided to play Daniel Boone for the weekend."

"No, no, it's not like that at all, really. I just ... I have to be in Neels Gap on Tuesday. It's important. Help me, please. Tell me what I need to do to get there. Preferably alive," I add, grinning.

Randall's glare softens a bit at my plea, but he's still fuming at what he thinks is some ridiculous, dangerous stunt. Finally, he nods. "Okay, but first you have to tell me who left you here."

"A friend of mine," I reply. "He owns Mountain Crossings at Neels Gap."

"Liam Crow?" he questions, clearly not believing me. "Liam left you here in those clothes, with *that* backpack?"

When I nod, he begins to laugh, a full-on belly laugh, which leaves him gasping for breath and sitting down on a nearby rock. "Oh," he finally gasps. "You must have really pissed him off."

"Yeah, I guess I did."

"Okay, so here's what we're going to do. I have to go to Hawk Mountain Shelter. I'll meet you there, and we'll spend some time going through your pack. I can show you how to use your stove, tent, and water filter when you get there.

"It's almost eight miles, which will leave you twenty-two miles to cover in the next two days. You should be able to make it there by nightfall. Take it slow and easy and be sure to take some breaks to eat, drink, and rest. Sign the trail register before you leave. Use your real name and the date so we can prove you were here, in case your family wants to sue Crow someday.

"Good luck, Hudson," he says, shaking my hand again. "I think you're going to need it." He walks off, still laughing to himself and muttering something about Liam and how he can't wait to talk to that asshole.

No one's using the register now, so I pull it out of its protected metal box and begin thumbing through it to find an empty spot to write my name. I'm not sure how long it's been since Ariella was here, five to seven days I imagine. I skim the dates quickly, trying to find her name, and there it is. Five days ago she was here, had added her name and the date with a few words below them, all in her very neat, very precise handwriting. With my finger, I trace her words.

Ariella Dobbs

Thursday, March 11, 2003

Terminus: an ending or a beginning?

My choice.

My eyes linger on her words. They're so like her—few in number but full of meaning and significance, with just a hint of strength, determination, and intelligence hidden beneath the surface. "Oh, my bella mente," I whisper to myself. "I'm so sorry, my love." I add my own entry beside hers.

Hudson Calder

March 16, 2003

Terminus: A second chance to get it right this time?

Please don't give up on me yet, sweetheart.

Your choice, always your choice.

She won't ever see this, I know, but it helps a bit to answer her, to tell the world I'm not ready for an ending. Closing the notebook, I reach to put it back into its container when a sudden gust of wind catches the pages, flipping them open. For a brief moment, I glimpse what looks like more of Ariella's handwriting. Quickly, I search through the back of the book until I find it. She's written me a letter, a whole page of her thoughts and feelings.

Dear Hud, it begins. The words are full of sorrow and pain, her devastation so clearly evident. I frown at the mention of the sales presentation. I knew she'd been nervous, but I thought she'd done a good job trying to explain a program based on theories and math calculations even the most intelligent person in the room would have been hard-pressed to understand. I remember glaring at Gia when she so obviously tried to hide her fake, bored yawn behind her hand.

But it's her mention of the lies and the love that broke her heart that has me feeling like someone just punched me in the gut. I didn't outright lie to her, but I did keep things from her. I lied by omission, and those lies hurt as badly as intentional ones.

I finish reading her letter. Although it doesn't have a happy ending, it does have a somewhat optimistic one. She says she's okay, and she will cherish what we once were. It gives me hope we can start again, hope she will give me a second chance.

It's time to start this journey. The sooner I make it to Neels Gap, the sooner I'll see her again.

The weight of the backpack pulls at my shoulders and back, but it's no match to the weight of guilt I carry. I ignore the pain, knowing her pain was so much worse than mine. With purpose and determination, I take my first steps northward on the Appalachian Trail.

I'm going to fix this, I tell myself. I'm going to make things right. We're going to be okay.

CHAPTER 27

His Pain

Date: Sunday, March 16

Starting Location: Springer Mountain, Georgia

Destination: Hawk Mountain Shelter

Total Trip Miles: 7.6

It takes over four hours to hike from Springer to Long Creek Falls, a distance of less than five miles. It is, without a doubt, the hardest thing I've ever done, at least physically. I stop repeatedly to catch my breath, shift the pack around, and simply sit. Walking uphill is almost impossible, and the downhills are even worse. The weight of the pack either pushes me forward or pulls me backward. How anyone can think this is fun, enjoyable, or worthwhile is beyond me.

I hurt. Everywhere. My feet are so tender and swollen I can barely take another step. I swear my back must be broken, but it's my shoulders that are the worst. The weight of the pack seems to be resting solely on them, and I wouldn't be surprised to learn Ariella, or Emma, or maybe even Susan, has a voodoo doll of me somewhere and is busy torturing it with long, red-hot needles to the shoulders.

Shaking my head at the ridiculous thought and image, I huff to myself. "Dear Lord, Hudson, the pain is affecting your mind now."

Long Creek Falls is a beautiful, secluded spot. The water tumbles over a series of ledges into a nice pool, deep enough for swimming, and is surrounded by rocks, perfect for sitting. The torture device on my shoulders falls with a thump onto one of those rocks when I shrug it off. Briefly, I worry I might have broken something but don't seem to have enough energy to care.

Shoes and socks come off next, and I groan at the sight of large blisters forming on my red, swollen feet. Into the icy water they go until they're so numb I can barely feel them. At least, it helps with the pain.

For some time now, I've been trying to ignore an increasingly uncomfortable rubbing in my groin. With no one around, this might be a good time to check out what is going on down there. As soon as I drop my pants, it becomes very obvious why hikers don't wear denim in the woods. Body sweat has soaked into the hard, bulky seams of the jeans and my silk boxers are bunched around my crotch. Everything down there is raw and inflamed. "Oh, fuck it," I mutter to myself, pulling off my shirt and wading into the icy pool. Maybe the cold water will numb my whole body.

To call it cold would be an understatement—it's icy, freezing, and blissfully numbing. When I can catch my breath again, I duck my head under, scrubbing my hair for a minute before rising with a gasp and a sob. I'm shaking. I want to blame it on the icy water, but I realize I'm close to crying. Maybe it's the sleepless nights, maybe it's the worry, maybe it's the physical exhaustion, or maybe it's the lack of food and water. Hell, maybe I'm a weak, wimpy, city boy who's in way over his head out here in the woods. I don't know, but I do know for the first time in a long, long time, I'm on the brink of tears.

The thought of twenty-five more miles like the last five is terrifying. "Get a grip," I scold myself. "There are hundreds of hikers, some twice your age, out here hiking the whole thing. And you want to quit after four hours? Man up. Use your head. Get some help. There must be something you're missing." Shaking my head because I'm talking to myself again, I start toward the shore.

There's a small bird hopping around on my discarded backpack. It cocks its head, watching me with a small black eye while I approach. Instead of flying away when I get closer, it hops over to the bottom compartment of my pack, pecking at the old canvas material. Maybe the pack smells like food to it, but the thunk, thunk of its beak hitting the canvas indicates there's something else in there. An idea forms as I stare at the source of my torment, and I hear Randall's question in my head.

"Oh, you didn't, you wouldn't, you couldn't have done something so devious, could you, Crow?" But even as I speak the words, I know he has.

I reach for the pack, unzipping the bottom compartment. Rocks— big ones, little ones, even gravel—fall out. Staring at the pile, I don't know whether to laugh, cry, or curse. Instead, I sit and begin going through each of the compartments on the pack.

I find a small tent, a new top-of-the-line, down sleeping bag, and a lightweight, sleeping pad. There's a valve at one end, and when I open it, the pad begins to self-inflate. A side compartment holds a soft, plastic water bladder with a drinking tube and an in-line filter. In the larger, middle compartment is a food bag, a first-aid kit, and a stuff bag with extra clothing. At the very bottom is a pair of hiking shoes with thin, wool socks tucked inside them and supplies for blisters. They're a whole size larger than I normally wear.

The last item I find is some kind of rolled up webbing. There's an envelope attached to it, and inside is a letter from Liam.

Hudson,

What you have in your hand is the belt to the pack. It attaches at the bottom. (I'm sure you'll be able to figure out how.) It shifts the weight of the pack from your shoulders, which are probably hurting like a bitch right now, to your hips. I hope you've also found the rocks, if you haven't, please empty the bottom compartment before you do any permanent damage to your back. I'd hate for my little cousin to take care of your invalid ass for the rest of her life.

And speaking of asses, Emma will have mine when she finds out what I've done, so after you leave, I'll be calling Randall with a heads up to give you some help when you get to Hawk Mountain Shelter. I hope you're smart enough to check these supplies and get rid of the rocks before you've gone that far, but if you haven't, then maybe you needed the pain to remind you to be more aware of everything and everyone around you, and that it's okay to ask for help. Or then again, maybe you've been too self-centered in your upper class, privileged world to care about anyone else. I don't want to believe that's true. I hope it's not.

After Ari told me a little about what happened in New York, I threatened to find you and kick your lily-white uka all over these hills. I wanted to teach you what real pain is. Guess I'll let the trail do my work for me.

Now, eat something. Fill up the water bladder and be sure to hydrate. Change your clothes. (Chafing hurts, doesn't it. Ha!) Doctor your feet.

Ari should be at Dicks Creek Gap on Tuesday. I'll be there to meet her midmorning and bring her home with me, hopefully by the afternoon. If what you told me is true, you two have a lot to talk about and some serious business to take care of.

In the meantime, enjoy the trail and the forest. The weather should be nice for the next few days, and it's a wonderful time to be hiking.

Liam

P.S. If I find out you've lied to me, I'm still kicking your ass all over these hills.

Holding Liam's letter in my hands, I survey the gear and supplies strewn haphazardly around me. Everything I needed to make the last five miles a pleasurable experience was right there on my back. Food, water, decent clothing, and a hip belt for the pack were just waiting to be found. Yet, here I sit, practically naked except for cold, wet boxers, blistered feet, sore shoulders, and an empty, growling stomach. The whole situation is ridiculous. The chuckle that escapes me is followed by another, and then another, until I'm laughing hysterically. I laugh until the tears run down my cheeks, until I'm so exhausted I have to lay back on the rocks to catch my breath.

"Well played, Liam Crow," I whisper. "Well played."

Taking his advice, I dress in the appropriate clothing he left for me, take care of my feet, fill the bladder with water, and start rummaging around in the food bag for something to eat. Cheese, crackers, and an apple disappear almost instantly. I only slow down after several handfuls of trail mix.

Much to my surprise, my little companion has stuck around, curiously watching me from a nearby bush. When I brush a few crumbs from my pants, he darts down quickly to peck them up. I edge a few more his way and watch while he devours those, too. I recall something Ariella once told me when I found her feeding birds on the cabin's porch one morning. She pointed out these small gray birds with their dark eyes, calling them juncos, and explaining they were her grandmother's favorite birds. My new friend looks just like those. When I finally pack up and prepare to leave, he flits back to his perch in the bush and begins to sing. I listen to his song as I hike north.

The next three miles pass quickly and, thankfully, with far less pain. The trail doesn't change much. Ups, downs, more ups, more downs. Liam was right, the weather is perfect, and the forest is awakening from its long winter sleep. It's a wonderful time to be hiking.

~ * * * ~

Randall is waiting for me when I arrive at Hawk Mountain Shelter. He smiles knowingly at my change of clothing. "How long did it take you to find the rocks?" he asks.

"Long Creek Falls."

"Damn. Five miles? You must have really been hurting." He laughs at my grimace, but it's a good-natured laugh, followed by a huge grin. "Well, let's get you fed and set up, okay?"

He pulls the gear from my pack, briefly explaining what each thing is and how it's used. The shelter is full, so he leads me to a small camping area close by where we set up my tent, inflate my sleeping pad, and roll out my down bag. In the clothes bag, he finds woolen tights and a long-sleeved pullover to sleep in, rain pants and a rain jacket, two more pairs of socks, and another pair of moisture-wicking, boxer briefs. "Top quality stuff," he nods approvingly.

Then, it's back to the table and a lesson on using the small camp stove, filtering water, and cooking dinner. We sit and visit while I eat, and he tells me a little about himself. He's open, friendly, and easy to like, plus he doesn't tease me too much about today's hiking fiasco.

I find out this is his third year to work as a ridgerunner, and when hiking season is over, he works part-time for Liam and takes classes at a nearby community college. He wants to be an accountant.

"I wouldn't have pegged you for a numbers guy."

"Most people don't, but I like numbers and order and figuring things out. I have a distant cousin who's a math genius. Went to MIT when she was like fifteen or something. Got her PhD at twenty on some papers she wrote about Chaos Theory. Not like I understand any of it," he adds laughing. "But she's kind of a hero to me and a lot of people around here."

While he continues talking, I consider his words about Ariella. I'm sure she has no idea the influence she's had on this young man or the respect people have for her. It's one more reason I'm glad I made the decision to move our company to the area, and one more thing I never told her. My regret list keeps getting longer and longer.

Although I try, I can't hide my sleepy yawn. He chuckles when I try to apologize, telling me it's been a hard day, and I should get some sleep. He suggests I take some pain medicine before turning in and reminds me to sign the register. Once again, he checks to make sure I know how to use my gear and if I have any other questions.

"I do have one. Liam left me a note saying he was going to call you. I didn't think cell phones worked out here."

"Most of them don't," he explains. "But I have a special one for the job, mainly for emergencies. He called me on it. You can usually get a weak signal on the top of most of the mountains. It's still really sketchy at best, though, and the weather can affect the signal, too.

"Good night, man," he adds before ambling off to his camp.

I watch him walk away. He's a good kid, easy natured but determined. He'd probably make a good employee when we get the company running again. I refuse to even consider any other possibility.

The shelter register is sitting on a small shelf on one wall. I take it to the table, flipping through it, looking for Ariella's entry. Her small, neat note is dated the 12th. She spent the night here, choosing to camp in her tent instead of staying in the shelter. The entry closes with a short mention of a nap at Long Creek Falls, and a friendly junco who sang her on her way. She's signed it "Ella," and I realize someone has given her a trail name.

I wonder if they chose "Ella" because it rhymes with Ariella or if it's a shortened form of Cinderella. Is she looking for a new Prince Charming because the one she thought she knew in New York turned out to be an evil troll?

"Get a grip, Calder," I mutter to myself, knowing full well how ridiculous my thoughts sound.

Picking up the pen, I add my own entry next to hers.

March 16, 2003

Learned a valuable lesson today. I'm not as strong or as smart as I thought I was, and asking for help doesn't show weakness. I rested at Long Creek Falls, too, and a little junco reminded me of you. Could it have been the same one? Someday we'll go there and listen to his song together.

I hesitate, not knowing how to sign it. I consider "Rocky" in honor of Liam's punishment and the difficult beginning of my hike but decide against it. Finally, I sign it, *Hud*. It's a nickname I hate but Ariella used it at Springer, and I'll use it until she can give me another one.

Thinking of her letter, I flip through the rest of the notebook but find nothing else in her writing. Another yawn reminds me I desperately need some rest. After placing the register back on its shelf, I make my way to my tent and welcome the relief of dreamless sleep.

CHAPTER 28

His Tears

Date: Monday, March 17

Starting Location: Hawk Mountain Shelter

Destination: Campsite just past Gooch Gap

Total Trip Miles: 18

"Hudson. Hey, you awake in there, man?" Randall's voice rouses me the next morning.

After my gruff, "Yeah," he continues. "Hate to wake you, but it's getting late, and you need to hit the trail if you're going to get some miles in today. I have to leave in a few minutes to go back to Springer, so I need to know you're okay."

"Getting up," I groan, my throat dry and gravelly. The sun is beating down on my little tent, and it's hot, I'm hot, my sleeping bag is hot. Crawling out of the tent is difficult but standing is almost impossible. I have to lean on my hiking poles just to maneuver myself up. The painful moan that escapes me is absurdly embarrassing.

Randall's anxiously watching me. I expect some kind of snarky remark but see only concern on his face. "Privy first," he instructs. "While you're gone, I'll start packing up your stuff and find something in your food bag for breakfast. We need to get some food, lots of fluid, and some ibuprofen in you."

With a nod, I hobble toward the outhouse. Moving helps, but I still hurt … everywhere.

He's moved most of my gear to the shelter table and is boiling water for breakfast by the time I return. After I change clothes, he starts loading everything into the pack, patiently explaining where to place everything to balance the load. He offers to take the clothes I was wearing yesterday to his car on Springer, an offer I gladly accept. Then, while I eat, he opens the guidebook and goes over the description of the trail, locations for water, and possibilities for spending the night.

The next shelter is seven miles away. I need to cover at least eleven miles today if I want to reach Neels Gap tomorrow, which means I'll probably be camping tonight. When he thinks I'm ready to start hiking, he prepares to leave. During March and April, he spends most of his time at Springer, greeting hikers who are beginning their hikes and stressing the importance of "Leave No Trace" hiking.

Shaking his hand, I tell him again how much I appreciate his help. With a last, "Good luck," he shoulders his small pack and heads south on the trail. His long, easy strides carry him from view within minutes.

I feel strangely emotional as I watch him leave. All my life, I've heard, "Boys don't cry." We're taught to suppress our emotions, to remain stoic and in control at all times. As if our masculinity depends on our ability to not show sorrow or pain. Ten days ago, I lost control of my life and my plans. I've been on an emotional roller coaster since then.

Maybe it's being outdoors away from all the trappings of civilization except for the bare necessities of life that has me feeling so vulnerable. Maybe it's the guilt. Or then again, maybe it's because I just plain hurt. Whatever the reason, I'm sad to see him leave. Sitting here isn't going to get me to Neels Gap, though. Swinging my pack around to my back and adjusting the straps and belt like he taught me, I grab my hiking poles and head north.

It's an unseasonably warm day. The forest is mostly hardwoods with very little leaf cover, and soon, my shirt is drenched. At my first snack break, I zip off the lower legs to my pants, leaving me in shorts. It helps some. The heat and the physical movement do wonders for my sore muscles. Soon, I'm walking freely down the trail, still sore in places but no longer stiff.

The physical release of hiking seems to do strange things to my head. Although I'm aware of the trail and my surroundings, all I can think about is Ariella. My body hikes, but my brain thinks. Over and over, I consider everything that happened in New York, trying to examine every word, every conversation, every incident that would have given me a clue about what Gia was doing. Nothing new comes to mind, however. It's the same thing I've thought about for the last ten days.

Thankfully the FBI had been investigating her for some time. When Agent Reynolds tracked me down at my parents' home where I was living and questioned me about my alleged involvement in her Ponzi scheme, I was finally able to understand some of her strange actions over the last two years.

Living in my old condo and posing as my fiancée lent legitimacy to her supposed investment company. She was smart enough not to have any clients in the Northeast. All her clientele were wealthy investors from the Midwest, close enough to recognize my family's name but not enough to actually know me. Her greed and over-reach were her downfall. When she implicated her Uncle Vincent, her house of cards collapsed. The FBI swooped in just in time to prevent her from leaving for Italy. I hope when the dust settles, she'll spend a very long time in prison.

I'm so occupied with my thoughts I don't see the snake until it's almost too late. It's a big rattlesnake. Stretched out across the trail enjoying the sunny spot, he barely moves at my approach. I have no idea what to do. Logs, bushes, and a narrow trail make it impossible to get around him. When I inch toward him, he moves slightly, flicking his tongue and following my movement, but he still doesn't move. Stomping my feet only makes him coil slightly. He's claimed the center of the trail and it's his—rushing hikers be damned.

Suddenly, the whole situation strikes me as funny, and I start laughing—at myself for ignoring my beautiful surroundings, at the snake for reminding me I don't always get my way.

I'm still chuckling when another hiker steps up beside me. When he sees the snake, he starts laughing, too, completely understanding the situation we're in.

"A friend told me to try this," he explains as he reaches for his water bottle. "The trick is to squirt enough water to make the snake uncomfortable but not make it mad enough to get defensive or attack." He pops the lid on the bottle and squeezes it gently. A steady stream of water shoots out, drenching the snake, who immediately slithers off the trail and disappears under a nearby rock. He grins at me as he puts the bottle away. "I guess it works. Enjoy your hike." And then he's gone, striding away along the trail and over a slight rise. He disappears before I can even say thank you.

For the rest of the afternoon, I concentrate on the trail and the forest around me. I enjoy the flowers and inhale their scent, watch the birds and listen to their song, feel the cool breeze dry the sweat on my face—and watch out for snakes. My worries of the past and future drop away as I focus on the here and now. Being in the moment makes me feel closer to Ariella.

It's late afternoon when I finally stumble into Gooch Mountain Shelter. Several hikers, all guys, are taking a break there. One is resting in the shelter, another is writing in the register, and two are eating a hot meal at the table. The smell of food makes me ravenous. Although Randall warned me about the dangers of not eating or drinking enough, I haven't stopped to do either in the last couple hours. Perhaps it's why I'm suddenly shaky and lightheaded.

Digging around in my pack, I finally get my food bag, pot, and stove out and set up on the table. I try to remember everything Randall told me about the stove, but when I finally get the pieces attached to each other, I can't remember how to light it. To make things worse, my hand is shaking so hard I can barely hold the lighter.

The hiker at the other end of the table is studying the guidebook and pays no attention to me, but his companion glances at me from time to time. Finally, he scoots down a little closer to me and, nodding at the stove I'm trying to light, asks if it's one of those new, ultralight, backpacking stoves.

"Sorry," I confess. "A friend loaned it to me, and I really don't know."

"Would you mind?" he asks, indicating the still unlit stove. "I've always wanted to play around with one of them."

I slide the stove across the table to him and watch him pretend to examine it. He turns a knob, then flicks the lighter, and a bright ring of flame appears at the top. "Cool," he says. My pan of water is sitting nearby, and he places it on top of the stand. "Nice pot, too. Lightweight titanium. Your friend has great gear.

"I'm Boyscout," he adds, reaching to shake my hand.

"Hud," I reply, shaking his in return. The hiker in the shelter looks up at my name, frowning as he studies me. He's a big guy, and his glare is intimidating. "Uh, Hudson," I add stuttering.

"You start at Springer?"

"Yesterday." I nod.

"We were there early this morning. You sign the register?"

"Yes …" I answer slowly, watching Boyscout, who has the strangest look on his face.

"You going all the way to Maine?"

His questions come quick and fast, giving me very little time to answer and no time to explain. I notice his three companions watching me closely. I'm beginning to feel very uncomfortable.

"No, I have to be in Neels Gap tomorrow. Liam Crow, the owner of Mountain Crossings, is expecting me. I'm, uh, I'm writing a little humor article for my hometown newspaper about the AT. Novice hiker trying to survive in the woods. That type of thing, you know." I laugh.

Something I said must have satisfied whatever doubts or questions they had about me because Boyscout smiles at me, adding a, "Good luck with that," and his fellow hikers return to their previous activities.

My dinner is finished cooking, and I dig into it, enjoying the rice, chicken, and cheese sauce. It tastes wonderful, and I try not to eat too quickly. While I'm eating, Boyscout and his friends begin gathering their gear. He explains they only have four months to complete their hike, so they have a goal of a least twenty miles a day.

He lingers behind when the others leave, purposely tinkering with his backpack. He seems undecided about something, but then sits back down across the table from me.

"Listen," he says. "I may have this all wrong, but if you saw the Springer register yesterday, you might have noticed a letter toward the back. It was written to someone named Hud. Apparently, this guy is a real scumbag who cheated and dumped a girl who is out hiking the trail to try to recover from everything he did to her. The AT chat groups and the Trail Journals website are full of people discussing her letter and some others she's written.

"Telling people your name is Hud makes them think you might be that scumbag and … well, let's just say you might not like their reaction. Anyway," he says, standing. "Wanted to give you a heads up. Have a good hike." With a final nod and wave, he walks away, leaving me thinking about his warning. I guess I need a new name.

I don't want to leave Gooch Shelter. I'm tired and would like nothing more than to roll out my sleeping bag and turn in for the day. But if I stop now, I'll have to hike sixteen miles tomorrow, and even I know that's impossible for me. So, reluctantly, I pack up my gear and start hiking again.

Two miles later, I cross a small forest service road at Gooch Gap. Randall highlighted the location of a small spring nearby and wrote a note in the guidebook to remind me to fill up my water bladder and bottle here so I would have plenty of water for the evening. He also said I would find several camping spots in the next couple miles. I top off my water containers and hike on.

Another hour and I'm done. All the aches and pains I thought were gone have come back with a vengeance, and I don't think I can take another step. When I spot a nice level area close by the trail, I stop and make camp. I get the tent up, maybe not as expertly as Randall, but it serves its purpose. Crackers, cheese, more trail mix, and dried fruit make my dinner. Water and ibuprofen are my dessert. I barely remember crawling into the tent before I'm asleep.

~ * * * ~

Something is touching my face. It's wet, cold, and slides across my skin with each breath. Barely aware of what I'm doing, I bat it away with one hand, only to be hit in the face with more cold water. Waking abruptly, I sit up only to find myself encased in the wet, sodden fabric of my collapsed tent. It's dark, it's damp, and it's cold. I'm miserable.

With an exasperated huff, I manage to open the zipper and crawl out. Getting upright is as hard as it was this morning. At least, there's no one around to listen to me whimper as I slide into my unlaced hiking shoes.

I have a small pouch for things I might need during the night. It holds some toilet paper, pain medicine, and a headlamp. The small LED light is attached to a stretchy headband meant to be worn across the forehead. When I turn it on, I can see most of the tent stakes have pulled loose from the soaked ground or the cords connecting them to the tent body are no longer taut. The top of the tent has fallen inward, creating an area in which water can pool. Given enough time, enough rain, and enough condensation from my breath, it's little wonder it started to leak.

With no other choice but to try and fix it, I restake, retighten, and readjust. When it's upright and taut again, I crawl inside, using a camp towel to mop up any standing water and thanking Liam for giving me a bag with a water-resistant cover.

My sleeping clothes are damp, but they're also wool and have remained warm. When I get back into my bag, I warm up quickly. Surprisingly, I find it hard to go back to sleep. I eat a trail bar, drink some water, and take a pain pill. Then, I have to get up and piss.

Thoroughly irritated, I toss and turn, finding it impossible to get comfortable. The wind has picked up a bit. It shakes loose the moisture from the pine trees I've camped under, and it falls like tiny drops of rain on my tent roof. Listening to the plink-plink relaxes me.

I've often heard the wind described as "lonesome," but I never thought about it very much. It was just wind; it made noise as it blew through the trees. But I think I understand now. Lying in my little tent, I listen to the wind blowing above me. It sounds lonely. It moans, and the trees groan as it moves through them. It's a melancholy sound—a sad sound, which only makes me more miserable and depressed. I think I may be lonesome.

My face is wet again, but it's not from the rain on my tent. This time, it's tears trickling down my face. I can't seem to stop them, and suddenly, I don't want to. "To hell with it," I mutter to myself, letting them flow in great, gasping sobs. I haven't cried like this since I was a child and my dog died. Wasn't this wrecked or emotional at my grandfather's funeral.

I've been angry, frustrated, enraged, irritated, and furious with everything that happened in New York, but this is the first time I've admitted to myself how sad and miserable—how lonesome—I've been. I miss my bella mente, and I can't wait to see her again.

With thoughts of her and the promise of tomorrow, I finally fall asleep.

CHAPTER 29

His Memories

Date: Tuesday, March 18

Starting Location: Campsite just past Gooch Gap

Destination: Neels Gap

Total Trip Miles: 30.7

Last night's rain has left the woods shrouded in fog and mist. Visibility is limited to a few hundred feet at best. Skeletal trunks of trees appear before me as I approach, then fade from view as I hike by. Unable to see very far on either side of me, I don't know if I'm above valleys or below mountains. Nothing exists beyond the misty bubble I move through.

Glimpses of the trail tease me as I walk. Flat and easy, it suddenly rears up in front of me, startling me with an abrupt climb. Then it descends, sometimes with a series of well-engineered switchbacks, others with a knee-torturing sharp drop.

The woods are quiet. No breeze to rustle the leaves, no birdsong to entertain, no small animals or insects to watch. Only the occasional drip, drip of moisture from the rain-soaked branches overhead and the squelch of my footsteps in the muddy path.

When the trail leads me through a little meadow, I find a small boulder to sit on and take a food and water break. The feeling of being all alone, of being separated from the rest of the world, intensifies as I sit and contemplate my misty bubble. It reminds me of post-apocalyptic novels I've read and survival movies I've watched. I can almost picture ragged zombies stumbling out of the dark forest around me.

Or maybe I'm in the *Twilight Zone* episode about the kid with mental powers who surrounded his little town with an impenetrable mist, cutting it off from the rest of the world. Ariella and I watched the episode together one night after picking up Chinese take-out. It led to a discussion about what "reality" was. Ariella had a theory that nothing existed except what our senses allowed us to experience. She argued we created our own reality based on what our brains perceived as real. I, of course, was thoroughly confused. "Like the Matrix?" I asked.

"Yes, but *reality* is no more 'real' than the *Matrix*," she explained. "Both are constructs; they're the same thing. Like the concept of time, the past and the future do not exist, have not existed, will not exist. There is only the here and the now.

Of course," she continued. "It could be just the opposite. There could be a whole other existence, which we are unable to experience because our input senses are so limited, and therefore, our brain doesn't process all the available stimuli, leaving us with a limited version of what reality actually is." Then she smiled at me, laughing when I shook my head.

Later, when I considered everything she'd said in our discussion, I marveled again at the beautiful and wonderful thing that was her mind.

My memories are interrupted when I notice a dark shape moving at the edge of the tree line. It disappears into the fog, then comes back into view as it meanders in and out of focus. Although I know it's not the ragged zombies of my earlier thoughts, I can feel my heart rate pick up and the rush of adrenaline as I try to decide whether to run, hide, or freeze. I've heard of wild hogs in the area. They can be dangerous, and so can the occasional black bear that roams these hills. I realize I have no idea what to do. None of my training, experience, or education has prepared me for dealing with a wild boar or a bear.

Frozen to the rock I'm sitting on, I watch with apprehension as the dark shape seems to move toward me. Finally, it steps out of the gloom and into sight. It's a buck, a big one. Still wearing his crown of antlers, he ambles into the small clearing, nibbling on grass or a leaf-covered twig. He stops abruptly when he sees me, staring with his large, dark eyes. He's a beautiful animal, majestic and graceful. Yet possessing an undercurrent of strength and power. I have no doubt his antlers and sharp hoofs could inflict some painful injuries.

He must decide this puny human is no threat to him because he slowly makes his way back into the tree cover. One blink and he's gone. Disappearing as if he never existed, as if he is no longer part of my reality.

The sun finally makes its appearance mid-morning. It burns off the fog, leaving a bright, clear blue sky. With a fresh breeze cooling my face, I cover the remaining miles toward Neels Gap. The mountains come and go. There's Big Cedar, Granny Top, and then Burnett Fields. I climb up and over each one, then drop down into another gap before ascending the next mountain. Jarrad Gap, Bird Gap, and Slaughter Gap all pass beneath my feet.

I eat. I drink. I rest. I take time to look at the flowers, the wildlife, the reality my brain is creating for me, but mostly, I walk. I walk toward the woman I hope is waiting for me at her cousin's home. The woman who needs to be told what is "real" and not the lies of another's reality.

The last obstacle of the day is Blood Mountain. As the highest point on the AT in Georgia, it tests my resolve as I slowly plod up its intimidating elevation gain. "Two more miles," I tell myself. "Just two more miles."

~ * * * ~

Liam is standing in the middle of his store, talking to a middle-aged couple when I burst through the door. He starts backing away as soon as he sees me.

"Rocks," I shout. "You damned motherfucker. You put rocks in my pack."

"Easy, easy," he urges, hands held out in front of him to protect himself.

"Easy?" I scream back. "There wasn't anything *easy* about it, you asshole. I thought I was going to break my back, and I'm not sure my shoulders will ever be the same again." Although I try to keep my angry façade, Liam sees right through it, and when he grins, I can't stop the laughter erupting from me. "You son of a bitch," I mutter, shaking my head at him.

The couple he was talking to are still standing close by, watching and listening to our conversation, as are most of the other customers in the store. The woman is staring wide-eyed at me, and her husband is frowning. Suddenly, I feel embarrassed for my language. "I'm sorry, ma'am," I apologize. "I wasn't raised to speak that way in front of ladies."

But she shakes her head, grinning when she tells me she has sons older than me, and she's heard it all before. "Besides, Mr. Easy," she continues. "I'd be calling him a motherfucker, too, if he put rocks in my backpack." With a grin, she holds out her hand. "I'm Dreamer," she says. "And this is my husband, Allday."

"Mr. Easy?" I ask while shaking their hands.

"Well, it was that or Rocky, and you're prettier than Stallone."

With a wink, a wave goodbye, and a "take it easy, Mr. Easy," they're out the door. I watch them walk down the steps, then turn north on the trail where it goes through the building. And just like that, I have a trail name.

I turn back to Liam, intent on finding out if she's here. One look at his face and I have my answer. This time, I'm the one throwing the right hook, and he's the one scrambling to avoid it. I'm screaming, cussing, threatening him with bodily harm right there in the middle of his store. One of his employees grabs me, and Emma gets in between us. Once again, she pushes us toward the back patio, telling us to sit. She disappears, returning with a cold beer for each of us and a prepared sandwich from one of their vending machines for me.

"Talk," she commands, then returns to the store, leaving us alone.

"You told me in your letter you would kick my ass if you found out I was lying to you, but you're the one who lied, Liam. Did you even try to find her?"

"Yes. I spent all morning and part of the afternoon with her. We even ate lunch together." Liam takes a long swig of his beer before facing me again. "She hiked into the gap right after I got there. She was with these two guys. Stop," he says, holding up his hand when I try to interrupt. "They're good guys. I'm glad she's with them. Safer that way. Anyway," he continues. "They headed into Hiawassee, and Ari stayed with me. I told her she needed to come home, talk to you and Susan, and get this business all straightened out."

"What did she say?"

Liam laughs, shaking his head. "She really went off on me. Said all she'd done for the past nine years was take care of *business*. Got right up into my face, even poked my chest with her finger." Grinning, he stops to take another sip of his drink. "She was one really angry woman."

"Ariella did that? Wow, doesn't sound like her. But she wouldn't come back with you?"

"No."

"Did you even tell her I was here?"

He studies me intently for a few moments before answering. "No, Hudson, I didn't."

Now I'm the one glaring down at Liam, but with a half-eaten sandwich in one hand and a beer in the other, I'm not as intimidating as he was. I'm tired, too. With a resigned sigh, I sit back down. "Why?"

"Three reasons. First off, I'd already made her mad by telling her what to do, and I was afraid if I said you were here, she'd leave and not talk to me at all. I really needed to speak to her. I know you told me some stuff when you first got here, but I wanted to hear it from her. And I'll admit I didn't believe you entirely."

"And the second reason?"

"She ..." Liam stares off at the forest, which surrounds the back of his building. I can tell he's trying to gather his thoughts. When he focuses back on me, I'm startled by the sadness on his face. "She told me she was trying to find herself, to find her soul. I had no idea how lost she'd become in your world. Did you know she took diction lessons because she was embarrassed by her accent? Did you realize she changed the way she dressed, what she ate, what she thought, just to fit into your world?

"She cried, Hudson. The only time I ever saw Ari cry was at Granny Cora's funeral. But I saw her cry this morning."

He pauses to look at me, gauging my reaction. But I can only stare back at him, stunned at his revelation and shamed at my lack of awareness. "I ..."

Shaking his head to silence me, he continues. "She told me she needed this hike, and I could tell she did. She's already different, changing, becoming more assertive and more self-confident. She's comfortable on the trail, knows what she's doing, and it shows. I liked what I saw, and I want her to continue to change, to become the competent woman I know she's capable of being. If it means with you, or without you, or with someone else, I don't care. I like you, you're my friend, but Ari comes first—she'll always come first."

Liam leans back in his chair, drinking his beer, watching me mull over everything he's told me. "I didn't know," I confess. "Never paid any attention. I guess you're right about me being wrapped up in my upper class, privileged world. I just ... Oh, God, Liam, I'm sorry. I'm so sorry. Please help me find her so I can make this right."

He doesn't reply, just stares at me, and I realize there's something else he hasn't told me. Although I don't want to know the answer, I have to ask anyway. "Reason number three?"

Nodding, he sets his bottle on the ground beside him. I get the impression he's readying himself for battle, and I'm going to be the one who gets attacked.

"I told you, if I found out you lied to me, I would kick your ass all over these hills. Well, I'm telling you now, if you want to see her, if you want to make this right, as you keep saying, then, you need to tell me the truth—all of it. You may not have outright lied to her, but you didn't tell her everything. You lied by omission, and that's just as bad.

"Ari told me a lot of stuff today, including the details of her visit to your condo and finding Gia there. It took a lot of courage for her to go there. She faced up to that bitch, even defended you, but Gia really did a number on her. Pulled all of her strings, played on all her insecurities. I think she would have stayed in New York and met with you and Susan if Gia hadn't been in the picture. So, let's start there. Why did you sell your condo to her, and why is she pretending to be your fiancée?"

"I ..." Hesitating, I try to get my thoughts in order. I knew very little of what Gia said to Ariella. I knew it was terrible, but I didn't know she defended me. Liam's right—it must have been very difficult for her.

"I didn't know it was Gia who was buying the condo," I start. "I was approached by a real estate broker who represented a wealthy client looking for a property overlooking Central Park. They offered me twice what it was worth and wanted to purchase the furnishings, too. It was a great deal, and I was already thinking of selling it, so I said yes. I'd hit a snag in funding for the business and thought I could use the money to tide us over for a while."

"But you didn't tell her?"

"No. I just ..."

"What?" he demands. "You just what?"

"I was embarrassed, okay?" I glare back at him. "I didn't tell her because I was embarrassed."

With a long sigh, I lean back in my chair, staring at the darkening sky overhead. "Ariella is the most interesting, unique person I've ever known. I was so in awe of her when we met. Her mind is so …" Pausing, I try to find the words to describe how I feel about her. "Her mind is so beautiful, Liam. It's ethereal, almost otherworldly. She doesn't think like us, doesn't see the world like we do. I wanted her to stay that way. I knew a little about her difficult childhood and her diagnosis. So, I had it in my head I would be the one to protect and provide for her. I'd give her everything she never had growing up."

Shifting in my chair, I sit up straighter, focusing back on Liam as I speak. "You know how hard raising capital is. I'm sure you jumped through hoops to get funding for this place. It's the same with our business. But I was supposed to be the money guy. I had the contacts, knew the shakers and the movers. I was the golden boy from the socially elite family. Getting investors was supposed to be easy for me. Except it wasn't, and I was getting desperate. The offer on the condo came at the right time. I left everything but my personal belongings and the art collection I inherited from my grandparents and moved into my parents' home."

"Why didn't you get another place?"

"I was already thinking about moving the business away from New York. The city is too crowded, too loud, and I thought she would be happier if she were closer to you and her other relatives. I also thought this might be a nicer place to raise a family. It seemed foolish to buy or rent something when my parents had plenty of room."

"Raise a family?" Liam asks with a smirk. "Aren't you getting a little ahead of yourself?"

"Well, maybe, but I do want that someday with her."

"I suppose this is another thing you neglected to tell her?"

"Yeah," I admit. "The list keeps getting longer and longer."

"When did you find out Gia was living in your old condo?"

"About six months ago. There was a mix-up in a delivery, and I went by to get my package. Gia was in the lobby getting her mail. That's when I learned she was living there." My beer is almost finished. I swallow the last little bit and place the bottle on the stone paving beneath me while I watch Liam.

I can tell he's thinking about everything I've told him. With a calculating look, he leans forward, resting his arms on his knees. "Hudson, Gia is pretending to be your fiancée. There are photos of the two of you on the piano. She's wearing an engagement ring. Her uncle announced your appointment as head of their new security division. There is so much more here than just a kink in your cash flow. What the hell is going on?"

"She's running a Ponzi scheme out of the condo. My family name and my address gave her a certain amount of credibility, and none of her investors are people from the East Coast who might know me. I think she realized the FBI was investigating her, and she was getting desperate. So, apparently, she convinced Vincent I wanted the position, and we would move to Italy together. She even told him I owned the company, that Ariella was just part of the development team.

"When Vincent made the announcement, I was as shocked as she must have been. He'd offered me a job several times in the past, but I always told him no. There wasn't much I could do while we were still on the stage in front of everyone, but as soon as we left the room, we went directly to his office and hashed it out.

"I don't know any more of the details, and the authorities have warned me not to talk about it until the investigation is complete, but I'm hoping she'll be going away for a long time."

Liam sits back in his chair, a stunned look on his face. "Wow ... What a conniving bitch."

"True," I agree with a wry smile. "She had all the details in place, or at least she thought she did."

"Wait." Liam leans toward me again. "How did she get you to take her to the charity ball?"

"Charity ball? I never took Gia to anything. Where did you get that idea?"

"From Ari. She saw the photo in the newspaper the next day. You were talking to Vincent, and Gia was standing beside you holding your hand."

"Oh, shit," I mutter, shaking my head as I remember what happened. "She never said anything. Why didn't she mention it?"

"Because it's Ariella, asshole. You told her you weren't going, then you show up in the photo spread holding hands with another woman. What did you expect her to do?"

"That's not what happened. I swear it isn't." The long day is finally catching up to me, and I can't stop my yawn. Leaning my head against the chair back, I stare up at the stars, which are beginning to make their appearance.

"We'd barely started our negotiations with Banca Italia. I was supposed to go out of town to meet with Vincent, but his assistant called and said his plans were changed, and he preferred to speak to me at the ball that night. It was the last minute, so I put on my tux and went. We were deep in conversation when I felt someone take my hand. I thought it was probably my mom, who wasn't expecting me to be there. I remember a photographer took our picture just then. When I turned to greet who was holding my hand, it was Gia.

"I remember pulling away from her quickly, surprised she was touching me. I was disgusted when I saw the photo because it looked like we were together. At the time, I had no idea why she would do something like that. She knows I can't stand her. Thinking about it now, I can see it was all staged. Hell, she was probably the one pretending to be the assistant."

Another yawn stops my account, and I look over to see Liam regarding me thoughtfully. "I thought she was a family friend," he finally says.

"She is, or was, I don't know." I shrug. "My mom never approved of her—thought she was too wild—but she was Kathryn's friend, so she was around some." Hoping he's satisfied with my answer, I don't say anything else. I should have known Liam wouldn't let it go. For a moment, I feel like a suspect trapped in an interrogation room as he stares me down.

"There's more between you and Gia than you're telling me," he finally says. "I warned you, Hudson, all of the truth. I still haven't decided whether I'm going to help you find Ari or not."

I can't stop the deep, resigned sigh that escapes me. He's right, of course, but sharing these memories is not something I want to do.

"Liam. It's personal and painful, and it was a really, really long time ago. Don't ask me to go there."

"Oh, my God," he exclaims. "How young were you? Did she—"

"No, no," I interrupt. "It wasn't like that. I was seventeen—it was completely consensual. It's just … Let's say it was a rude awakening."

"I think Gia may have said or at least hinted about your shared past when Ari talked to her. I could tell there was something she was hiding when she told me about the visit. You know you'll have to tell her," he adds sadly. "You can't keep things from her anymore."

"I know, and I will. I promise." With a defeated sigh, I lean back in my chair once more, staring up at the dark, star-filled sky. For a moment, I wonder if Ariella is watching the stars, and if so, is she thinking about me? "I just have to find her first," I whisper to the lights above me.

The evening has cooled, and Liam lights the fire pit between us. I pull my chair closer to its welcome warmth. Emma joins us with nachos and another beer for each of us. We eat, they talk, and I listen, yawning from time to time, trying to fight off sleep. I'm not very successful because I awake suddenly to find Liam leaning over me and shaking my shoulder.

"Hudson. Hey, can you listen? I have two things I need to tell you. I'm sorry, I should have said this before, but I'm telling you now. Before I left Ari, she told me she loves you."

I stare up at him. "She did?"

"Yes, she said she loved you and always would. And now I know you love her, too. But the very last thing I asked her was what I should tell you if you came looking for her. She laughed at me and said you wouldn't because you were going to Italy with Gia. Then she said, 'If Hudson shows up looking for me, you know what I'm doing and where I am. If I'm important to him, he can come find me.' She should be in Franklin in three, maybe four days. You can rest here until then, and I'll take you to her."

"No." The word bursts from my mouth before I fully realize what I've said.

"What?" Liam asks, clearly confused by my answer.

"No, I don't want you to take me to Franklin. I want to find her. On the trail, I mean. I want to follow her and find her, just like she said I should. I want to show her how important she is to me. I want to keep hiking."

He stares at me a long time before finally nodding. "Okay, you can start tomorrow, but for now, let's get you into bed. You're going to need your rest."

"Wait for me, my bella mente," I whisper in my head as I follow him. *"Please wait for me. I'm coming."*

CHAPTER 30

More than a Beautiful Mind

Date: Wednesday, March 19
Starting Location: Neels Gap
Destination: Whitley Gap Shelter
Total Trip Miles: 36.9

During breakfast the next morning, Liam shows me a hiking schedule he's prepared if I want to intercept Ariella. He doesn't think I can catch her by the time she reaches Franklin and believes the best I can hope for is to make it to Nantahala by the time she does. It's a little over a hundred trail miles away. I'll have to average fifteen miles a day if I want to get there in time.

"You don't have to do this," he reminds me. "I called a trail angel to pick her up when she gets to the road crossing at Winding Stair on Friday. Tator will take her into town where I've made reservations for her at the Franklin Motel. We could call and get you a room there, too. Your car is still in the parking lot. You can be there in little over an hour."

His offer is tempting, especially with my lingering muscle soreness, but I want to keep hiking. I want to follow her. I want to see what she saw, do what she did, and experience what she felt. If I left the trail now, I would never understand this part of her. If I've learned anything since starting at Springer, it's that I only knew and appreciated the small piece of her I was focused on, the part I wanted to protect and provide for. I didn't accept her as a whole person. As a grown woman accomplished in so many more ways than I acknowledged. I also want to read her shelter entries. Since Boyscout mentioned them to me, I've wondered what else she's written. I don't want to miss this opportunity to know her better.

"No. I need to do this. I *want* to do this. She needs to know she's important enough for me to come find."

"Okay," Liam reluctantly agrees. "But you should understand this is going to be a lot harder than walking from Springer to Hawk Mountain, even without thirty pounds of rocks in your pack. Which reminds me," he continues with a smirk. "When did you finally figure out something was wrong?"

"Long Creek Falls," I reluctantly confess.

His smirk turns into a howling belly laugh. "Five miles?" he gasps when he can speak again. "It took you five miles? Oh, you must have been hurting so bad."

"Laugh it up, you asshole. I'll get you one of these days."

"Yeah, you probably will, if Ari doesn't first." He grins back at me. "In the meantime, let's make sure you survive the next week." Still chuckling, he leads me into the back room of the store where he has gear laid out for me.

"You're going to have to balance the need for speed versus safety," he explains as he points to the gear on the table. "The lighter your pack, the faster you can hike, but you run the risk of not being prepared if you get caught in bad weather or some other threatening situation. Not carrying a tent lightens your pack by at least three pounds, but means you have to stay in a shelter each night. You can cowboy camp as long as the weather is decent.

"Then there's the food situation. A stove, fuel, and cook kit will add a pound or more. If you don't carry one, you'll have to eat cold food like jerky and trail mix. There are some decent trail bars out there, and we can put those in your food bag. But unless you want to go into town to resupply, your bag is going to be really heavy. Something else you need to consider."

Over the next twenty minutes, Liam and I discuss all the gear options and make some final decisions. The tent is left behind as well as the cooking equipment. A small fire-starter kit is tucked inside the titanium pot and added to my growing pile of gear. This will give me the ability to heat water over a campfire if the need arises.

My clothes are kept to a minimum: convertible pants, a short-sleeved shirt, a long-sleeved shirt, woolen sleeping top and bottoms, rain pants and jacket, two pairs of socks, a knit cap, and a change of underwear. Everything can be layered if the weather turns colder.

"Water weighs over eight pounds per gallon, so only carry what you need to get you to the next source. This time of year means plenty of water everywhere. Which reminds me," he continues. "Wash when you can. It helps with the chafing and the odor. You're going to be pretty ripe by the time you get to Nantahala."

He laughs when I roll my eyes.

Then we start on my food. The bag gets heavier and heavier as we add each day's allotted rations.

"I don't like this," Liam mutters, frowning. "There has to be a better way." He picks up the guidebook, looking at the notes he's written for me in the margins. "Here." He points to the fifth day. "You'll be coming into Winding Stair Gap early that morning. I'll get Tator to meet you there with food for the next three days."

"You don't have to. I can carry it."

"You say that now but wait until you put all this on your back. He won't mind; we help each other out all the time. Anyway, I kind of owe you," Liam admits with an embarrassed grin.

Chuckling, I agree with him and accept his help.

An early lunch, another shower, some clean clothes, and I'm ready to go. Liam's right—the pack is heavy but nothing like the old one with rocks in it. Although I wanted to continue carrying what I assumed, and then was told, was Granny Dobbs and Ariella's old backpack, Liam persuaded me to use a newer, much lighter, internal-frame pack. It rests securely on my hips, fits closer to my back, and gives me a more stable center of gravity. "You'll be less likely to fall," he assures me when he follows me outside.

"There's something I've been meaning to ask you," I tell him, pointing to the large tree that grows near the parking lot. Hundreds of pairs of boots and hiking shoes dangle from its branches. "What is that?"

Liam chuckles when he sees what I'm looking at, then sobers quickly. "It's a lot of broken dreams," he says. "Every year people quit their jobs, put their lives on hold, and spend a lot of money to follow the dream of hiking the Appalachian Trail. They start at Springer, then get here three days later, only to realize being in the woods is not what they expected. So, they 'go off trail.' They don't quit. Most of them tell themselves they'll come back, but they rarely do. Hiking boots are heavy and smelly. They get rid of them by throwing them up into the tree."

For a moment, we both stare at the tree, watching the broken dreams sway in the breeze. With a clap to my shoulder, Liam ends our moment. "Go get your dream, Hudson," he tells me. "And be careful."

The AT passes through an open breezeway in the middle of the old stone building, then continues on past the back patio of Liam's home. There it starts a long, slow pull up the mountain. It seems to go on forever. I walk, and walk, and walk. Sometimes, my mind distracts me with runaway thoughts— regrets from the past, hopes for the future, goals for the present. At the center of them all is Ariella. Always Ariella. Other times, I concentrate on the trail, being careful where I place my feet and hiking poles.

If the trail is difficult and my pack heavy, at least the weather is wonderful. It stays warm and sunny with a gentle breeze and low humidity. I wonder how miserable it would be in bad weather. At least I haven't hiked in the pouring rain yet.

I reach the side trail to Whitley Gap Shelter late in the afternoon. Liam suggested I spend the night there rather than push on another five miles to the next shelter. It makes for a shorter day, but the difficult trail has left me exhausted. With a relieved sigh, I drop my pack on the shelter floor.

Twenty minutes later, I'm set up, pad and sleeping bag rolled out, gear stored neatly nearby. I take Liam's advice and do a quick wash before pulling on my sleeping clothes. My hiking pants and shirt are hung from nails on the shelter wall for a good airing out. Picking up the shelter register, I take it with me to the table while I rummage in my food bag for something to eat.

I find her entry quickly. She's written a short note about hiking in the rain and falling on the slippery trail. It's signed "Ella" and dated the 15th. "You were here just four days ago. You were here," I whisper into the silence around me. I think about her sitting on the wooden platform, eating at this table, and writing in this notebook.

"Did you write anything else?" I wonder as I flip through the back pages. And then I find it, a whole page filled with her neat handwriting. She's addressed it to *Hud,* and as I start to read it, I'm very glad there's no one else with me in the shelter because this one breaks my heart.

I knew her childhood was difficult. She told me Granny Dobbs raised her after her mother's death. I knew there were bullies, and I knew she always felt different. But I had no idea the terrible scars those tormentors left. Here was a lovely young woman who thought of herself as weird, bizarre, and strange. She'd never been told she was beautiful or even pretty.

I called her beautiful, but even I failed her, too. It was her mind I was referring to. Had I never told her how beautiful she was, both inside and out? She was radiant the year I took her to my parents' charity ball. Did I tell her how lovely she was that night? As hard as I try, I can't remember.

Thinking about our time together makes me realize how ridiculous it was to try to keep our relationship on a friendly, strictly business level. Although we saw each other almost daily, I was careful to make sure none of our activities would seem like a date. There were no romantic dinners, no holding hands, and no long walks along the river. Had she even been to a nightclub, I wondered? Had she ever done anything a normal twenty-some-thing-year-old woman would do?

Then, after keeping my distance for years, I spent the night with her. I'd been so intent on my plans, on my wants, on my needs, on what I saw as our future that I'd forgotten the present. No wonder she'd believed the lies Gia spewed at her. I'd done nothing to make her believe otherwise.

Blinking my eyes to clear them of tears, I read the rest of her entry. It's a terrible description of a unique child left alone in a horrible situation. It's also a testament to the indomitable will she possesses. She speaks of the patterns and shapes in the lonely room and the safety she found in them. Then describes the changes she made in her behavior to satisfy the people who were neglecting her.

I realize she'd still been changing herself to please others while she lived in New York. The knowledge she'd done all of it to fit into my world, to become something she wasn't just for me, feels like a punch to the gut. I left her alone much too often. This time, I was the one neglecting her.

"I'm sorry," I murmur to the empty space around me. "I'm so sorry, love." Turning back to her previous entry, I write my own beside it.

March 19, 2003

Please stay safe. No more falls.

You told LC I wouldn't follow you, but I am.

I'm following because you're the most important thing in my life.

I'm coming, my love. I'm coming.

I sign it with my new trail name, *Easy.*

The sun set while I was writing. As the temperature dropped, a foggy mist formed. I watch it creep its way into the meadow, and then slowly engulf the shelter behind me. Shrouded in its sound-muffling blanket, the woods around me are quiet, desolate, forsaken. There are no shapes or patterns to distract or entertain, only numbing whiteness.

"Goodnight, my bella mente," I whisper as I crawl into my sleeping bag, but the loneliness around me doesn't answer.

CHAPTER 31

A Really Angry Woman

Date: Thursday, March 20
Starting Location: Whitley Gap Shelter
Destination: Tray Mountain Shelter
Total Trip Miles: 56.2

I've always heard that roosters crow the sun up each morning. I wouldn't know. I've never lived anywhere near a rooster. Apparently, though, songbirds also like to welcome the sun. They wake me this morning, long before the sky is barely light enough to be called dawn. My first reaction is irritation. A couple more hours of sleep would be wonderful. Rolling over, I will myself to relax, but every time I close my eyes, they pop open again. Finally, I lie on my pad, letting my eyes wander over the graffiti-covered walls of the shelter.

Someone has carved "Daniel Boone slept here" on one of the logs. I smile when I read it. Although the shelter has definitely seen better days, it's not quite that old.

A sense of peace creeps over me. Perhaps this is the way we were always meant to start the day—sung into wakefulness by beautiful birdsong. No blaring alarm clocks, no ringing telephones, no traffic noises, just the sounds of nature and a glorious sunrise.

I have a very long day ahead of me. It's over nineteen miles to Tray Mountain shelter where I plan to spend the night. I rise, pack, and hike out.

Although I spent the night alone, I don't spend the day alone. This is prime hiking season, and according to Randall, as many as a hundred hikers a day can start at Springer during the six-week span from March 15 to May 1. As soon as I reach the main trail, I join an almost constant stream of hikers heading north. Some I pass as they sit taking a break. But most seem to be hiking faster than I am. I soon learn to quickly step aside as they approach me from the rear. After a Boy Scout troop and then a high school hiking club pass me, I realize this is also spring break and one of the reasons the trail is so crowded.

I'm a little embarrassed to be so slow. Although never a big fitness buff, I've always been active. My family loved skiing and sailing. I swam, played tennis, and lifted weights from time to time. I always considered myself healthy and in shape. Nothing seems to have prepared me for hiking with a backpack though. "It's just walking," I tell myself. Yet it's not.

Midway up one particularly difficult, rocky climb, I stop for a break, taking the opportunity to catch my breath and drink some water. Hikers pass me. Most are friendly, wishing me a good hike or nodding and saying hello. It's so unlike the city where no one catches your eye or speaks. I find myself smiling at each person.

A group of two women and two men approach me. I must look a little worse for wear because the man bringing up the rear stops and asks if I'm okay.

"Yes, just taking a breather. The hill and the rocks are kicking my ass."

He laughs along with me, nodding as he quickly glances over my new clothes and gear. "You new to the trail?" he finally asks.

"Never backpacked before starting at Springer four days ago." I nod.

"Thought so." He chuckles. Shifting both hiking poles to his left hand, he thrusts out his right. "I'm Stronghold," he says.

"Easy," I reply, standing and shaking his proffered hand. He has a firm handshake, a short military buzz cut, and an engaging, friendly smile. Glancing uphill at his trailmates, who have continued hiking, he shifts from side to side, clearly debating something in his head.

"You know," he begins hesitantly. "There's a real art to hiking up a rocky trail." Nodding toward the last woman, he continues. "Just Jen has short legs. If she tried to move from rock to rock, she would soon be exhausted. She's learned to take shorter steps. This way, she's only moving part of her body weight with each step. If you move from rock to rock with longer strides, you end up lifting your entire weight each time. Pretty soon, you're exhausted, and your legs are killing you."

I watch the woman he indicated, and as he described, she takes much smaller steps, moving in an almost zigzag direction as she ascends the hill. It looks easier, smoother, and almost effortless.

"Thank you," I say, turning back to Stronghold. "You've been a great help. I'll take your advice."

"You're welcome," he replies. "Good luck, Easy. See you up the trail." Then with a last grin, he follows his trailmates. I watch him leave, weaving his way over, around, and in between the rocks, and then I follow.

Thirteen miles and several hours later, I arrive at Blue Mountain Shelter. Shrugging out of my pack, I flop in a tired heap on the sleeping platform and groan when I realize I still have at least six more miles to go. The trail has been a roller coaster all day—up hills, down hills, dropping into gaps, climbing out of gaps. Even though I've made sure to snack and drink regularly, I'm starving and craving something hot to eat.

Liam has included a couple dinners in my rations. I decide to take the time to build a small fire and boil the water needed to rehydrate one of them. I'm hoping the hot meal will help me get through the rest of the miles waiting for me. His small fire kit works quickly, and soon, I have a full pot of water boiling. After I dump the noodles and sauce mixture into the pan, I set it aside to finish. With fifteen minutes to wait, I pick up the shelter register and thumb through it.

I notice an entry by Yellow and Wonderland. Two names I've seen in other registers. Boyscout's name is there, too, along with his three companions. They appear to be keeping to their twenty-miles-a-day schedule. Of the entries dated yesterday, I laugh when I see a cartoon of two huge backpacks with tiny, stick-thin legs hiking along the trail. Underneath are the names Ghost and M&M and a note about being back on the trail.

Dreamer and Allday were here, too. They signed the register with a short limerick. It reminds me of the one I read at Springer.

I don't see anything signed by Ella, though. Perhaps she didn't stop at this shelter. With a few more minutes to wait, I idly flip through the rest of the notebook. Her unmistakable handwriting covers more than three pages at the very back of the register. Surprised, I begin to read her words.

If last night's entry broke my heart, this one flays the very skin from my body. Her words are fierce, furious, ferocious. A complete thesaurus couldn't contain enough synonyms to describe the feelings of rage and despair that are poured onto the pages she's written. They lash out at me, cutting through my bravado attempts to prove myself worthy of her. Accusations, insults, and blame all wrapped in words of hopelessness and wretchedness. All this—because of me.

She mentions the scarf I bought her. Describes the wonderful day we spent together at the street fair in New York, and then my asking her to wear it on the last day. How devastated she was to find the real reason behind my request. Apparently, she brought it with her on the hike to remind herself how something so beautiful can hide so much ugliness.

She writes of confronting "that" woman, of the photos of the two of us displayed on my old piano, and the large diamond ring thrust so proudly into her face. There is a brief comment about watching me arrive at the condo while she hid in the shadows across the street. Calvin told me she'd just left, and I looked for her but never saw her standing there. What a shock it must have been to see me enter the elevator and go to the condo she thought I was sharing with Gia.

The last page is a condemnation of me and my efforts to steal the business. The papers I neglected to have her sign, the remarks by Vincent about my "staff," diminishing the important roles Oliver, David, and Susan played in the formation of our business and product.

Everything is written in the vaguest of terms. There's no way anyone else would know who she's referring to, and her words are wrapped in enough profanity to make a sailor blush. I've heard her curse a few times but never anything like this. I can't help the slight chuckle when I read them.

As terrible as her entry is, as horrible as I feel when I read it, still there is a bit of hope in the last paragraph. It's a warning to me, and perhaps to anyone else who thinks they can deceive a naïve woman. It's also a promise. She will not go down without a struggle; she will not give up the business or her intellectual property rights. My efforts to cheat her will cost me dearly, not only monetarily but my reputation and my social standing. This woman scorned is not giving up without a fight.

I recall Liam's words about her changing, becoming more assertive, more aggressive. This is what he was talking about; these are the changes he noticed. I'm suddenly thankful he didn't make her return but recognized her right to choose her own path. I'm glad she's angry and ready to fight for herself, even if I'm the cause of the anger. When I find her, I'll explain everything, beg for her forgiveness and try to show her I've changed. All I want is for her to be happy—with or without me, or with someone else—I only want her to be happy.

My determination to catch her renewed, I finish my dinner, pack up my gear, and start hiking again. I still have six miles to go before I sleep.

~ * * * ~

"Hey, Ghost, I found their entry. Looks like she was here a couple days ago."

There's a guy sitting in front of the shelter when I finally reach Tray Mountain. His size matches his voice—big. He has the register open in front of him and is reading the writing there. "Looks like she's hiking with someone named Yellow. Hope for your sake it's another woman and not a man." His booming laugh stops abruptly when he glances up to see me standing in front of him. "Sorry, man," he continues, "Thought you were my buddy. He must still be in the shitter."

Nodding, I sit on the bench across the table from him, fumbling to retrieve my food bag from my pack. "There still room in the shelter for me?" I ask.

"Sure," he answers. "Ghost and I can scrunch over a bit. I'm M&M, by the way," he continues.

"Easy," I answer. "Saw your drawing in the register at Blue Mountain. You the artist?"

"No, that would be Ghost." Frowning, he studies my face. "Don't remember seeing you there yesterday. You camp out somewhere?"

"No, I spent the night at Whitley."

"Wow, that's some big miles today. You must be like some lean, mean, hiking machine or something."

M&M's words bring a grin to my face. "No, no." I shake my head, chuckling. "I'm anything but. Just trying to catch up with someone by the time they reach Nantahala, and I only have about six days to do it."

"Ah." He nods his head wisely. "Same with my buddy, Ghost. His fiancée is out here hiking, and he wants to surprise her. I came along to keep him company. You chasing a woman, too?" he asks with a smirk.

"Actually, yes," I admit.

M&M responds with a big, friendly laugh. He seems good-natured, and I feel comfortable around him. Ghost joins us while we continue to talk. Although not as tall or as muscular as his friend, he still carries himself with a certain air. I get a feeling of strength and determination from him. When

M&M makes some off-handed remark about spending so much time in the privy, Ghost tells him it's better than squatting in the desert.

"You guys ex-military?" I ask.

"Marines," Ghost answers me. "Just got out."

"Thank you for your service," I tell them both. "I met another guy today who looked like he might have been in the armed forces. He gave me some good advice about surviving steep, rocky climbs. Said his name was Stronghold."

"Yeah, he came through here earlier," Ghost replies. "Nice guy."

When I'm finished with my food, I haul my gear into the shelter and set up next to Ghost and M&M. There are several other people in the shelter, too. They're friendly and nod when I introduce myself. It's already dark by the time I clean up and change clothes. My last thoughts are of Ariella. I wonder where she is and what she did today. Sleep comes quickly.

CHAPTER 32

Important Enough to Follow

Date: Friday, March 21

Starting Location: Tray Mountain Shelter

Destination: Plumorchard Gap Shelter

Total Trip Miles: 71.1

Although everyone starts around the same time this morning, it doesn't take long before we're scattered out along the trail. I'm surprised when I end up spending most of my time with Ghost and M&M. I expected them to be much faster than I am—they're certainly fitter because of their military background—but at one of our frequent rest stops, M&M explains he's recovering from a bad fall.

"Yeah." He laughs. "We were going down that nasty hill right before you hit Neels Gap. I was busy stuffing my face and not watching where we were going. Next thing I know, I'm bouncing down the trail. Twisted my ankle pretty bad, but at least, I didn't lose my candy." With a huge grin, he reaches into a side pocket on his pack, pulling out the biggest bag of candy I've ever seen. "Have a handful," he invites before dumping a generous portion into his mouth.

"M&Ms?"

"Best candy in the world," he replies, grinning. "And a good trail name, too."

Ghost joins us during our break. He's quieter than M&M but seems just as friendly.

"How far you thinkin' about going today?" he asks. I can hear a slight Southern drawl when he speaks, and I wonder where he's from.

"Plumorchard. It's about fifteen miles. I'm not carrying a tent, so unless the weather stays this nice, I need to make it to a shelter."

Ghost nods while studying the trail guide. "Looks like Kelly Knob is coming up soon. It's supposed to be really tough. Then we drop into the gap where US 76 crosses the AT. You needin' to go into Hiawassee to resupply?"

"No. I have someone meeting me at Winding Stair in three days. He's bringing me supplies there."

Ghost studies me intently for a moment. He's a bit intimidating, and I wonder if he was an officer. "You *are* in a hurry. She must be important." He grins.

"She is," I assure him.

Kelly Knob is as hard a climb as I've had so far. Rocky and steep, we huff, and puff, and rest. I remember to take small steps and wind back and forth across the trail rather than try to go straight up. Stronghold was right—it makes the climb much easier. When we make it to the top, we're rewarded with amazing views. Ghost believes the mountains we see far to the north could be the Smokies. "They're a hundred trail miles from here," he states. "We should be there in a week or so."

His remark reminds me of Ariella and her time traveler theory. Will I hike those misty, blue mountains with her, or will I be back in New York without her? Our future is still unknown.

The flat summit of Kelly Knob makes a great resting spot, and the three of us decide to eat an early lunch there. "First lunch" as M&M calls it. I find out he's a big Tolkien fan. I also learn he's first aid trained. "The Navy provides medical doctors and personnel for the Marines, but each ground unit has its own first-aid specialist. My job was to stabilize the wounded until they could be evacuated."

When I ask if he plans to do something in the medical field now that he's left military life, he discusses his plans to become a physician's assistant and return to the small, rural community he grew up in. "There's an old clinic there," he explains, "but they can't keep a doctor on staff because it's too isolated, and there isn't enough money to pay for a full-time MD. I can see patients as long as I'm under the supervision of a doctor. There's one in Asheville who's willing to work with me."

"You sound like you've got this all planned."

"Well," he acknowledges, "there's not a lot to occupy your mind over there, so I've had plenty of time to think about it. Just have to get through a bunch of classes." He grins with a shrug.

The four miles to Dicks Creek Gap passes quickly, mainly because it's downhill most of the way. We're surprised to find the parking lot and the picnic area very crowded. The Boy Scout troop that passed me yesterday is putting on a feed for hikers. Several tables are loaded with chips, cookies, and fresh fruit. Water, canned soda, and fruit juice fill ice chests. Scouts and their leaders man several grills, and the tempting aroma of sizzling hamburgers and hot dogs causes my stomach to growl with hunger.

"Oorah! My kind of trail magic," shouts M&M before he jogs to the nearest empty table, shrugs off his pack, and heads to the serving line.

Ghost and I follow at a slightly slower pace. "You ever see anything like this before?" I ask him, still amazed at the food, the people, and the party going on around us. They even have music playing.

"No," he answers. "But I'm not lookin' a gift horse in the mouth. Come on. I'm starving."

One double meat, double cheese with all the fixings hamburger, two hot dogs with mustard, relish, chili, and cheese, two bags of chips, and one apple later, I'm loosening my too-tight pants and groaning in absolute bliss as I watch M&M devour a second plate of cookies that a young, awestruck Boy Scout has handed him.

"I'm not sure I can get up," I moan while resting my head on the table.

"We probably should take a long break here," Ghost agrees. "We still have plenty of time to get to Plumorchard."

Movement at the other end of the parking lot catches my eye. A county sheriff's car and a Georgia State police car have pulled in. We watch three officers get out and begin to walk through the crowd, speaking to groups of hikers as they make their way toward us.

"I wonder what's going on?" M&M mutters.

"Afternoon, gentlemen," the deputy greets us as he sits at our table.

"Officer." Ghost nods. "Is there a problem?"

"Just out warning everyone. A woman hiker was threatened by two men when she came through here three days ago. We're asking everyone to be aware of their surroundings and reminding them to hike with a buddy."

Ghost's body stiffens at the news, and I'm reminded his fiancée is hiking the trail. "Was she hiking with another woman?" he demands. "Was she hurt?"

"No, no," the deputy replies. "Single woman, hiking alone. Darnedest thing, though. See that rock face along the creek over there, just above where the boulder juts out." He points across the road where the trail continues. "She heard them talking and climbed the cliff to get away from them. Even kicked some rocks down on them." The deputy chuckles a little to himself. "Tough little lady. Made one of the men mad though, and he tried to climb up after her."

I'm still examining the cliff face he indicated, worry nagging at me that he could be talking about Ariella. A single woman hiking alone and the date sounds like it could be her.

"What happened?" I hear M&M ask the officer.

"The guy fell and hurt his leg. She got away and made it to Plumorchard where she told everyone what happened. The shelter register has a pretty good accounting of the incident if you want to read it when you get there."

"And the guy?" Ghost prompts.

"Oh, we have a lead on him. A doctor in the area contacted us after reading about it in the paper. He treated a man who said he injured his leg in a fall. He'll be picked up soon. Still, it helps for people to be on the lookout for anyone acting suspicious or—"

"Officer," I interrupt. "Do you know what she looked like? Medium height, long dark brown hair, dark eyes, goes by the trail name Ella?"

He frowns at me, examining me closely with an intimidating stare. "You know something about this, son?" he finally asks.

"No. I mean ... Yes," I stutter as his glare gets more intense. "Liam Crow, the guy at Mountain Crossings?"

"Yeah, I know him. Go on."

"His cousin is out here hiking by herself. She has long, dark hair and goes by Ella. He'll be worried to death when he hears about this."

"I'll let him know. Thanks. You guys stay safe now, ya hear?" With that reminder, he leaves and moves on to the next table.

This time, it's Ghost who's staring at me intently.

"What?" I ask.

"Does Liam Crow know you're out here chasing his cousin?"

"Yes. In fact, he's the one who gave me the new gear and is helping me catch her."

"Okay, okay," he says. "Just needed to know you aren't some crazed stalker or something."

M&M, who has been watching our exchange, starts to laugh at the two of us, but Ghost silences him with a quick glance. Seems neither one of us wants to be on the receiving end of his glare. M&M doesn't back down

233

as quickly as I did, however. Cocking his eyebrow, he answers Ghost with a long, drawn-out, "Yessss, Sirrrrr."

Ghost has the decency to look contrite. "Sorry, M. I guess I'm worried about Al. I know she's with some other hikers, but I won't be happy until we catch her. Didn't mean to go all officer on you."

"It's okay, Bucky. My ankle's good. Let's step up our game and go find your girl."

Nodding, Ghost stands and hefts his backpack. We join him and cross the road together.

The trail to the shelter is fairly easy. Or maybe it seems that way compared to the climb up Kelly Knob. Ghost forges on ahead, leaving M&M and me to bring up the rear.

"So, Markham's your real name?" I ask. "Mine's Hudson."

"Yeah." He stops, holding out his right hand. "Markham Mitchell Manning. Nice to meet you, Hudson—"

"Calder," I finish before shaking his hand. "And Ghost is Bucky?"

Markham grins. "Actually, it's Travis Buchman. Allison, his fiancée, calls him Bucky from time to time. He's okay with her saying it, not so much with me though."

"Where did the name Ghost come from?"

"Oh, that's a good one," he assures me as we start walking again.

It's a bit long and involved, too. Something about Travis being a Marine sharpshooter, sneaking into destinations, taking out his target, and then leaving as quietly as a ghost. He keeps me entertained all the way to Plumorchard Shelter.

~ * * * ~

Travis has his food bag, trail guide, and the register spread out in front of him when we join him at the shelter. "We're three days behind Allison," he explains. "If we skip going into Franklin to resupply, I think we should be able to catch them before Nantahala. How much food do you have, M?"

Markham and I dump our food bags on the table, and Travis begins sorting through everything. "You said you were getting more supplies at Winding Stair?" he questions me.

"Yes. Here," I add, handing him the itinerary Liam prepared for me. "Would this help?"

Travis nods. He examines Liam's notes, does some calculations of his own, and sorts through the food one more time. "Okay, I think I have a plan. It's 63 miles to Nantahala. We can make it there in four days if we push it, and if we don't go into Franklin to resupply. We should catch Allison and Ro … uh, Yellow, somewhere before then. And your girl—?" he adds, glancing at me.

"Ella," I answer his unspoken question.

"Ella, too."

For the next ten minutes, we study Travis's plans, discussing mileage, trail difficulty, and food supplies. If Tator brings me enough, we should be fine skipping Franklin. Travis thinks his fiancée will probably have extra food, and I'm sure Ariella will, too. The last day hiking to the outdoor center could be a long, hungry one, but it'll be worth it if we can find the girls.

Markham pulls out three hot dogs and three oranges he picked up at the hiker feed, and we share those for our dinner. While we eat, I flip through the register and find Ariella's recounting of the incident at the road crossing. It's frightening to read, and even more so because it happened to her. It seems so unlike her, but having read her last angry letter, I'm not really surprised.

Other hikers have added to the page, calling her brave and lucky. Wonderland calls her a badass, take-no-shit hiking girl. When I read her remarks to Travis, he laughs, telling me she must be someone special for Allison to like her. While we're cleaning up and preparing to turn in, I casually flip through the rest of the notebook and find more of her writing in the back. Wanting some privacy when I read it, I decide to wait until later.

It takes almost an hour for everyone in the shelter to settle in and prepare for the night. Finally, when I think everyone is asleep, I grab my headlight and slip out of the shelter, register in hand.

There's a bright, almost-full moon overhead. It bathes the meadow surrounding the shelter in its silvery glow. Slipping around to the back, I find a rock to sit on and lean against the outside wall of the shelter. Then, I open the notebook.

If Ariella's letter about her childhood broke my heart, if her angry message left me raw and bleeding, this note crushes my soul. She shares three things that happened to her, three events that opened a new direction, a new pattern for her life. In her words, I read pride for standing up to the bullies, not only the two who sought to hurt her at the road crossing, but all the ones in the past, especially Gia in New York. They will never make her feel inadequate again.

She hopes I would be proud of her for speaking to the group at the shelter, and I am. I can see her so clearly, bravely facing her fellow hikers and relating the scary events. I'm sure there were plenty of questions afterward, and I imagine her answering them all in her clear, logical manner.

Then she confesses she loves me and says she's sorry she didn't tell me when I spent the night with her. I'm not sure I noticed she didn't say the words back to me. I'd been so wrapped up in my vision of how our life would be I never questioned or doubted she didn't love me. How could she not?

I could spend the rest of my life on my knees begging for her forgiveness, and it wouldn't be enough. Yet I don't have to—because she forgives me. It's written there for the whole world to see. She forgives me and wishes me happiness. Her love is strong enough to let me go, if that's what I want. She has a journey to make, with or without me—she's going forward. And then, she tells me goodbye.

Heartbroken and soul crushed, I clutch the notebook to my chest. I'm not ready to say goodbye. I'm not ready to make my journey without her. Bent over with arms wrapped around myself, I give in to my misery, my loneliness, and my guilt. I'd do anything, give up everything, to be a time traveler and change the past.

There's a rustle in the dry leaves at the edge of the cleared area around the shelter. Startled out of my despair, I look into the woods to see two small eyes glowing in the moonlight as they peer back at me. With a blink, they're gone, only to reappear a short distance away. Some small night animal, I tell myself. It happens two more times, then three. Stare, blink, disappear, reappear somewhere else. I find myself mesmerized by their movement. Gradually, my heart slows. The peace I felt yesterday morning seeps slowly into me.

Sighing, I lean my head back against the shelter wall and stare at the sky above me. I've rarely seen so many stars. The last time was probably when I stayed with Ariella at her granny's cabin when we came down for Liam's wedding. One night, we took an old quilt outside and, after spreading it out over the damp grass, had lain down and watched the stars overhead.

It was the peak of the Lyrids meteor shower, and the sky was filled with shooting stars. In between the streaks of light, she pointed to the constellations above us and kept me entertained with Cherokee stories about the stars.

I wanted to kiss her that night. I should have kissed her. I should have done so many things. Thinking of kissing her reminds me of our first kiss.

We'd been toasting our business success with the champagne I brought. It went to her head quickly. She was giggly, silly, and clumsy with her chopsticks. I took them from her, laughing at her awkward attempts, and began feeding her myself. Distracted by her chocolate eyes, I missed her mouth, leaving a little sauce on her lip. I leaned over and kissed it away. When I pulled back, she was staring at me, eyes wide with surprise, lips quivering slightly. Then, I moved closer and kissed her again. It was a real kiss this time. Her lips were soft and full beneath mine, and somehow, we ended up standing with our arms wrapped around each other. This time when I pulled away, she was smiling shyly at me. "Hudson," she whispered, her voice all low and breathy. "Why did you wait so long?"

"Because I'm an idiot," I whispered back. And then I kissed her again. The kiss led to many more, not only on her lips but every part of her. I knew she had very little experience with boyfriends, love, or sex, for that matter, but she was eager and so responsive to everything we did.

Our first time was slow and unhurried. I wanted her relaxed and ready before we joined our bodies, but it was difficult to restrain myself. It'd been over four years since I'd touched a woman. As soon as I realized I was falling for her, I quit dating completely. No one was as interesting or as fascinating as she was. Now I was here, in her bed, all her beautiful caramel skin exposed to me, ready for me to touch, to kiss, to explore with fingertips and lips. By the time she welcomed me into her body, I was shaking with need.

We fell asleep afterward, arms wrapped around each other, blissful in our exhaustion. Sometime later, she woke me. This time, it was *her* kisses on my skin. *Her* fingertips and *her* lips that explored. She was as passionate and needy as I was, almost demanding in her actions. Her gasps and moans only fueled my desire. Any thoughts of restraint were quickly forgotten.

Later, I lay half-sprawled on top of her, eyes closed, head resting on her chest, listening to her steady heartbeat. I opened my eyes to find her left breast in front of me. Blowing on her nipple, I watched in fascination as the skin rippled and hardened rapidly. This close, I could see the tiny bumps covering the areola. I leaned over, kissing the swell over her heart, adding a tiny bite at the end. Ariella shifted and giggled. I looked up at her, grinning like a naughty boy caught stealing cookies, and marveled at the beautiful, happy woman who smiled back at me.

Thick, luxurious hair covered the pillow around her. Her face was flushed, cheeks a rosy pink, and lips swollen from our kisses. Luminous eyes framed by dark lashes watched me in the dim light of her bedroom. In her face, I saw my future, saw all our tomorrows. We would make our big sale and move our company closer to her home. Eventually, there would be marriage, a house, and children to fill it. I would tell her tomorrow, after our signatures were on the contract with Italia. I would share my thoughts and my plans for our future.

"I love you, my bella mente," I whispered to the woman beneath me. "Now and for always, I love you."

She didn't say it back then, but she did in the register I still clutch to my chest. Opening it, I turn back to her words, reading them over one more time. I realize there is some hope in her last two paragraphs. She wants to be important enough for me to search for. She would choose to make her journey with me rather than without me. Perhaps it's not goodbye after all.

The eyes are once again watching me from the edge of the nearby woods. They seem to grow larger as I stare at them. Dark and luminous, they remind me of Ariella's eyes that night in her room. "I love you, Ariella," I whisper into the darkness around me. "You're important enough to search for, and when I finally find you, we'll make this journey together."

The eyes stare at me for a moment longer before they're gone. I hear the soft pitter-patter of retreating footsteps in the dry leaves before the night is quiet once more. Tired from a long day of hiking, I welcome the warmth and comfort of my sleeping bag. Tomorrow, I'll resume walking toward the woman who can heal my heart and soul. For now, I let the blissfulness of deep sleep work its magic on my worn-out body.

CHAPTER 33
The Fall

Date: Saturday-Monday, March 22, 23 & 24,
Starting Location: Plumorchard Gap Shelter
Destination: Siler Bald Shelter
Total Trip Miles: 110.5

Like a man possessed, or perhaps obsessed, Ghost sets a punishing pace for
the next two days.

Exhausted from days of big miles, hard trail, and the emotional turmoil
from reading her letters, I somehow manage to sleep through most of the
hikers' morning preparations, waking only when my sleeping bag becomes
too warm. Markham is packing his gear when I finally rise and stumble my
way to the privy. I'm sore, my feet hurt, and my back is stiff. I may be a young
man, but I move like an old one. Even his friendly "good morning" does little
to improve my mood.

"Ghost?"

"Left before dawn," he tells me. Then he asks if I need him to stay.

"No, I'll be fine. Go ahead. I'll catch up."

Nodding, he shoulders his pack and leaves the shelter. I notice he limps slightly as he begins hiking, and I wonder if his ankle is giving him trouble. Thirty minutes later, I follow him.

My trail guide mentions an old, gnarled oak tree that marks the state line between Georgia and North Carolina. I pass it some four miles later. It's strange looking—all bent over and growing close to the ground with a crown of antler-looking branches at one end. If I were thru-hiking, I'd probably be celebrating the completion of my first state, but my journey is a different one, and I barely take time to notice it as I walk by.

Ghost and M&M are taking a break in the grassy meadow beyond the oak. As soon as I sit, I'm handed his large bag of candy and told to eat my fill. The sweet, chocolatey treat never tasted so good.

Travis doesn't seem to be able to sit still. Trail guide in hand, he paces the area, muttering about miles, and food, and the girls. Markham watches him warily, and then, finally fed up with his agitation, tells him to go. "Easy and I will rest a little longer, and then meet you on the trail somewhere."

When Travis hesitates, M&M yells at him again. "Go," he demands. "You're driving me crazy with your pacing." Without a backward glance, Ghost takes off.

"Is he all right?"

"Yeah," he finally answers. "He's been in a real temper since we heard the news about those guys at the road crossing yesterday. Ghost has this driving need to protect, ya know. Protect his fellow Marines, protect his fiancée, protect his sister—protect your girl," he adds, grinning. "I guess his father was a real abusive piece of shit, and he blames himself for not taking care of his mom and sister. Course, he was just a kid himself, but … Well, that kind of stuff sticks with a guy."

I consider his words, nodding slowly to myself. When I turn to answer him, I find him examining me closely. "Your girl, is she going to be happy to see you?"

"I hope so."

"What did you do?" he asks quietly.

"Everything and nothing," I finally reply with a long sigh. "Took her for granted mostly. We were in business together. I had everything planned out—money, marriage, children, our future. Everything I wanted. Problem was I forgot to include her in the planning. Thought I was *protecting* her from the ugly parts of life," I finish with a disgusted huff.

Shaking my head, I stare down at the ground between my bent knees, absently plucking at the grass growing there. M&M says nothing, letting me gather my thoughts. "Someone from my past reared her ugly head, and because I wasn't open and sharing with her, she believed the worst and left. Now, she's out here hiking, convinced I'm a cheater and a thief."

"What do you intend to do when you find her?"

"Grovel," I admit.

"Sounds like a plan." He laughs, reaching for his backpack. "Come on," he adds. "We've got a mountain to climb, and I understand it's a real doozy."

He's right. Standing Indian Mountain is a huge, hulking monster of a mountain. We walk and walk and walk. Sometime during the long, never-ending uphill trek, Markham gradually pulls ahead of me. I seem to be getting slower and slower. To make matters worse, I'm hungry. I've heard about "hiker hunger." It's a constant need to fill a stomach that never seems to get full. I didn't expect it to hit me this soon though. Thinking about yesterday's trail magic from the Boy Scouts only makes my stomach growl louder.

Mid-afternoon, I stop and examine my food bag. I'm carrying only enough for the rest of today and tomorrow. The extras have been added to Travis and Markham's rations. I'll be resupplying the day after tomorrow when I meet Tator. I snack, drink, and move on.

When I finally get to the shelter near the top of the mountain, Ghost and M&M aren't there. They've decided to hike another mile or two and are waiting for me at a camping spot farther along on the trail. With a weary sigh, I trudge on.

The aroma of cooking food greets me even before I reach their camp. Ghost takes one look at me and quickly removes my pack, handing me a pot full of piping hot beans and rice topped with corn chips and cheese. He's even prepared a large bottle of sweet lemonade. I have to make myself eat slowly.

While I eat, they finish setting up camp. They're using their tent as a ground cover and unroll our bags and pads on top of it. The weather's nice, and we'll cowboy camp tonight. Travis takes care of my gear, arranging everything neatly and conveniently beside my bed. He doesn't say much, just glances at me from time to time. I'm not in a mood to talk to him either. When I'm finished with my meal, he takes the pot, cleans it, and packs it away.

Finally, he sits down on the log beside me. "Sorry about today," he says. "I really need to be alone sometimes. You, uh … You okay?"

"Yes, just hungry and really tired."

He nods his head in answer, then shifts nervously before he speaks again. "I thought maybe if we did a couple more miles today, it would make tomorrow a little easier."

"Sounds reasonable," I answer, still not warming up to him.

"Well, okay," he finally says. Standing, he points to a trail that leads off to the side. "There's a nice spring down there. You should probably clean up, and then turn in. It's been a long day, and we've got another long one tomorrow."

Still sitting on my log, I look up at Travis. He's a good-looking guy, fit and muscular from years in the service. Blond curls peek from under a battered cowboy hat. He stands like a Marine officer, talks and moves like someone who's used to giving orders and being obeyed. I can see Markham sitting on another log behind Travis. He's watching me, a slight smirk on his face as if he suspects what I'm about to do. Standing, I face Travis, coming to attention. "Yesss, Sirrr," I answer, mimicking M&M's answer from yesterday.

Markham howls in laughter and nearly falls off his log. I'm laughing as hard as he is. Travis looks back and forth between the two of us, trying to maintain his scowl, but soon he, too, is laughing with us. "Assholes," he mutters, shaking his head as he walks to his bedroll. "Go to bed."

Tension relieved and friendship restored, we do just that.

~ * * * ~

The second day of "Travis Buckman's Forced March," as I call it in my head, begins at the crack of dawn.

Sleeping outside was a new experience for me. With nothing above me but sky, I stargazed until I could no longer keep my eyes open. The temperature dropped sometime during the night, and I found myself pulling the hood of my sleeping bag snug around my face, leaving only my nose exposed to the cold night air. Exiting the warmth of my down bag was an exercise in stubborn determination.

I feel better today. A hot dinner and a solid night's sleep make for a happier hiker. The trail helps, too. It drops down off the mountain in a series of long, gradual switchbacks that are easy on the knees and back. My pack is the lightest it's been. With very little weight from food, water, and gear, I almost forget it's on my back.

Ghost is in a much better mood. Maybe it's the big miles we're doing, or maybe because we're one day closer to his fiancée, but he stays with M&M and me most of the time. He makes sure we eat, drink, and take rest breaks more often, too.

The hardest climb comes twelve miles into the day. Albert Mountain rears its steep, rocky face in front of us. A few log stairs are built into the trail, but it's mostly a hand-over-hand rock scramble up the almost straight cliff. At times, I'm so bent over my face is only inches from the ground.

The fire tower on top offers a great place to rest and cool off. Markham takes off to the edge of the woods, saying he has a date with a bush, while

Travis and I climb the tower. The cool breeze dries our sweat as we gaze at the forested mountains spread out before us. I'm still a little uncomfortable around him and try to think of some topic to start a conversation.

"M&M told me he wants to go into the medical field now his service is over. Do you have plans?" I finally ask.

Ghost nods, still staring at the view before us. "I always wanted to be a teacher. Before I joined the Marines, I planned to get an advanced degree in history with an emphasis in military campaigns. Thought I would teach at the university level.

"I grew up around guns—it's hard not to when you're from Texas," he explains with a slight smile. "And I was always fascinated by everything concerning the armed forces. My nana wasn't very happy when I left graduate school and enlisted, but I wanted to serve my country. I thought I was keeping us safe from our enemies."

"And now?" I prompt after he doesn't speak for several minutes.

"Now, I'm not so sure," he finally continues. "I knew I would probably have to kill people. But they weren't *real* people. They were the nameless, faceless enemy, and I was good with it. When they made me a sniper, it all became personal."

He shifts around to face me, watching my reaction as he continues his story. "When you look down the scope of your rifle, you see a person. They're someone's husband, brother, son. I killed them. I squeezed the trigger of my gun and watched my bullet enter their head and blow the back of it off. They weren't nameless or faceless anymore."

I stare at him, speechless by the painful truth of his revelation. "Travis, I didn't realize … I didn't know—"

"Don't," he interrupts. "It's okay. I'm okay. But you can understand why I don't want to teach military history anymore," he continues with a slight smile. "I still want to teach, but now it's going to be art. Painting and drawing have helped me deal with some of my issues. I want to get certified as an art therapist and use it to help other vets like me."

Turning his attention back to the scene before us, he stares off into the distance, lost in his thoughts and memories. I say nothing, thinking about the two men I'm hiking with. Both are a few years older than me, both have served their country under some of the worst conditions, and both of them have decided to use their talents and interests to help other people. *What have I done?* I ask myself. Building the business and making money don't seem as important as they once did.

We pull into Rock Gap Shelter as the sun sets. It's the end to a long, tiring, eighteen-mile day. Depending on how much time Allison and Ariella spent in Franklin, it's very possible we will catch them tomorrow or the day after. It makes the long miles worthwhile. Travis cooks our last meal. With only snacks left in our food bags, my resupply tomorrow can't come quickly enough. Markham and I unpack and set up. An hour later, we're asleep.

~ * * * ~

When you get up with the sun, you start your hike early. The problem with starting early is getting to your destination *way* too soon. With only three miles to Winding Stair Gap, we arrive long before Tator does. I'm not sure when Liam asked him to be here, but I know it wasn't *this* early. We can't skip this resupply, and we can't hitch into Franklin and risk the chance of missing him. We're stuck.

Travis is antsy again. He paces, mutters, and scowls at the empty parking lot. Markham and I watch calmly from our seats at the picnic table while we eat a trail bar. Finally, when I can't take any more, I call him over.

"Take this," I say, emptying the contents of my food bag on the table. "Take what I have and go. This and what you have left should get you and M through today and maybe tomorrow. By then, you'll have caught up with

Allison and maybe Ella, if they're together. I'll wait for Tator and start as soon as I can. If he has any extra food, I'll bring it, too."

Travis can't seem to make up his mind. He glances at the food, at M, at me, at the clouds rolling in overhead.

"Go," I urge. "Go find your girl. I'll be fine."

Finally, he nods. "Okay," he agrees and begins gathering up the food on the table. "Looks like the weather is getting colder. You gonna be all right?"

"Yes."

"You got enough clothes?"

"Yesss, sirrr." I laugh. "Wool long johns, hiking pants, and rain pants to put over them. Wool sleeping shirt, two T-shirts, and my rain jacket to cover those. A knit cap and a hood. Extra pair of socks for my hands. I'll be fine, Ghost. Just go."

"Wayah Bald is ten miles," he tells me. "We can camp inside the tower on top if the weather turns bad or push on to Cold Springs Shelter, which is another six miles from there. Depending on conditions, we'll meet you at Wayah or we'll leave you a note there."

"Sounds good," I agree.

"Be careful," he adds before he and M&M make their way across the road and into the woods on the other side.

With nothing to do but wait, I crawl up onto the top of the table. The temperature is dropping, so I pull out my sleeping bag. Then, using my pack for a pillow, I fall asleep.

~ * * * ~

"Hey," a voice wakes me. "You Hudson?"

"Yes," I mutter, sitting up with a groan.

The older man standing in front of me smiles. "Sorry to wake you. Name's Tator," he explains, holding out his hand for me to shake. "I have

247

some supplies for you, but you might want to reconsider staying on the trail. Looks like a pretty nasty storm headed our way. I can take you into Franklin, and you can wait it out there, if you want."

"Can't. The two guys I'm hiking with went on ahead. One of them is trying to catch his fiancée. They're almost out of food and need the supplies you have."

Tator grimaces at my explanation. "Do you know the girls' names? Maybe they're still in Franklin, too."

"His fiancée is Wonderland. She's hiking with someone named Yellow. Ella may be with them, too. Have you seen them?"

"Yeah, brought them back here late yesterday afternoon. I'm guessing they probably spent the night at Siler Bald. Should be on their way up to Wayah by now."

I frown at his news. "And the storm?" I ask. "Why did they start if bad weather is coming?"

"Not sure they knew," he answers. "The weather forecast said the storm would track north of us. They were predicting cold temperatures and the chance of some snow, but nothing like they say we're going to get now. You really need to think about staying here. It's going to be pretty nasty up there on the top." Glancing northward toward the mountain looming above us, he continues. "If you're going, you need to start soon. There's a rocky ridgeline part of the way up. It's exposed and open to the wind and rain. When it starts freezing, it's going to be very dangerous.

"If you make it past the rocks, you can hole up in Siler Bald Shelter or even Wayah Tower. But I really wish you'd reconsider. No one's sure how bad this storm's going to be. The mountains make everything much worse."

I listen to his warning. My brain tells me to stay, but it's overruled by my longing to see Ariella again and the knowledge that Travis and Markham are relying on the supplies I'm supposed to be bringing.

"I need to go," I tell Tator. "They're expecting me and need the food you have."

"Okay." He nods. "Let's get you loaded up and on your way."

Tator's van is full of supplies: food, first aid, stove fuel, anything a hiker might need. He helps me pick out enough food for three people for three days. Although we opt for the lightest possible choices, my food bag is still heavy when we finish. I can tell he's not happy about my decision, but he helps me into my backpack and gives me some tips on balancing the load.

"I'm going to call Liam when I get back to my house," he tells me. "I'll tell him you went on and his cousin is still hiking, too. If this turns into a full-blown blizzard, we'll at least know where you are."

"Thanks for your help," I tell him. Then I cross the road and hike out.

The physical movement warms me quickly, and I'm okay for the first mile. As soon as the trail begins climbing and I leave the shelter of the forest, conditions begin to deteriorate. The wind is blowing hard out of the north, and I'm hiking straight into it. The temperature drops dramatically.

I find a small copse of trees, which provides some shelter from the wind, and quickly strip out of my pants and shirt. My wool long johns and top go on first, followed by my pants, long-sleeved shirt, and then to be safe, the rain pants and jacket. I pull my knit cap over my head and secure the rain hood over it. Extra socks cover my hands.

Feeling much warmer now, I eat a quick snack and drink my fill. Then it's back to hiking.

Another mile passes. The trail is steep and exposed, and I feel drops of moisture from time to time. I'm not worried, however. I'm warm, fed, and sufficiently hydrated. Most of all, I'm feeling strong and confident. I keep climbing.

Almost before I realize it, I'm on the rocky ridgeline Tator warned me about. There's no trail here, just white blazes painted on the sides and tops of huge boulders. Arrows point the way over, under, and around rocks the size of cars and small houses. My progress slows to a crawl, literally. Standing is almost impossible in some places, so I crouch, crawl, and sometimes wiggle my way through the rocky maze. I'm on the top of one boulder, about halfway through, when I feel the first sting of ice.

Indecision glues me in place. Looking behind me, I can see down the way I've already come. Ahead of me is more of the same, yet I can also see the end of the ridgeline and the beginning of a more normal dirt trail. Do I go back, or do I go forward? Standing there, braced against the wind, I wait to see if the ice gets any worse. It doesn't, so I resume hiking. I've gone another quarter of the way upward when the storm hits in earnest. Sleet pours down in a solid sheet. It pings off the rocks, bouncing around almost like hail. I'm off my feet and lying flat on my stomach as quickly as I can. There is no staying here. Somehow, I need to either make it to the end of this rock pile or manage to find a corner or crevice where I can shelter.

Inch by inch, I creep across the rocks, sometimes on hands and knees, sometimes on my stomach, pulling myself along with hands that are quickly becoming numb. The most difficult stretches are those requiring me to lower myself down to a rock below me, or hop from one rock to another over a small open space. I can imagine that this would be fun on a warm, sunny day—almost like a rock jungle gym. Today, it is not fun—it's dangerous, and I'm scared. The first time I have to jump across to another rock, my foot slips when I push off. I manage to land safely, albeit on all fours. My knees hurt, but I'm not seriously injured. I take a few moments to catch my breath, willing my heart rate to slow down. The end of the rocks isn't far away; the dirt trail is just beyond them.

The sleet slows down, and the first flakes of snow begin to appear. I can see into the valley below. The storm hasn't hit there yet. The edge of the ice-laden cloud is beginning to slide down the mountain into the town. Above me is all white—clouds, snow, and a massive storm boiling in from the north. It's beautiful in its own way, but I don't have time to watch it right now. I need to get off the rocks, onto the trail, and into the next shelter. Standing,

I look for the blazes, tracing their path across the rocks, and planning a slow, careful, safe route. I creep across them. One rock done. Two finished, and then three. I'm almost to the end when I hear a shout behind me. Turning quickly, I look, worrying someone is in trouble and needing help.

In a split second, I know it is the wrong thing to do. Turning has thrown me off balance and my feet slide across the ice-shrouded rock. I try to stop myself with my hiking poles, but they find no grip on the surface. They skitter across the top, flying in opposite directions even as my feet skid toward the edge of a boulder.

With a desperate lunge, I throw myself onto my stomach, grabbing at anything protruding from the rock face. There is nothing. The ice has coated everything with a smooth layer of slick evenness.

I'm sliding … sliding.

The edge of the boulder looms closer, and I can feel my legs dangling into the nothingness below me. A final twist throws me onto my side, my backpack slowing my descent slightly. I can see a rock ledge below me. If I can land on it, I might be able to stop my fall there. It comes too quickly though, and I hit it much too hard. A sharp pain rockets through my leg and it gives way, tumbling me forward. I can see a rough edge of rock rushing toward my face. At the last minute, I manage to turn my head, the left side of my face taking the brunt of the impact. It scrapes across the coarse granite, the skin burning as it shreds. Pain blooms around my eye and jaw. The sharp taste of blood fills my mouth.

Still, I fall.

A scream born of pain and fear escapes as I watch the rocks rush up to meet me. I land on my left side. My backpack absorbs some of the impact and cushions me from the hard surface upon which I'm lying. Stunned, shocked, and gasping for breath, I stare at the small patch of sky I can see through the opening in the rocks above me. The snow is blowing sideways, and for some strange reason, I find this to be funny. The chuckle that escapes me brings on a searing wave of fresh pain. Another scream, and then another.

Somewhere deep in the recesses of my logical brain, a voice is urging me to try to get into my sleeping bag. It tells me I need to protect myself from the cold until someone comes to save me. It hurts too much to move, and I'm already very, very cold.

"Ariella, my beautiful bella mente," I whisper into the freezing air around me. "I'm sorry, so sorry." My words seep away from me, leaking out through the rocks where the wind grabs them, flinging them away into the cold, uncaring winter storm.

CHAPTER 34

The Rescue

Ariella

Date: Tuesday, March 25

Starting Location: Siler Bald Shelter

Destination: Siler Bald Shelter

Total Trip Miles: 110.5

Throughout the long night, Allison and Markham take turns watching Hudson. While one sleeps, the other sits beside him, checking his vital signs and making sure he's warm and resting comfortably. His face and hair have been cleaned. The wounds covered in antibiotic ointment and wrapped in bandages. They've closed the long gash on his forehead with surgical glue. Although his eye is still swollen and the bruising will take a long time to disappear, Allison doesn't think he's broken any bones around his eye or his jaw. She assures me the blood in his mouth was probably from his lip.

The most troubling injury is his broken leg. After a great deal of discussion, they decide to set the bone. It needs to be cleaned, sterilized, and stabilized. It's a procedure Allison has done many times. She and M&M examine it closely, plan each step, and gather the supplies they need. Then, with all of us restraining him, they pull and snap the bone back in place. Hudson awakens with a scream.

Allison is prepared for him to regain consciousness. She's crushed several ibuprofens and dissolved them into a small amount of water for him to swallow. I dribble it slowly into his mouth while he stares up at me, swallowing roughly around each sip. One lone tear trickles down his cheek, and I kiss it away, telling him how much I love him and how everything is going to be fine. He doesn't try to speak but grimaces from time to time while Allison finishes her work on his leg. He watches me until his eye slowly closes and he goes back to sleep.

I refuse to leave his side. No Filter makes me put on all my layers of clothing, gives me hot soup to drink, then wraps me in my sleeping bag. I sit, holding Hudson's hand, watching his face in the dim light of the candle lantern until I eventually nod off.

I wake in the cold silence of the shelter. The wind has stopped blowing, and we're wrapped in the hushed stillness that follows a heavy snowfall. Markham is sitting on Hudson's other side, and he nods and smiles at me when he sees my eyes are open.

Behind him, I can see Travis, Allison, and Rosemary wrapped in their down bags, sound asleep. I must have laid down sometime during the night because I'm stretched out on the floor beside Hudson. Confused, I sit up, looking around for the other two men. That's when I realize my head has been resting in Curly Dan's lap. "Sorry," I mutter, wiping drool from the side of my mouth.

"It's quite all right," he answers. "Rather, it is I who owe you and Hudson an apology." He's using his very proper British accent, and I frown, not understanding his meaning. "I'm afraid he may have fallen because of me."

"What?" I'm still confused.

"No Filter and I were following your Hudson up the ridgeline. He was doing quite well, in spite of the sleet and snow. Smart chap. He was staying low, crawling when he needed to, and moving slowly and carefully. He was very close to the end when I slipped and inadvertently cried out. We saw him turn toward the sound, lose his balance, and then fall. So, you see, Miss Ariella, I'm responsible for his condition, and I am deeply sorry."

"Oh, Dan, no." Twisting myself around, I wrap my arms around him, hugging him through our multiple layers of clothing and sleeping bags. "It's not your fault. You couldn't have known he would fall. Did you and No Filter get to him first?"

"Yes. We hurried as much as we could under the abysmal conditions. He'd fallen onto a rock ledge. Ron lowered me down to him, and I managed to get him into his sleeping bag. Then I tried to lift him high enough for Ron to grab the bag. We were having a devil of a time until Ghost and M&M arrived. With all four of us lifting and pulling, we managed to get him back on top, and then off the rocks. I'm afraid our jostling was quite painful, however."

I cringe to think what it must have been like for him. Glancing back, I watch Markham take his temperature and listen to his breathing and heartbeat. "Everything okay?" I ask, keeping my voice to a whisper.

"Yes." He nods back to me. "I'm sorry, too, Ariella. We shouldn't have left him at Winding Stair by himself. We should've stayed together. An extra hour or two wouldn't have made any difference in the long run. I guess I've forgotten how quickly the weather can change in these mountains."

"What was he doing there?" I ask, confused by his confession.

"Waiting for supplies. Liam Crow arranged for Tator to bring him food so he wouldn't have to go into Franklin. He was trying to catch up to you before you got to Nantahala. And we were trying to catch Allison, too."

I nod, putting all the pieces together. They click into place, forming a pattern of events in my head. "Then Liam and Tator know we're all up here on the mountain somewhere. Liam would know I wouldn't stay on Wayah Bald—it's too exposed. So, he'll assume either Cold Springs Shelter or here. This is the most likely place, given our late starts. I think we can expect some type of rescue attempt later tomorrow."

Looking around for No Filter, I start to ask where he is when something Dan said finally registers in my brain. "Wait." I frown. "Who's Ron?"

Curly grins at me, chuckling softly. "He never told you? It's No Filter's real name. He's outside boiling water," he adds, nodding toward the tent curtain beside us.

I let my gaze wander around our little enclosure. The fabric barrier has done a good job keeping the wind out, and the layers of plastic and ground-covers are sealing out the cold beneath us. While not warm, it's at least cozy with the flickering glow of the candle in its holder. Standing, I stretch, trying to loosen my cramped muscles. "Going to the privy," I explain when I duck outside the curtain wall.

I'm immediately struck by intense cold. The air I suck in burns its way down my throat. No Filter has all the stoves going and is boiling water over each one. They're grouped in a circle close to him, and I can actually feel the heat radiating from them. He grins at me when I join him.

"I should have moved these inside," he says. "It would've put out some heat, but I was afraid of making too much noise."

"Travis and the girls are asleep right now," I tell him. "Markham and Dan are watching Hudson."

"Curly feels awful about what happened."

"I know, but he shouldn't. It wasn't his fault. I'm just glad you were there to help Hudson. So, hot water?" I ask, after several minutes of silence.

"Wind's died down," he finally says. "Which usually means the temp is going to drop like a rock. The coldest part of the night is in the next couple of hours. We're going to start feeling it really soon. So, hot water for the bladders and for some soup and hot cocoa."

It's still very dark outside the shelter overhang, but the sky must be clearing because I can see a few stars in the sky. The snow in the meadow glows in their dim light. Although it's hard to judge, I'd guess there's at least three feet of snow on the ground.

"Wow," I mummer to myself.

"I know," he whispers back to me. "It's beautiful but deadly."

Several more minutes of silence pass between us as we stare at the scene. The clouds must be dissipating because moonlight paints a shimmering path across the pristine whiteness.

The water is boiling, and No Filter turns off the stoves. I hold the bladders open as he pours the water into them, then screws on the lids. We use one pot for hot chocolate and empty several packages of dried soup into another.

"Thanks, *Ella*." He grins. "Or is it *Ariella*?"

"You're welcome, *No Filter*." I grin back. "Or is it *Ron*?"

His answering chuckle matches mine. "Ronald Ulrich, at your service," he says, extending his right hand and bowing slightly.

"Ariella Dobbs at yours," I reply, shaking his hand. "Well, I came out here to make a quick trip to the privy," I explain as I start to step away.

"Ariella ..." Ron stops me before I leave. "I need to know if that's *the* Hudson Calder in there."

"Yes. But how did you know?"

"I worked for the caterer who did the food for several of his parents' charity functions. I thought he looked familiar. After the sun comes up, Dan and I are going to hike up to the summit of Siler Bald and try to make an emergency phone call. When the authorities contact his family, I'm sure they'll insist on speeding up the rescue efforts."

"You have a phone? Will it work out here?"

"Yes, and yes. After what happened to Rock Dancer, we've made sure to carry a phone capable of sending emergency messages. He tried it a few hours ago but couldn't get any response. With the storm dying down, we'll have a better chance of reaching someone, especially from the summit."

"The snow's really deep, Ron. Are you sure you'll be okay?"

"We're going to take the side trail to the top. Most of it is protected by forest, and it should be easier going. Dan and I have hiked in these conditions in the Sierras. We'll be fine. Now, I better get these water bladders inside before they cool off." He crawls behind the fabric curtain, and I hand him the bladders followed by the pots of hot chocolate and soup. I hear him whisper to Markham as they begin to pass them out.

With our conversation over, I'm suddenly very cold. When I step around the corner of the shelter to use our makeshift privy, my legs sink into snow up to my knees. I can't imagine how deep it is out in the open, unprotected area of the meadow. I want to tell Ron and Dan not to go, but Hudson needs to get to a hospital, and I have to trust they know what they're doing.

When I reenter the shelter, I find Allison has replaced M&M. I'm shaking uncontrollably, and she frowns in disapproval. "Get into your sleeping bag, Ella. I don't need another patient."

My bag is situated beside Hudson. When I crawl in, I find a warm bladder at my feet. The heat feels amazing, and before I finish yawning, I'm asleep. The next time I open my eyes, I'm staring into familiar green ones. "You're awake," I exclaim, sitting up quickly.

"Come back, please. I need to look at you."

Lying down, I situate myself on my side, facing him. I watch him watch me.

"Ariella," he finally says after a long, drawn-out sigh. "I'm sorry. Everything Gia told you, everything you thought was happening, was a lie. All of it was a lie, and I'm so sorry."

Touching my fingertip to his lips, I urge him to stop. "It wasn't all your fault, but you need to rest. Shh, don't talk."

"Not talking, not telling you everything, not sharing, is what got us into this situation. I should have—" He swallows roughly. There's a small bottle of water nearby, and I grab it, letting a small amount trickle into his mouth. "Thank you," he croaks, swallowing again.

"How are you feeling?"

"Head hurts," he finally admits. "Leg hurts. Feels like I got hit by a bus." His slight chuckle turns into a groan of pain. "Do you think I could have some more pain medicine?"

The shelter is empty except for the two of us and Markham, who's sleeping in a far corner. When I peek around the curtain, I find Travis, Allison, and Rosemary sitting at the wooden table.

"Hudson's awake and asking for pain medicine. Can he have more?" I ask Allison. With a nod, she tells me there is some ibuprofen in a small cup next to him.

"I'm heating him some broth, too. It'll be ready in a minute," she continues.

I help Hudson sip the dissolved pills. When Allison enters, she checks his vitals. "You're running a little fever and your blood pressure is low, but otherwise, you seem to be doing okay, considering the nasty fall you took yesterday. We've set your broken leg and cleaned the wounds on your head. You have a concussion, so please rest and not too much talking. Okay?" She finishes with a smile. "I'm Allison, by the way."

"Nice to meet you, Allison. Thank you for taking good care of me."

"You're welcome, Hudson. See if you can get a little of this broth down, and then I want you to rest again. No Filter and Curly Dan are trying to contact the authorities with his emergency phone. We hope to get you out of here this afternoon. You'll need your strength when they start moving you."

Hudson manages to sip most of the broth. After he's finished, Allison hands him a plastic bottle with a large letter "P" written on the side. "This is Travis's 'I'm-not-getting-out-of-the-tent-in-the-middle-of-the-night' bottle." She laughs. "I thought you might be getting uncomfortable and would like to relieve yourself."

Allison laughs again when he stutters an embarrassed, "Thank you."

"I'm a nurse. I've seen it all," she reminds him before leaving.

Afterward, he falls asleep quickly. Travis brings fresh hot water bottles, and we place them around Hudson, making sure he's warm enough. Then, we leave to let him get more rest. I join everyone else at the picnic table where Travis has cooked a meal. I'm starving, and the hot food tastes so good.

The storm has passed, and the sky is a fresh, clear blue. Clean, undisturbed snow covers the meadow in front of the shelter as well as every limb, branch, and twig. The bright sunshine transforms everything into a sparkling kaleidoscope of shimmering white. It's breathtakingly beautiful, but like everything in nature, it can be deadly, too.

Recalling No Filter's words from the night before reminds me of their trek to contact help. When I look around for them, I realize they're still nowhere in sight. "How long have they been gone?" I ask.

"Almost six hours," Travis answers me. "I expect we'll hear something very—" He stops, listening intently. "Soon." He grins.

The whining sound of motors gets louder and louder, and soon, four snowmobiles burst from the woods and come to a quick halt in front of the shelter. The driver of the first one jumps off, rushing to me, before picking me up in a bone-crushing hug.

"Dear God, Ari. I've been so worried about you," exclaims my cousin. "And Hudson," he continues with a rush. "Where is he? How is he?"

"He's inside and is doing as well as can be expected."

Liam takes off his helmet and looks around quickly. He surveys the curtain we've pieced together from tents and nods in appreciation. "Good job," he tells me before ducking inside the sheltered area.

He's kneeling beside Hudson when I enter. I hear only bits of their murmured conversation, but he tells him how sorry he is. Hudson makes some kind of joke about rocks not being his friend, and my cousin grimaces. Before I can ask what he means, Liam starts explaining what will happen in the next hour or so.

"There's a medevac helicopter on its way. It'll be tight, but they think they can land in the clearing. They're going to take you to the hospital in Gainesville. An orthopedic specialist is on his way from Atlanta. He and the other doctors will examine you there. Your parents are on their way, too."

"Ariella and the others?" Hudson asks.

"The snowmobiles are capable of holding four people. We'll buddy up and get everyone off the mountain and back to Franklin."

"No, no. I want her with me. We've been apart too long, and I need to talk to her. Please," he begs. "Don't leave me."

"Easy, easy," Liam tries to calm him. "My truck is in Franklin. I'll take her with me to Neels Gap, get her fed and cleaned up, and then drive her to Gainesville. She'll be there by the time the doctors get finished with you."

"But—"

"He's right," I interrupt before he becomes more agitated. "There won't be room for me in the helicopter, and I do need a shower and something to eat. We'll get there as soon as we can. I promise. I'm not leaving you again. I'll come."

Our conversation is cut short by the whump, whump of a nearing helicopter. It lands in the clearing, throwing up a whirlwind of snow. Two medics emerge, running into the shelter with a stretcher and other medical equipment. Allison meets them, and they start examining Hudson.

The rest of us step outside and begin cleaning up and repacking our gear. In no time, they've strapped him to a stretcher, inserted an IV, and secured him in the helicopter. I'm barely able to kiss him goodbye and promise to see him soon before they lift off in another flurry of swirling snow. Behind me, I can hear my friends gathering everything and loading the snowmobiles, but I don't join them. Instead, I stand knee-deep in the aftermath of the storm, watching the man I love fly away from me.

"I'm coming, love. I'm coming," I whisper to the departing helicopter.

CHAPTER 35

The Journey Is the Destination

Date: Wednesday, March 26
Starting Location: Siler Bald Shelter
Destination: The Journey
Total Trip Miles: Forever

Contrary to what Liam told Hudson, it was actually the next day before I arrived at the hospital in Gainesville. After the helicopter left, we dismantled our tent curtain, rolled up and stored the plastic sheeting, and packed away all our gear. The search and rescue team that responded to Curly Dan's emergency call were driving heavy-duty, multi-person vehicles. Each one was capable of holding up to four people. I rode behind Liam, with each couple settling in on the other three machines. With all our gear, it was a tight fit.

They'd cobbled together a route from Franklin using forest roads, trails, and open meadows. It took them to the AT cut-off trail below Siler Bald summit where they met and picked up Curly Dan and No Filter. We took the same route back, and it was slow going. The deep snowfall hid all kinds of obstacles. No one wanted another injury, even if it were minor.

Although Liam offered to let everyone stay free of charge at Neels Gap until the snow melted and conditions improved, they decided to stay in Franklin. A quick warm-up was expected, and the three couples planned to continue their hike. We exchanged phone numbers and email addresses, and then—amid hugs, a few tears, and promises to keep in touch—I climbed into Liam's truck and left behind six people who were very special and very dear to me. Strangers once, they were now my best friends—all of us brought together by our journey on the Appalachian Trail.

It was dark when we finally arrived at Neels Gap. Emma had a hot meal waiting. I ate, showered, and collapsed on the bed in their guest room. Although worried about Hudson, exhaustion took me, and I slept soundly until the next morning.

We're eating a quick breakfast the next morning when I realize Emma and Liam are staring at me. "What?" I ask.

"You cut your hair," Emma says. "I can't believe it. You actually cut your hair, and it's curly."

Running a hand through my short locks, I grin at her. "Yeah, did it in Franklin. I've worn a knit cap for so many days I've actually forgotten about it."

"What did Hudson say?" she asks.

"He never really saw it. We were all so bundled up."

Emma continues to search my face. "I like it," she finally says. "You look different. Part of it is probably the hair, but I think you've lost weight, especially in your face. I wonder if you'd like to use some of my makeup, just a bit on the cheekbones and eyelashes," she finishes tentatively.

I smile back at my cousin-in-law. "I'd like that. Thank you, Emma."

Not only does Emma help me with my hair and makeup, but she insists I borrow several outfits to take with me to see Hudson. "You can't wear your hiking clothes in the hospital," she reminds me. She hugs me goodbye, wishes me good luck, and waves when Liam and I drive away.

Hudson's parents arrived sometime during the night. When we ask at the desk, we learn they've moved him to a private, VIP suite. The nurse escorts us through to his rooms after she finds our names on the admittance list. Both his mom and dad hug me when we enter. "He's been anxiously waiting to see you," Patricia tells me, ushering me toward the bed.

"You came." He smiles slightly, his lips still too swollen to move very much. He holds out a hand toward me, and I take it, moving closer to his bed. The bandages on his face have been changed, and he looks cleaner, but when I place my hand on his cheek, I can feel the heat radiating from him.

"You're flushed. Do you have a fever?"

"Some," he admits. "Allison and Markham did a great job, under the circumstances. The doctors were impressed, but still, the conditions weren't the cleanest. I probably have some infection in some of the wounds. The antibiotics should take care of it soon."

"And your leg?"

"Orthopedist said he couldn't have done any better setting it." He reaches down to thump the cast encasing his leg. "He wants to offer Allison a job," he finishes with a cough. It's followed by another. This one is deeper and rougher sounding.

"Hudson?"

Patricia steps up beside me and hands him a cup with a straw. "We're keeping a close watch on his lungs," she tells me. "No signs of pneumonia yet."

Liam leaves after a short conversation with Hudson and another hug for me. I'm reminded to contact him if anything happens.

Hudson sleeps most of the day. He wakes from time to time, talks a little, manages to eat and drink small amounts, but returns to sleep quickly. Sometime during the night, his fever peaks. I wake to find him surrounded by a doctor and two nurses, who are bathing him with tepid water.

Patricia holds my hand as we watch, squeezing it from time to time when the deep bruising on his body is revealed. His whole left side is black and blue. It's much worse than I expected. His private nurse insists we go back to sleep, promising to wake us if he worsens.

When I emerge from the guest suite the next morning after taking time to shower, fix my hair, and apply some of Emma's makeup, I find him sitting up in bed looking and feeling much better. The dressing covering his left eye has been removed, and although it's still swollen and very bruised, he's able to see just fine, he assures me.

He frowns at me slightly as I walk closer. Then his eyes widen as he takes in the changes in my appearance. For a moment, I falter, the small child who needs to please others rearing its scared head. But then she's gone, and the more confident woman who found herself on the trail emerges once more.

"You look amazing," he tells me, his gaze roaming over every part of me. "I always loved your long hair, always thought you were beautiful, but now, you're just … Now, you're stunning."

A pleased, silly giggle escapes me, my inner nerd rolling her eyes at the sound. I'm not used to compliments on my appearance. To hear him gush about my looks is both gratifying and slightly uncomfortable. "I donated it to Locks of Love," I explain, running my fingers through my curls. "And when she cut all the weight off, it curled. It still feels a little strange, but I like it," I continue.

Hudson smiles at me while I talk, but when I finish, there's an awkward silence between us.

"Hudson—"

"Ariella—"

We both start and stop at the same time. When he waits for me, I continue. "Why are you here? Why aren't you in Italy with Gia?"

"I'm here because I love *you*, because you're worth following. I'm here because I was a self-centered fool who thought he was *protecting* you, *shielding* you from the everyday messiness of business and life. I'm here because I forgot what a strong, amazing, capable woman you are.

"Ariella," he reaches out to take my hand, drawing me closer to him until I'm standing next to the bed looking down into his troubled eyes. "You are the most important person in my life. Nothing else matters but you. The business, the money, the prestige? I'd give up everything, do anything, for you."

"But Gia—"

"Lies, all lies. An elaborate scheme by a horrible, manipulative person. One I hope is going to prison for a very long time."

Dragging a chair closer to his bed, I make myself comfortable. "Okay, start at the beginning and tell me everything."

And so, we talk. Something we should have been doing all along. He leaves nothing out, patiently answering all the questions I ask, and making no excuses for his mistakes and misguided actions. He explains Gia's Ponzi scheme. How she pretended to be his fiancée to lend respectability to her swindling racket. Apparently, she would entertain prospective clients in the condo from time to time. She left no detail undone. Even hanging men's clothing in the master suite and stocking men's toiletries in the bathroom. The old family pictures and the Photoshopped new ones displayed on the piano were the finishing touch.

He details the lies to her uncle Vincent and how there was, and is, no position waiting for him in Italy. Then, he explains his questioning by the FBI and his hopes for her arrest and prison time.

"So, you had no idea who was buying your condo?"

"No, it was all done through a realtor. The money was wired to my account, and I signed the papers. I left everything but my personal belongings and the art collection."

"And you used the money to keep the business going?"

"Not all of it. I'd hit a slow period with investors. I used most of it to keep us afloat until more money came in. Then I paid myself back."

"Hudson," I hesitate, leaning toward him for emphasis, "Gia told me you are the sole owner of the business. She said you stripped your trust fund to buy out all the other investors and the business is yours. She warned me

I would ruin you financially if I protested or tried to interfere with the sale to Italia."

"That fucking bitch," he murmurs to himself before glancing at me. "Sorry for the language," he adds, smiling sheepishly.

I answer him with a shrug. "It's okay. I seem to be using that word and others like it a lot more frequently myself."

"I know." He grins back at me. "I read some of them in your shelter entries. What a potty mouth you have, Miss Dobbs."

It's my turn to be embarrassed. "Uh … Even the one where I was mad?"

"Yes. And you have every right to be angry." Hudson reaches for my hand, making me drag the chair even closer. "I'm sorry. I don't think I can say it enough or often enough, but I'm really sorry for everything that happened. I'll spend the rest of my life making it up to you, if you'll let me."

"You might live to regret your statement, Mr. Calder."

"Never," he assures me with a smile.

Pulling my hand away, I lean back in the chair. "I have more questions."

"Ask."

"The papers I was supposed to sign. Did you forget?"

"Yes and no. I did forget about them that night but only because I was distracted by a beautiful woman."

"Hudson—" I interrupt him. "Stop the charming act. Those papers were to protect both of us from being taken advantage of. Why didn't you tell me to sign them?"

"Because they weren't needed."

"What?"

"I don't own any of the business. It's yours. None of my money is invested in it. I'm one of your paid employees, just like Oliver and David. Only you can sell any of our products. The investors own thirty-five percent, but you own the rest."

"When were you going to tell me?"

"When we signed the contract with Italia."

I stare at him, confused by his words, wondering why he would do something like that. We built the business together—my ideas, his management. He'd worked as hard as me.

"Why?" I finally whisper.

Staring at the ceiling, he sighs deeply before reaching up to rub his face, only to be stopped by the swelling. When he finally turns to look at me, I can see hesitation and regret on his face. "This is going to sound really elitist and snobbish, but I promised to tell you the truth, so here goes. You remember we met at your eighteenth birthday party?"

"Yes."

"I was looking for an idea to use for my graduate project."

"Yes."

"And you let me build a business model based on your theories."

"Yes."

"We saw each other from time to time and corresponded when I had questions but nothing more. We were both busy with graduate school and our papers. I've told you I was intrigued. However, you were so much younger, and so ... different." He glances at me, an apologetic look on his face, but I wave him on.

"I never thought the business or our friendship would go beyond a school project or a casual acquaintance. Then, four years ago when it became obvious this could be more, Dr. Albright took me aside and warned me to be careful with my feelings and business dealings with you. He was concerned you wouldn't fit into my lifestyle and people in my social circles would think I was taking advantage of you. He didn't want you to get hurt.

"I tried to follow his advice. Tried keeping you separated from the rest of my life. I dated women from the social groups I was expected to date from. Did the traveling, appearances, and events, everything my parents required of me. That didn't work out so well, but I did make sure no one could ever say I was cheating you. The business is all yours. I work for you."

I don't know how to answer his truthful confession. Gia's words about my suitability for Hudson repeat in my head as I gaze back at his worried face.

"Ariella? Say something, please."

"When I went to your condo and saw Gia, I argued with her that you wouldn't cheat me out of the business. I told her you weren't that kind of person. But there were two things she said that convinced me she was telling the truth.

"The first was that I wouldn't fit in your society. She said you needed and deserved a woman who could help your career. Someone who knew how to act, how to dress, knew which fork to use. A woman who could speak to people without looking like a frightened mouse all the time.

"She's right about that. I will never be comfortable around many of your family's friends. I can learn how to dress and which fork to use. I'll never be a frightened mouse again. But I won't fit—I never will. You need to understand that if you want any kind of future with me. It would hurt too much if I ever found out you were embarrassed by me. I refuse to change who I am and where I came from."

He's shaking his head by the time I'm finished. "No, no," he argues. "None of it is true. You could never embarrass me. I swear I don't care about social standing or someone to advance my career. None of it's important to me."

"I'll never live in New York City again," I warn him.

"I don't want to either," he counters. "In fact, I thought maybe we'd talk about moving to Georgia or maybe North Carolina. The business could be done anywhere, and I wondered if you might like being closer to Liam and the rest of your family."

"I'd like that," I admit with a smile but quickly sober when I remember what else I have to ask him.

He must see the seriousness in my face because his smile slips away and a worried frown takes its place. "You said there were two things," he begins before I stop him.

"Yes, and this is difficult for me to talk about. I want the truth from you, all of it. I can't trust you until you tell me what I need to know."

He nods, acknowledging how earnest I am.

"You left a mark on my neck when we made love in the shower the last morning. Gia saw it. She became extremely angry and said some things about your prowess in the bedroom. Then she mentioned you liked to mark your conquests, and I probably had a love bite over my heart. How did she know? How would she know what you're like in bed?"

His face pales even more as he listens to my words. "Oh, God," he mutters to himself. "That bitch. That fucking bitch," he curses, staring at the ceiling.

"Hudson," I repeat, rising from the chair. "You told me there was no one else for a long time. I will *not* be lied to."

"Wait," he demands as I start to leave. "I didn't lie. I haven't touched anyone else in over four years. I couldn't, not after I knew I loved you."

"Then how did Gia know those details? Did you have a relationship with her?"

"I wouldn't call it a relationship exactly."

"Hudson," I warn.

"I was seventeen," he finally says. "Seventeen and horny as hell. I'd kissed a few girls, even did a little groping in the back seat. But not much more—besides watching some porn in our dorm rooms. My parents were pretty strict about dating and appropriate behavior. Going to an all-boys school means there aren't a lot of girls around." He glances at me, hesitating until I nod for him to go on.

"I'm sorry. This is difficult for me, too. It was eleven years ago, and I've tried to forget everything. Anyway," he begins again. "It was spring break my senior year. Our parents took Kathryn and me to Europe for a skiing trip. Gia and her family were there, too. It'd been awhile since we'd seen them. She's Kathryn's age, three years older, and never had much to say to me. Mom didn't like her—said she was too wild, but my younger self thought she was attractive and intriguing.

"The families ate dinner together one night. When we were leaving, she slipped me her room key. I snuck into her room later. She answered the door completely naked, and it was very obvious what she wanted. I didn't say no." He stops again, and I watch him gather his thoughts, knowing this is as difficult for him as it is for me.

"I spent every night with her. She, uh … She liked it rough, really rough." He glances at me, worried I'll be disgusted, but I just nod, and he continues. "She'd tell me what to do, and, well, there was a lot of biting and some … Shit, Ariella, I can't," he yells, hitting the bed with his fist.

Hudson faces away from me, breathing heavily. When he's more composed, he turns back to me.

"I was completely infatuated, thought I was in love." He laughs ruefully. "I begged her to wait for me. Told her I'd join her at college. We could get an apartment and be together. She just laughed. Said I was a pretty good lay, but I needed to grow up a lot. I've hated her ever since and never tried to hide it. Kathryn found out and blacklisted her. I've wondered if this was all an elaborate plan to hurt me and my family. It would be like her to do that. The woman is fucking mental.

"I'm sorry you got caught up in all this," he adds after calming down. "I thought it was all behind me. I would never want you to be hurt by my past actions."

Moved by his difficult confession and his heartfelt apology, I bend over his bed, laying my head gingerly on his chest. He wraps his arms around me, hugging me to him while one hand slowly rubs up and down my back. "I know that was difficult to remember, but thank you for telling me," I whisper before placing a kiss on his cheek. We stay that way for a long time, enjoying the pleasure of being so close again.

"Ariella?"

"Hmm?"

"In the last letter you wrote at Plumorchard Shelter, you said you had a journey to make. You said you'd like me to make it with you. I want that, too. Can you … Will you let me be your companion on the journey?"

I raise my head, smiling at the love I see in his eyes. "It might be a very long journey," I warn him. "It could last fifty, sixty years."

"Fifty, sixty, a hundred, a thousand years wouldn't be long enough. I love you, Ariella. You and that beautiful mind of yours."

"I love you, too, Hudson. But I have one last question for you."

His smile disappears, and his eyes widen with panic at my words. "Tell me." I grin. "What's this about rocks not being your friend?"

CHAPTER 36

A Future of Wonderful Possibilities

Date: September 11, 2015

Starting Location: Asheville, North Carolina

Destination: The Future

Total Trip Miles: Just Beginning

Years ago, I stood on the summit of Springer Mountain and stared at the vista before me. Spring was slowly creeping its way into the valleys below, but winter still gripped the mountaintop. I gazed at a future that seemed as bleak and cold as the wind that tossed the dead leaves at my feet and nipped the chilled skin on my face.

Devastated by what I thought was Hudson's personal and professional betrayal, I'd escaped to the mountains of Georgia to deal with the ruin of my life and to hopefully find some small bit of peace.

When I met Dreamer on Springer's summit, she'd told me Prince Charmings were nice to have around, but I was a strong, confident woman who was capable of making her own dreams come true. I hadn't believed her at the time, but hiking the trail brought back the real me I'd lost in New York.

It gave me more than just my vanished self-confidence. A loving husband, two amazing children, a wonderful extended family of good friends and business associates were all part of my life because of the Appalachian Trail.

Now, standing in the doorway to our bedroom, watching that loving husband, I have to wonder if I could actually time travel, would I go back and tell that sad, younger version of myself that everything was going to be all right? Would I let her know how her hike would forever change her life? *No, probably not,* I think to myself. *That journey was hers to discover and I have my own waiting for me.*

Smiling, I make my way into the room and sit beside Hudson on the end of our bed. He glances up at me with a grin before resuming his activity. Hudson is trimming his toenails. It's such an ordinary thing, this little piece of personal grooming, but it's always struck me as intimate, too. Something you would only be comfortable doing around a spouse or longtime lover.

I remember the first time I watched him cut his nails after we'd been living together for a few months. Although he'd tried to persuade me to share an apartment with him when we first moved our business to Asheville, I resisted. I wanted to reset our relationship, to start over and let it develop in a more normal way. I wanted to be wooed.

We began dating. He taught me ballroom dancing; I taught him to two-step. I made him homemade meals; he took me to fancy restaurants. Hudson gladly gave me the hearts and flowers, wine and candy I wanted. We explored the area around our new home, and then—when his leg was properly healed and strong enough—we began doing short hikes on the Appalachian Trail.

"What is that beautiful mind of yours thinking?" he asks, interrupting my musing.

"About the first time I watched you trim your toenails."

My dear husband frowns at me for a moment, searching his memory for something he's probably forgotten. "Remind me, please?"

Taking the clippers from him, I stand, turning to face him and stepping between his now open legs. "Do you remember this?" My lips trace the outline of his jaw, then ghost over each eyelid. "And this?" A peck to the tip of his nose. "And this?" I kiss him—deeply, thoroughly—only pulling away when I need to breathe.

"Well, I'm not sure that I do," he teases. "Maybe you should remind me again?"

"Oh, you!" I laugh. "You had finally persuaded me to share an apartment. It was a Sunday morning. We were lying in bed, reading the paper, you sat up and began trimming your toenails, and that's when I knew."

"What did you know?"

"That …" Pausing, I try to find the words. "That our relationship had survived its difficult start. We'd left our winter behind us and entered a spring full of wonderful possibilities."

I can see the love in my husband's face as he smiles at me, and I know my smile matches his. Throat tight, I run one hand through his chestnut curls, watching his eyes close in pleasure as I lightly scratch his scalp. At forty, Hudson is still a handsome man. Our active lifestyle has kept him lean and fit, and he regularly works out in our home gym.

"Is that why you gave me these?" he asks, opening my other hand that still holds the clippers.

"No." I chuckle. "Those were to spare you the horror of losing another blackened toenail."

Laughing, we both remember his panic at finding one of his nails turning black after a weekend of hiking. I'd warned him his feet might swell and to make sure his nails were short and his shoes big enough. He ignored me and learned a painful lesson. At our wedding on Granny's porch two years later, I gave him the clippers engraved with the date. He carried them from Springer to Katahdin on our honeymoon hike.

Hudson takes them from my hand, running his fingers over the numerals. "I wonder if anyone else has ever received engraved nail clippers as a wedding present." He laughs at my grin. "Such a *unique* gift."

"From such a strange and weird mind," I add.

"No!" He doesn't let me demean myself. "You know how I feel about labels. You are amazing, wonderful, and maybe a bit *unique* at times, but always beautiful, and never, never strange or weird."

Hudson is laid-back and easy-going as a father. The only time he's ever lost his temper with our daughter was when she came home from kindergarten one day and called her two-year-old brother a weirdo because he refused to talk. He'd yelled at her, and then sent her to her room in tears. Later, after he calmed down, they'd had a long private conversation. I never found out what he said to her, although I suspected it might have been something about my bullied childhood. It made a lasting impression because she'd never used derogatory labels again and was always quick to defend anyone she thought was being harassed. She became her little brother's staunchest protector and defender.

Before I can answer, he pulls me down for another kiss, another deep, thorough kiss that leaves me breathless again. With a quick flip, he has me on my back, his weight pressing me into the mattress.

Soft, feathery kisses make their way down my neck while his hands slip their way under my shirt. "How much time do we have before our guests start arriving?" he whispers into my ear.

"I don't think—"

"Mom! Dad!" Cori's loud voice echoes down the hallway. "Siler needs your help."

With an exasperated sigh, Hudson rolls off me and sits up but not before whispering that this conversation will resume later. With a smirk, he stands and adjusts his clothing just before our daughter bursts into the room.

"He got into the stuff on the bookshelves in the library and some of it fell off."

"Cori, what have we said about using inside and outside voices?"

His eight-year-old mini-me has the grace to look apologetic for a fleeting second. "Sorry, Dad," she manages to mutter before her younger brother follows her into the room.

"It is a physical impossibility to get *into* stuff on a bookshelf," he says, frowning at his sister. "And one book fell off, not some," he continues before turning to Hudson. "Sorry, Father."

"No problem, buddy," Hudson reassures him.

"What do you have there?" I ask, motioning to the large book he's trying to carry. "Cori, help your brother."

She takes the heavy book from his arms, and once again, I marvel at the differences in my two children. Coraline Dobbs Calder didn't cry when she was born—she screamed. She was loud, rambunctious, and full of energy. It was months before she slept all night. Hudson and I existed in a semi-zombie state for weeks until he insisted we hire a night nurse. I resisted, afraid it meant I was a bad mother, but the prospect of a full night's sleep, and the argument we would be rested and energized to spend all day with our new daughter, did the trick. Even after Cori started sleeping all night, Mrs. Morris stayed on. Four years later when Siler was born, she became a trusted nanny to our two children.

Siler was the complete opposite of his sister. Shy and retiring by nature, he inherited my dark hair and eyes. It was those eyes that stared at me as I held my son only minutes after his birth. Those eyes told me raising this little boy would be completely different from raising his sister. It wasn't without worry, however. He rarely cried, and although able to communicate his needs with looks and gestures, he didn't speak until he was two.

Hudson worried about him, but I knew he didn't need to speak—Cori did all his talking for him. Then one day, he spoke—in complete sentences, with proper grammar, and a stubborn refusal to use contractions. Each word was clear, distinct, and pronounced with a slight English accent. We could only guess he picked it up from being around Daniel so much.

"Is that an old photo album?" Hudson asks after taking the book from Cori.

"Yes, Father," Siler answers. "Can you remind me who some of these people are?"

Crouching down to his level, my husband studies the serious face of our son. "You worried about tomorrow, Siler?"

"A little," he admits.

"It's okay to be nervous, and you know you don't have to do this. Everyone will understand if it feels too big or too scary."

"But Mr. Daniel and Mr. Ron asked me to be the ring bearer."

"Yes, they asked because it's a special day for them, and they want you to be part of it. That's why they won't be upset if you decide you don't want to."

"Because they love me?"

"Yes. It's your decision, son."

"Can we look at the photos first before I decide?"

"Sure." Hudson settles on the floor, hefting the large album onto his lap. He smiles when I slide off the bed and sit next to him.

On the cover of the album are the words:

Appalachian Trail

March 11, 2003 - September 12, 2003

Siler crawls into my lap, settling between my crossed legs. Both children have seen this album before, particularly Cori, who loves looking at the old photos. So, I'm surprised when our normally restless, can't-sit-still daughter flops down beside Hudson.

She grins at his questioning glance. "I want to see it again, too. It's a good story."

"It is," he agrees before opening to the first page. *Springer Mountain, Georgia* is written at the top. There are several photos looking down into the green valleys below the summit. An older, middle-aged couple smile at the camera in two of them.

"Who are those people?" Siler asks. "Should I recognize them?"

"They're Dreamer and Allday, two people your mom met on the day she started hiking. She took those pictures, and they took the others. When their hike was over, they sent copies to us. And no, Siler, you've never met them."

"Will they be at the wedding tomorrow?"

"Yes, they'll be there. They're part of our little hiking family."

"She's the one who gave Mom her trail name," Cori adds, leaning over to tell Siler. "She thought Mom said Ella, like in Cinderella."

"And then she named me Mr. Easy," Hudson adds. "Because your Uncle Liam was mad at me and put rocks in my backpack, and it wasn't easy to carry them."

"But you should have been called Prince Charming, like in the fairy tale," Cori continues grinning. "Look," she says, already jumping to another topic. "There's Uncle Travis and Uncle Markham standing behind Mom."

I wasn't aware of it at the time, but Dreamer snapped several photos of me as I stood on the summit. One of those captured Travis and Markham in the background as they prepared to leave.

"Why do you look so sad, Mother?" Siler whispers, examining the photo more closely.

"She was upset with me," Hudson answers. "You know how we've always told you to talk and share your feelings so there are no misunderstandings? Well," he continues after Siler nods, "I forgot to share things with your mom, and the misunderstandings made her sad."

"Oh," he says, wide-eyed. He glances first at me, and then at his father. "Then you were not really a Prince Charming."

"No, I wasn't." Hudson chuckles at his observation before winking at me. "She didn't need a Prince Charming to rescue her, though. She's the one who rescued me."

He continues to turn the pages while our children look at the photos, pointing out and discussing places they've been to or heard us talk about. I've labeled most of the photos, adding short notes describing what I did or saw. Most of the early pictures were taken by Dreamer and Allison. We added a few after Hudson was released from the hospital.

"There is Uncle Liam's store at Neels Gap, and Great-grandmother Dobbs' backpack hanging on the wall."

Siler leans over, examining the photos more closely. "I like his store, Father."

Our son has always been fascinated by Mountain Crossings. If we'd let him, he'd spend hours examining the merchandise sold there.

"When will Uncle Liam, Aunt Emma, Brandon, and Bryan get here?" Cori asks.

"Sometime this afternoon. Did you help your mom get their rooms ready?"

"Yes, sir," she answers. "And I picked up all the toys around the pool, too."

"Thank you. That was a nice thing to do."

My daughter grins back at her dad, her dark-blue eyes sparkling. "But Mama says you have to clean it and do the chemicals."

"Oh, she did, did she?" He laughs at her teasing, then smiles at me. "Well, then we should hurry up and look at the rest of the pictures."

While Hudson and the children examine and discuss more of the photos, I let my mind wander to those first few months after he was released from the hospital in Gainesville. His parents flew us to New York, and we spent the next two months taking care of all the business details that were put on hold when we'd both left. One of the first things I did was give Oliver and David each a ten-percent share in the company. Then, we'd lured Susan away from her law firm with a generous salary and a ten-percent share. Hudson became the CEO, but I was still the single largest shareholder.

We were excited about moving from New York and eagerly began researching sites in and around northern Georgia. We finally settled on Asheville, North Carolina. The weather, the thriving art scene, and the proximity to a wide variety of outdoor activities made the town a perfect choice. With several colleges and universities in the area, we were guaranteed a skilled labor force when we began expanding. The expansion came quickly.

Before Hudson left New York to find me, he and Susan met with representatives of the US military. The war with Iraq highlighted the need for better computer security. They turned to our company for help. Suddenly, we had more work and more contracts than we could handle. We hired staff, then hired more staff.

We also signed a very lucrative contract with Banca Italia Internazionale the week after we returned. Hudson speculated Vincent wanted to forestall any legal actions we might take against him and his niece.

Gia was arrested. Her assets were seized, and eventually, through a long, drawn-out plea bargain, everything was sold to reimburse the people she cheated. The rest of her family distanced themselves from her, and she was sentenced to fifteen years in federal prison. Both of us were questioned and gave statements about our interactions with her. Hudson never saw her again, but I did.

I never told him I went to her sentencing. I needed to see if the haughty, designer-clothes-wearing bully still existed, and, if she did, could she still affect me. From the back of the courtroom, I watched her shuffle to her place in front of the judge. What I saw was a broken, disheveled young woman in an ill-fitting prison jumpsuit who meekly admitted to her crimes and read the apology to her victims that her plea bargain required. I stood as she was leaving, and my movement caught her eye. For several long moments we stared at each other. Her lips clenched, and for a brief second, I saw resentment on her face. Then, the jailer pulled on her arm and she was led from the room.

I felt nothing. Her power was gone, and I felt neither anger nor bitterness, only a slight sense of sadness at a life wasted because of greed. We dismissed her memory from our lives and never spoke of her again

"See this." Hudson's voice brings me back to the present. He's pointing to a photo of a wide-open grassy meadow. "It's the top of Max Patch. Your mom and I hiked up one evening. The wind was blowing so hard we couldn't keep the tent up, so we cowboy camped under the stars."

"Did you get cold?" Siler asks.

"A little, but it was beautiful. We watched the full moon come up, and then the fireflies came out and danced for us." My husband glances at me with a smug smile. Our memories include another type of mating dance on top of Max Patch, but we don't share those with the children.

"Fireflies are awesome," Siler whispers.

"I like this one," Cori declares, indicating another photo. "You're feeding the wild ponies, Mom."

"That's Grayson Highlands in Virginia. Some people think it looks like the Scottish moors. We thought you and Siler might like to go next month when the weather gets cooler. They have lots of fireflies there, too," I add, smiling at my son.

"Oh, look at this one," he says. "It looks like a flying saucer taking off. See," he adds, pointing to the curving ramp leading up to the observation deck on top of Clingman's Dome in the Smokies. "These are the centrifugal force lines. If they kept going around and around and faster and faster, it would just whoosh, pop up into the air."

Siler illustrates his words by spinning his arms around and around before throwing them up into the air. For a fleeting moment, I see the serious science professor he will probably grow up to be, but then he giggles, and he's our little boy again.

Hudson turns the page, and there we all are.

One weekend toward the end of June, I surprised him with a much longer road trip. This time, we drove to Harpers Ferry. The historic town at the confluence of the Potomac and Shenandoah Rivers is considered to be the halfway point of the Appalachian Trail. It's also home to the Appalachian Trail Conservancy, a nonprofit organization dedicated to managing the trail.

We drove to the historic rock building housing the organization's offices, and standing there in front getting their photos made for the 1,000 miles thru-hiker album, were the six people who saved my husband's life on a cold snowy day outside Franklin.

Although we were in touch by email and the occasional phone call, I hadn't seen any of them in almost three months. Except for Ghost and M&M, Hudson didn't really know the girls or Curly Dan and No Filter, and barely remembered them through the haze of pain and confusion. There were hugs, tears, slaps on the back, talk, and more talk. We booked rooms at a nearby hotel, checked in, cleaned up, and explored the small town.

My children examine the photos taken during the three-day reunion. No Filter has kept his head shaved, but his mustache is longer and drooping below his chin. Dan has hair again, and it's curly. Travis and Markham are both sporting beards. Rosemary's hair is longer and in braids, but Allison has kept hers short. Everyone is much thinner than they are now.

"They look so different," Cori says.

"Where are Dreamer and Allday?" Siler asks. "I thought you said they were part of the hiker family."

"Oh, they are," his father reassures him before turning the next few pages. "They hiked in right before we left." The last photos are taken in front of the headquarters as we were saying goodbye. The older couple are with us, grinning as they have their picture made for the halfway mark.

We met our friends several more times during their journey to Katahdin. Each visit is captured in the pictures, carefully labeled, and preserved in the album we study.

The only train station on the AT is located just north of Pawling, New York. All four couples caught it one weekend and met us in New York City. We invaded the Calders' home, the laundry and showers in almost constant use. To thank them for their hospitality, No Filter cooked dinner one night. It was a four-course feast complete with wine, coffee, and digestifs. Hudson's parents were so impressed they began serious discussions about helping him open a restaurant. His successful restaurants in New York and Asheville are the result of their collaboration.

It was cold and rainy the day we met them on Mt. Washington. We opted to ride the cog railway to the top rather than risk the sometimes-dangerous hike up the mountain. Siler leans closer to the photos, carefully examining the train and its trailing plume of black smoke. "I want to ride that someday, please."

"It was fun," Hudson tells him. "Especially when the hikers we passed dropped their pants and mooned the train."

"Hudson!" My husband just laughs at me while Siler glances between us, confusion on his young face.

"I'm sorry, son, your mom's upset with me for talking about mooning. You see, when someone bends over and sticks their bare bottom up, it's called mooning. And it's a tradition for the hikers to moon the people riding in the train as it goes by."

I'm not surprised when Cori starts giggling so hard she can barely sit up. "Mooning," she gasps. "Bare bottoms are moons."

Siler frowns and shakes his head. "That is disgusting."

"You're right, it is," I tell him. "Now let's get back to the pictures and the story. Uncle Liam and his family will be here soon. I'm sure the boys will want to get into the pool. And, by the way, not a word to anyone about mooning." Siler solemnly nods. I know he'll never say a word, but the glint in Cori's eyes tells me she'll soon be sharing the story with Brandon and Bryan.

Hudson turns the pages, describing the pictures taken by Allison at places along the trail. Mountain views, rivers, streams, a few photos of shelters, both new and old. In some pictures, they are carefully crossing streams, hip-deep in the rushing water. Sometimes, the trail is cut logs crossing a swampy, boggy area; in others, it crosses wide-open mountain summits.

She's documented their hours' long, torturous journey through the boulder-strewn, infamous Mahoosuc Notch in Maine. Looking at them brings back painful memories of my husband's fall. There's a sign announcing the start of the Hundred Mile Wilderness. It warns hikers to enter only if they are prepared and carrying enough food for ten days. Allison included photos of wildlife they encountered: a moose or two, birds, snakes, and even a black bear.

As the weeks and months pass and they travel north, spring turns to humid summer, and summer to magnificent fall. The lush forest greens change to reds and yellows, oranges and gold. Our friends traveled from winter to spring, from summer to fall.

And then they arrived at Baxter State Park in Maine.

As soon as the doctor declared Hudson's leg well enough to resume normal activities, his goal had been to rebuild his strength and fitness levels to the point he could climb Katahdin. Under a therapist's guidance, he'd worked hard, knowing the ascent of the northern mountain would probably be the physically hardest thing he'd ever done. And it was.

Our friends arrived the evening of September 10th. We were waiting for them in the two shelters we'd reserved. We partied late, eating, drinking, talking, and listening to the stories of their great adventure. Although I was delighted for our friends, there was still a part of me that envied their hike. Hudson must have sensed my longing for the trail because later that night, he promised we would make the journey together, and we did. Two years later, we spent our honeymoon hiking from Springer to Katahdin.

It took us almost five hours to reach the famous sign at the northern terminus of the Appalachian Trail. The dirt pathway gradually changed to a steep rock climb. In some places, foot and handholds made of steel rebar were drilled into the sheer cliff face. In others, the men formed a chain, passing and hauling the women over rocks taller than we were. We pulled, pushed, and scrambled our way to the top.

The weather was perfect. The sky a crystalline blue, dotted here and there with pure white clouds. Below us, forests and mountains painted in the glorious hues of autumn stretched as far as we could see, broken only by the shimmer of small lakes and ponds.

There was a sense of awe, an almost reverence, as we approached the iconic sign. We touched it, each person wrapped in their quiet thoughts as they reached the long-sought goal. Dreamer had a small pebble with her that she had picked up and carried all the way from Springer. Physically exhausted and overwhelmed at the completion of her journey, she broke down and cried when she added it to the rock cairns near the sign.

Then it was picture time. Allison and Dreamer took photos of each person, then each couple, then the group as a whole. There was a moment of silence for Rock Dancer when No Filter and Curly Dan placed his memorial stone near the last white blaze at the base of the sign.

"Why is Uncle Markham down on his knee?" Siler asks, pointing to one of the last pictures on the page. "Did he fall?"

Before I can answer, Cori explains. "No, he's proposing to Aunt Rosemary. When a man wants a woman to marry him, he gets down on one knee and asks her."

We were gathering our things, getting ready to start the long descent back to the shelters, when Markham surprised us all by dropping to one knee and asking Rosemary to marry him. Over the months of the hike, their relationship advanced from pen pals to lovers, but no one suspected how serious their love had become. When a shocked Rosemary gasped out a tearful, "Yes," Markham pulled out a ring made from duct tape, wire, and a bright yellow

M&M candy. At their marriage six months later, he presented her with a more permanent version fashioned from platinum and a large canary-yellow diamond.

The original ring is preserved in a small cube of clear resin. It sits in a place of honor beside their official wedding picture on a shelf in her law office in Blowing Rock, North Carolina where they moved as soon as Markham finished his medical studies. Their son, Henry, is Cori's best friend.

Allison and Travis settled there, too. Attracted to the small town and its beautiful surroundings, she eventually went to work with Markham. His dream to provide affordable, quality healthcare to his childhood community became a true success story. Their twin girls inherited Travis's looks and Allison's love of the water. I knew they, too, would be in the pool as soon as they arrived.

Travis stayed true to his dream of teaching art. After completing his educational training, he joined the faculty at the small local school, teaching 7th through 12th grade art classes. An art gallery on the city square exhibits his paintings, and they're attracting attention from galleries as far away as Los Angeles and New York. Once a week, he still drives to Asheville to teach an art class to local veterans.

"I can't wait until Aunt Rosemary gets here tomorrow," Cori interrupts my memories. "Henry is going to teach me how to do a somersault off the diving board."

"Not without an adult watching," I warn my water-loving daughter. "You and Henry are still too young to be in the pool by yourselves."

"I know, Mom," she replies before jumping up and running from the room when the doorbell rings.

"That's probably Liam and his family." Hudson stands. "I'll help them with the suitcases and get them settled. You two okay?"

Siler is still studying the last of the photos in the album, but he glances up and nods before returning to the pictures. "We'll be down in a minute," I tell him.

There are only a few more pages of photos in the album. They show us hiking back down the mountain and saying goodbye the next day. Everyone will be here tomorrow when Ron and Daniel get married. We're expecting a larger crowd for the party afterward. Some are friends from the college where Dan teaches, and some will be from Ron's restaurants. Hudson's parents will be here, too. My little boy is quiet, lines creasing his forehead as he examines them closely.

"Siler. What are you thinking about?"

"Rings, circles," he answers. "May I show you?"

Rising, I walk to my desk and return with a pad of paper and some colored pencils. When I sit down beside him, he crawls back into my lap. I wrap my arms around his small body and he leans against me, sighing in contentment. I know this is one of his "safe" places.

Picking up the green pencil, he draws a circle in the center of the page. "This is me," he explains. Then he makes another circle in red that overlaps the green one, and a blue circle that touches both.

"This is you and Father. The red one is Cori." He continues to draw. "Here is Uncle Markham, Aunt Rosemary, and Henry. Then Uncle Travis, Aunt Allison, and their daughters." The circles overlap as he draws and lists the people. "Uncle Liam and his family, Dreamer and Allday, Grandmother Patricia and Grandfather Richard." Soon the whole page is covered in interlocking circles.

"Do you know what you've drawn?" I ask.

"No. Does it have a name?"

"Yes. It's called the Flower of Life, and some people believe it symbolizes the creation of all things." Picking up one of the pencils, I draw lines connecting points where the circles overlap. "You can find all five of the

Platonic solids within the circles. Cubes, and tetrahedrons, and octahedrons." I name them as they take form within the circles he's drawn. "Dodecahedrons and icosahedrons."

I can hear him whispering the names to himself, liking the way the letters and sounds roll around in his head and on his tongue. I find myself doing the same thing.

"I'd like to know what it represents to you, Siler."

I wait patiently while he stares at the paper. He's always needed time to think before he answers a question. We've learned to give him all the time he needs. My long braid is draped over my shoulder, and he wraps one hand around it, rubbing its silky softness between his fingers. It's a self-soothing habit he's had since infancy.

"I think it shows how I am a part of everything and everyone," he finally tells me. "And I think it is pretty, too," he adds, glancing up at me with a grin.

"I do, too." Leaning over, I plant a kiss on his head before lifting him to his feet. "How do you feel about tomorrow?"

"Good. I am not worried anymore, and Father says I look very handsome in my suit and tie."

I laugh, and he smiles at me.

"Come on," I tell him, rising and taking his hand. "We have guests to greet and a party to prepare for. You should share your circles with Uncle Travis when he gets here. I bet he can show you how to color them and make them even prettier."

Hand in hand we leave the room, ready to welcome our friends and a future abundant with wonderful possibilities.

CHAPTER 37

His Beautiful Mind

Siler

Date: Sunday, March 11, 2035

Starting Location: Springer Mountain, Georgia

Destination: Unknown

Total Trip Miles: 0

The rocky lookout point at the edge of the mountain is still there. I stare out at the misty blue hills in the distance and the green valleys below, Mother and Father beside me. His arm wraps around her shoulders as he hugs her close to him, reminding her of the time he stood here all alone and wished he could turn back time.

"If you could really time travel, would you go back and change anything?" he asks her.

She shakes her head, smiling at his teasing face. "No. It's been an amazing life. I have an amazing husband, two amazing kids, and an amazing grandchild on the way. I'm very happy with the way things turned out."

"You're amazing." I hear him whisper before he presses his lips to her forehead.

I look away, giving them a bit of privacy. My parents have always been affectionate, their deep love and appreciation for each other apparent to everyone. Although Mother just turned fifty-six and Father is now sixty, they're still healthy and active. The lines on their faces are evidence of a happy life—well lived and well loved. Even though Father sports a few gray hairs at his temples, they only make him look more distinguished. The long braid I loved so much as a child was cut long ago, but Mother's hair is still as dark and thick as it was when she was younger.

This isn't the first time I've stood in this spot. Four years ago, when my sister, Cori, and her new husband, Henry, started their honeymoon hike, all my extended family gathered to see them off. Their first child, my nephew, will be born two months from now.

My cousins, Brandon and Bryan Crow, made the hike with them. Their humorous, often awkward account of accompanying an amorous, newlywed couple on the trail turned into a best-selling novel. They're currently hiking the Pacific Crest Trail and busy taking notes for their next book.

I'm brought back to the present when Mother reminds me to sign the register. When I reach the rock that houses it, a young woman is sitting there writing. She glances up at me, and I feel an instant shock of recognition even though I know I've never seen her before. Perhaps it's because she has the same dark hair and skin tone as my mother.

"*Osiyo Uwoduhi*," I whisper to myself because she is very beautiful.

A startled look passes across her face, and her eyes widen in surprise. "*Wado*," she replies. Now I'm the one staring in surprise when she thanks me in Cherokee.

Collecting myself after several awkward moments, I hold out my hand. "Siler Calder."

"Rachel Green," she replies, standing to take my hand in hers. She doesn't shake it, just holds it while we stare at each other.

"Do you, uh … Do you have a trail name yet?" I finally manage to stutter.

"My father, Randall, calls me his little flower, so I thought I would use his nickname, *Atsilvsgi*."

"*Uwoduhi Atsilvsgi*," I slowly pronounce it, changing it to "beautiful flower." Rachel flashes me a smile, a slight blush spreading across her cheeks, before asking if I have a trail name.

"No, I thought I'd let the trail give me one."

She nods. "So, you're hiking north?"

"All the way to Katahdin."

"Me, too," she whispers before handing me the register. "I'm finished. You should sign it so we can get started."

I scrawl my name under hers, then hug my parents one last time. Mother has tears in her eyes when she tells me to be careful but have fun. When I reach out to shake Father's hand, he pulls me into a crushing hug. With a glance toward Rachel and a knowing wink, he lets me go but not before reminding me to remember everything I've been taught about the woods.

Hefting my backpack, I take my first steps on the Appalachian Trail. Just before it makes a sharp turn, I look back at my parents one last time. They're still standing at the edge of the lookout point. Behind them, the ancient hills, ridges, and forests of the Appalachian Mountains stretch out until they disappear into the distant horizon. They were formed long before I was born and will exist long after I am gone. I see the past, the present, and the future just waiting to be explored and experienced.

With one last wave to the man and woman who gave me life, I turn and walk north, following spring on the Appalachian Trail.

ACKNOWLEDGMENTS

First, thank *you*. Thank you for choosing this book and taking a chance on a new author. The idea for this story formed over twenty years ago. It went through many different versions before settling into this final form. I'm very happy to share it with you.

Thanks to my pre-readers, Ipsita, Lynda, Donna, Denise, Judy, MJ, and all the other members of the fandom, whose love for this story encouraged me along the way. Thanks to Lisa Hollett for her suggestions. A very special thank you to Sally Hopkinson who edited and proofread through every version. I admire your patience and expertise.

Thank you to my husband and hiking partner for making this journey with me.

And finally, a special thanks to Bellebiter. You told me I could do this. I'm glad I listened.

Hike On!

Janet